THE LEOPARD'S LINES

KARL C. KLONTZ

ISBN 978-0-9963918-1-8

Cover design by Sensical Design & Communication
Cover illustrations by Katharine Asher

To my wife, Sarah, who shows me
what it means to be loved every day.

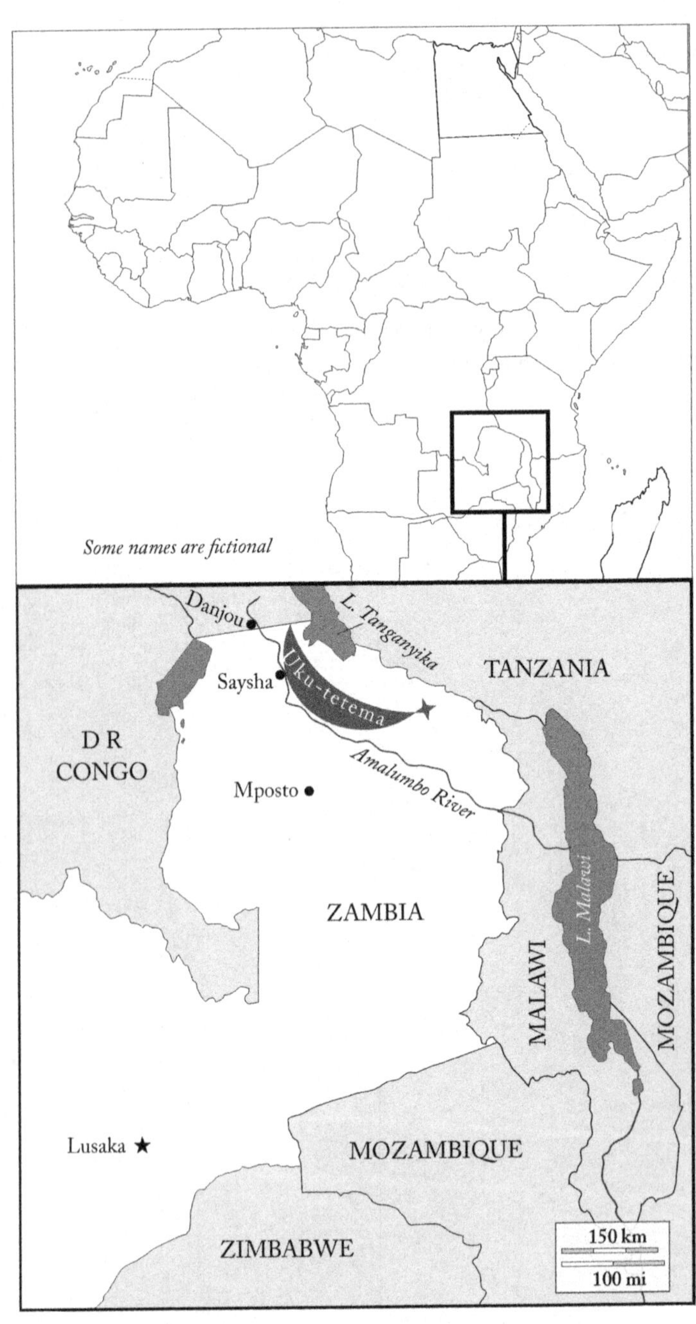
Some names are fictional
Danjou
L. Tanganyika
TANZANIA
Saysha
Uku-tetema
D R
CONGO
Amalumbo River
Mposto
ZAMBIA
MALAWI
L. Malawi
MOZAMBIQUE
Lusaka
MOZAMBIQUE
ZIMBABWE
150 km
100 mi

Glossary of Select Words from Bemba Language*

amalumbo – praise

ingwe – leopard

mzungu – person of European descent

nudume – brother

tata – father

uku-tetema – to twinkle

* Commonly spoken in northeastern Zambia

I

THE WOMAN'S HEAD looks like a spent firecracker.

I kneel on the dirt floor of the hospital to examine her more closely. Her hair has vanished to expose burned tissue from forehead to nape of neck. Along the circumference of destruction is a rim of missing skin. Taut blisters mark second-degree burns while in more severely burned areas, straw-colored serum oozes like sap from an injured tree. Partially spared, her eyebrows and lashes are singed.

This is what a head burned in a bonnet hair dryer looks like.

"She needs fluids," I tell my assistant, Innocent Mbewe. "Start an IV immediately."

Candlelight is all I have to decipher the lettering on a piece of paper I've extracted from the patient's clasped hands. Squinting, I read the words…

Dear Dr. Paul Rider:

This burn was intended for me, not the woman before you.

Please take care of her. I will pay the hospital for the care she receives.

In the meantime, please come to Danjou to see me as soon as possible.

It is urgent you do so because my life is in danger…as is yours.

Annette Wilson

"Who's Annette Wilson?" I ask the patient.

She blinks and groans but says nothing.

"She speaks only French," Innocent Mbewe tells me. He translates my question and delivers her response: "She doesn't know who Annette Wilson is."

"But this message," I say. "It's directed to me. How can she *not* know Annette Wilson?"

I look at the burned woman more closely. "I don't recognize her. Is she from our village?"

"No, she's from Danjou," Innocent replies.

I know the name well. Danjou is located two hundred fifty kilometers to the northwest just over the border in the Democratic Republic of the Congo, or D R Congo as we call our neighbor. Four months ago, shortly after I came here to become medical director of this hospital, I drove to Danjou to purchase supplies. It was an arduous day-long journey in a four-wheel-drive vehicle.

I'm the sole medical doctor here in the village of Saysha located in northeast Zambia. The hospital where I work was founded twenty-five years ago by an Australian physician lovingly referred to as *tata* Murphy who recently passed away. Although English is the official language of Zambia, villagers here speak a Bantu language called Bemba, and in Bemba the word *tata* means "father." After learning of *tata* Murphy's death in an online recruitment notice, I left a job at a clinic in the Amazon rainforest of Ecuador to come to Zambia. I serve as an interim medical director until a permanent replacement is recruited. I supervise a cadre of fifteen "paramedics," a term coined by *tata* Murphy to refer to caregivers who, with few exceptions, lack a high school education and come from families of subsistence farmers. Innocent Mbewe is one of the paramedics. Together, we uphold the hospital's unwavering mission of delivering care to the poor by the poor. The hospital has an agreement with D R Congo wherein severely ill persons who live near the border who can't afford care can come to our hospital without need of a passport.

"The patient's brother drove her to our village and then returned to D R Congo," Innocent informs me. "Before he left, he told me that his sister was burned at a hair salon in Danjou. A spark from a hair dryer exploded liquids in her hair."

Innocent lights an additional candle as night falls.

Electricity is absent in Saysha. Because the municipal grid doesn't come here, we rely on a diesel-powered generator to charge laptops and cell phones, to run a refrigerator in the pharmacy, and to power a ventilator when we need it. Internet access is limited to a single hotspot at the hospital, but the connection is intermittent.

I lift the tattered message I extracted from the patient's hands and read it again. Turning it over, I find only wrinkles and stains. I grow angry. "How can this be?" I blurt. "A patient who comes from a town two hundred fifty kilometers away with a message telling me my life's endangered yet provides no phone number or contact information for the woman who wrote it. This is outrageous!"

"Leave it be," Innocent says. "It's likely a hoax."

I'd like to think it's a hoax, but I see no reason for it to be one. From morning to night, I treat severely ill patients housed in the dozen huts that comprise our hospital. The huts are made from tree trunks or wood planks and have thatched roofs. The only exceptions are a small pharmacy constructed from bricks and corrugated tin and a roofless laundromat made from cinder blocks. Patients here lie on mats atop dirt floors. Although *tata* Murphy envisioned a maximum census of fifty patients, we routinely exceed that number. With no other hospitals nearby, we turn no one away thanks to funding from an Australian foundation *tata* Murphy created before he died. In the five months I've worked here, never have I seen an unsatisfied patient; to the contrary, gratitude is the rule.

"I'm going to Danjou first thing tomorrow morning," I tell Innocent.

"No, you mustn't! It's too dangerous there!"

"But I feel I *have* to. Something tells me this message is genuine."

Agitated, Innocent strides to the door.

"Where are you going?" I demand.

"Do not go to Danjou!" he repeats before leaving the hut.

I slip my arms under the burned woman and carry her with the intravenous line to a ward where she'll share floor space with other severely ill patients.

I BEGIN WALKING to the shack I inhabit, but before I reach the perimeter of the hospital grounds two boys rush up to me.

"*Nudume*, have you heard?" one calls. "They're coming!"

The boys are breathless from running. Fondly, I think of them as "blue shirt" and "green shirt" because of the colored shirts they consistently wear. Both are eleven years old and live in a dormitory for orphans maintained by the hospital. When I first moved to the village, they called me *tata,* but I insisted they drop the title for *nudume*, which means "brother" in Bemba.

"Who's coming?" I ask.

"The soldiers!" Benji declares.

Benji wears the green shirt. His face is bright, and he has dreads that fall to each side like merry waterfalls. His love for animals inspires him to become a ranger in the future at a national park, and because rangers often dress in green, that's his favorite color.

"I've heard nothing about soldiers coming," I tell him. "What's this all about?"

"They're passing through our village to go to the border with D R Congo," Oscar chimes. "There's trouble in Danjou!"

My heart accelerates as this is the second time in less than half an hour that I've heard about trouble in Danjou. For weeks, news has reached us about strained relations in Danjou and surrounding areas because of a recent discovery of diamonds in the region, but the report of Zambian soldiers traveling north to the border represents an abrupt worsening of events.

"Who told you soldiers are coming?" I ask Oscar.

"Innocent Mbewe," he replies. "We just saw him as he was walking home."

Now I understand why Innocent objected to my decision to go to Danjou. I'm puzzled, however, that he made no mention of soldiers while we evaluated the burn patient.

"Do you want to stay with us to watch the soldiers pass?" Oscar asks. "They will be coming soon, Innocent says."

"I'd like to stay, but I need to get some things done at home," I reply.

A worried look comes over Benji. "Innocent told us you're going to Danjou tomorrow, *nudume*. Why are you doing that?"

I'm annoyed with Innocent for sharing this decision with the boys. "It's complicated," I tell them. "But I won't be gone long."

"Will you drive the truck to Danjou?" Oscar asks, his face inquisitive.

I know why he inquires: Oscar has a passion for vehicles. If I ever need to find him when he's not in school, I needn't look further than a spot under a mango tree where we park the hospital's lone vehicle, an old flatbed truck which *tata* Murphy bought years ago. When the truck requires maintenance or repair, Oscar is present to assist the mechanics. One day, he tells me, he'd like to own a garage and fix cars. In his room at the orphans' quarters, a magazine photo showing a mechanic working on an engine hangs from the wall above where he sleeps. The mechanic wears a blue shirt, and for that reason, Oscar does the same.

"Yes, I'll drive the truck to Danjou," I tell Oscar.

"The oil and petrol levels are fine. We checked them today," he tells me.

"Thanks for telling me, Oscar. That's good to know."

I leave the boys in the village to continue walking home. Although the moon is in the first quarter of its cycle, it casts sufficient light for me to see a path that takes me away from the village through thick bush toward the river. As I near my shack, I ignite a kerosene lamp for additional light. I keep a whistle between my lips which I blow every few steps. It was given to me by the hospital staff with the instruction that I blow it while walking to or from my shack in darkness to ward off predators.

My choice of where to live is not popular among the paramedics. Upon arriving in Saysha, I told them that the home in the village vacated by *tata* Murphy was not the right place for me to live. As an alternative, I proposed to build a dwelling along the Amalumbo River that skirts the village because, metaphorically speaking, flowing water helps me move on in life. I made that insight while working in the Amazon rainforest. My job there entailed treating employees of a multinational corporation called TransNational Oil that tapped vast tracts of rainforest for its oil reserves. The house I lived in had bamboo walls and a roof made from banana leaves. It stood on stilts and straddled a tributary of the Amazon River which afforded solitude and spectacular wildlife sightings.

After receiving reluctant approval to build on a bluff above the Amalumbo River, I asked Innocent and several other paramedics to help me build the hut. We sank young tree trunks into the ground and threw mud at them to form walls. Grasses from marshes along the river formed the thatched roof. I added a small covered patio in back which overlooks the river, and it wasn't long before a shoebill stork built its nest on my roof. The two of us sit in our different worlds looking over the river and wilderness that extends northeast to the border of Tanzania and Lake Tanganyika. As the village's sole *mzungu*, or person of European descent, I respect the privacy of the village and find solace in living apart from it.

I reach the clearing before my hut and notice all is not well. Stalks of grass that formed a wall around the latrine have been knocked to the ground to expose the privy. Clothes hung to dry are strewn about. Inside the hut, my cot is overturned and dishes and cutlery litter the floor, but nothing appears to have been stolen. Oddly, the only area left undisturbed is a small table in a corner where I keep a bar of soap, a washcloth, and my toothbrush. Beside these items is an addition that makes my skin tingle: a tube of blood with a label reading, *Biohazardous Material—Handle with Caution.* When I pick it up, I find the tube is cold, as if it had been removed recently from an ice pack or refrigerator.

What puzzles me is that while the place appears to have been ransacked, nothing of value was taken. Remaining on a small shelf in clear view are my passport, a silver necklace, and a watch, leading me to conclude that whoever disheveled my belongings did so not to steal but to warn.

But what are they warning me about?

And what message could possibly be conveyed in a *cold* tube of blood?

I UNDERSTAND INNOCENT Mbewe's discomfort at hearing the name, Danjou. For the paramedic, it stokes memories of escape from his native D R Congo three years earlier. As a subsistence farmer there, he witnessed the killing of an elephant one day on his land. Three men from his village brandishing machetes emerged from a grove of trees at the edge of Innocent's farm and surrounded the animal. While one man distracted the elephant, the remaining two plunged blades into the animal's sides, repeating the stabs until the behemoth slumped. Even as the elephant gasped for air, the men severed its tusks for personal gain—all because the elephant had plundered the men's fields of maize.

Distraught, Innocent reported the killing to authorities at a nearby reserve. The killers were fined but weren't imprisoned because the judge ruled the attack didn't constitute poaching—killing strictly for the sale of animal components—but, rather, retribution for the elephant's marauding of crops. After paying fines, the three farmers meted out a justice of their own, beating Innocent to near-death. A cousin of Innocent's found him in a field and ferried the young farmer in an oxcart to the nearest town of Danjou, but lacking funds to pay for medical care, the cousin hired a driver to transport Innocent across the border to our hospital in Saysha. After recovering, Innocent gained asylum in Zambia. To thank the hospital for saving his life, he apprenticed as a paramedic under *tata* Murphy and remained in Saysha thereafter.

Late as it is, I hurry to Innocent's hut. The village is silent now. Even the fires used earlier to cook dinners outside have faded to embers.

I stoop before a doorway and whisper, "Innocent, are you there? We need to speak!"

I repeat the summons several times before the paramedic appears. He steps outside to join me.

"I'm sorry to disturb you," I say, "but something happened."

"What is it, *nudume*?"

"While we were at the hospital with the burn patient, someone raided my home."

"Did they steal anything?"

"No, but they left something very odd."

He tilts his head.

I extract the tube of blood from my pocket and show it to him. "This was *cold* when I found it."

He takes it from me. "It has warmed," he observes.

"Because it was in my pocket as I rushed here."

He reads the warning. " 'Biohazardous Material.' We don't use such labels here."

"Nor tubes like this," I add.

By convention, lavender top tubes of the sort I hold are used to collect venous blood specimens tested for blood values such as red and white cell counts. The tubes contain an anticoagulant that keeps blood from clotting prior to testing.

"You're right, *nudume*: the lavender top tubes we use here are plastic with screw-off caps whereas this one is glass and has a rubber stopper."

"And the sizes differ as well; ours are smaller than this one." I slip the tube into my shirt pocket again and button it securely.

"How did it come to be cold?" Innocent asks.

At the hospital pharmacy we have a generator-powered refrigerator to keep our vaccines cold. On occasion, we store a sample of blood, tissue, or fluid in it for a short time before someone drives it to a large town called Mposto to have it shipped to a diagnostic center in Lusaka, but those occasions are rare.

"We need to ask our paramedics if anyone knows about this tube," I say. I lean closer to him and lower my voice so that it's barely audible. "And I want you to ask around to see if anyone saw a stranger about the village earlier today or someone who may have gone to my shack while we were at the hospital."

"I will ask, *nudume*."

I thank Innocent and back away to give him space before I address the next matter. "Who is this Annette Wilson that sent the message to me with the burn patient?" I ask him this because I know he has many contacts in Danjou from his days of living near the town.

He frowns. "I've only heard of this woman. She's from Ireland and keeps an apartment in Danjou."

"What does she do there?"

"She works for a private group."

"Doing what?"

"Taking photos."

"Of what?" I feel as if I'm drilling teeth or extracting a sliver from deep within a toe; progress comes painfully slowly.

He becomes agitated. "I do not know!"

I've pushed him beyond his comfort zone. "Thank you, Innocent." I prepare to leave.

"I hope you're not going to Danjou tomorrow as you said earlier. Did you hear the soldiers' trucks roar through the village twenty minutes ago?"

"No, I was at my home at the time."

"So, don't go to Danjou!"

"I won't go alone," I tell him.

My reassurance has failed. His face is heavy with concern as he turns to leave.

2

I SLEEP IN fits, haunted by the realization that someone scouted my shack to know when to storm it. I have two theories for why they did so—robbery or harassment—but the facts don't support either well. If burglary was the intent, the robber was incompetent given his failure to abscond with the valuables I'd left in clear view. Which leaves harassment; perhaps pillaging my belongings was a statement or a threat of some kind, but for what, I don't know. During the five months I've worked at the hospital, not once has a patient expressed discontent with the care received. To the contrary, gratitude has been the rule.

As for the tube of cold blood I found, it fits neither theory—robbery nor harassment.

Of more concern to me at the moment is the intruder's shredding of the mosquito net above my cot. In the darkness, critters buzz about me. A burning coil does little to dispel them, and I wave my arm about futilely. In this area, mosquito-borne infections are common, particularly malaria, although I've treated patients with yellow fever and dengue, too. While I take prophylactic medication to thwart malaria and have been vaccinated against both yellow fever and dengue, the vaccine for dengue is a relatively new one with a spotty record of protecting against the four different strains of virus that circulate, which leaves me susceptible to an infection that, in its severe form, causes fever, bleeding, and fatal shock.

In the distance, from across the river, I hear the sounds of hyenas battling a pack of wild dogs over a kill, most likely an impala. The hyenas emit a high-pitched growl I find eerily similar to that of cats in battle while the dogs, likely outnumbering the hyenas, issue staccato clattering yelps. After a while, the battle ends, and all is silent save for the chirp of a cricket that has found its way into my shack. I lift my head to assure myself that the grated metal doors at front and back are locked to protect me from the outside world.

Unable to sleep, I get up and light a candle. I use what remains of my laptop battery to review a job announcement for a physician in rural Indonesia. A week ago I managed to connect to the Internet long enough to discover the job opening. I complete the application now and save it just before my battery runs dead. At the next possible opportunity, I'll submit the application electronically.

In flickering candlelight, I sit on my cot to look through the grates of the back door upon the Amalumbo River. Moonlight shimmers from the surface of what looks like a silver ribbon winding along a black backdrop. When children visit to sit on the patio overlooking the river, I benefit from their sharp eyes and keen awareness of wildlife. The other day, Benji, a master at spotting animals, pointed out an elusive deer-like waterbuck along the shoreline. I was intrigued to learn that the waterbuck is a skilled swimmer that produces a scent in water that repels crocodiles. Although my knowledge of animals isn't as deep as his, he listens with rapt attention when I tell him about my experiences in the Amazon rainforest tracking jaguars with members of an indigenous tribe.

SUN FROM THE river reflects onto the ceiling of the patio roof. I sip tea prepared over a kerosene stove in my shack. Breakfast consists of flatbread baked over hot stones in the village, and to spruce it up, I add jam which I purchased from the sole grocery store in Saysha, a sparsely-stocked facility with the braggadocian name, *North Zambia Trading Center.*

As I eat, I look for the hippopotamus that frequents the river in the early morning. I spot it at a bend a hundred meters upstream. Only his head is visible, a dark knob just above the surface. A gargantuan mouth opens before the animal disappears under a swirl of water marking the site of its descent.

The Amalumbo River runs fifteen hundred kilometers from its origin in D R Congo to Lake Malawi. Through Zambia, much of its course traverses desolate lands where few humans live. For this reason, the river is a haven for wildlife, so much so a bill has been introduced in the National Assembly to designate a portion of the river and thousands of square kilometers to the northeast as a national park. The bill is hotly contested by the mining sector which seeks to tap the area's minerals. With the recent discovery of diamonds along the river in D R Congo, the mining companies, some with international operations, have stepped up pressure to defeat the bill.

I finish breakfast and go to the courtyard out front to pump water for the day. Before building my shack, I paid a drilling company to bore a hole to determine whether a source of drinking water could be tapped. The drilling proved to be productive by striking water at eight meters which supplies ample potable water. I work the handle now to top off a small reservoir for bathing and drinking purposes before I fill several bottles to take with me to the hospital.

I begin workdays by recharging the batteries of my laptop. Since a generator at the hospital provides the only electricity we have in Saysha, I try to get there early to plug in. This morning, however, there's no power because we've run out of fuel for the generator. I'm told that someone has just rushed off to the depot in the village to get more but it'll be twenty minutes before they return. I set the laptop aside and turn to my next task: meeting with the paramedics to examine patients. I find the paramedics huddled outside in uncharacteristically energetic chatter.

"Good morning all," I greet them.

Immediately, they give me their full attention.

"*Nudume*," one calls from the rear of the group, "we heard about what happened at your home last night and are very concerned."

"As am I," I say. "We need to discuss this before we see our patients."

The fifteen paramedics step closer to form a tight cluster.

"Let me begin by asking whether anyone noticed a stranger take the path to my shack last evening as darkness fell."

Heads shake.

"What about anything else that may have been unusual yesterday?"

A paramedic with a round face steps forward. Her name is Cynthia and she's one of four female paramedics. "*Nudume*," she says, "a small aircraft landed in the distance yesterday. I saw it descend, but I don't know if it was an airplane from the Interior Ministry."

"What time did you see it?" I ask.

"Mid-afternoon."

"Were you able to see any markings on the airplane?"

"No, only that it had two propellers."

"And did you hear it take off again?"

"No, but that may be because the evening wind blows away from Saysha, carrying sounds with it."

The observation, while intriguing, is not unprecedented because aircraft from the Interior Ministry fly over our region occasionally to conduct resource surveys. On rare occasions, they land on a field several kilometers west of Saysha to carry out their work.

"I'd like you to follow-up on what you saw," I tell Cynthia. "Please check with the Interior Ministry headquarters to see if an aircraft of theirs made a landing yesterday in our area. Let me know what you learn."

"Yes, *nudume*."

"Now to the matter of the blood," I continue. "Does anyone know where the tube of blood I found in my shack came from?"

Heads shake.

"Well then, after I discovered it last night, I brought it to the hospital and left it in the refrigerator with a note asking Katrine to prepare a smear of it using standard stains."

Katrine is a technician in the lab who runs blood tests. She's meticulous with her work and arrives early every morning. After graduating from secondary school, she completed training as a medical technician in Lusaka with financial backing from *tata* Murphy. Although hospitals in the capital wooed her, she returned to Saysha to be near her aging parents. Although our resources are limited, she makes the most of them with unending patience. Because we can't afford an automated blood cell counter, she prepares blood smears manually and uses light microscopy to report her findings.

"Would someone ask Katrine to come join us?" I ask.

A paramedic hurries to the lab and emerges with a young woman wearing a white coat.

"Katrine, good morning," I call to her. "I trust you saw the sample I left in the refrigerator last night?"

She stops behind the group, a short woman whose face I barely see over shoulders. Bodies soon part to form a channel that allows Katrine to face me unimpeded.

"Yes, *nudume*, I just finished examining the specimen. The results are unusual."

Mumbling erupts.

"Hang on, folks," I say. "Let Katrine continue."

"I don't believe the blood comes from a human," she declares.

The mumbles escalate.

I raise a hand. "Please, let's hear Katrine."

"Using a standard stain," she explains, "I noticed many more immature red blood cells than I'd expect to see in a human blood sample."

"By 'immature red blood cells,' you're referring to 'reticulocytes,' I presume?" I ask.

"Yes, red cells freshly produced by the bone marrow. These cells normally take a day or two to assume the appearance of mature red cells and are larger than their mature counterparts."

I nod. "Very true; please continue."

"So I prepared a second smear using a stain called 'new methylene blue.' It turns RNA in red blood cells purple."

For the benefit of the paramedics, I interject: "Mature red blood cells don't have residual ribonucleic acid, or RNA, in them whereas immature ones do." I turn to Katrine. "What did you find?"

"I saw a good deal of purple streaking in the reticulocytes, indicating the presence of RNA. This is why I'm sure they were immature red cells."

"But there are a number of conditions and diseases in humans that can lead to elevations in the number of reticulocytes," I say. "For example, previous bleeding or even anemia can cause the bone marrow to rev up its production of red cells, leading to increases in the reticulocyte count."

Katrine frowns, telling me she's not convinced. "But there is something about the purple streaking I saw that makes me suspicious this is not human blood. It was far more prominent than anything I've ever seen."

"So, what does this mean, *nudume*?" a paramedic asks.

"I'll think about our next step," I say. "In the meantime, we mustn't let this matter interfere with our work. We've many patients to see."

If I've put their minds at ease, mine swirls with concern. Too many events have happened to dismiss them as innocent: a message has announced my life is endangered; my shack has been ransacked; a tube of blood left with my possessions has produced suspicious results on laboratory analysis; and an airplane has been sighted in the vicinity of our village. I'm worried these events are connected somehow to work I did in the Amazon rainforest of Ecuador before I moved to Zambia.

The airplane sighting troubles me especially because if it was the means by which the blood was delivered to Saysha, it would indicate the specimen came from afar. Even though I know online mapping software and satellite images make it relatively easy to pinpoint specific geographic sites, I'm still concerned that the sender found my elusive shack.

I formulate my next step, one I'll take before I leave for Danjou.

THIS MORNING AS the paramedics and I begin examining patients, we see the sickest first along with those admitted overnight. A six-year-old boy who came to the hospital in the middle of the night with severe diarrhea and a diagnosis of cholera continues to receive intravenous saline because he can't keep oral fluids down. A middle-age man with malaria has been started on appropriate drugs.

While I'm confident now treating patients with tropical diseases, my training in the U.S. provided little experience in this realm. After completing two years of a general surgery residency, I switched to a residency in emergency medicine because I wanted to be able to move about freely. After completing my residency, I worked in the emergency department of a Boston hospital for three years where I saw little in the way of tropical diseases. A divorce and no offspring led me to abandon the job and move to Washington, D.C. where I accepted a two-year consulting position with the Peace Corps. Much of my time was spent in poor nations evaluating the health of volunteers and the systems that provided them with medical care. I found it liberating to live out of a suitcase while moving from nation to nation, a change I welcomed after my marriage failed.

My stint with the Peace Corps motivated me to complete a one-year degree at the London School of Tropical Medicine and Hygiene. Toward the end of my studies, a professor offered me a two-year position in the Amazon rainforest of Ecuador funded by a company called TransNational Oil. The job entailed taking care of oil workers and overseeing a clinical trial involving a new malaria vaccine. I accepted the job and, in doing so, gained first-hand experience treating diseases I'd studied in London. Moving to Zambia came as a natural sequel.

The paramedics and I stand now before the burn patient. Last evening, after carrying her to this space, I evaluated her from head-to-toe with another paramedic named Bristol. We concluded the burn was confined to her head and neck, but much of it consists of third-degree burns, meaning all layers of the skin have been damaged. In some spots, muscles have been burned, too, a serious situation that will strain our ability to provide her with the treatment she requires.

Bristol reports now that the woman's night was uncomfortable notwithstanding the receipt of pain medications. An intravenous line continues to deliver saline. The burn oozes less than last night but looks more raw and charred. I see daunting hurdles ahead—pain alleviation, wound debridement, infection control, skin grafting, and physical therapy, all for a woman who sits on a mat atop a dirt floor. With minimal anesthesia resources and a metal table for an operating suite, we'll do what we can to help her.

We complete our rounds on patients which leaves the paramedics free to undertake their clinical chores. I pull Bristol aside to talk quietly. He's good-natured, attentive to patients, and shows empathy for those in pain. He's also dependable, which is why I seek him now. I tell him about my plans to drive to Danjou and ask him to lead the paramedics in my absence. He's not happy with what he hears.

"I understand your concern," I tell him, "but I feel compelled to find the Irish woman who sent me the note with the burn patient. If I don't return by tomorrow night, call my mobile." I hand him a slip of paper. "And if I don't answer after three attempts, you're to report to the American Embassy in Lusaka that I'm missing. Here's their number."

I leave Bristol to go to the laboratory to find Katrine. She sits before a microscope examining a blood smear. "Katrine, got a minute?" I ask.

Generous with her time, she turns to me.

"We need to call our friend," I say.

"Raymond?" she asks.

I nod.

Raymond Chabala is one of the sharpest physicians I know. After earning his medical degree, the Zambian native traveled to Germany to complete a residency in pathology followed by a PhD in biomolecular mechanisms from the Max Planck Institute for Medical Research. He then returned to Lusaka to run the diagnostic laboratory at the university hospital. I met him briefly there several months ago on a trip to Lusaka. Katrine, in turn, met Chabala while she trained to become a medical technologist in the capital. She broke his heart when she declined a job offer to remain at the university hospital. Not infrequently, we consult Chabala on difficult laboratory issues, and his staff runs tests for us at no charge.

"I think I know why you want to call him," Katrine says. She points to the refrigerator. "It regards the blood sample you found in your shack, doesn't it?"

"Yes, I'd like to see if he'd look at it."

Together, we place the call and reach him readily.

No conversation starts without his jocular reminder that he'd hoped Katrine would've taken the job he offered after she graduated. Katrine is gracious and thanks him for his confidence in her.

"Listen," I say, "we need your help." I explain the nature of my request.

"Let me get this straight," he says. "You want us to determine whether the blood you discovered in your home came from an animal or a human?"

"That's right. I trust Katrine's suspicion that it may have come from an animal, and I'd like to get your confirmation of that."

"Far from me to disagree with Katrine," he chuckles. "But we'll take a good look at it."

We make arrangements for Katrine to ship the sample to Lusaka.

"Can't thank you enough," I tell Chabala. I leave the laboratory knowing the blood is in good hands.

I'VE TOLD ONLY two paramedics of my decision to travel to Danjou: Innocent Mbewe and Bristol. I'm sure they'll spread the word before long so I'd like to hit the road before my departure becomes a topic of general conversation.

I waste no time in collecting my backpack from the office beside the pharmacy before I go to the flatbed truck parked along the hospital perimeter. It's a school day but for some reason the students are out early. I see two of the older orphans walking toward me now. They greet me with beaming smiles.

"*Nudume*, we're excited!" one announces.

Thandi is a tall, lanky girl. Still finding her legs, she stumbles sometimes while walking but usually catches herself. Despite being only twelve, she carries on as an adult. This is because her parents died from HIV/AIDS several years ago, leaving her to fend for herself until the hospital provided her space in the orphans' quarters.

"What are you excited about?" I ask her.

Unable to restrain herself, her friend, Amu, exclaims, "Teacher Daniel told us we'll help you install solar panels on the pharmacy roof soon. We can't wait!"

Short for "Amukasana," Amu glides when she walks. Among the village girls, she's the most athletic. She lost her mother at childbirth and her father from tuberculosis when she was eight. Before he died, her father taught Amu how to play soccer, or "football" as it's called here. In the open spaces between hospital huts, I often see her juggling a ball with ease. When no ball is available, she kicks a dried coconut. She's the only girl who plays in games the boys organize, yet she stands out as one of the best players. When it comes to choosing teams, she's selected among the first.

"I'm so glad you'll help me with the solar panels," I say.

Four months ago, when I drove to Danjou to purchase medical supplies, I came upon a hardware store going out of business. They'd reduced their prices dramatically, so I bought the supplies needed to build a small solar power system at the hospital. Frustrated we had only one generator, I wanted to produce more electricity. The supplies have been sitting around since then because I've been too busy to install them. When a teacher named Daniel at the school learned of the supplies, he asked if the older students could help with the project as a learning experience. I thought it was a brilliant idea.

"When will we do the work?" Thandi asks.

"Soon," I promise. "I'll speak to teacher Daniel to set a date."

I leave the girls and hurry to a mango tree under which we keep the flatbed truck. Purchased by *tata* Murphy two decades earlier, the vehicle has endured years of journeys over inhospitable roads, yet the engine and suspension have been maintained.

I throw my backpack into the cab and take the wheel. Even though I drive slowly through the village, I leave a dirt plume behind me. The end of the hot dry season is here, and the earth is parched. Normally, the rains would've begun but climate change has upended norms. For three years in a row, far less rain has fallen than expected, leaving rivers low. In the south, the mighty Victoria Falls has diminished to a trickle. Locals tell me they no longer visit the falls because they're sad to see it so depleted; even tourism at the World Heritage Site sags significantly.

Before long, I leave the village behind. Folklore holds that the road from Saysha to Danjou began as a trail eons ago etched into the earth by elephants, zebra, and other animals that migrated along the Amalumbo River. Each year as grasses turned brown during dry season, animals moved north to greener pastures near Lake Tanganyika only to return with the rains. As humans settled the area, the animals retreated to less populated land east of the river, creating a swath that, to this day, hosts a rich array of wildlife.

As I drive, I'm grateful the rains haven't begun because the route to Danjou becomes impassable when wet, even by truck. As it is, barely a kilometer out of Saysha, I slow to negotiate ruts so deep the truck sways back and forth like a ship at sea. In the dirt, I see fresh tracks from the military convoy that passed through Saysha last night on its way to the border with D R Congo. Behind my seat on a rack, a Vektor R5 rifle used in earlier times by the South African military reminds me of the need to remain vigilant at all times. The hospital acquired the weapon as a gift years ago from a grateful patient who underwent surgery for a ruptured appendix. Shortly after I moved to Saysha, a paramedic who happened to be a former soldier himself insisted I learn to fire the rifle and store it in my hut as a defense against animal incursions. For target practice, he took me into the countryside to shoot mangoes.

Gripping the wheel, I round the first of a series of hairpin bends that take me up a hill and down again into a ravine where I negotiate a dry creek bed only to face another hill. The sequence of ascents, descents, and ravine crossings repeats itself several times while, to my right a hundred meters away, the Amalumbo River churns through a narrow canyon. In my mind, I envision an aerial view of the area looking like a fish skeleton with the river being the spine and hills radiating from it the ribs. Scaling each hill is a stomach-twisting venture, for the road is narrow and slippery and has no guard rails. Presently, the ravines are dry, but with the onset of rains they become torrents that gush into the river.

I stop at a summit to stretch. Removing the rifle, I step outside and peer through its scope at a small tree below in a ravine. Hanging from a branch is a half-devoured carcass.

"Most likely a kudu, *nudume*," a voice calls from the bed of the truck.

Startled, I turn to find Benji standing on the flatbed. He shields his eyes from the sun as he peers at the tree, adding, "It was caught by a cheetah, I believe." He jumps to the ground.

Astonished, I ask: "What are you *doing* here, Benji?"

I start toward the rear of the truck but before I reach it, I see a pair of feet drop to the ground from under the chassis. A second boy appears.

"Oscar!" I call.

He hurries to Benji's side where the two stand sheepishly.

I stoop to look under the truck to see how Oscar managed to hide there. A space that normally holds a spare tire has been vacated to make room for a small body. Ropes fashioned into a pair of handles hang from the chassis. I'm reminded of a news story about a teenager who survived a flight unharmed from mainland United States to Hawaii by hiding in the landing gear of a jumbo jet.

I approach the boys with exasperation. "This isn't right!" I admonish them. "You shouldn't be here!"

They cower. Along one side of Benji's head, the dreads press his face as if they'd been flattened during transport.

Hearing no response, I glance at a wooden crate secured in a forward corner of the flatbed. I've seen the crate often, a container used to house tools. Presently, it's covered by a burlap sack.

I point to the crate. "So, that's where you hid, did you?" I ask, an indictment more than a question.

"Yes, *nudume*," Benji admits.

The boys sulk at my displeasure. "Shall we walk home?" Oscar asks sorrowfully.

"*Walk*? We're two hours from Saysha by truck!" I point to the ravine. "You'll end up like one of those carcasses down there if you walk." I try to contain my anger but fail. "Oscar," I shout, "you betrayed me with your knowledge of this truck! You picked a dangerous spot in which to hide, and I would've been responsible for you if you'd fallen out!"

The boy lowers his head and, after staring at the ground for a moment, begins to cry. The remorse is infectious for Benji follows suit. Tears fall to the ground to form tiny craters in the dirt.

I approach them and place a hand on their shoulders. "We'll travel to Danjou together," I tell them. "Come into the cab with me."

I take my seat, but I notice the boys remain outside the passenger door. "Get in!" I call. "Why are you waiting?"

Oscar approaches the lowered window. "*Nudume*, will you allow me to sit beside you?"

"Of course, why do you ask?"

He demurs. "You're angry with me. I've never heard you shout before."

I grasp the wheel and look out my window. I've broken a promise I made to myself not to berate children the way my father reproved me.

Early on, I attended public schools in the Hudson Valley of New York where I grew up. During seventh grade, I rode with my father to school each day. Along the way, he warned me regularly that if I didn't rank in the top five percent of my class he'd send me to boarding school. After dropping me off each morning, he'd rush to catch a train to his investment banking firm on Wall Street. To my father, educating a child was no different than investing venture capital; the goal of each was to maximize returns. Because I fell short on his metrics for performance, he considered me a failed investment. Boarding school was a last-ditch attempt to salvage his investment, even if it meant doling out more funds. So off to New Hampshire I went to begin eighth grade.

I was miserable and did poorly there. When I came home for breaks, my father rebuked me constantly. Although he'd never been in the military, he adopted a drill sergeant style to address me, shouting orders and implementing curfews. One summer between my sophomore and junior years, a buddy from school visited me at home. Following the visit, he asked whether I'd read the novel *The Great Santini* by Pat Conroy. I checked it out from the library, and I couldn't put it down because it read like a biography of my life. In it, a demanding Marine fighter pilot father commands his family as if they're a military unit under his control. I realized then that I'd never meet my father's expectations.

The revelation led me at Thanksgiving during my senior year to avoid going home. Instead, I caught a bus to New York City where I spent the weekend. When I didn't show up at home, my mother called to ask where I was. I told her I couldn't stand being shouted at by my father any longer. My younger brother and sister joined my mother in a chorus of protest, but I held firm; returning home would only reignite my father's wrath.

On Thanksgiving night, I left the seedy motel I'd checked into in the Bronx and ate a burger at a fast-food joint. I was fortunate to find the place open as everywhere else was shuttered. At a table beside me a homeless man nibbled on a sandwich in an effort to extend the meal to closing time. After leaving the joint, I declined the overture of a hooker and spent the next few hours walking the streets listening to my iPod. One song spoke to me in particular, Simon & Garfunkel's *Sounds of Silence*, a piece from a previous generation my mother had introduced me to months earlier. Its lyrics brought me solace, as in: *Hello darkness, my old friend I've come to talk with you again.* As I listened to the song, I realized that in growing up we're never really taught how to be alone. To the contrary, lessons abound in social interaction—manners, greetings, appropriate responses, protocols—but few address loneliness and how to deal with it.

On the streets of New York City that Thanksgiving night, I realized being alone and being happy were compatible. Although I didn't recognize it at the time, I'd begun my journey in life as a vagabond.

I CARESS THE gearshift in the flatbed truck and look at Oscar standing outside with Benji. "How will I shift gears without you?" I ask Oscar.

He wipes his eyes, smiles, and enters the cab with Benji close behind.

Our bodies press together. Immediately beside me, Oscar places a hand on the gearshift with eager anticipation. Far more comfortable holding wrenches and screwdrivers than pencils, he shifts gears for me whenever we drive together. It's a custom we've practiced to perfection.

Not long after we set off, however, the hand drops and I take over the shifting. I'm not surprised the boys have fallen asleep: the heat, the crying, and the discomfort they endured in their former quarters have done them in.

After two more hours of driving, I stop for another stretch. The hills have given way to savannas where termite mounds, some reaching twenty feet in height, project skyward like rockets ready to launch. Others more rounded than pointed host subterranean colonies with termites that excavate rich soil which allows grasses, shrubs, and trees to grow beside them. These green zones attract grazers, and with a herd of antelope feeding off to one side, I sit still to watch them.

Beside me, the boys stir. They disentangle and sit erect. Wiping sleep from their eyes, they turn their heads one way, then another, leading them to spot the antelope.

"Puku," Benji mumbles, pointing out the window.

The adults stand just beneath three feet at the shoulder and weigh between one and two hundred pounds. They're sandy brown with lighter underbellies. Some twenty pukus congregate presently under a grove. While some eat, others watch warily.

"They have no horns," Benji observes, "which means they're females. The males are elsewhere guarding territory."

Oscar motions to leave his seat.

"Wait!" Benji says. He raises an arm to keep Oscar from leaving. Peering out the window, he says, "Do you see the giraffe in the distance?"

I crane my neck to follow his arm. Well beyond the grove, I see another collection of trees above which the head of a giraffe projects.

"You have eagle eyes, Benji," I tell him.

Oscar can wait no longer. "Let me out!" he demands.

With the opening of a door, the pukus prepare to flee. The boys slip out quietly but soon freeze.

"When the rainy season comes," Benji whispers, "the pukus will migrate to higher lands to avoid the flooding river."

I look at Benji and envision him wearing a green ranger's uniform within ten years.

I open my door and get out, sending the pukus away. As they sprint, they emit a shrill whistling sound.

We disperse to relieve ourselves before resuming our journey. Grasslands are replaced by barren fields where huts with thatched roofs dot the landscape. Evening arrives, and in the distance to one side, I see the distinct motion of arms rising and falling at a bore hole which provides well water. We pass a solo bicyclist and then a pedestrian. More walkers appear, many of them women balancing loads on their heads. Anticipation wells within my companions as they grow restive from the journey.

Along one side of the road, a clearing with countless poles fashioned from tree trunks stand to mark the site of a weekly outdoor market where farmers and merchants gather to sell crops and handicraft. When we see a store and then a brick building, we know civilization lies ahead.

After crossing a gully, we climb a hill but before reaching the summit, we come to a convoy of military vehicles parked along both sides that leaves only a narrow channel to traverse. A soldier from the Zambian armed forces controls a gate. I stop before it and wait for the soldier to approach.

He holds an assault rifle as his eyes dart from me to emblems on my windshield that prove the vehicle is current in paying required taxes to travel the nation's roads.

"Destination?" he asks.

"Danjou," I tell him.

He frowns. "Purpose of visit?"

"To meet a woman from Ireland."

"Her name?"

"Annette Wilson."

He looks across the seat at the boys. "Why are they with you?"

"I'm taking care of them. They live at a hospital where I work in Saysha."

"Are you a doctor?"

"Yes." I reach for a black bag on the floor beside Benji's feet and show him my stethoscope.

The display sets the soldier at ease. "I've heard of your hospital," he says. "I'm from a village not far away." He leans closer but only after looking both ways. "My mother is ill and short on cash. Can she be seen at your hospital?"

"Yes, we'll evaluate her," I reply.

He nods. "Good, my brother will bring her to you. Your name, doctor?"

I present my passport.

He glances at the photo before returning it.

"Your stay in Danjou must be brief! It's not safe there." He steps back, raises the gate, and waves us on.

We crawl forward, passing machine gun-mounted Humvees,

multi-mission wheeled vehicles, and a heavy equipment transporter with a tank as its payload.

The boys' eyes widen. "Is there war, *nudume*?" Oscar asks.

"Precautions only," I reply.

From the summit we see the lights of Danjou below. By virtue of having electricity, it seems much larger than Saysha, but it's not a large town by most standards. A border crossing before us prevents us from proceeding.

I park the truck and take the boys to a small building that serves as the border control office for Zambia. I offer my passport to the sole official inside. After stamping it, he points to the boys. "What about their passports?"

I explain the situation as to how the boys have come to travel with me and that I intend to return to Saysha with them the following day after a brief visit to Danjou.

He appears to understand my dilemma. "D R Congo may not allow them to enter without passports," he warns.

"I understand. We'll go home if that's the case."

We return to the truck and begin driving toward the border control office for D R Congo located a kilometer away. Before reaching it, however, I stop at a bend in the road where we can't be seen by personnel in either office. Darkness has fallen now as I address the boys: "I want you to hide again as you did before. Otherwise, we may not be able to enter D R Congo."

The two leave the cab to return to their positions.

Satisfied they can't be seen, I drive to the crossing where I purchase a visitor's visa. After leaving the office, I proceed to a gate where a soldier checks my paperwork. He peers into the back of the truck.

"Cargo?" he asks as he holds my passport.

"None," I reply.

He circles the vehicle, and my heart races. Handing me the passport, he says, "Go."

The gate opens and I heave a sigh of relief.

Houses and stores populate the road with increasing density as I drive, and I become worried when I pass a car pulled to the side to be inspected by soldiers. I stop along a darkened section well beyond them. Circling the truck, I summon Oscar and Benji to the cab because I don't want them to be discovered in their hiding places should we be stopped. They nestle beside me closer than ever.

As we enter Danjou proper, we see soldiers stationed on every street. Some wear helmets and others tan berets. Automatic weapons are prominently displayed.

"Keep your eyes out for a hair parlor," I tell the boys.

Most stores have closed for the day, leaving the town eerily quiet. A goat crosses the street and forces me to stop. As I wait, the flashing lights of a hotel catch my eye. I make a direct course to it and park before its entrance.

"Let's see what we can learn here," I tell the boys.

A single light bulb illuminates the hotel lobby. It wobbles from a ceiling fan and casts shifting rays through cigarette smoke rising from an attendant behind a counter.

"*Bon soir*," the man says, rising from a stool.

"Good evening," I reply. "I'm looking for a woman from Ireland by the name of Annette Wilson. Would you know where I can find her?"

"Your name, sir?" the man asks.

"I'm Dr. Paul Rider."

Politely, he offers me his hand which I shake. I get the feeling that westerners are seldom seen here or, alternatively, that he's pitching for me to stay at his hotel.

"Who is it, again, you seek?" he asks.

He leaves his station and comes around the counter to join me. He's small and wiry, little more than a hundred pounds, and his head barely reaches my shoulders. His white-collared shirt is frayed at the neck. He smiles now to reveal a set of teeth that seem to be too large for his mouth yet appropriately sized for his gargantuan jaws.

"I'm looking for Annette Wilson," I repeat. "She's a photographer who has an office in town, I'm told."

"But she's not a guest here?" he asks.

"No, she has an apartment."

"Then, I wouldn't know her," he says apologetically. "You see, Danjou is a town that's too large to know everyone but small enough not to get lost in." His politeness fades. "But this is no time to be searching for anyone because we're having trouble currently."

"What sort?"

"We have unwanted intruders."

"Who are they?"

"Extremists."

"From where?"

"Other nations."

"What are they doing here?"

He smiles, a feckless gesture to change subjects. "Our restaurant is serving lovely food," he says. He acknowledges the boys. "And I'm sure they're hungry."

Oscar taps my side. "*Nudume*, we *are* hungry."

As am I, for during the journey, I gave my meager lunch to the boys. I struggle now between mission and appetite. The latter prevails.

"Dinner it'll be," I say.

Our man beams. Raising an arm, he beckons us to accompany him to an airy room with tables and a stool-lined bar. At the far end of the room, a swinging door opens to a kitchen where steam rises from kettles. A chef pokes his head through the doorway to scan the attendance of his restaurant. He acknowledges us with a look of satisfaction.

Two other parties currently partake in dinner. One consists of a group of six who sit two tables away from the one we've been assigned. They speak in hushed tones and alternate between German and English. Beyond them, a lone traveler sips a beer as he shifts his eyes frequently from a travel guide to the room about him.

A waiter delivers menus. "Drinks?" he asks.

The boys are shy. "Water," Oscar says.

"But can it be sparkling, *nudume*?" Benji asks me.

I indulge the boys: "Of course, make it bubbly," I tell the waiter.

The boys wriggle in delight as our server leaves.

"You may have anything from the menu you like," I say. "Breakfast is a long time off."

"Where will we stay tonight?" Oscar asks.

"I'm not sure. We have more searching to do for the Irish woman."

"Is she your friend?" Benji asks.

I have no ready answer other than: "I'm not sure."

We order, and I'm pleased to see the boys wash their hands at a sink in the corner of the room. With the arrival of dinner, they use their fingers to form balls from a white dough-like paste called *nshima*, a staple prepared from maize. They dip the balls into sauce served with their meals while I cling to the custom of using a knife and fork. Midway through the meal, I see the party of six prepare to leave. I address them now.

"Excuse me, would any of you know a woman named Annette Wilson?"

When they shake their heads, I resume my meal, but I hear a jarring sound of utensils strike ceramic at the table of the lone traveler. I look over and see the man staring ahead with an ashen face.

After finishing our meals, I pay the bill and lead the boys out of the restaurant into the hotel lobby to leave.

"It is getting late, sir," our host calls from the counter. "It will not be safe in the night."

"We'll not dally," I assure him.

Outside, as I unlock the truck, I hear footsteps rush across the gravel. It's the traveler from the restaurant.

"Sir!" he calls urgently. "We need to speak!"

His accent tells me he's French. I open the door to the truck and tell the boys to get in.

"What is it?" I ask the man.

"The woman you spoke of inside, Annette Wilson, I know her!"

"You *do*?"

He angles his body between the truck and me and, as a spy might huddle with another, whispers, "I met her this past week. I work for a wildlife protection group in France, and I've been visiting the area for business. I know she's in grave danger."

"Why?"

Agitated, he glances both ways. "No time for details! They may be watching me. Just go to the circle down there, pass half-way around it, and continue on. You'll see a clinic on one side and a cement factory on the other. The street then narrows and you'll find a series of tin sheds side-by-side. Stop at the one with an orange light outside and ask for Felice."

"Who's Felice?"

He grasps my arm. "Do as I say! A curfew takes place shortly, and you must be off the streets."

Quickly, he retreats into the night.

I seek refuge in the truck where I find the boys anxious.

"Who was that, *nudume*?" Oscar asks, one hand clutching the gearshift.

I start the engine. "I don't know, but we must drive a short distance."

I follow the directions—circle, clinic, cement factory. The street narrows, and we come to dilapidated dwellings. The air reeks of sewage and trash. I park before a shack with an orange light above its doorway.

"Stay put, keep the doors locked, and honk if you need me," I instruct the boys. "I'll return shortly."

I leave the truck and cross an open gutter emitting a putrid odor. A mangy dog curled beside the shack lifts its head but makes no move to threaten me. I knock on a door which rattles with each rap.

An elderly woman appears. She has grey hair, bent fingers, and gnarled knuckles.

"Felice?" I ask.

"*Oui*," she replies.

"Do you speak English?"

"*Un peu*," she says, followed by, "a lee-tle."

"I'm looking for Annette Wilson."

"Who are you?" she asks. Suddenly, her English improves.

"Dr. Paul Rider. I work at the hospital in Saysha. Annette sent a message asking me to see her urgently."

Nodding as if she's familiar with my name, Felice juts her head through the doorway to look both ways before motioning me to enter.

I step into a single-room dwelling with a tin ceiling only inches over my head. A mat and pillow occupy the floor while another section holds a kerosene stove and assorted pots, pans, and utensils. In modest fashion, a board covers a commode in a corner. I suspect the products that pass through that commode and others like it in neighboring shacks emit the odor I smelled from the open gutter outside.

Felice bolts the door behind me. "Annette in trouble," she says.

"What sort?" I ask.

"Men try to catch her but she get away."

"Who were these men?"

"Extremists!"

"From where?"

"Another country!"

"How do you know Annette?"

"I clean office where she works."

"What office is that?"

"Animal office."

"What does she do with animals?"

"Take photos."

"She's a photographer?"

"Yes."

The response is consistent with what Innocent Mbewe had told me. Mindful of the boys, I say, "I need to see Annette. Where is she?"

"Hiding."

"Where?"

"You call her. Ask to see her."

"I don't have her number!"

"I give it." The woman retrieves a slip of paper and hands it to me.

I dial the number scribbled on it. A voice answers after the first ring. "Yes?"

"Paul Rider calling. Is this you, Annette?"

"Oh, God, yes, Paul! I'm so relieved to hear from you! You must be at Felice's."

"Just arrived. Where are you?"

"Felice will show you. Come now!"

I leave the phone to my ear after she disconnects. Everything's truncated here: discussions, sentences, and—I look about—living standards.

"Annette said you'd take me to see her," I tell Felice.

She goes to the table from which she collected the scrap of paper but now opens a drawer. She extracts a large cumbersome key that appears to come from the middle ages.

"We go!" she says.

Outside, a military jeep passes with a loudspeaker blaring full bore.

"Curfew begin in ten minutes," Felice tells me.

She turns to pursue a narrow gap between sheds, but I stop her before we enter it. "Wait, I must get my companions."

Bewildered, she pauses.

I return shortly with Oscar and Benji who receive a once-over from Felice before she resumes the lead. We follow her through a maze of ramshackle dwellings that makes me think of the *favelas* of Rio de Janeiro only this slum is comprised of single-story tin or wood-scrap structures that span flat terrain as opposed to the hillsides of Rio. Surprisingly agile, Felice maneuvers with ease, and I find myself trailing the boys. Along the way, I hear babies cry, radios blare, and brooms sweep.

At the outskirts of the tenements, we come to a church surrounded by brick houses.

"Convent," Felice whispers. "Nuns keep Annette." She leads us to a metal gate that opens to a cemetery. The boys suddenly fall back.

"*Nudume*, I'm not going there!" Oscar insists, pointing to moonlit gravestones.

Across the cemetery, the lights of a passing troop carrier streak the night. The flare of a spent cigarette makes an arc from truck to ground.

"You must come!" I whisper. "Stay close."

Felice inserts the key into a cavernous hole and with a heave opens a creaking gate. We step into the cemetery and, to Oscar's chagrin, the gate closes behind us.

We pass graves with plaques, plastic flowers, and mementos. At the head of one, a candle burns beside engraved letters dedicated to a fallen baby. Oscar squeezes my hand.

At the center of the cemetery, we stop before a large sarcophagus. Formed from sculpted limestone, the vault sits atop a thick marble slab. At one end, a crawl space is visible between limestone and marble.

With traffic silent at the moment, I hear mumbling inside the vault. To my ear, it sounds like a woman's voice.

"*Nudume*," Oscar whispers, "the place is haunted! I hear a voice in there!"

Felice kneels beside the vault. "Madam, we're here!" she whispers.

When a pair of feet emerges from the crawl space, Oscar and Benji hide behind my back. Before long, a female body resurrects itself in full form.

The woman who stands before us looks about nervously as if preparing for an ambush. She affords only a brief glance at me before she turns in a complete circle to scan our surroundings.

"Did the men come to your house looking for me?" she asks Felice.

"No."

The answer reassures her. She brushes her skirt, straightens her blouse, and runs a hand through her hair. Never before have I seen moonlight mix with auburn.

"Dr. Rider," she says, looking at me in earnest, "it's good to see you again."

I draw back. "Forgive me, but have we met?"

Her shoulders relax although her vigilance remains. "I'm Annette Wilson." She offers her hand.

As I shake it, bodies peel away from my back. Something calms the boys, for they stand beside me now. Perhaps it's the tone of Annette's voice or her resolve to trust us, or perhaps she's merely proven herself to be human rather than ghost.

"I'm not saying we've *actually* met," she explains. "But I feel I know you well."

"How can that be?"

"I'm familiar with the work you did with jaguars in the Amazon rainforest, and I respect it enormously."

I feel my past well up and seek to tamp it, but my eyes are drawn to a search light that illuminates the church and convent. A quick glance reveals it comes from a jeep on the street behind us.

"Get down!" I order.

Our bodies hit the ground just before the light passes. I hear a groan from Felice and worry that she has injured herself. I can't attend to her, however, because the light sweeps over us repeatedly as if its pilot has discovered something of interest.

Seconds turn to a minute before gunfire erupts from the area where I saw the jeep. A voice shrieks, and the light extinguishes. The jeep races into the night.

I maneuver to Felice's side. "Are you alright?"

She grasps a knee. "I hurt it when I went to the ground. I remain here after you go."

"No!" Annette insists. "I won't leave you!"

"What if the light has allowed them to see us?" Felice counters. "You *must* go and I will stay to delay them." She reaches for Annette's hand. The two peer at one another.

"I'll call you later tonight," Annette promises.

We retrace the path to the gate. In the silence, I whisper to Annette: "Who are these men that are after you?"

"Militants," she replies. "They've put me on their kill list, one you occupy as well."

I find the descriptors "militants" and "extremists" insufficiently precise to understand who these men are, but I let the matter slip for now.

"Why am I on a kill list with you?" I ask.

"Because they view us as enemies."

"My work as a physician puts me on a kill list?"

"No, what you did with jaguars in the Amazon put you on the list."

"I don't understand!"

"I'll explain later!" she snaps.

I grasp her arm as she reaches for the gate. "How do you know about the militants' kill list?"

"Someone I know discovered it online."

"*Who*?"

"We need to go!" she pleads.

We rush from the cemetery to the tenements which provide anonymity in their passages. After reaching a point deep within the maze, Annette stops along a walkway so narrow only one person can pass at a time. Beside me, cigarette smoke wafts through a crack. I hear voices inside the dwelling.

"We can't stay in this town!" I whisper to Annette.

"What choice do we have?"

"We have to escape!"

"*How*? There's fighting in the streets and soldiers everywhere!"

"And the curfew, *nudume*," Oscar adds. "I understand a little French and I heard them say on the loudspeaker that no one's allowed on the streets."

"We'll find a way!" I insist. I place a hand on Oscar's shoulder. "I'm assigning you and Benji very big jobs."

"What are they?" Benji asks.

"You, Benji, will collect the rifle from the truck and you, Oscar, the machete from the crate."

Benji's eyes widen. "What do we do with these things?"

"You'll carry them as you walk to Zambia with Miss Annette."

"*Walk* to Zambia?" Annette scoffs. "That's five kilometers from here! We'll be apprehended because of the curfew!"

"You'll go through countryside where no one'll see you," I tell her. "How well do you know Danjou?"

"Quite well."

"Can you confirm, then, that countryside runs parallel to the road which comes here from the border? That was my impression as we drove here."

"You're right, but there are animals and dogs wandering about in the bush."

"The boys will have weapons," I remind her.

"You're allowing me to use the rifle?" Benji asks.

"Yes, to protect yourselves," I reply.

Well before I arrived in Zambia, Benji had learned to fire the weapon. With his dream to work as a ranger in a game reserve one day, he convinced *tata* Murphy to teach him how to use the rifle. He even accompanied me one day into the bush during my training with the weapon to show me how well he could shoot it.

Annette looks at me with appall before addressing the boys: "What year in school are you?"

"Nearing the end of primary," Benji announces.

Annette glares at me.

I confront her before she protests. "We'll meet at the border control office at the entry to Zambia. This means you'll have to skirt the control station for D R Congo. As you know, the two are separated by a kilometer. I'll come in the truck and find you at the Zambia control office."

"I don't like this plan!" Annette declares.

I grow impatient. "Then offer another one!"

She's quick to do so: "We can hide in the truck until morning and then make a run for the border!"

"What if someone finds us tonight?" I ask.

She suggests alternatives: returning to the cemetery, checking into a hotel, or hiding with the nuns. For each, I remind her that the militants could find us.

She grimaces and clucks her tongue. "Alright, then, I'll go with your plan, but reluctantly!"

We set off again through passages and turns. Along one strip, I slip into a sewage-filled channel. One sock turns wet. Shoe sloshing, I catch up to the others who wait at the truck.

I unlock the door to retrieve the rifle. In the meantime, Oscar scrambles along the flatbed to the crate where he extracts the machete. Moonlight flickers from its blade.

I reach across the cab and file through the contents of the glove compartment. Pulling out a flashlight and a box of matches, I hand them to Annette. "Is your phone charged?" I ask her.

"Enough for the night."

"Keep it close," I tell her.

We stand in silence, Annette between the boys.

"Put your weapons down for a moment," she tells them.

After they do so, she takes the boys' hands and forms the beginning of a circle. She nods at me to fill the void, but I remain apart. Having driven the better part of a day to find her and, in doing so, put the boys at risk, I'm in no mood to partake in her circle.

She nods again, only more forcefully.

I capitulate.

"Thank you, Paul," she whispers.

My hands slip into those of the boys on each side of me. Their flesh is warm. Silence flows from the circle.

A full minute passes before headlights streak the night in the distance. We drop hands and take cover behind the truck. Before long, a military Humvee roars by.

"Time for you to go!" I say. I point into the darkness across the road. "And that's where you begin. Remember, I'll meet you in Zambia at the border station. Don't leave without me!"

The boys approach me. In their eyes I see a border of a different kind, one that separates childhood from manhood. They know they've come to that line and are about to cross it.

Together, they encircle me with their arms, and I look to the stars.

3

ANNETTE AND THE boys left me only moments ago, yet I feel they've been gone forever. I begin to question my plan to send them by foot to the Zambian border. A better idea would've been to flag a military vehicle to escort us in our truck to Zambia, but with a curfew in place, I doubt that would've worked. And deciphering extremists from military isn't clear here; flagging down the enemy would be disastrous.

I douse my doubt with a turn of the ignition. Leaving Felice's shack, I backtrack to the circle where I follow a road further into town. Before leaving with the boys, Annette asked that I swing by her office to pick up two large boxes she'd left on a loading dock. I keep an eye out for the landmarks she provided. Only a few lights flicker now as the hour grows late.

I pass a market, church, and small fountain before I find the two-story building. It is blue in front and has yellow balconies along its sides. I park behind it with the flatbed backed to a loading dock.

The boxes are where Annette said they'd be. Because they're heavy, I push each across the dock onto the truck. Before driving off, I text Annette…

Boxes collected

She's quick to reply…

In bush walking toward border.

I'm relieved to have such ready contact with her.

Setting off, I come to a screeching halt to avoid a soldier who runs onto the road. He motions with an assault rifle for me to leave the truck. By the time I do so, other soldiers from a troop carrier parked in the dark have stepped onto the road. They converse in French as they approach me with weapons raised.

An officer steps to the fore and speaks to me.

"I'm sorry, but I don't speak French," I tell him.

He comes close enough to tap my shoulder with the tip of his rifle. I obey his command to place my hands on the truck.

I'm groped from neck to ankles. My cell phone is taken.

"Give that back!" I shout.

"Shut up and turn!" the officer commands. His English is decent. "Passport!" he demands.

I ask for permission to retrieve it from the truck.

After inspecting the document, the officer barks, "Why did you break the curfew?"

"I'm a medical doctor on my way back to Zambia. I have ill patients there to take care of."

"Why did you come here?"

"To collect supplies for my hospital."

"What kind of supplies?"

"An inflatable raft," I reply.

He points to the rear of the truck. "Is it in the boxes?"

"Yes."

He orders his men onto the flatbed where they rip apart the boxes. One lifts a section of deflated rubber and the other an outboard motor.

"It's a Zodiac," I inform the officer.

He shows no interest in my cargo. "Take him to headquarters!"

A rifle pokes my side. "Get in!" a voice commands.

"My passport and phone!" I plead. "Give them to me!"

"They'll go to headquarters," the officer replies.

I board the flatbed with two soldiers who pin me into the middle seat. We make a U-turn and pass through the center of town. Before long, we come to a makeshift compound with tents and vehicles. A sentry raises a gate. After a short drive, we stop. I exit with the soldiers before a large tent.

Inside, an officer sits at a desk. Surrounded by soldiers with assault rifles, he takes my passport and phone from a soldier who accompanied me.

"I want those back!" I tell the officer.

He shakes his head and tells me to sit in a chair across the desk from him.

"Why've I been detained?" I ask. "I'm a doctor with ill patients in Zambia, and I need to return to take care of them as soon as possible."

He stands, a big man with a pistol at his waist and an insignia identifying him as a colonel. He flips through my passport. "A visitor's visa, I see, issued only three hours ago. Why so little time in our nation?"

"I came here to pick up a Zodiac raft," I tell him.

He wrinkles his brow. "A *raft*? Why would you need one at a hospital?"

"We serve a number of remote villages accessed by river."

The answer appears to satisfy him. He walks to a map of Africa on a tripod.

"You came to a dangerous area to collect the raft," he says. He sweeps a hand across the Horn of Africa. "We've seen an influx of Islamic militants from this region into our nation recently. They've already carried out attacks in Kenya in recent years and are moving south now."

"Why have they come here?" I ask.

"For money." He places a finger along the border between D R Congo and Zambia. "Diamond mining is lucrative."

"I've heard there's mining along the Amalumbo River."

"Yes, and the Islamic militants have turned Danjou into a miners' town. Teams depart at dawn to work the mines and return at night to sleep in shanty towns."

"Is it true a village nearby burned recently?"

"Yes, it was set fire by the militants in retribution for village elders refusing to allow their youth to work in the mines." The colonel stands, rounds the desk, and sits on its edge just inches from me. "Why are you helping the militants?" he asks.

"That's preposterous!"

He remains calm. "Come now, the militants value children highly as laborers and sex slaves. A large bounty goes to those who sell them children."

I smell the remnants of the colonel's last meal. It's as foul as the notion of a bounty on minors.

"You *do* know about the bounty, don't you?" he asks.

"No, I wasn't aware of it, but I'm not surprised given the nature of the group."

His eyes narrow. "You're not selling children?"

"Of course not!" I try to stand but his arm forces me back.

"Why do you lie?" His voice is unnervingly steady.

"I'm telling the truth! Why would you think I recruit children for Islamic militants?"

"Because, you sold two boys tonight, didn't you?"

I break out in a sweat. "What boys are you talking about?"

"Please, Dr. Rider, don't take me for a fool. A hotel receptionist informed us you had dinner with two boys this evening. Did you want to fatten them before the sale?"

"You can't be serious! If I were selling boys, would I parade them through a hotel?"

"You were careless," he replies. "More importantly, where did you get the boys? We checked with our border control officers to see if they recorded the entry of two boys with you earlier this evening. They stated you came alone. Did you smuggle them in or acquire them locally?"

"The boys you're referring to are orphans who live at the hospital where I work! They snuck onto my truck without my knowing it and accompanied me here. After I discovered them, I hid them in the truck when I entered your country because they didn't have passports."

"Where are they now?"

I inspect the colonel's uniform more closely. His insignia is haphazardly sewn and his shirt and trousers are a mismatch in fabric and color. When he breathes, his lips part enough to reveal a gold-capped incisor. It matches the glimmer of a garish bracelet around his wrist.

"Give me my phone," I repeat. I point to it on the desk.

He lifts it and runs a fingertip across it. "What's your password?"

"I'm not telling you!"

"Password!" he repeats.

"My phone's private!"

He draws his pistol. Around us, soldiers tense.

I relent.

The pistol returns to the holster. Manipulating the touch screen, the colonel asks: "Who's this person you just texted to say you'd picked up the boxes?"

"A woman who donated the Zodiac to my hospital."

He looks at me. "What's her name?"

I say nothing.

The pistol appears again. "Name!"

"Annette Wilson," I reply.

He spits at my feet. "Annette Wilson? How do you know her?"

"I don't, really; I just met her tonight for the first time."

"She's an instigator! Her photos bring trouble!"

"What photos are you referring to?"

"You know what photos I speak of—ones of poachers she posts on social media to stir trouble!"

"I commend her for her work," I say. "I don't think a rhino should be killed for its horns."

The colonel's nostrils flare. "You know *nothing* about our lives here! Many of our people have little to eat other than bush meat. It keeps them alive!"

"What are they going to do after they've killed all the game?"

He shakes his head with disdain before returning his attention to the mobile. "Why's Miss Wilson walking to the border?"

"Because her life's endangered here!"

"Of course it is! She brought danger on herself with her photos!" His eyes heap rage on me but abruptly turn to the ceiling as a helicopter's whir becomes audible. He addresses his soldiers. All but one rush from the tent.

In the meantime, gunfire erupts outside as the roar of the whirring intensifies.

"Get out!" the colonel yells.

I start for the exit just as an explosion obliterates the tent. My ears ring and pain shoots across my arm. Blood stains a sleeve below my shoulder. Crawling to the overturned desk, I find the colonel on his back. He shows a series of penetrating wounds across his head. One, a gaping hole along the temple, spurts arterial blood.

"Colonel!" I shout.

His lips quiver and he moves a leg but says nothing.

I look at my arm. It's bleeding from a laceration but not enough to keep me from attending to the colonel. For a moment, I debate whether to plug the spurt from his head or try to escape.

I look up and see the remaining soldier is still alive. He's just raised himself and appears dazed. About us, canvas litters the ground like a deflated lawn Santa at Christmas. Billowing smoke blurs the stars.

"Hey!" I shout to the soldier, "go to the truck and get my medical bag!"

He looks at me aimlessly. Beneath his helmet, his face is youthful but paralyzed by fear.

"Understand English?" I yell.

He shakes his head.

Gathering my shirttail, I wrap it about my index finger which I insert into the colonel's wound. The flow slows but doesn't cease. I sink the finger deeper. It scrapes bone before bouncing off brain.

Around us, the pace of gunfire slows. Vehicles are heard leaving the compound.

I shout at the soldier again only to find him weeping. Using my head, I summon him to my side. "Hospital?" I ask him.

He nods.

I free my hand, strip off my shirt, and rip it to produce a band that I tie around the colonel's head. "Let's go!" I tell the soldier.

Together, we carry the colonel to my truck, one of the last vehicles remaining in the compound. We lay the colonel across the seat where I bend his knees enough to allow me to drive. Across from me, the soldier props the colonel's head on his lap.

Just then, I realize my phone remains in the tent. I race from the truck to the canvas folds. Using moonlight as I can to guide me, I get on my hands and knees to search the folds. I sweep a hand under each one and my pulse quickens when I feel something. It's my passport. Tucking it away, I resume my search for the phone but quit when gunfire erupts again.

Returning to the truck, we drive to the exit of the compound where I see two soldiers removing their uniforms in exchange for civilian clothing. A jeep races by along the main road with the words *Forces Armées de la République Démocratique du Congo* on its side.

Beside me, the soldier points the direction I'm to go. After speeding through a ghost town, I see an illuminated red cross ahead. Before long, we stop before a small hospital where, to my relief, a gurney lies outside. With the engine idling, I park and rush around the truck to help the soldier unload the colonel. Together, we transfer him to the gurney. I motion for the solider to wheel our patient inside.

After the soldier departs, I speed away, resolute this time to swerve around any barriers that may appear. Fortunately, the road's deserted with not a single checkpoint in place. I race along the center to avoid the erosions that pock each side. Save for my headlights and dashboard, the world is pitch-black from what I assume is a power failure outside.

When I reach the border, I note the distance traversed: four kilometers. I crunch the numbers in my brain: If Annette and the boys have maintained a pace of three kilometers an hour and have taken a course that parallels the road, they're likely to be somewhere between the two countries' check points. By instinct, I reach for my phone to call Annette but remember I've lost it. For a moment, I think about doubling back to look for it again but dismiss the idea as too dangerous.

Before me, a lowered pole at the D R Congo crossing prevents me from proceeding. With no sign of anyone present in the roadside office, I maneuver the truck around the side of the gate to resume my way. When I reach the Zambia control station, I find it attended and lit.

I park and hurry inside. A sleeping official awakens.

"You can't enter D R Congo now," he says groggily. "Their border crossing has been closed due to an emergency."

"I just came from there!" I tell him. "I want to enter Zambia to return to my home in Saysha." I place my passport on the counter. "Have you seen an Irish woman and two boys traveling with her?"

He ignores my question and looks at me inquisitively. "Did you say you *came* from D R Congo?"

"Yes, I drove around their roadblock since no officials were present."

"And you live in Zambia?"

"Yes, in Saysha. I direct the hospital there." I give him a moment to arouse further. "An Irish woman and two boys," I repeat. "Have you seen them?"

"No."

I fret and look about. I lament not having written Annette's phone number on a slip of paper, for if I'd done so, I could ask the officer to call her for me.

"From where are they coming?" he asks.

"From D R Congo but through the bush; this is just about the time they should arrive."

He sits bolt upright, as if an electric shock has entered his derriere. "They're coming by *foot* through the bush?"

I nod.

"Why didn't they come with you?"

"Because it would've been too dangerous; there's gunfire in Danjou."

He's unconvinced. "But the bush is dangerous!"

I lift the passport and place it in his hands. "Please, may I continue into Zambia? I'll search for them up the road."

He opens the booklet, glances at the photo, then at me, finds a blank page, and stamps it. "What about your friends? Why not wait for them here?"

"I'll come back if I don't find them up the road." A thought comes to me: "Are the Zambian soldiers still up the way? I saw them there last night."

"Yes, they'll remain there as long as unrest continues across the border."

"Very good, I may or may not see you again," I tell him and turn to leave. "If my friends arrive while I'm gone, notify the soldiers."

"Let's hope they're safe," the man cautions. "We've had a cheetah around here that recently killed a child in a village nearby."

I RUSH TO the truck but before leaving the Zambia border station, I rev the engine because I know that if Oscar is around he'll recognize the roar. Slowly, I creep forward. With no traffic present, I carve arcs across the road to shine the headlights into the bush. Periodically, I stop to allow the beams to pierce the darkness where

I think I may have seen movements. When nothing pans out, I move on while I listen through open windows.

I recall from the evening before that only a kilometer separated the border station from the area where the Zambian military was camped. With each meter traversed and no sign of Annette and the boys, I grow more concerned. Mentally, I prepare to return to the border station to wait for them there if the soldiers report no sightings.

And then I hear it: a gun shot. The explosion is a familiar one—a low-pitched blast followed an instant later by a deep-throated but less intense mechanical echo. I've heard the sequence repeatedly while firing the Vektor R5 rifle, the very weapon Benji carries tonight.

I stop and rush outside. "Benji!" I shout.

I leave the road and begin trekking in the direction from which I heard the shot but soon find myself tangled in a thicket of brush that sends thorns into the clean shirt I put on before reaching the border crossing of D R Congo. I used the stop to dress my wound as well, noting then it didn't need sutures.

"Oscar! Benji! Annette!" I shriek.

No response.

I disentangle from the bushes and return to the truck with the hope that honking will draw their attention. Instead, it brings a military vehicle around a bend ahead. After stopping before me, three soldiers leap from it while a fourth rises from the interior with a machine gun trained on me. I lose all sight on account of a blinding search light.

"Announce yourself!" a soldier calls.

I provide my name and affiliation with the hospital in Saysha. For good measure, I raise my arms.

The search light dims. The three soldiers stand before me with weapons drawn. "Why are you here?" one asks.

I take him to be an officer. "I'm looking for a woman and two boys who were supposed to meet me at the border crossing after coming by foot from D R Congo. Because they weren't there when I checked for them minutes ago, I decided to search for them along the road here."

The officer directs me to lower my arms which I do gratefully.

"Identification," he orders.

I produce my passport and explain the events of the past twenty-four hours. It brings expressions of disbelief.

"Are you armed?" the officer asks.

"No."

"So it wasn't you who fired a gun moments ago?"

"You heard it, too?" I ask. My hopes surge with the realization that the military hadn't fired the shot. It reaffirms my thought that the Vektor R5 rifle produced the blast.

"Yes, we heard it and then the blare of your horn." He adjusts a strap over his shoulder that carries his rifle. "It wasn't a good decision for your partners to come by foot."

"I agree but at the time we made our decision, we thought it was the best action to take given the unrest in Danjou."

He inches forward at an angle before stopping alongside me. I feel as if I'm newly conscripted and under the intense inspection of a drill sergeant.

"No," he asserts, "during conflict, the best option is often to stay put."

"That was out of the question," I reply. I stand straight to convey respect. "I didn't even feel safe in the company of the D R Congo national forces!"

The officer draws closer still, so close I feel the warmth of his breath. "Where did you encounter them?" he asks.

"They stopped me along the road in Danjou for violating the curfew. They took me to a makeshift headquarters on the outskirts of town."

He spurts air at me which delivers spittle across my cheek. "Those weren't national forces that detained you!"

"Sure they were! They were in uniforms."

Even as I look forward, I sense his eyes run up and down me. Condescension seeps from his gaze.

"Those were militia *rebels* that detained you, not national forces! The army just captured Danjou from them moments ago!"

"Rebels?" I repeat. "Do you mean Islamic militants?" I swivel to look at him.

He greets me with a shaking head. "You know nothing about geopolitics here!"

He backs away and goes to the roadside where he extracts a stalk from a sheath of grass. Slipping it into his mouth, he returns.

"Let's talk geopolitics," he says as the stalk bobs from his mouth. "A local militia captured Danjou a week ago from Islamic militants who'd seized it days earlier along with the diamond business. National forces were called in because of atrocities committed by both sides. Tonight, the *Forces Armées de la République Démocratique du Congo* finally liberated the town from both groups."

"Was it the national army that blew up the militia headquarters where I was detained?" I ask.

"Yes, the attack came by air and land."

"And almost killed me," I note.

"You shouldn't have gone to Danjou in the first place!"

It comes to me now: No colonel in a national army would wear a garish gold bracelet on duty. For that matter, disciplined soldiers wouldn't strip uniforms for civilian clothing in the midst of battle.

"So, with your colleagues missing," the officer says, "we must launch a search team. But first, we'll fire flares."

He sends a colleague to the vehicle from which the soldier returns with the requested supplies. Loading a flare, the officer shoots it into the air. It makes a long ascent before arcing into the bush.

I step away from the three, cup hands to mouth, and shout, "Benji, Oscar!"

"They won't hear you unless they're close," my interlocutor says. "The bush acts like soundproof panels; it absorbs noise. This is why we use flares."

He loads another and fires it.

We wait several minutes without a response.

"Come, we'll organize a team," the officer says. "Bring your truck to the convoy. We'll meet you there."

I wait for the soldiers to depart. When they're out of sight, I scan the darkness. Its emptiness extinguishes hope.

I steer the truck to the convoy where, unlike the day before, tents are propped between vehicles along the roadside. At the far end of the convoy, I notice soldiers encircling a flame that rises above their heads.

I park the truck and walk to the gathering. As I approach it, I see the orange embers that race skyward come from the end of a bundle of grass that burns at one end. When I reach the soldiers, I squeeze my way through the pack to the center.

"Oscar!" I shout when I see who holds the torch. I stumble as my foot catches a soldier's boot.

"*Nudume*!" Oscar volleys. He hands the torch to Annette and rushes to me with Benji close behind. I wrap my arms around the boys.

"We saw the flares," Oscar tells me. "They led us here."

"After the lights went out along the road," Benji adds, "we used the stars to navigate." He points to the sky. "You can see the Southern Cross clearly." He raises both arms and crosses one over the other to trace the constellation. "We followed the long axis in a southern direction to find the border of Zambia."

"Was it you who fired the rifle?" I ask him.

"Yes, *nudume*, because I saw spots of a cheetah not once, but twice, so I shot into the air."

I lift my eyes to Annette. Sputtering flames from a dying torch cast shifting light across her face. Relief vies with concern in her eyes.

"Hello, Paul," she says.

Her tone is formal, the sort a chair of a corporate board might use to address members at a quarterly meeting.

"I'm glad you're safe," I tell her.

She turns the palm of her free hand up to expose her cell phone.

"Yes, I know," I say. "Mine was taken from me. I'm sorry."

She glances at the few soldiers who remain. "We need to talk," she says.

The officer with whom I'd spoken earlier appears. "Madam, with apologies for interrupting, I need to ask whether you have a visa to be in Zambia."

"I do," she says, removing her passport from a cloth carrier that hangs from her neck.

The officer flips through the pages until he finds the target of his search. Looking at Annette, he says, "I see you've been to our country repeatedly."

"Yes, for business."

He returns Annette's passport. "We can offer you a tent but our exercises will awaken you at dawn."

"Your offer is a kind one," Annette replies, "but we'll be on our way."

"Annette, it's a very long drive to Saysha," I say. "The road is perilous at night, and I think it'd be better to stay here tonight."

"I'm a confident driver," she replies.

"Confidence isn't the issue; visibility is."

"You must trust me, Paul, just as I trusted you in Danjou when you set us afoot through the bush."

I'm annoyed by what I perceive as her prim demeanor, one that falls short of prissiness but still irritates me. "Why the rush to leave?" I ask.

She eyes the boys before turning her scorn on me. "This is a matter to discuss alone."

I look up at the stars to find the Southern Cross. In the past few months, I've come to know the stars from tutorials the orphans have given me. At school, teacher Daniel told them to prepare a presentation that describes constellations viewed from the southern hemisphere. To prepare, the orphans have rehearsed repeatedly before me under nighttime skies.

If the Southern Cross could take momentary form on earth, the four of us—Annette, Oscar, Benji, and I—would form its four points. The boys are stationed in neutral territory between Annette and me as if they sense an axis of hostility separates the two of us.

"Who *are* you exactly?" I ask Annette, free to speak more at will now that the soldiers have gone.

"You ask as if we've never met," she replies.

"An encounter at a cemetery and a sprint through a tenement barely constitute an acquaintance."

"Look, I'm sorry I drew you to Danjou, but I had little choice. You're the only one I know who can help me."

"From the message you sent with the burn patient, it appears you've drawn me to more than just Danjou; you've put my life in danger."

The boys look at me abruptly.

"Please, Paul, can we continue this discussion alone?"

"Where do you propose we talk?" I ask her.

"In the truck as we drive to Saysha." She glances at the boys. "Let's see if we can make the back comfortable enough for them to sleep while you and I drive."

She extinguishes the last embers of the torch using her foot. As she does, I look at her intently. Her skirt is wrinkled, her blouse sullied, and her hair disheveled yet not unbecomingly. There's a presence to this woman, one that neither strife nor challenge dissolves.

"Alright," I say. "We'll drive through the night."

We start for the truck, but before we reach it, we come to a supply tent. A stack of folded blankets occupies a table. With no one to ask, Annette removes four of them and, in their place, deposits several Zambian bills. At the truck, she makes a pass along the sides to test the integrity of the rails. Satisfied, she lowers the tailgate. It releases a cloud of dust.

"The Zodiac!" she sings, tapping the rubber folds. "Let's slide it and the motor toward the crate to form a bedding area for the boys."

Excited, the boys leap onto the truck to help build their nest. In short order, they nestle beside the crate with blankets beneath them. The Zodiac and motor form an outer border to keep them from rolling along the flatbed.

"This is good!" Oscar calls.

"Alright," I tell them. "We'll leave for Saysha now. If you need us as at any time, tap on the roof or shout, and remember, no fooling around back here." The fatigue in their eyes tells me sleep is the sole item on their agendas. Closing the tailgate, I take the driver's seat with Annette across from me.

We leave the convoy for open country. With the moon descending, darkness deepens to leave the headlights piercing the night like lasers. In the silence, I watch dragonflies flare across the beams and listen to insects strike the windshield. Beyond the headlights is a subtle beauty of its own, one formed by evanescent contours of passing trees, ghostly hills, and soft transitions of earthly black to heavenly starlight.

When I sense Annette looking at me, I turn to find her eyes. They're large and sad.

"Thank you, Paul, for coming to get me," she says.

I look ahead as my heart heaves. I allowed myself once to be lured by physical beauty and the velvet of a woman's voice. It didn't end well.

"Let me at least tell you who I am," she continues.

"Please," I say.

She resettles in her seat as if to organize her thoughts.

"I'm a photojournalist," she begins. "Eleven years ago, I came to Africa for the first time. A travel magazine sent me to Tanzania to write a story. While on assignment there, I witnessed something that changed my life. It happened while I was returning to the capital after going on safari. My driver and I had stopped for a break under a grove of acacia trees in a remote section of the country where elephants wander from one reserve to another. There was a jeep parked in the same area, and when we heard a loud shout from the bush, we went to see what it was about."

She pauses to look out her window. A hand rises to cup her mouth as if to prevent her lips from moving.

"Go on," I say.

The hand drops. "After walking around a large bush, we saw two elephants, a mother and her calf. They stirred in half-sleep on the ground thirty meters ahead under a tree. Another shout called our attention to three men perched nearby behind a termite mound. They held rifles pointed at the elephants. Startled by the shout, the mother tried to get up but was felled by a series of bullets. She slumped to the ground in moans. As she shifted her weight to try to stand again, a second volley followed to her head. This time, she was stilled."

Annette leans forward and glares through the windshield. "I began screaming at the men. Although my driver tried to restrain me, I slipped free and ran to them and began kicking dirt onto their boots. When they laughed at me, I struck one in the mouth. He returned the favor with a blow to my belly. I folded to the ground."

She takes a deep, slow breath.

"My driver hurried to my side where he emptied his wallet as a bribe to free me. One of the men took the money as the other two approached the elephants. Assisted by my driver, I slunk to our car, but not before stealing a final glance at the scene behind us. I saw the men severing the mother's tusks while, beside them, the calf shrieked as it turned in countless circles."

Annette shakes her head and leans back.

"You were fortunate to escape," I say.

"With nightmares since . . ."

"Did you report the incident?"

"Yes, we stopped at a game reserve to speak to a ranger. I gave him the details of what happened, and he promised to relay them to authorities."

"Did you get any follow-up?"

"Nothing, but I learned later that poaching events like this happen all the time."

She turns to me with her arms raised. "At the turn of the twentieth century, there were several million elephants in Africa but we're down to about half a million now." One arm drops while the other remains elevated. "What I saw changed my life. After completing my assignment, I quit my job with the travel magazine and became a freelance photographer. I focused on poaching and licensed killing of African wildlife." She lowers her second arm.

"Hazardous job," I note.

She removes her cell phone and taps the screen. It alights with a photo. "Take a look."

With one hand on the wheel, I hold the phone with the other and see a photo of a rhinoceros. It stoops on the ground with its two front legs folded at the knees while the back legs remain extended. I've seen warthogs do the same, often in rest, but the rhino is clearly in a different situation as a man stands beside it with a chain saw buzzing across the animal's horn.

"They shot him in the heart first," Annette informs me. "The rhino had just enough blood flow to allow him to kneel while they severed the horn."

I return the phone.

She slaps it onto her thigh. "All of this because idiots believe the horn is an aphrodisiac."

"What do you do with the photos?"

"I sell, publish, and display them as I can."

"And that earns you a living?"

She's silent for a moment. "Almost."

I inquire no further into the privacy of her finances.

"Someone helps me with the rest," she volunteers.

The seatbelt unclicks and I feel Annette's hand graze my arm. "It's someone who's quite ill," she says, "and he needs your help, Paul." Her hand remains on my forearm.

"Who are you speaking of?" I ask.

She re-buckles. "His name is Xavier Treadwill, and he lives on the other side of the river from you in Uku-tetema."

I'VE NEVER BEEN to Uku-tetema, let alone across the Amalumbo River. Upon arriving in Saysha, I was warned to avoid the vast expanse of Uku-tetema because of its dangerous terrain and wildlife; the crescent-shaped region was to remain terra incognita. Translated loosely as "to twinkle," the word *Uku-tetema* is an apt one because, like a sliver of new moon or the faintness of distant stars, the land is seen by few.

Residents of Uku-tetema, an area roughly the size of Rhode Island or Yosemite National Park, belong to an ancestral tribe and are spread among a number of villages. The social fabric is a tapestry of family, clan, and kinship where elders resolve disputes while those that can't be settled are relegated to a tribal chief. With few exceptions, traditional healers care for the ill, and Western medicine is unknown. In recent decades, residents have increasingly adopted Bemba as a language although many continue to rely on an ancestral dialect.

"Uku-tetema," I voice as I drive. The tip of my tongue plucks my teeth as I say the name.

"Yes," Annette replies. "Xavier Treadwill lives there."

"Is a he a *mzungu*?"

"No, he's black with pure Zambian roots."

"How do you know him? Westerners don't visit Uku-tetema."

"I'm an exception because I work for Xavier."

"Doing what?"

"I take photographs of poachers so he can share them with authorities. He provides me with armed guards when I'm in the field."

My curiosity is piqued. "Tell me more about this man, Xavier Treadwill."

"He's the son of a former Uku-tetema chief and one of only a few from the region to be educated outside his homeland."

"Yet he lives in Uku-tetema?"

"Yes, by duty, he claims. He couldn't stand idle as poachers decimate the wildlife of his homeland."

"What makes him think he can stop them?"

"He's determined, persistent, and wealthy."

The juxtaposition of "wealth" and "Uku-tetema" intrigues me. "What's the source of his wealth?"

"He's a software engineer."

Sensing a disconnect, I ask: "Yet he's from Uku-tetema?"

Annette relays the details of a rags-to-riches life that conjures characters from novels by nineteenth century author, Horatio Alger. In Xavier Treadwill we have a boy of humble origin who left Uku-tetema for Lusaka at the age of seven to begin school. The move resulted from a confluence of the death of Xavier's mother, which left his distraught father overwhelmed with raising six other siblings, and the offer of a missionary passing through Uku-tetema to shepherd Xavier through studies in the capital.

I feel a sense of communion with Xavier when I learn that he, like I, attended boarding school, and I grant him credit for earning a scholarship to attend Oxford University in England. After receiving a degree in engineering, he added a doctoral degree in computer science from Stanford University to his portfolio. Endowed with an entrepreneurial spirit, he launched a start-up in Silicon Valley that designed software to encrypt digital communications. He sold it three years ago for over a billion dollars and moved back to Zambia.

"Why did he return to Africa?"

"He wanted to help others in his nation get better educated. Upon returning, he started a school in Lusaka for disadvantaged children but was distracted by reports of rampant poaching in Uku-tetema. The killings led him to return to his boyhood home a year and a half ago to address the problem."

"Has he succeeded in fending off poachers?"

"To some degree, but it's a complex problem requiring multi-faceted solutions, many of them economic in nature. When thinking about factors that contribute to poaching, I envision a pyramid, the base of which consists of impoverished individuals for whom farming or other means of employment fail to provide adequate income to feed themselves and their families. For these people, hunger drives them to kill rhinos, elephants, lions, and other wildlife, not only for meat but for the lucrative horns, tusks, and fur. To address this problem locally, Xavier began funding farming cooperatives throughout Uku-tetema to foster improved agricultural practices while, at the same time, he employs hundreds of young men and women to serve as wildlife rangers to monitor and protect the animals in his homeland. In schools, he's introduced modules to foster an appreciation for the rightful place of wild animals. We've seen dramatic declines in poaching recently as a result of these interventions, but that's been the easy part; dealing with the higher levels of the pyramid has been more difficult."

"Higher levels?" I ask.

"Yes, those entwining international markets with insatiable appetites for ivory and horns. In this realm, Xavier deals with a far more sophisticated and resourceful set of poachers and economic forces. It's a constantly changing milieu with evolving killers and techniques employed, and in the end, a final solution will come only from cooperation at national levels." She sighs. "In the meantime, a new nemesis has emerged in the form of Islamic militants who've come to Uku-tetema from the Horn of Africa to raid our wildlife; that's a problem that'll require solutions of an entirely different sort."

" 'Islamic militants,' " I repeat, recalling the lecture the colonel delivered at the militia compound in Danjou.

I wait for her to say more but she folds her arms across her chest and sinks into her seat. For now, the night has taken her away, and I don't know when she'll return.

I THOUGHT ANNETTE might sleep, but she doesn't. "Even before Xavier fell ill," she tells me, "he asked me to contact you to help him deal with poachers."

"How did he know who I was?"

"He saw online reports of your work with jaguars in the Amazon. He thought the techniques you used could help him battle poachers in Uku-tetema. For that reason, after *tata* Murphy died, he ensured you received an announcement for the job opening in Saysha. He celebrated when you accepted the position and has been waiting for the right moment to meet you since you arrived. When he became ill recently, he pressed me to contact you as soon as possible."

"Why didn't he contact me directly?"

"He was convinced it would only endanger you further."

I begin to connect mental dots now that explain how my life and Xavier's have come to intersect. From what Annette has said, Xavier faces a problem with poachers in his homeland of Uku-tetema. Having read about my efforts to protect jaguars in the Amazon, he worked behind the scenes to lure me to Zambia, and having succeeded, now seeks my help to address his poaching problem. I assume his enemies have learned I've been tapped to help protect Uku-tetema, and for that reason my name was added to a jihadist kill list.

Annette has watched me through my mental dot connecting. She addresses me: "Your work with trip lines follows you, Paul."

So it appears. The concept of using a trip line to stop jaguar poachers in the Amazon rainforest seemed innocent enough when I conceived the idea. It came to birth after a dishwasher employed by the company I worked for approached me in the Amazon to ask if I might evaluate his ill father. Because the worker hailed from a tribe deep within the forest, I had to hike with him an hour to reach his village. I found an elderly man there stretched along the ground on banana leaves. Wearing a loin cloth, he had a gaping wound in the back of his calf while the entire leg above it was beet-red and swollen.

"*Mi padre*," the dishwasher said, pointing to the man.

I squatted beside him. After donning a glove, I probed the wound with my finger. It drew little response, even as I pushed deep into his leg.

"*La cocaína*," my companion noted.

"*Sí*," I replied. He was referring to the fact that his father, like many others in the indigenous community, chewed coca leaves to dull pain and ward off hunger.

It wasn't long before I felt an object lodged against the man's tibia. I asked my co-worker to brace his father's leg while I inserted a pair of forceps into the wound. After digging around and making several attempts to extract the object, I finally secured it and twisted it out.

Holding a stubby bullet in the air, I asked the dishwasher how his father had come to be shot.

The man's face lengthened. "*Cazadores del jaguar*," he replied.

Although my Spanish was elementary, I understood what he said: Jaguar hunters had shot his father.

He explained further: Security guards from the oil company routinely hunted jaguars for their pelts which brought big money on the black market. Because the dishwasher's father revered jaguars for their power and grace, he placed himself in the line of fire to dissuade the guards from shooting the cats. In doing so, he took a bullet to the leg a week earlier.

After learning about the poaching, I approached local managers at the oil field to inform them about what had happened. Rather than express concern about poaching or the injury that resulted from it, they questioned my use of company resources to treat a man who wasn't on the payroll. When I requested to speak to someone higher on the ladder, I was referred to the company's regional office in the capital of Quito. An exchange of emails with officials there proved fruitless. Persevering, I contacted corporate headquarters only to receive a response that someone would look into the matter.

In the meantime, I persuaded a supervisor at the oil field to call a meeting of security guards. In dispassionate tones, I asked the men to refrain from shooting jaguars because it placed members of the indigenous population at risk. The request was received with jeers.

A week after the meeting, while walking home from the clinic, I saw two guards sling a dead jaguar into a jeep. Stooping among the foliage, I peered at the scene to make out a bullet hole in the cat's head. After loading the jaguar, the men tucked their rifles into the jeep and drove off.

It wasn't the last cat to be killed. As the weeks passed, I heard from the dishwasher that poaching had become more frequent as men from far off came to the rainforest in pursuit of jaguar pelts. I decided then to try to do something to protect the cats.

As a premed in college, I majored in physics and spent summers in labs that conducted research on light and sound. One project dealt with invisible lasers—lasers which produce electromagnetic radiation in wavelengths invisible to the human eye. A version of the technology is used in stores to sound chimes when customers disrupt invisible beams across entryways.

My work with invisible lasers inspired me to build a trip line to deter jaguar poachers. Relying on contacts in the U.S., I ordered an invisible infrared laser that I attached to the inside of a birdhouse. I then affixed the birdhouse to a tree trunk five feet above ground so the beam projected across a flat clearing which poachers used to access an area of rainforest frequented by jaguars. The clearing was the size of a basketball court located a kilometer beyond the outermost oil rig in a desolate area that few humans traversed. Directly across the clearing from the birdhouse, I installed a sensor that detected disruptions of the infrared beam. With each disruption, the sensor triggered a high-frequency alarm audible by cats but not by humans or dogs. I chose a height of five feet for the laser beam because I wanted only humans to set the alarm off. To my knowledge, there were no horses or cows in the area.

I chose an alarm frequency dogs couldn't hear because I'd seen guards enter the rainforest with German Shepherds. I was afraid that if a dog heard the alarm, it might get spooked enough to make the guards suspect something was awry. To ensure jaguars fled to safety at the sound of the initial alarm, I installed a series of relay sensors deep into the rainforest that triggered more alarms in cascade fashion. Rechargeable batteries served as the power source for the electronic equipment, which meant I had to devise a steady source of electricity to recharge the batteries. To do that, I put solar panels on the roof of my house to provide backup power for times when the company's generators failed.

In the months after I installed the alarm system, no jaguars were killed. With tepid optimism, I emailed my contacts in the U.S. to thank them for helping me secure the equipment. Unbeknownst to me, one of the contacts relayed my story to a wildlife protection group who, in turn, published a story online. Shortly after the piece went live, I was summoned to my employer's regional office in Quito. I was met there by a high-level executive from TransNational Oil headquarters in Houston, Texas who expressed disappointment I hadn't allowed the company to work through standard channels to address the issue of jaguar hunting.

"Those channels produced no results," I told him. "I had to design a warning system to protect the jaguars."

"We didn't hire you to protect animals," he told me. "We pay you to take care of our oil workers."

"That's what I've been doing."

"Perhaps, but your activism tarnished our firm's reputation at a vulnerable time."

"It's not my fault that one of your tankers struck a rock and spilled millions of gallons of oil along Canada's shoreline," I replied. "I suspect what I've done for Ecuadorean jaguars may have gained us favor among environmentalists."

"But that's not our constituency! The folks we care about are those who buy fuel."

I was put on probation for generating unfavorable press for the firm. Any further demerit would lead to immediate dismissal.

A week after the meeting, the supervisor of guards at the oil field stopped me outside the clinic one morning to demand that I dismantle the alarm system. When I refused to do so, he pushed me to the ground. I told him I wouldn't stoop to his level by fighting him.

That afternoon, I went online and applied for the position of medical director at the hospital in Saysha, Zambia that I'd heard about several days earlier. The announcement came none too soon because shortly after the supervisor of security guards had pushed me to the ground, I received a notice that I'd been fired by TransNational Oil for malicious activities. I departed Ecuador for Zambia six months before my contract with TransNational Oil was due to expire but was relieved to leave.

WE'RE A THIRD of the way from Danjou to Saysha, and with a gauge showing the main fuel tank near empty, I flip a switch to access a reserve tank. It'll allow us to reach Saysha where we maintain a fuel depot.

I bring the truck to a stop. "Let me check on the boys," I tell Annette.

They're fast asleep in their den. After making a round of the truck to check tires, I find Annette at the wheel.

"Take a break," she tells me. "I'll drive now." She has the seat pulled forward and her hands on the wheel.

Grateful, I occupy the passenger seat and lean back. It's two-thirty in the morning and while I long to sleep, I want to test the conclusions I drew earlier from connecting mental dots. "You've said repeatedly that my life's in danger. Is this because poachers know that Xavier wants me to help protect wildlife in Uku-tetema?"

Yes," she says. "With the Internet, they know what you did in the Amazon and they communicate closely. They know who their enemies are, and you're one of them. Your arrival in Zambia set off alarms in poaching circles, all the more so because of your choice to reside near Uku-tetema. It's become 'ground zero' for wildlife protection efforts in Central Africa."

" 'Ground-zero'?"

"There's a battle raging for the control of Uku-tetema with international money at stake."

"It's Zambia's land," I remind her.

"Borders lose meaning when it comes to wealth generation. In Africa, map lines can be little more than artifacts of colonial rule."

I wonder whether the bitterness in her voice stems, in part, from Ireland's struggle to separate from Britain.

"With the discovery of diamonds in D R Congo," I say, "I've heard mining interests are keen to explore the Amalumbo River along its course near Uku-tetema."

"Yes, it's a battle between mining and animals, and the miners are well-connected in Lusaka. They're fighting a bill in the National Assembly spearheaded by Xavier Treadwill to turn Uku-tetema into a national park. If the bill passes, no commercial development will be allowed on the land."

"How are votes lining up?"

"It's too close to call." She pivots in her seat. "This is why you need to see Xavier as soon as possible. He's been feeling weak recently, and that's impeded his ability to travel to Lusaka. His lobbying efforts are critical there."

"How old is he?"

"Thirty-eight."

"And how long has he been ill?"

"About a month."

"What are his symptoms?"

"Weakness, largely, but also something strange: pins and needles in his feet that've become so uncomfortable he feels like he's treading on hot coals."

"Does he have back pain?" I wonder about a pinched nerve.

"Not that I've heard of."

"Diabetes?"

"Not a chance! He's exceptionally healthy. Had he chosen to, he could've played professional football in Zambia, but his business interests steered him elsewhere."

"Has he seen a physician?"

"Yes, an internal medicine specialist in Lusaka, but so far there's been no diagnosis."

"He needs a neurologist."

"Funny you say that," she replies. "He was going to see one

but had to cancel the appointment after receiving a threat on his life if he returned to the capital."

"Who threatened him?"

"He's looking into that as we speak."

"With the help of the police, I trust."

"He reported the threat, for sure, but he also prefers to work alone; that's his way. He has technical skills that you'll learn about when you visit him in Uku-tetema."

"Can he come to Saysha to see me there?"

"No, it'd be too risky," she replies. "He's safe in Uku-tetema, but only with armed guards."

DAWN BREAKS AND I drive the final miles to Saysha. Beside me, Annette rests her head on my shoulder. While changing drivers at the last stop, the boys asked to join us in the cab. Too sleepy to man the gear shift, Oscar relinquished his seat to doze beside Benji.

Although the night's been long, my heart is quiet like daybreak. For the past hour while Annette and the boys have slept, I've watched the stars dim and the sky lighten. I can't explain why, but morning in Africa is an awakening as much as a start of a new day. As night surrenders to an axial earth, the first glow brings renewal, even this morning after little sleep.

I drive slowly to prevent the ruts from waking the others. For now, creaking joints and a moaning engine carry the discussion. In the rear view mirror, Annette's face occupies the lower portion. It's the first time I see her in daylight, and in the absence of moonlight, her auburn hair flirts with red. Her eyebrows are a shade redder than her hair and her lashes more so. Freckles sprinkle her cheeks. With her hair pulled back to one side, her bare ear shows no sign of being pierced. Her hands, crossed at the wrists, display no rings. She wears a pleated skirt, lace-up boots, and a khaki blouse with epaulets. Simplicity and functionality elevate to elegance, leaving jewelry out of the equation.

Caution steers my eyes back to the road but for visual relief, I savor views of the austere landscape. When we reach the summit where I stopped the day before to take my first break, I notice the kudu carcass no longer hangs from the tree in the ravine below. I presume the cheetah Benji spoke of has returned to devour the remains. Its disappearance is a beat in the cadence of life: give and take, come and go, live and die. In Africa, this cadence differs from ones I've experienced elsewhere, and it makes me wonder whether the difference stems from the continent still being in transition from a cataclysmic separation from Pangea.

In the distance, I see the huts of Saysha. As if by instinct, the boys awaken.

"*Nudume*, we're home!" Oscar announces.

Annette lifts her head. For an instant, she blushes to acknowledge that my body has been her support. Leaning forward, she collects her hair before splaying it over her shoulders. "So, this is Saysha?"

"Haven't you been here, Miss Annette?" Benji asks.

"No, it's my first time."

I'm not surprised to hear this. Her work photographing poachers takes her to lands where big game resides, and while the marshlands around Saysha are rich with birdlife, poaching isn't a problem here.

"How long will you remain in Saysha, Miss Annette?" Oscar asks. He and Benji no longer stare at her the way they did after first meeting her. Their trek through the bush of D R Congo has bonded them.

Annette glances at me before answering. "I really can't say how long I'll stay. I'll discuss the matter with Dr. Paul."

We enter the village where the rituals of morning are underway: bucket filling with water, patio sweeping to clear debris, and cattle shepherding to pastures.

"Boys, I'll drop you off at your quarters so you may prepare for school," I say.

"*Nudume*, can we skip school today to assist Miss Annette?" Oscar asks. He looks longingly at his new friend.

"No, I want you to go to school because teacher Daniel has something fun for you to do today."

"What is it?" the boys ask in unison.

"You'll help me install solar panels on the roof of the pharmacy."

"We'll do that today?" Oscar asks gleefully.

"Yes, so make sure you get to school."

The boys bump shoulders and grin.

"As for us, Annettte, I suggest we wash and grab a bite to eat at the hospital. We'll find room for you in the visitors' quarters should you like to rest."

"I'm fine, Paul, but what about you? You slept very little."

"I'll nap after I see our patients with the paramedics."

After we park, I dismiss the boys only to see Bristol hurrying toward the truck.

"*Nudume*!" he calls, "are you not tending your phone?"

"I lost it last night," I explain. "I'll go to Mposto soon to replace it."

"So this is why Dr. Raymond Chabala from Lusaka couldn't reach you!"

I raise my eyebrows. "Chabala called?"

"Yes, he has results on the blood specimen you sent him. He said—" He turns abruptly as Annette walks around the front of the truck. "Good morning, madam." He backs away deferentially.

I introduce the two, informing Annette of Bristol's position as lead paramedic.

"A pleasure," she says, offering a hand.

The paramedic shakes it but quickly returns to the matter of Chabala's call. "He said the results were most unusual."

"In what way?"

"He agreed with Katrine's assessment. Here, let me play his voice mail."

Over the speaker comes Chabala's voice . . .

Hello Bristol, please relay this message to Dr. Paul. I wasn't able to get through to him.

I had my staff examine the blood we received from the hospital. Our results agree with those from your lab. In particular, the prominence of reticulocytes and the staining pattern they exhibited lead us to believe the blood likely came from an animal.

Interestingly, I asked a veterinarian colleague to examine the smear and he said it looked like cat blood. Unlike in humans, in whom residual RNA in reticulocytes remains a day or two, in cats RNA remains for up to three weeks.

To get a definitive answer for the source of the blood, we'll run tests on DNA from white blood cells. I'll be in touch soon.

Bristol slips the phone into his pocket. "*Nudume,* why would someone leave cat blood at your home?"

"Let's not rush to conclusions," I reply. "It's still a presumption that it's cat blood, but we don't know for sure. In the meantime, please text Dr. Chabala to let him know I lost my phone and that he may continue to relay messages through you."

"Yes, *nudume.*"

"Very well, let's assemble the paramedics in twenty minutes to see patients."

Annette waits until Bristol has gone before she confronts me. "*Cat* blood? Not good, Paul!"

I say nothing because I'd rather not exhume my past.

THERE'S EDGINESS AMONG the paramedics as we assemble. It stems not only from the results Chabala conveyed but also from the arrival of a *mzungu*.

I address the latter issue because Annette's arrival has come as a surprise to all. "As I'm sure you've heard, we have a visitor. Her name is Annette Wilson, and she accompanied me from Danjou because of unrest there. Miss Wilson is a photojournalist who'd like to write a story about our hospital. Please give her your cooperation should she approach you with questions."

"How long will she stay?" a paramedic asks.

"To be determined; she's balancing a number of deadlines which calls for her to be flexible."

I skip the matter regarding Chabala's call to broach the subject of patient care. Before I can do so, an arm rises.

"Yes, Cynthia," I say.

The paramedic with the round face who reported seeing an airplane land in the distance two days ago steps forward. "*Nudume*, as you requested, I checked with the Interior Ministry yesterday to ask whether any of their airplanes had landed in our region recently. They were unaware of any."

"Thank you for checking."

"But there is more," she adds. "I called the Department of Civil Aviation to ask if they knew of any landings near Saysha two days ago."

"How did they respond?"

"They said a flight plan had been filed for a Cessna to visit our area."

"A flight from where?"

"Lusaka."

My pulse accelerates. "Two days ago?"

"Correct."

"Did they say who operated the aircraft or what the purpose of the flight was?"

"That was confidential, they said."

Detecting more unease in the group, I thank Cynthia and redirect the discussion to patients admitted to the hospital during my trip to Danjou although it takes all I have to keep my thoughts from straying to what Cynthia just reported. I learn that a child with pneumonia has been admitted along with an adult with bloody diarrhea from a flare up of ulcerative colitis, a disease involving recurrent episodes of inflammation of the large intestine.

After examining the new patients, we start for the hut where the burn patient resides but before getting there, I ask a paramedic to summon Annette from the visitors' quarters. While driving to Saysha from Danjou, she had asked for permission to visit the woman with me. Sensing guilt on her part for being the one spared injury, I granted her wish. With the boys asleep in the back of the truck as we drove, she described the events that led to the explosion in the salon.

It was first thing in the morning when Annette arrived for her appointment, her second visit to the salon since setting up an apartment in Danjou. An employee she hadn't seen before escorted her to a chair set apart from the others. It was an odd choice, Annette thought, because the other chairs that comprised the central section of the salon were vacant. Not only that, but the woman she followed appeared to be anxious, looking about nervously as the pair walked toward the distant chair.

Just as Annette reached the chair, her phone rang. Because it was an important call, she excused herself to converse outside. By the time she returned inside, business had picked up to the point that the odd-chair-out was occupied by another client. Seated by the owner in a central chair this time, Annette settled back to have her hair washed only to be jolted by an explosion from the isolated chair. Shrieks followed as the scent of burnt hair filled the salon.

Turning, Annette saw a flame engulfing a woman's head within a hood. In the pandemonium, she rushed to the chair and, following an electric cord to its outlet, disconnected it. All the while she screamed for someone to call an ambulance. Using a towel as a hot pad, she tried to lift the scalding hood, but it was fused to the woman's scalp.

In time, Annette found herself alone in the parlor with the woman who now slumped under the hood. To her horror, she watched the force of gravity free the woman's head from the hood but, in so doing, it ripped a rim of skin from her scalp, leaving charred tissue dangling from the hood like strips of burnt bacon. When Annette tried to arouse her, the woman remained silent with eyes rolled up. A siren grew louder by the moment as Annette clutched the woman's hand. The sights and smells made her think she might vomit, but she managed not to do so. After what seemed like far too long a delay, EMTs rushed the woman away on a stretcher.

Outside the salon, Annette thought about driving to the hospital to file a report but stopped short when she noticed the worker who'd escorted her initially to the separate chair was speaking into a phone nearby. Because the employee faced a wall as if to shield her discussion, Annette approached her until she heard the words *Mademoiselle Wilson*. Freezing, she listened more closely.

Fluent in French, Annette was appalled to hear the woman apologize for failing to target *Mademoiselle Wilson* with the explosion. Fleeing the scene, Annette rushed to her office where she gathered her laptop and assorted files. While she was there, she received a text from Xavier Treadwill that read . . .

> *You're on a jihadist hit list! Leave Danjou before they kill you! And get ahold of Paul Rider somehow. Tell him he's on the same hit list and that I need him more than ever.*

While rushing out of the office, Annette ran into Felice who was arriving to begin her cleaning duties. Having befriended the grandmotherly woman over the past months, Annette told her about what had happened at the salon and the conversation she'd overheard after the incident. Felice advised her to go immediately to her home in the shanties to hide. In the meantime, Felice went to the emergency department to tell the victim about a hospital across the border in Zambia that treated patients for free, a hospital where her nephew, Innocent Mbewe, worked as a paramedic. While there, she gave the patient's brother a hand-written note that Annette had penned before Annette went to Felice's shack. Felice implored the brother to make sure I received the note in Saysha.

ACROSS THE HOSPITAL grounds, I see Annette leave the visitors' quarters. She's accompanied by the paramedic sent to summon her. I use the opportunity to assign a small group to examine the burn patient with me; the remaining paramedics are instructed to wait outside until we complete our examination. I take this action to reduce the risk of introducing pathogens into the patient's hut. Although the dirt floors of our hospital have mats on them, we take precautions as we can to reduce the likelihood of infection in immune-compromised patients.

Accompanying me to examine the patient are Annette, Bristol, and Innocent Mbewe. Each has a different mission—Bristol, as lead paramedic, to maintain an awareness of the status of all patients; Innocent to continue providing day-to-day care; and Annette to work with the demons that taunt her with remorse and guilt.

Before we enter the hut, I introduce Annette to Innocent Mbewe. Despite his reserved nature and deep privacy, he welcomes Annette graciously.

"My aunt, Felice, in Danjou is very grateful for your friendship," he tells her.

"As I am for hers," Annette replies.

We don masks, gloves, and shoe covers before entering the hut. Inside, the burn patient sits atop a surgical drape. A soothing gauze with anti-infective compounds covers her burn.

Speaking in French, Innocent introduces the patient to Annette. The woman shows no signs of recognizing her which suggests to me that shock from the explosion prevented her from registering Annette's presence in the salon.

Annette addresses the woman and, for my benefit, translates: "I told her I'm so sorry about what happened and that I wish her the speediest of recoveries."

My attention is diverted from Annette to the patient's labored breathing. "Innocent, has she complained of shortness of breath this morning?"

The paramedic relays the question.

The woman nods and, with hoarseness, says, "*Oui.*"

"When did she start having trouble breathing?" I ask.

"Last night," Innocent conveys.

The patient coughs.

"What does your physical examination tell you?"

"Her temperature is normal, and when I listen by stethoscope, I hear no rales or rhonchi." He refers to crackling and gurgling sounds that often accompany pneumonia. "But," he adds, "she's wheezing."

"I'll listen in a moment, but first please update us on her status."

"Her pain is under control, but she has lost five pounds since coming to us." With care, he removes the gauze from the wound. The exposed burn causes Annette to flinch.

"As you see," Innocent continues, "the wound is clean without signs of infection. We continue to debride it daily to remove dead tissue."

"And the plan moving forward?"

"We'll continue to monitor her for signs of infection, and I'd like to discontinue the intravenous line today because she's able to drink fluids. We'll introduce foods shortly to ensure she receives sufficient calories."

"Is her urine output adequate?"

"Yes."

I remove my stethoscope and listen to her heart and lungs. My faith in Innocent's skills is reaffirmed as I hear distant wheezing.

I step back to ponder this exceptionally challenging patient. Before undergoing skin grafting, she'll need meticulous care to prevent life-threatening complications. I'm concerned one such complication has begun.

"The combination of hoarseness, wheezing, and labored breathing suggests to me she likely inhaled damaging products of combustion from the explosion," I say. "I worry her airway is inflamed."

At times, the paramedics engage me in vigorous discussion about diagnosis and treatment, but at this juncture Innocent Mbewe defers to me.

I continue: "While one part of me thinks it could be useful to pass an endoscope into her airway to see whether the tissue is inflamed, another warns me this procedure is too hazardous given our limited access to mechanical ventilation should she stop breathing."

"So, what do you advise, *nudume*?" Innocent asks.

"Let's supplement her breathing with oxygen and monitor her closely for now. If the wheezing worsens, we can treat her with inhaled corticosteroids to combat the inflammation of her airways. We can also give her antibiotics if signs of pneumonia develop."

I lead the way out of the hut to rejoin the other paramedics but notice Annette has remained behind. Peeking into the hut, I find her holding the patient's hand.

"With your permission," she says to me, "I'd like to stay here for a few more minutes."

I leave her there. Her compassion is far more than anything I can offer the woman from our limited medical arsenal.

AT THE PERIMETER of the hospital grounds, I see older students from the primary school approaching with teacher Daniel. They march with deliberate speed as if eager to begin a project long in waiting.

"Good morning, *nudume*!" they call.

I smile at the group that encircles me. "Are you ready to install solar panels?" I ask them.

A chorus of cheers follows.

To undertake the project, teacher Daniel and I have assigned students to teams, one to attach panels to the roof of the pharmacy and a second to wire them to batteries and meters inside the building.

As the teams assemble, Amu and Thandi approach me with frowns. "It's not fair what happened!" Thandi declares.

"What do you mean?" I ask.

Thandi plants her feet in defiance. "Oscar and Benji accompanied you to Danjou while Amu and I remained here."

About a month after I'd arrived in Saysha, I noticed a gender-based feud had developed among the four oldest orphans who lived at the hospital, the point of contention being the amount of time I spent with Thandi and Amu versus Oscar and Benji. Any deviation from equality, slight as it may be, ignited resentment.

"I didn't *invite* the boys to go to Danjou!" I tell Thandi. "They snuck onto the truck and announced their presence only after I'd traveled a distance."

Crossing her arms, Amu exclaims: "You should have sent them home!"

"Impossible! We were in the bush where carcasses hang in trees."

"So, let the boys hang there!"

A moment passes before a crack parts Amu's lips. It's followed by laughter. A wrong hasn't been righted, but a gap in the ledger of gender equality has been narrowed.

"Go on!" I tell them. "Get to work."

Three hours later, an electric circuit connects solar panels on the roof of the pharmacy to rechargeable batteries inside. Running more cables, we install lights in the space. The time comes to test the system.

I call a boy on crutches to step forward. Despite his disability, he has showed unfailing effort throughout the project. Two years earlier, *tata* Murphy amputated one of his legs because of cancer. We recently received funding to purchase a prosthesis for the boy.

I ask the boy to flip a switch. Lights turn on to whoops and applause.

I allow the celebration to run its course before leading the group outside where I draw a rectangle in the dirt.

"What is that, *nudume*?" a student asks.

"It symbolizes a battery," I reply, "one like those we placed inside the pharmacy." I don a stern look. "It's important you know that each battery is a potential bomb."

I add a "+" and "-" above the rectangle. "As you noticed, each battery has two terminals. You must *never* connect the terminals of a single battery with anything metal because the battery could explode and you'll be hurt badly. In fact, I don't want you to approach the batteries without permission from teacher Daniel or me."

Heads nod.

With the project completed and dusk approaching, Daniel dismisses the group.

I use the time to look for Bristol. I find him in a ward nearby attending to a patient. "Bristol, can I have a word with you?" I ask.

We step outside. "I need to go away for a few days," I tell him.

"Again?" he asks. "Where to this time?"

"To Uku-tetema with Annette." I explain myself before his thoughts wander: "Annette has asked me to evaluate a sick friend there. I agreed to do so."

"But Uku-tetema is forbidden land, *nudume*! You mustn't go!"

I say nothing. Forbidden as it may be, I'm convinced Uku-tetema holds the answers I seek.

BRISTOL AND ANNETTE join me in the truck as we drive through the village. Evening has come and fires burn outside huts for dinner preparation. After passing the last of the dwellings, I continue a short distance until the bush prevents us from driving further.

We go to the back of the truck where Bristol and I hop onto the bed and drag the Zodiac to the tailgate.

"Take care not to rip it," Annette cautions.

Together, we lower it to the ground. Aligning its folds for three to carry, we trek toward my shack. From my position in front, I blow the whistle at every bend with the approach of night.

Perspiration soaks us by the time we reach my home. We place the Zodiac at the top of the bluff overlooking the river.

"Let's carry it down there in the morning," Annette suggests.

A second trip brings the outboard motor and fuel tank. We huddle to make final plans.

"You'll bring your medical bag to Uku-tetema, right?" Annette confirms.

"Yes, I'll have it ready to go," I reply.

She stirs. "Xavier requests you bring some casting material as well."

"What for? Did he injure himself?"

"No, but he says it's imperative you bring it."

"Why?"

"He told me you'd be applying a cast to your arm."

"What for? That makes no sense!"

"Believe me, I asked him why, but he was in a rush to hang up. He said he'd explain his reasoning when he sees you."

I shake my head. I ask Bristol to have Innocent stop by the hospital in the morning before we leave to pick up some padding and a roll of fiberglass casting tape.

Annette and Bristol prepare to depart. Glancing at my watch, I address Annette: "You said Xavier's men will meet us at sunrise tomorrow, right?"

"Yes, up the river," she replies. "We can't be late!"

A specific site has been selected where we'll meet a group of armed guards who'll be waiting to drive us to Xavier's lodge deep within Uku-tetema.

"Get some sleep, Paul," Annette says. "Tomorrow will be a long day."

After Annette and Bristol leave, I open my laptop which is fully charged now thanks to the solar panels we installed earlier. I grow impatient while the laptop boots up. A series of clicks brings me to a photo on my hard drive that I've obsessed about over the past day. It shows a rack of tubes containing blood or serum. Affixed to each tube is a manufacturer's label. I snapped the photo a year earlier at the clinic I worked at in the Amazon, a photo taken from an angle that allows me to see the tops and sides of the tubes.

Nervously, I retrieve the lavender-topped glass tube which held the blood I discovered in my shack. Before going to Danjou, I asked Katrine to transfer the blood from the glass tube to a plastic one of the type we use at the hospital. A courier then drove the blood to Mposto to have it shipped to Raymond Chabala's lab in Lusaka. While at the hospital today, I picked up the original glass tube at the lab.

I zoom in now on one of the lavender-capped tubes in the photo. Like the tube beside me, it has a rubber stopper that's indented in the middle for needles to pierce.

Zooming in further, I read the small print along the top of one of the labels . . .

©Hacienda Vacutainer
Whole blood
REF 421569

Heart racing, I compare what I've seen to the tube beside me. The labels are identical.

I know the name *Hacienda* well. It's a manufacturer of laboratory equipment based in Quito, Ecuador. While running the clinic in the Amazon, I placed several orders with the firm for supplies.

I return my attention to the photo, this time to examine print along the side of the label:

Hacienda Pharmacia, Avenida del Comercio,
Quito, Ecuador
6.0 ml

I've already scrutinized the tube beside me to know it carries identical wording.

I reproach myself for failing to observe these details the instant I discovered the blood in my shack. At the time, my attention had been diverted by the label that read, *Biohazardous Material—Handle with Caution*, a label I almost never see on tubes of blood.

"*Shit*!" I whisper, horrified by the notion that the tube of blood delivered to my shack almost certainly came from the Amazon. *Hacienda Pharmacia* is not a large player in the international market, and all of its sales are confined to South America. I know this because, while visiting the firm's headquarters in Quito one time, I met with a sales representative who spoke at length about the young firm.

I pace the dirt floor of my hut as I think about Cynthia's report of a Cessna landing outside Saysha on the very day I discovered the blood in my shack. More than ever, I want to know who was in that airplane and why they came here.

I walk to the front and back of the shack to lock the metal gates. For the first time ever, I stoop to look under my cot before I retire for the night. I find a spider web but nothing more.

4

LACKING MY CELL phone, I rely on my internal alarm to awaken. It brings me into the predawn darkness. After lighting a candle, I make hot tea for a caffeine fix to prepare for travel.

I empty my backpack of items I took to Danjou and replace them with clean clothes. Turning to my medical bag, I check to see that it contains syringes and containers for collecting specimens.

Based on what I've heard about Xavier's symptoms—weakness for a month plus a sensation of pins and needles in his feet—I compile a mental list of causes of peripheral nerve damage which could explain his symptoms: trauma, infections, cancer, and metabolic or nutritional disorders, among them. When I take his history, I'll ask sensitive questions regarding alcohol consumption, number of sexual partners, and illicit drug use, too.

From outside, I hear voices. I look through the doorway to find Thandi and Amu leading Annette toward the shack. I greet the party but also ask why Annette hasn't come with Innocent Mbewe. Last night before Bristol left my shack, I asked him to go to Innocent's hut to request that he travel with us to Uku-tetema so he could ferry blood or other specimens to the hospital should I decide to collect them.

"Innocent will be here shortly," Annette tells me. "In the meantime, I wanted to get a head start to let you know that I invited the girls to join us on our trip to Uku-tetema."

"They can't go!" I exclaim.

"Why not? The Zodiac carries eight people and Xavier's caravan will have more than enough room for them."

"But you told me it's a dangerous journey!"

"I gave the decision much thought," Annette replies.

"What thought could you have given it? You barely know Amu and Thandi!"

She smiles at the girls. "I'd say we know each other rather well. We stayed up late talking."

"I braided Miss Annette's hair," Thandi announces, pointing to the interlocking cords.

"That's nice, but braids don't make up for the fact that you and Amu are twelve years old—far too young to go on such a hazardous trip."

"Yet Oscar and Benji were old enough to go to Danjou?" Amu asks.

I grit my teeth. "We discussed that yesterday!"

Annette steps forward. "Paul, I invited Amu and Thandi because there are some younger girls in Uku-tetema I'd like them to play with."

"This isn't a play date!"

Annette looks at me with patience but says nothing.

Sighing, I relent. "So be it. Let's get our supplies down to the river."

We begin with the fuel tank and motor. When we return for the Zodiac, we find Innocent Mbewe has arrived.

"Good morning," he chirps. He tells me he's brought the casting material as requested.

"Great, let's take it down to the river."

Carrying the Zodiac requires all of us to navigate the steep trail, but we reach the river intact. Extracting a pump, Annette begins inflating the boat. As the Zodiac takes shape, she assigns Thandi and Amu to relieve her while she attaches the motor to the rear, ensuring it tilts forward to prevent the propeller from striking the ground.

We slide the boat into the river. After the others have boarded, I remain ashore to keep it from setting off into the current. Satisfied with the motor's performance, Annette tells me to hop in.

For a moment, the current whisks us downstream but the force of the motor quickly reverses course. Instantly, Annette displays her skills as she directs us to deeper water where she weaves a path between floating debris.

For the briefest moment, I see the head of the hippopotamus I view each morning at its bathing station. Disturbed by our approach, it disappears beneath the surface. Even in the dry season, the segment of the river we traverse is deep enough for the animal to submerge. As we motor further, low ridges along the shorelines grow into cliffs that squeeze us like vices. I grow claustrophobic until the shrill cries of birds nesting along the cliffs divert my attention. Thankfully, sections of sandy shoreline appear between cliffs.

Suddenly, the river becomes sliver-thin and turns dark brown. On each side are more cliffs but unlike those we passed earlier, these cast off wing-like ledges that stretch toward the center of the river only feet above the water. If we're to pass through the gap that approaches, it'll require Annette to thread a needle. I glance at Amu and Thandi to ensure their life jackets are secured.

Rather than dissect the gap, Annette eases the Zodiac to one side and glides under a ledge. The water about us is calm on account of a slab upstream that shunts the current elsewhere. After a tense journey, we've found a tranquil inlet albeit one that pins us under a ledge.

"We're here," Annette announces. She maneuvers the Zodiac to a point where light streams through a hole above her to set her hair ablaze. Climbing through the hole, she secures the boat with a rope. Before long, her head pops through the hole to beckon us to pass the bags to her. One by one, we clear the boat before filing through the hole, but with my six-foot-three frame, I'm the least graceful to do so.

Standing on the ledge, I note the Zodiac is hidden below us. Beside me, the hole reminds me of blow holes along volcanic seashores where raging swells force jets of water skyward. It makes me wonder whether similar eruptions occur here during torrential rainstorms.

"Listen carefully," Annette says. "We'll leave the Zodiac here and climb a path to meet our drivers above." She leads us to a wall where a transverse fissure cuts through a cliff to reveal sky above. Slowly, we ascend the fissure, an arduous climb in which our bodies and bags bump the sides. The air inside the passage is cool and moist, one which supports a luxurious crop of lichen and moss along the walls.

As we climb, it dawns on me that these are my maiden steps in Uku-tetema. I wonder whether every step hereafter in this mysterious land will be as challenging, each breath as burning, and each heartbeat as pounding as the ones now. Breathless when I reach the summit, I gasp.

Before me, a plain stretches as far as I can see. Upon it, thousands of wildebeests graze on golden grass. There's a symphonic motion in their undulating bodies, blowing manes, and swaying tails. Sunlight glows through plumes of fine hair along their necks. Their muzzles, long and wide in Romanesque style, make me want to rub my cheek against them as I would with a dog. Something about their gait is humble; perhaps it comes from the head held low. While some run with good speed—in the distance I see hooves kicking up dirt—their legs seem dainty compared to their plump abdomens.

"Isn't this something?" Annette asks, standing a few steps below me along a slope that drops to grasslands.

Only then do I notice four Land Rovers parked under trees at the base of the slope. They're vintage vehicles with spare wheels mounted to hoods, winches attached above front bumpers, and dual, square-paned windshields. Their headlights look like huge bug eyes set back from rounded fronts along each side. These are the Land Rovers from Africa-of-old, ones which roamed savannas, scaled hills, and washed under waterfalls, rugged vehicles more at home on dirt than asphalt.

"I like wildebeests," I tell Annette. "I find them endearing."

"The blue variety is especially handsome, don't you think?"

"Blue?"

She explains: "The horns differentiate two types of wildebeests. Blue ones have horns that jut to the side before rounding back toward the skull whereas those of their black counterparts curve forward and then turn up toward the sky." She sighs. "Isn't it cute how their ears project from beneath their horns?" She grazes my side. "Time to go; the drivers are anxious to leave."

"Why are there four vehicles?" I ask. "Two would suffice."

"Decoys," she responds. Her face tightens. "We've come under intense surveillance by drones recently. A week ago, one fired a missile that took out a Land Rover, but fortunately the driver survived."

"*Drones?* Where are they coming from?"

"We suspect from forces opposed to Xavier's drive to turn Uku-tetema into a national park. They appeared after the bill calling for the park was introduced in the National Assembly."

We reach the Land Rovers. The drivers, four in all, are dressed in khakis that match the one Annette wears. Their faces wear looks of caution. One acknowledges me with a nod before scanning the sky.

"We'll split up into two vehicles while the remaining two go solo," Annette announces. "And we'll take different routes to the lodge."

Thandi and Amu, out of earshot, play beside the Land Rover furthest away. Thandi runs a finger through dirt caked along the vehicle's side while Amu flicks stones with her feet.

"Come *nudume*," Thandi beckons.

I go more to summon her than to see why she calls but when I arrive, I'm taken aback by the drawing she's done with such frugal resources: a wildebeest mother and calf.

"That's incredible," I tell her. "Absolutely beautiful."

She wipes her finger between tire treads before accompanying me to the others. Assignments are made and we split up, Annette and the girls in one vehicle and I in another.

"Let me take Amu or Thandi," I suggest.

Annette shakes her head. "No, I'm following Xavier's instructions. He thinks they'll be safer with me."

Feeling like a marked man, I get into the last vehicle in line. My driver, a stocky man who's yet to say a word, waits patiently at the wheel while the others disburse. I watch them set off in different directions across the plain.

"Ready, Dr. Rider?"

I welcome my driver's words. "I'm in your hands."

Finally, he turns with a grin. "My name is Henry."

"Paul." I squeeze forcefully to match the firmness of his grip.

Scattered by the vehicles that departed before us, the wildebeests form a black haze on the horizon. With the exception of isolated umbrella thorn acacia trees, the plain grows grasses of varying lengths. At one point, a red sheen appears, and when I look out the window to search where the color comes from, I see grass stalks whiz by, some reaching the window where I rest my elbow. Among them is a species bearing reddish-brown flower complexes with hairy spikes.

"What's the red-colored plant?" I ask Henry.

"Herringbone grass," he replies, "or, if you prefer its scientific name, *Pogonarthria squarrosa*. It grows in disturbed areas."

"I'd hardly call this 'disturbed.' It seems pristine to me."

"By 'disturbed' I mean a busy area where antelopes and other grazers pass. Because they don't like the taste of herringbone, they leave it untouched."

I'm impressed with Henry's knowledge, and as the kilometers pass, I learn he was born in Uku-tetema about the same time as Xavier but in a different village. Unschooled until his late twenties, he enrolled in a program Xavier began that teaches adults with no previous education how to read and write. Students also study the geology, ecology, and zoology of Uku-tetema so they can work for Xavier subsequently as wildlife experts in what Xavier hopes will be the country's next national park.

It becomes clear to me that, despite his late education, Henry is academically-inclined. At one point, he stops the car and beckons me outside to show me footprints.

"Look carefully," he says, leading me along a patch of sandy soil. He points to two prints several feet apart. "Both were made by an elephant which has four toenails on its front feet and three in back." He stoops to point to fine lines comprising the prints. "If you compare the marks left by the two front feet, you'll notice differences between them, one having more vague markings than the other. These stem from the elephant withholding weight from its injured leg." Anger defines his expression. "The animal was a victim of poaching."

"Causing him to limp," I say.

He nods. "The poachers slashed the elephant's leg with a machete before we could stop them."

Later, he instructs me further before we climb a range of hills. After peering out the window, he brings the Land Rover to an abrupt halt. "Follow me," he says, reaching for a rifle.

We leave the Land Rover to climb a grassy knoll overlooking a swamp where a herd of sleek antelope feed.

"Black lechwe," Henry whispers.

They resemble deer but are thinner and especially agile in water. Their forequarters remind me of the chests of greyhounds, rib-lined pulmonary machines designed to oxygenate fast-twitch muscles. In back, powerful hind legs that lift the hips higher than the rest of the torso permit the lechwe to leap through water with uncanny ease. They do so now, hopping effortlessly across the swamp.

"They're spooked," Henry notes. He has me crouch low as he does. He holds the rifle ready to fire at any time.

While my eyes follow the herd, I feel a nudge.

"Over there," Henry whispers, pointing the barrel at a patch of grass beside the swamp where a single lechwe stands between two lions. Even from a distance, I see the brown fur on the lechwe's back and side stands in response to fear while the white of its underbelly heaves with the animal's respirations. Like a cornered dog, it holds its tail between its legs as its eyes dart one way and another in split attention between lions and escape route. Pivots of its head make it look as if the antlers pirouette.

Bolting for the water, the lechwe streaks across grass but is snared by claws that sink into its rear. Its hind legs fold under the lion's weight. Instantly, a second lion attacks from the front, this in the form of jaws that pierce the lechwe's neck.

I want to close my eyes for, as a child, whenever I watched television shows of African wildlife, I turned away at scenes of one animal killing another. Cruelty—*is* it cruel when a wild animal kills another for survival?—was too much to process.

But here things are different: I'm older, action is live, and fascination reigns. The lechwe squirms in a final attempt to escape, but the jaws in front and back only tighten, making escape impossible. Blood streaks from the lechwe's neck and abdomen while its eyes, once filled with terror, close. Limpness brings the animal flat on the ground.

"Life's cycle," Henry says.

The lions, aware of our presence, glance at us with calculated caution, teeth and claws committed to the kill. Theirs is to remain, ours to depart, so ever so gently, we stand and back our way out. The lions' meal will be taken in private.

FROM 1953 TO 1963, the British colony and two protectorates that ultimately formed the nations of Zambia, Zimbabwe, and Malawi were united in the Central African Federation. Dissolution of the federation occurred when Northern Rhodesia seceded to become the Republic of Zambia in 1964. Underpinning the new nation was fervor for self-government under a constitutional democracy. Blessed with major deposits of copper that turned the nation into a leading exporter, the new country had a robust economic foundation upon which to build a representative government.

Henry relates this history as we drive the final kilometers, ones that are deceptively arduous because, even though the terrain we cross is a savanna, rocks and gullies litter the region and force us to drive slowly. I listen to Henry's accounts and am intrigued most by the portrayal of Uku-tetema's residents as fiercely independent people who shun the shackles of central government. Having played a key role in securing Zambia's independence, Xavier's grandfather, an Uku-tetema tribal leader, was rewarded with a proclamation that Uku-tetema would remain autonomous for a century. With pride, Henry reminds me that, because of this accord, forty-seven years of self-rule remain for Uku-tetema.

I learn that freedom, independence, and autonomy run deep within the Treadwill bloodline. After Xavier's grandfather died, Xavier's father became chief of Uku-tetema and continued to protect the region from exploitation by commercial interests. The untimely death of Xavier's father when Xavier was ten years old left Xavier as titular chief, but it wasn't until Xavier reached the age of twenty-one that he assumed full powers, ones he exerted even as he pursued an education and career in England and the United States. As his grandfather and father had done, Xavier rejected pressure from mining interests to open Uku-tetema to exploration. After diamonds were discovered along the Amalumbo River in D R Congo, aggressive foreign groups failed in a push to get Xavier to permit mining along a section of southwestern Ukut-tetema where the river formed the region's border. His unwavering passion to protect the wildlife of his homeland inflamed tensions and led to calls in the National Assembly to annul what remained of Uku-te-tema's self-rule. In response, Xavier rallied sponsors in the National Assembly to introduce a bill to turn the region into a national park.

We reach the perimeter of the Treadwill estate with the sun low. Henry calls the terrain "miombo woodlands" after the word *miombo*, a Swahili term referring to a genus of trees that grow in tropical and subtropical south-central Africa. He tells me the genus that dominates the area sheds its leaves to conserve water for a short time during the dry season. But now, with rainy season due to begin, new leaves grow, many of which are aflame in gold and red which reminds me of fall back home.

Henry attends to his phone briefly. "They're waiting for us at the lodge," he informs me.

For the first time since beginning our journey, we drive along a road, one comprised of dirt and stones that leads through a forest of low-lying oak-like trees. Above their tops at one point I see a giraffe feeding on leaves and, later, an elephant wrapping its trunk around branches which it strips free.

Shortly, I appreciate why Henry used the word "lodge" to refer to our destination. Before us stands a large, curved, three-story structure made from stone, mortar, and wood. The stone component takes the form of buttresses that support massive logs positioned horizontally one atop another to create walls with cream-colored mortar filling their gaps. Along the second floor are balconies with pillars made from young trees. In the center of the circular driveway before the lodge is a fountain encircled by a wall of stones similar to those used for the buttresses.

"When was this built?" I ask Henry.

"A hundred fifty years ago," he replies, "although not by the Treadwills but by a British businessman residing in Malawi who wanted a vacation home here."

"How could he afford such a grand place?"

"He owned a timber business in Malawi." He points ahead. "The beams came from a tree called the yellow commonwood, or *Afrocarpus calpatus*. It's an evergreen that grows up to sixty meters and has a trunk as wide as three meters. The owner used buffaloes to drag the logs all the way here from Malawi."

"How did the Treadwills come to own the lodge?"

He looks at me apologetically. "Uku-tetema can be unfriendly to outsiders."

I leave it at that, not because I'm offended but because we've stopped beside the fountain, the last of the four Land Rovers to arrive. Through arching water, I see the front door to the lodge opens as a tall figure appears. He's bespectacled and bald, although not in the fashion that aging or shaving would configure. Rather, there are patches of thin hair on his scalp in a pattern that suggests hair loss of an acute nature.

"Come," Henry says to me, "a round of introductions."

Before I reach the stairway to the lodge, the tall man has descended. "Paul Rider," he says, extending a hand. "I'm Xavier Treadwill."

I didn't allow his descent to go unnoticed. During medical training, I learned that a patient's gait offers clues to diagnoses. In this instance, Xavier took the dozen or so steps gingerly, appearing to be weak rather than unstable or uncoordinated. Based on this observation alone, my initial impression is he suffers not from an ailment of the central nervous system but, more likely, from a systemic illness that produces generalized weakness.

"It's a pleasure to meet you, Xavier," I say. "Annette has spoken highly of you."

"As she has of you, Paul," he replies, "which puts us in rarified company given her high standards."

His accent is a blend of Central African, European, and American English, one I find soothing and sophisticated. His physical features, in contrast, are pure-African—high cheek bones, sleek jaws, and ears close to scalp. If I had to describe his physique with a single word, it would be "lithe." Notwithstanding his illness, he's lean, supple, and graceful.

Yet all is not right with him. There's a languid movement of the eyes and his shoulders slump below the level I'd expect for an athlete. He shifts from one leg to the other and back again as if discomforted by his feet. "Please come in," he says. "We've much to discuss."

An attendant has carried my bag into the lodge while another stands at the top of the steps with a tray in hand. "Please, take a drink," he tells me. "It's hot today."

I find the fresh lemonade has been prepared with just the right sweetness.

"Let's join the others in the sitting room," Xavier says.

The foyer we enter is expansive with massive beams lining its ceiling. I fall in love with the beams because they're meaty and dark and I suspect each could tell magnificent stories about visitors who've trod beneath them. For their part, the walls are adorned with photographs of, I presume, Treadwills going back several generations. Animals play a prominent role in the photos but not in a manner one would find in a lodge frequented by hunters. To the contrary, wildlife here are in pristine habitats—a gazelle standing on a grassy plain; a buffalo with low sweeping horns and flared nose holding two yellow-billed birds on its back; and an African civet whose black bands around the eyes give it the appearance of a raccoon. Conspicuously absent are weapons or trophy kills; here the trophy is the living animal in full glory.

We come to an enormous sunlit room lined by bay windows overlooking a watering hole at the base of the hill on which the lodge sits. Two adult giraffes have stopped to drink. The two use different techniques to lower their heads to the water, one spreading its front legs in full extension to the sides while the other keeps the front legs together but bends them at the knees.

"*Nudume*!" Amu calls. "You've arrived!"

She and Thandi rise from the floor to greet me with hugs, leaving behind two younger girls with whom they've been playing.

"Welcome, Paul," Annette says, remaining seated beside a window. "I trust your journey went well."

"It did," I reply. "Henry was a masterful guide."

"Yes, he is," she says.

I look at Annette intently because the tone of her voice and her expression convey concern, but I have no chance to decipher why because Xavier beckons the young girls to meet me.

They appear before me instantly, one stepping forward to shake my hand before the second follows suit.

"My six-year-olds, Sheena and Shauna," Xavier announces.

They're identical twins from what I see. Both are dressed in red and white candy cane dresses. After shaking my hand, they stand side-by-side with heads tilted at similar angles to look at me. Their eyes are bright and eager, and they wear wide smiles that reveal missing front teeth in the same spots. Cornrowed pigtails host happy red bows that bob about as they giggle. Their café au lait complexion leads me to look about the room for their mother.

"Do you need something?" Xavier asks.

The question surprises me because I'd glanced about in a manner I thought was subtle enough to escape notice. "No," I reply, "I was just looking for Innocent Mbewe. Has he arrived?"

"Yes, he's downstairs freshening." He addresses Annette: "I trust the rest of you would like to do the same now that Paul is here."

Annette stands. "That'd be nice. I'll take Amu and Thandi to their room to get them started. In the meantime, perhaps you and Paul would like to chat."

This is the source of Annette's concern, I conclude: She's eager for me to evaluate Xavier's health.

"Works for me," I say. "That'll give me a chance to finish this lemonade."

Xavier instructs the twins to play on their own. To Annette who passes, he says, "Paul and I'll be in my office if you care to drop by."

"I'll do that because there's a matter I'd like to discuss," she says.

I worry again about what Annette has on her mind. Although I've been with her less than forty-eight hours, I've gathered a sense of her thinking and emotions, both of which tell me something has set her off kilter.

Yet there's another reason I fret: I've come to like being around her. I realized this when we parted ways after arriving in Saysha, she to rest and I to see patients. The parting brought an unmistakable longing to reunite: I wanted the comfort of having her rest her head upon my shoulder; I missed looking into the mirror to see her eyes even if they were closed while she slept; and I lamented the loss of our bodies pressing into each other with each bump in the road.

I'm not so young to allow bliss to reign, however. Pain from my last relationship remains, and I warn myself that escape from Danjou hardly constitutes a basis for attraction. Yet the resentment I harbored initially for Annette drawing me into her affairs has been replaced by a dawning awareness of her person, and I like the colors of the dawn. A limited lesson it may be to draw from, but in my life I've done a good deal of traveling, particularly since becoming a doctor, and I've learned that compatibility on the road is a fair litmus test for a lasting friendship. Annette and I have traveled well so far.

I watch her walk across the foyer with Thandi and Amu. When they reach a staircase leading to a floor below, it is I who receives Annette's glance, not Xavier. It prompts the man beside me to shoot his eyes my way, but I display neutrality.

"Very well, Paul, shall we?" he asks.

My host leads me across the foyer to a closed door. Leaving it shut, he runs a hand along its deep purple surface as if stroking a beloved pet. "Do you know the wood?" he asks.

Admiring the dark violet-black streaks that run through it, I answer, "Not at all."

"It's called *Bois de Rose*. It's native to Madagascar but can no longer be purchased because of its scarcity." With an index finger, he traces a streak and looks at me. "In the past month, I've developed lines like these."

"Where?"

"Come, I'll show you."

We enter a conference room where laptops line the perimeter of a massive oval table. Two young men, oblivious to our entry, keep their eyes locked on their monitors. In like fashion, Xavier ignores them as he escorts me across the room to a private office.

"What's going on out there?" I ask, pointing toward the door.

"In due time, Paul, but first allow me to get straight to business."

"Yes, we need to talk about your health. Perhaps you should start by—"

"No, it's not my health I want to discuss first. It's another matter."

"Of course, what is it?"

He sits in a swivel chair behind a handsome desk carved from another tropical hardwood, but rather than speak, he spins around to face a garden outside his window. Colorful flowers flame the foreground while a mahogany look-alike called a Khaya tree frames the backdrop.

"I love my country deeply, Paul," he tells me now. "I'm not a traitor."

"I know you're not! Why would you say that?"

"Because, some of my countrymen claim I'm treasonous, including some in very high places. They say I'm a traitor because I value animals more than humans. Can that be?"

From the look on his face, I see he genuinely seeks my view. "Both must be held with reverence," I tell him.

"Exactly! This is the point I stress to my fellow citizens and those in the international business arena: It *is* possible to live side-by-side with our magnificent creatures but doing so requires us to relinquish land to them."

"I understand you've succeeded in getting the National Assembly to introduce a bill to do just that with Uku-tetema."

He nods. "I have, indeed, and I can't thank Annette enough for helping me get that done."

I search him for clues as to whether his relationship with Annette is confined to work or extends beyond that. "She's very capable," I say, "which makes me curious why you sought me."

"For two reasons," he replies, "one being because I need your help as a physician, but that's not the principal reason."

"What is?"

He eyes me intensely. "I seek your passion for animals. I felt it vividly when I read about the work you did with jaguars in the Amazon rainforest. I want you to share that passion with me in Uku-tetema."

"The technology I applied in the Amazon was targeted to protect jaguars only. I'm not convinced the same techniques would work in the open plains of Uku-tetema."

He smiles patiently. "You're missing the point, my friend: It's not technology I seek but *passion!* I ask only that you share it with me until the vote takes place in the National Assembly."

"Passion only goes so far. History has shown time and again that the call of hearts is silenced by the force of muscle."

"Which is why we need to combine the two, and I believe you're a man who does that!"

A knock comes on the door.

"Come in," Xavier says.

Annette steps in to join us, taking a seat beside me. To me she says, "I received a call from Bristol just before you arrived."

"Oh, what did he say?"

"He told me Raymond Chabala had called to report that tests of DNA from the blood left at your shack identified it definitively as jaguar blood."

"Oh, *God*, are you sure?"

"Chabala was absolutely confident in the results."

Xavier leans forward across the desk. "Paul, we have no jaguars in Africa. They're native to the Americas."

"I know that." I feel the world close in on me, as if tentacles from outer space squeeze the globe into a smaller ball. I envision one tentacle pulling me from Africa back to the Amazon.

Xavier leans back in his chair and sighs. "All of this is my fault, Paul, and I'm sorry I've placed you in this position. Had I not lured you to Africa to seek your help with my problems, you wouldn't be endangered as you are now."

"It was *my* decision to come to Africa, Xavier."

"But you wouldn't have known about the job in Saysha had I not intervened. Not only that, but I had Annette rope you into my sphere."

"She asked me to see you because you're ill," I remind him.

"Yes, that's true, but the fact remains you're a marked man now because of what you did with jaguars in the past and because we know each other now."

"But of all the people who might object to your efforts to protect Uku-tetema, why is it that *jihadists* placed us on their hit list?"

Xavier points to the door. "Earlier, you asked me what was going on out there in the conference room."

"I did, yes."

He removes his glasses, wipes them clean, and then replaces them. The cleaning makes his eyes look as big as melons now. "The cybersecurity skills my assistants and I have are among the most sophisticated in the world. If there's an answer *anywhere* online that explains why you, Annette, and I have been placed on a jihadist hit list, we'll find it." He points to the door again. "My assistants are working on the issue now, and they've made tremendous progress. If you're willing to help us, I'm absolutely certain we'll get to the bottom of this matter before long."

TEA HAS BEEN served and I hold a steaming cup before the window in Xavier's office. From behind me, I hear the tinkling of metal on ceramic as Annette and Xavier stir their cups.

"*Jaguar* blood!" I vent, unable to dispel the report from Chabala.

"Did you tell your ex-employer that you were moving to Zambia?" Annette asks.

"No, but they found out through the grapevine. An assistant of mine at the clinic in the Amazon emailed me after I left to tell me that a supervisor learned about the move."

"So, if someone in Ecuador wanted to send you jaguar blood, they knew where to find you," Xavier states.

"True, which is why I really want to know who was in the airplane that landed outside Saysha three days ago."

Xavier coughs up his tea. "What did you say?" He sets his cup on the saucer.

I tell him about the paramedic who'd seen an airplane land outside Saysha on the day I discovered the blood in my shack. "She's a great paramedic," I add, "dependable in every regard. She called the Department of Civil Aviation to ask if they knew of landings near Saysha."

"And what did they tell her?"

"They said a flight plan had been filed for a Cessna to fly from Lusaka to our area, but they couldn't reveal who flew the plane or the purpose of the flight because it was confidential."

Xavier adjusts his watch, wipes a speck of dust from his desk, and checks the status of his morning shave by running a finger under his chin. "Why didn't you tell me this earlier?"

"I just met you an hour ago!"

Worked up, he points to Annette. "You could've told her and she would've passed it on to me! This is extremely valuable information!"

"Xavier, calm down," Annette says. "You have the information now."

He glares at Annette before going to the door. Opening it, he calls, "Alexander, before you leave today, I need to speak to you about an aviation matter." He returns to his seat where he breathes deeply. "A simple task like that—getting up and walking—has become a chore."

"I'll address your health in a moment, but first a question for Annette." I turn to her. "With jihadists and militiamen battling in Danjou, why didn't get you out of town earlier?"

"Because I asked her to remain there," Xavier replies. "She was collecting information about the two groups because both have been a problem with poaching."

"But it was perilous to be there!" I retort.

"Peril is unavoidable! What's important is how one manages it. I had a group of armed guards there in case Annette needed them."

I stomp the floor. "You had guards in Danjou?" Glowering at Annette, I confront her: "Why didn't you call on them that night we were together?"

"I almost did, but I had to balance their safety with the dangers we faced."

"Still, I wish I'd known there was an option for help before I sent you and the boys into the bush!"

Xavier lifts a hand. "Paul, I understand your anger. I jeopardized your life by asking Annette to lure you to Danjou, but I saw it as the most expedient way to bring us together." His expression softens. "As I said, I need you."

I gather my wits. "It was a close call in Danjou."

"Understood." Xavier's eyes widen. "But it was a profitable venture. It took us to the militia's compound."

"Your guards followed me there?"

"Indeed, they were just outside while you were detained there, all the while prepared to raid the place if you needed help."

"How did they know I'd been detained?"

"We monitored radio bands used by the militia. We heard a dispatch stating you'd been taken to the compound."

"Were your guards present when the militia compound was attacked?"

"Nearby, yes, and they were about to come to your rescue but then saw you load an injured soldier into your truck."

"That was the colonel. Did your guards follow us to the hospital?"

"No, they entered the compound to search the place. They found two cell phones there, one belonging to you and the other to the colonel."

"You found *my* cell phone?"

"Yes." He reaches into his desk and hands it to me. "As for the colonel's phone, it chronicled a battle against the jihadists for control of the diamond business as well as his anger for Annette and me for obstructing his militia's poaching activities in Uku-tetema."

Annette stands. "I'll leave you two alone as I need to check on the girls." She departs the room.

To Xavier, I say, "So, as I see it, you have *three* opponents: jihadists, militiamen, and a domestic political faction in the National Assembly who seeks to defeat your bill to turn Uku-tetema into a national park."

He nods. "But let's be clear: The groups use different means of opposition—jihadists and militiamen resorting to forced entry onto my land while parliamentarians rely on democratic processes. And another difference: Those in the National Assembly have our nation's welfare at heart while, clearly, that isn't the case for the other groups." His face brightens. "But enough of these heavy matters! There's a lighter one we must celebrate!"

"What's that?"

"That you allowed Amukasana and Thandi to come here! My twins are ecstatic to have them vist. They long for new friends, and I feel guilty for moving them here from the U.S."

"Where's their mother?" I ask. Immediately, I know I've been rude.

Xavier looks away.

"I'm sorry, that was not for me to ask," I say.

"No, no, you had the right to ask because, after all, you're fostering orphans in Saysha." He returns his eyes to mine. "You and I are alike in having lost our wives."

I see Annette has informed him of our discussions while driving from Danjou to Saysha. "My loss came through divorce," I say. "What about yours?"

"Death," he replies.

I blink hard. "I'm sorry..."

"Don't be; I'm moving on." He smiles wanly. "It makes us brothers of a sort as we're men on our own."

"Divorce makes me a lesser brother." When I see him frown as if he expects an explanation, I add, "I screwed up my marriage; I take all the blame for it."

I READY A pad and pencil. "Tell me about your illness," I say to Xavier.

He proves to be an excellent historian, providing the right amount of detail without belaboring any particular point. I appreciate, too, that he's precise with dates and durations of symptoms.

I learn his illness began abruptly a month ago with weakness and easy fatigability. This was followed a few days later by what he calls "magnified sensations" in his legs. By that, he means that anything that touches his legs produces an exaggerated sensory response. Then a feeling of pins and needles began to bother him in his legs, especially in the soles, so much so that when he walks he feels he's treading on hot coals.

"That's not all," he adds. "Strange things happened with my skin. My palms became scaly and I developed a rash around my mouth; even my tongue is tender at the tip."

He grows discouraged. "What worries me most is hair loss. It began falling out two weeks ago, mostly from my head but also from my eyebrows and even from my limbs." He rubs his bare arm before holding out his hands. "And see these—the white lines across my fingernails?"

I examine them. "Yet, Annette told me that you've been healthy until recently," I say.

"That's right; I rarely see doctors because I haven't needed them."

"What about medications or dietary supplements? Do you take any?"

"No." He anticipates my next question: "And I rarely drink and never use illicit drugs."

I go through a list of symptoms that covers the entire body. He denies each with the exception of insomnia and a feeling of being more anxious than normal. "But that's probably stress-related," he explains. "God knows it's stressful here."

I ask him a second time whether he experienced any gastrointestinal symptoms early in his illness. He shakes his head emphatically.

"What about green urine?" I add.

"No! That's the second time you asked me that! What's the deal with green urine?"

"I'll explain after I examine you."

I check his blood pressure and pulse, both of which are normal. Examining his head, I corroborate the hair loss. One eyelid droops perceptibly. Around his mouth I see raw red skin that's tender to the touch. When I ask him to grimace, he exhibits weakness of the facial muscles.

I close the blinds to look into the back of his eyes. His optic nerves have shrunk in size from normal. "Have you had any visual changes?" I ask.

"No," he replies. "Why do you ask?"

I describe the optic nerve finding.

He shrugs. "I haven't needed glasses for anything, not even for reading."

Probing his tongue, I elicit tenderness at its tip but there's nothing visually abnormal about it. Examination of his neck, including the thyroid gland, is unremarkable.

I ask him to strip down to his underwear. He sits on the desk now as I listen to his heart and lungs. Both are normal. Holding his arms out, I confirm hair loss again but my attention turns to the white lines across his fingernails that he showed me earlier. A single line located halfway between the tip and cuticle is present in several nails, but none shows any depressions. When I press the lines, they disappear only to return upon removal of pressure.

"Have the lines moved?" I ask him.

He thinks for a moment. "I believe so... outward with nail growth."

His reflexes are normal. Lifting a cushion from a chair, I place it on the desk and ask him to lie down. I find nothing notable with his abdomen, genitals, or lymph nodes. Using a toothpick and cotton swab, I test his sensory perception and confirm that both pokes and brushes along his legs elicit more sensation than I'd expect to find.

I move to the end of the desk and place a palm against his sole and ask him to push against my hand.

"Oooh, that's tender," he says.

"The sole?" I confirm.

"Yes!"

I ask him to stand on the floor.

Rising from the desk proves to be laborious. "I'm telling you, I'm weaker than normal."

While he's in the standing position, I test his coordination by asking him to touch my finger as I move mine. He performs adequately, as he does walking a straight line with heels placed before toes. When I have him stand with legs together and then ask him to close his eyes, he shows no tendency to fall. However, he's unable to walk like a duck from a squatted position. "My soles," he complains. "They're sore!"

"Get dressed and then let's talk," I say.

He puts on his clothes.

"I think I know what you're going to tell me," he says. "I've read about my symptoms."

"What did you learn?"

"I'm a casualty of climate change."

I wait for him to explain, but he, too, appears to be in wait-mode.

"To be honest, climate change was the last thing on my mind," I say.

"I'm not surprised; that would be true for any doctor who examined me, yet I have no doubt that, ultimately, it's made me sick."

"Why do you say that?"

He crosses his legs, groaning as he does. "Many, including myself, believe Africa will bear the brunt of climate change even though we're responsible for only a tiny fraction of greenhouse gas emission. Actually, the harm has already begun. Consider the African elephant: Adults can drink over 200 liters each day, and with recent droughts here and elsewhere, animals are forced to migrate to areas where their lives are endangered even more than before."

"What does this have to do with your illness?"

He looks to the ceiling. "You see that beam?"

I look up. "Yes, it's beautiful, just as all of them are about the lodge. Henry told me they came from Malawi."

"That's correct, but they've become infested recently with a type of beetle that's eating them. We've never had this beetle in our area until the last few years, ones which have been drier and hotter than normal. My guess is the beetle extended its range as a result of changing climate."

"Are you saying the beetle caused your illness?"

"No, I'm saying I was poisoned by a pesticide we used recently to treat the beams in the lodge."

"Alright, now we're thinking along the same lines," I say.

He sits forward. "Are you convinced as well that pesticides made me sick?"

"I'm convinced you've sustained damage to your peripheral nerves, ones that come off the spinal cord and run to distant parts of the body, including the legs."

"Can pesticides do that?"

"They can if they contain toxic heavy metals."

"That's exactly what I concluded!" he affirms. "I believe the pesticide we used in the lodge contained arsenic. I probably inhaled a good deal of it over the days it was applied. "

"You told me earlier you saw an internal medicine specialist in Lusaka before you received a death threat. Did he test you for arsenic poisoning?"

"He submitted blood for testing but he said nothing about looking for arsenic."

"Did he share the blood test results with you?"

"Yes, he told me that my kidneys and liver are normal, as is my blood sugar."

"That's helpful because kidney disease can cause those white lines on your fingernails. They're called 'Mees' lines.' "

"Yes, I discovered photos of them online and also read that arsenic poisoning can produce them. That's why I'm guessing I was poisoned by arsenic."

"It shouldn't be a *guess*," I say. "Let's check the pesticide that was used to see if it contains arsenic."

"I already checked; it *does* contain arsenic." He opens his laptop and produces a photo of a container of pesticide. On the label is a statement advising caution because of the presence of arsenic.

"Has anyone else become ill since the pesticide was applied?" I ask.

"Not that I am aware of."

"What about your daughters?"

"They're fine."

I frown. "I'd expect others to have become ill if a pesticide was the culprit." I point to a photo of the twins on the wall behind him. "Especially them; children are particularly vulnerable to heavy metal poisoning."

"But they weren't around when the pesticide was applied. I sent them away before the first application took place."

"What about your staff who frequent the lodge?"

"I put them on leave because I didn't want them to be exposed to the process."

"Yet you remained here?"

"I couldn't leave the lodge unattended while workers traipsed about. They came from Mposto and I wasn't sure I could trust them being here alone."

"What precautions did the workers take while they applied the pesticide?"

"They wore masks, gloves, and gowns."

"Did you do the same?"

Furrows form across his forehead. "Not to the same extent."

I pause to think. "You may be right about arsenic, but we need to confirm the diagnosis."

"How do we do that?"

"We'll look for heavy metals, including arsenic, in urine and blood samples." I lean forward. "I asked repeatedly whether you've had green urine because thallium, another heavy metal, can turn urine green sometimes. Not only that, but thallium poisoning causes an illness remarkably similar to the one you're experiencing."

He nods. "I think I read something about that on the net. It causes hair loss, too, right?"

"Yes, it can. Do you know whether thallium is allowed in commercial products in Zambia?"

"I have no idea."

"The reason I ask is because many nations have banned its use commercially in light of its toxicity. Nonetheless, thallium-containing products occasionally get onto the market, particularly as rat and mouse killers. Do you have a problem with rodents here?"

"No more than usual, thanks to cats we keep around."

"Nonetheless, we need to check your storage areas for rat killer products to ensure none contain thallium."

"We can do that," he replies.

"And let me ask you this: Do you have any hobbies?"

"Hobbies?" he repeats. "Like what?"

"Wood working…airplane modeling…these sorts of things."

"Paul, I have twins! I employ hundreds of people! And I'm fighting poachers! As much as I'd like to have hobbies, there's no time for them!"

"I inquired only because arsenic and thallium are not the only things we need to be concerned about; other substances can damage peripheral nerves, including chemicals in glues and solvents used for hobbies."

"You're the doctor, Paul," he replies.

I draw blood from him before extracting three plastic vials from my bag. "I want you to fill these with sequential urinations. Ideally, we'd collect a twenty-four-hour specimen to test for heavy metals, but let's go with these for now."

"Where will they be tested?"

"In Lusaka; my hospital is not equipped to test for heavy metals."

"How do you plan to get them to Lusaka?"

I think for a moment. "You said earlier the company you hired to treat the beams came from Mposto, right?"

"Yes."

"How difficult is it to get there from here?"

"To Mposto?" he asks.

"Yes; if we can get them there, we can use overnight delivery to send them to Lusaka."

He scoffs. "I can have them flown to Lusaka directly from here."

"How can that be?"

A patient smile, all too familiar now. "I keep an airplane with my own pilot. You tell me where you want the specimens to go, and I'll have them delivered."

"Ideal, but I'd like Innocent Mbewe to accompany the specimens as he's familiar with the lab that runs the tests."

"Very well." He points to the vials on his desk. "I'll fill them by morning."

I prepare to depart but stop at Xavier's summoning.

"Did you bring material for casting as Annette asked you to do?" he asks.

"Yes, and I'm puzzled that she said you wanted me to apply a cast to one of my arms. What's that all about?"

"I'll explain tonight," he says. He stands and joins me at the door. "I need to check my pantry for rat poisons."

A HOT SHOWER is beyond luxury; it's celestial.

In Saysha, heating water over a kerosene stove for bathing purposes is cumbersome and costly, so what I do is stand under a metal tank outside my shack that's heated by the sun and let water run over me as I lather. But here in Xavier's lodge, I feel as if I'm in a hotel because my room has a shower with hot running water and a drain. I relax under its stream as my muscles unwind.

Before retiring to my room after examining Xavier, I received a schedule from my host for the remainder of the day. It called for rest followed by a short meeting in his office; cocktails in the sitting room; dinner; and, finally, private time.

I dress in fresh clothes and make my way back to Xavier's office where I join a young man seated beside Annette as Xavier occupies the swivel chair. A liter-sized water bottle stands before him, its level halfway.

"You look refreshed, Paul," Xavier says.

"I feel like a new man," I admit.

He addresses the young man in the room. "Alexander, please meet Dr. Paul Rider, the physician who oversees the hospital in Saysha."

The young man stands and we shake hands. He's rail thin, little more than tendons, bones, and skin, and if there's muscle to be found, it's disguised as another anatomical part.

"Alexander works for me," Xavier says. "He's a software engineer trained in Lusaka but born and bred in Uku-tetema. I'm very proud of him."

Yet another rootlet sprouting from Uku-tetema to the outside world, I learn.

"Very well, please sit, gentlemen so we can get started."

I take my place beside Annette who, like I, has bathed and changed clothes. She wears a cotton dress with a modest neckline before which hangs a thin gold necklace bearing a cross.

"Hello, Annette," I say, "good to see you again."

She places a hand on mine on my thigh. With a gentle squeeze, she smiles. I look at Xavier to see if he's noticed the touch but he hasn't because the desk blocks his view.

"Paul," he says presently, "I've asked Alexander to join us because he has important information to divulge. Let's go to the conference room to talk about it."

We sit at the oval table where two laptops have been placed side-by-side. From my seat, a view through a window at the far end of the room displays a large penned-in area outside where two elephant calves are hard at play. About them are mango trees that provide shade from the late afternoon sun. Above the elephants, boughs laden with green fruit hang from long stems which sway in the breeze.

Alexander begins: "I believe Xavier told you earlier that we recovered a cell phone that belonged to the colonel at the militia compound where you were detained." His diction and manners are formal, ones I attribute to my presence but also to the seriousness with which young professionals in this country approach the opportunity to climb out of poverty that's held their families back for generations.

"Yes," I say, "Xavier told me you found the colonel's mobile."

"Well, that was not the only one which provided valuable information. We acquired one from a jihadist as well."

"How'd you get it?"

Alexander loops around the table to occupy a space across from where we sit. "Yesterday afternoon, a group of jihadists entered Uku-tetema from D R Congo with the goal of plundering our rhinos sixty kilometers from the lodge. We were prepared for their arrival, however, because we'd monitored a listserve used by a jihadist cell in Danjou."

"How'd you know about the listserve?" I ask.

Alexander turns to Xavier as if to ask how much detail to divulge. His supervisor comes to his aid but not before gulping from his water bottle.

"Alexander spent two years working for me in Silicon Valley. During that time, he collaborated closely with DARPA." He pauses. "Are you familiar with the acronym?"

"I've heard of it but can't recall what it stands for," I reply.

"Defense Advanced Research Projects Agency. It's a U.S. government entity that invests in breakthrough technologies to advance national security. DARPA hired my company to execute many of their initiatives. As such, Alexander became privy to sensitive information regarding extremist groups worldwide. It was through these channels we discovered the jihadist listserve and the hit list that includes your name."

With that, Xavier defers to Alexander who, in turn, lifts a remote. A press of a button brings the two laptops to life, one displaying text in a foreign language and the other in English.

"What you're seeing on the left," Alexander says, "is a command in Arabic from a jihadist commander to conduct a raid of Uku-tetema to collect rhino horns. The command is translated into English on the right."

The command orders the invaders to secure a minimum of five horns and specifies when to conduct the mission. Three jeeps will ferry twelve heavily armed militants. The horns are to be sold on the black market and the funds to be deposited into a designated account.

Alexander continues: "With this information, we sent twenty armed guards to sites frequented by our rhinos. At the same time, another team monitored border crossing points with D R Congo to look for jihadists traveling toward Uku-tetema."

I feel a set of eyes zero in on me. They belong to Annette who, I suspect, seeks clues as to whether the trip line system I used in the Amazon to protect jaguars might work in Uku-tetema. In the briefest of glances I afford her, I register a palette of colors I find attractive—brushed hair with a wave emanating from a part along one side; blue eyes; and freckles which appear more lustrous than before.

"Indeed, our border team spotted three invading jeeps," Alexander continues. "They entered Zambia from different locations before meeting at a spot from where they entered Uku-tetema. They drove straight to an area frequented by rhinos. However, before they arrived, our guards had taken strategic hiding positions there. I will show you a video now of what transpired. The video was taken by one of our guards."

One laptop goes dark while the other begins a video depicting grassland leading to a muddy watering hole in the foreground. Blurry reeds frame the scene in a way that suggests the video was shot from among them. In the distance, seven rhinos approach the watering hole, among them a calf.

"Look closely," Alexander says. "Those are southern white rhinos." He allows the video to run as he speaks, his voice lowering to a whisper as if he stands among the reeds. "All rhinos—so called 'black' and 'white'—are actually gray in color. The designation 'white' originates from a mistranslation of the Afrikaans word *weid*, which means 'wide' in English. The main difference between white and black rhinos is the shape of their mouths. While black rhinos have a pointed upper lip used to pluck fruit and leaves from branches, white rhinos possess a flat, wide lip to graze on grasses. Early English-speaking settlers in South Africa misinterpreted *weid* as "white," which explains why white rhinos are called by that name today."

Alexander pauses. It's clear he's memorized the cadence of the video because even though he's blinded to the screen, his words mirror the unfolding events. "As you can see, a bull takes the lead as the rhinos approach the mud hole while the cows encircle the calf. After grazing in the hot sun, they cool themselves in mud which acts as a sunscreen and bug repellent."

The animals enter the mud hole and lower themselves to a point where their eyes barely clear the surface. Some swish their tails, creating expanding rings that collide.

"Note their ears," Alexander says. "Do you see how they fall back on the head only to rise in listening mode? Rhinos have exquisite hearing." He bends forward from the waist, rapt with what he can't see but feels in the core of his being.

I glance at Xavier. He's not watching the video but, rather, eyeing Alexander with pride. Silently, I credit my host for nurturing a deep respect in his staff for the animals of his land.

Suddenly, three jeeps with roll bars appear from the side of the screen. They turn abruptly toward the mud hole and speed forward through the grass. The roar of engines causes the rhinos to leave the hole but before the last has exited gunfire erupts.

The jeeps disperse but continue toward the rhinos. In each vehicle, a man clad in a red bandanna stoops just below the level of the windshield to assess the source of return fire while another unleashes an automatic rifle in a wide swath. The camera's zeroing-in on a windshield confirms the bulletproof nature of the glass as not a single crack is seen.

Shouts come from the jeeps which halt abruptly. In a flash, bodies eject from the chasses to take cover behind the vehicles. In a momentary lapse of gunfire, the rhinos take refuge among the reeds.

Gunfire resumes and a body is seen falling to the ground beside a jeep. From the rear of each vehicle, a militant crawls forward into the driver's seat. In rapid sequence, the jeeps back up and then spin around to flee with only their roll bars visible above the grass.

Gunfire ceases. In the silence, Alexander whispers: "The guards are looking through binoculars at the area where the militant fell."

The camera focuses on a patch of grass where blades are seen parting beyond the mud hole.

"The militant is moving!" Alexander exclaims.

Guards leave the reeds to advance through the grass in an arrow-like motion that reminds me of geese flying in the late autumn sky.

A shout is heard.

"That's a guard," Alexander announces. "He warned the militant in French and Arabic that he will be killed unless he surrenders immediately."

A body rises from the grass. It's the militant, and one of his arms is bloodied.

A short distance before the militant, a guard's head appears.

Alexander: "The guard is ordering the militant to raise both arms."

The arms rise, but they hold a rifle that fires at the guard. Shots ensue and the militant falls.

The arrow in the grass advances further, only more slowly now. Another shot is heard. Before long, a guard stands with the militant's weapon. The remaining guards encircle their comrade. Slowly, the circle closes like a tightening noose. In the center, a guard lifts the injured militant in his grip. The militant's shirt is soaked with blood.

"The enemy!" Alexander proclaims. Sweat lines his forehead and the screen goes black.

"Where's the man now?" I ask.

Alexander rejoins us to take a seat beside Xavier. "He is with the hyenas."

I crinkle my brow.

Alexander explains: "In Uku-tetema, we believe those who are cruel to animals should be left to animals."

Xavier stirs. "Alexander has omitted telling you that we tried to save the man, but he bled to death in the grass. That's where we left him."

"However, there *was* an item we preserved," Alexander quips. He lifts a cell phone. "The militant was careless to have carried this."

"Indeed," Xavier agrees, "because it revealed valuable secrets." He sits up straight. "You see, we can penetrate virtually any cell phone service provider in the world regardless of whether they use encryption technologies. In Silicon Valley, we developed products that use laser-fast algorithms to decode these systems. National security agencies around the world allied with the U.S. rely on our technology."

Xavier nods at Alexander. "Let's show Dr. Rider the power of our system."

A laptop alights. It lists in tabular form a series of calls and texts, ones I recognize immediately as my own.

"Here we have two weeks' worth of your communications," Xavier notes.

I stir uncomfortably.

"I'm sorry, Paul, but nothing's private any longer," he continues. "As eyes are the window to the soul, cell phones are a verandah to the mind and heart; from this verandah, an onlooker may peer into a house to see and hear the most intimate expressions and conversations."

He scrolls to a call I placed ten days earlier and clicks on it. A box with an arrow appears on the screen. "Shall we listen to the voice mail you left your sister?" he asks.

"I don't think that's necessary," I say.

He smiles awkwardly before clicking the arrow.

In the clearest of voices, I'm heard telling my sister that I won't return to the U.S. to see my father in the aftermath of his diagnosis with terminal cancer. "The Great Santini," I tell her, "has received what he deserves."

Even though they're my words, I'm struck by the bitterness with which they're uttered.

"And now, a text," my host says.

"Please, Xavier," Annette interjects. "You've made your point!"

"No, one more item," he insists. His face is stern, like a hunter's after striking a target but not fatally.

A text appears on the screen…

For the first time, I want to stay put.

"I share this," Xavier continues, "because it illustrates an important point: A single interception may not disclose the perspective one needs to fully understand content." His eyes bore in on mine. "What did you mean by this text, Paul?"

He's revealed a text I hold most personal, one I sent to Annette last night after she and Bristol helped me carry the Zodiac and motor to my shack.

"It's a private matter," I reply, "one immaterial to my role as your physician."

He shifts his eyes from me to Annette and back again as if to snare any glance or communication between us. An awkward stillness engulfs the room, one in which air currents cease.

"Paul… Paul," Xavier says, reaching out to squeeze my shoulder. "Please don't take this too seriously. I mean no harm by exposing your texts and calls. I use them simply to point out that something one person may perceive as intrusiveness is valued as a treasure trove by another. I trust I've convinced you that I can evade firewalls erected by service providers to protect clients' confidentiality."

"I'm convinced," I assure him.

A new list appears on the screen.

"So, let's move to a new dataset, one collected from the jihadist's cell phone. As you can see, we have before us his calls, texts, and emails."

I scan the list with lingering resentment for what Xavier has exposed of my life.

"Let me get straight to the point," he says. "This jihadist was the commander of the cell based in Danjou."

He scrolls through a spreadsheet with columns listing phone numbers, email addresses, individuals' names, and, in some instances, GPS coordinates or locations of recipients at the time contacts were made. I recognize only one of the locations, Mogadishu, Somalia's capital; the other names are foreign to me: Hargeysa, Kismaayo, and Boosaaso, among them.

A click brings a name to the fore: International Mines, LLC.

"Hey, I know that name!" I say. "They're a subsidiary of the company I used to work for."

"That's correct," Xavier replies. "Their parent corporation is TransNational Oil, and their headquarters are located just outside Houston, Texas, not far from TransNational's U.S. main office."

"Was International Mines listed on the jihadist's cell phone?" I ask.

"Not as such; what we found was a telephone number that belongs to a temporary office International Mines set up in Lusaka."

"That's outrageous! Why would a jihadist have that number on his phone?"

"We're hoping you'll help us find the answer."

"*How*?"

He grins. "By placing a cast on your arm; that's why I asked you to bring the supplies with you."

WHEN IT COMES to cocktails, I prefer fruity mixed drinks. A dash of liquor with a blend of crushed ice and tropical fruits such as guava, coconut, and/or pineapple cruises me into happy hour; the merrier the name of the drink, the tastier I find it.

It's cocktail hour at Xavier's lodge, and I'm with the group that assembled earlier in the sitting room. Sipping a vanilla mango mojito, I'm relieved to see Amu and Thandi watch zebras drink from the watering hole below.

Innocent Mbewe is present as well and appears to be comfortable in his new surroundings. He holds a beer as he carries on in animated fashion with Xavier about how African professional football players are faring in European leagues. Xavier continues with his drink du jour although ice now accompanies his water. The animation of their discussion gives me hope that Xavier has turned the corner from whatever ailment afflicts him. Although I'd like to interrupt him to ask how casting my arm could possibly help learn how the telephone number for an office of International Mines in Lusaka appeared on a jihadist's cell phone, I'll wait until after dinner for the explanation. In the meantime, I seek a quiet spot beside a bay window where I watch an antelope join the zebras at the watering hole.

"That's a male Sharpe's grysbok," Annette says from behind me. She joins me at the window with a glass of wine. "See the short horns? It's easy to confuse it with a common duiker which is just a bit larger."

"Are there animals you *don't* know?" I ask her.

My compliment falls flat.

"Paul, we need to chat," she says.

"I'm all ears."

"Raymond Chabala just called a few moments ago as I was coming here from my room."

I check my phone. "That's funny, he didn't call me."

"Did you tell him you have your phone back?"

"No, that's why." I put the phone away. "What did he say?"

"Matters become more complex every time he rings."

I brace myself. "What's it this time?"

She takes a drink. "The jaguar blood was radioactive."

"My God! What do you mean 'radioactive'?"

"It contained traces of radioactive phosphorus in it!"

"Do you mean P-32?" I ask.

"Yes, that's the term he used."

I'm familiar with radioactive phosphorous, also referred to as 'P32 'or '32P.' During medical school, I did a stint at the National Institutes of Health in Maryland where I labeled enzymes from the digestive tract with P-32. Before starting the job, I took a required week-long course in radiation safety.

"What led them to look for P-32 in the blood I sent them?" I ask.

"A lab technician happened to walk past a Geiger counter while going to store the remnants of the specimen and it set off an alarm."

I take a swig of mojito and allow the rum to pickle my mouth. "Why'd someone add P-32 to the blood?"

"To harm you," Annette suggests.

"I'm not convinced. If harm was the purpose, they picked the wrong element; others could've done far more harm."

"I'm not a nuclear scientist, but P-32 sounds bad enough."

"Not really; the half-life of P-32 is just 14 days, meaning half the radioactivity present in the blood initially will be gone in two weeks. After ten half-lives, or 140 days, radioactivity will disappear totally. I'm wondering whether Chabala's staff tested the blood for other forms of radiation."

"He mentioned something about a scintillation counter—did I get that right?—showing no other radiation was present."

"That's good, a scintillation counter would've detected more dangerous forms of radiation than that produced by P-32."

"So, you're not worried that your staff handled the specimen in Saysha?" Annette asks.

"I'm not happy about it," I reply, "but my technician, Katrine, wears gloves and a lab coat whenever she works with blood. That would've reduced her exposure to radiation emitted by P-32 which, in general, doesn't pass through skin. Ingestion of the radioisotope, of course, would've been another matter, but that didn't occur."

THE CALL TO dinner comes from a bell chimed by a member of the kitchen staff who holds a candle in her other hand.

The twins spring from the floor where they've been playing with Amu and Thandi and rush to an adjoining room, narrowly missing a butler who carries a tray with empty glasses.

"Come," Xavier calls. "Supper is ready."

The last rays of dusk show me to the dining room, a space where intimacy trumps size. Once again, tropical woods carry the theme as a magnificent table stretches some thirty feet across the room. Places for six have been set at one end while four await the children at the other.

Along one side of the room is a Demilune table that holds two large bowls of water and a stack of towels. After washing hands, we sit. Xavier has assigned me to a chair beside his at the head of the table with Innocent Mbewe and Alexander as my neighbors while Annette takes a place across from me. For a moment, I ponder the asymmetry of the assignments only to see a tall wiry man enter the room. He apologizes for being late and washes his hands before stopping at Xavier's side.

"Martin, please meet our guests from Saysha, Dr. Paul Rider and Mr. Innocent Mbewe," Xavier says. For my benefit, he adds: "Martin is a pilot. He will fly Innocent Mbewe and the clinical specimens to Lusaka tomorrow morning."

Innocent and I shake hands with Martin before he sits beside Annette. The children, in the meantime, giggle from their private space. Xavier calls to the twins and puts a finger to his lips. "Annette," he says after the room falls silent, "would you lead us in prayer?"

Heads bow as I process the awkwardness I feel. I'm not a spiritual man by most standards, much less a church-goer. While I have vague rumblings about worlds beyond, I leave the rumblings in lonely corners where they reside without nurture or interference.

"Let's still our minds," Annette begins.

She allows the silence to deepen before she speaks, and when she does, she gives thanks for destinations reached, friendships commenced, and a safe place to gather for the night. For the food to be served, she gives particular thanks, acknowledging that we're no different from the crowd of thousands in the desert who were fed through the breaking of seven loaves. Her words are elegant, gracious, and reverent.

"Amens" follow and napkins unfold. From the head of the table, Xavier says, "In wealthy countries candlelight dinner is a romantic event, but here we dine by candles to save precious electricity generated by our wind turbine and solar panels for our computer tasks. I invite you to enjoy your dinner in our soft evening light."

Dinner consists of *nshima*, steamed vegetables, and a small portion of fish. As we eat, Xavier draws his guests into discussions that cover topics ranging from wildlife to Uku-tetema's history to present day politics. At one point, with tea before us and plates cleared, he points to an oil painting on the wall. It depicts a windswept island with a hostile coastline against which crashing waves send whitewater skyward. Above the cliffs encircling the island, a lush carpet of grass gives way higher up to rocky outcrops that lead to a stark plateau forming the island's center. Along one section of grass are the remains of what appears to have been a castle. A majestic horse stands beside the remains.

"Annette is the artist," Xavier announces, "but she's too shy to admit to it." He cringes playfully as if the woman to his right might slap him for revealing a secret.

Immediately, I ask myself why Xavier would display a painting by Annette in his dining room, but with further thought, I remind myself that, as a photojournalist, Annette relies on artistic expression in her work products, ones which Xavier shares with others routinely. "It's beautiful," I say.

"What do you find appealing in it?" Annette asks.

I search for words. "The austerity and loneliness speak to me."

She looks at me in earnest. "What do they tell you?"

I sip my tea. "It's not so much what they tell me but, rather, that they *renew* me."

"You're an introvert," she states. "Rejuvenated by being alone…"

"Could be," I reply.

"Has it always been that way or did something happen to bring it about?"

I hear cups touch their saucers as eyes turn my way.

"Can an event create an introvert?" I ask.

"That's what I'm asking you," she replies.

I seek my shell. "I suppose it could." I lift my cup and hold it to my lips to keep them from divulging more.

Annette dabs her mouth. "I'm sorry," she says. "I was rude to put you on the spot. I become emotional when I discuss the painting because if I were ever to leave Africa, it'd be to return to the island."

An uncomfortable silence ensues only to be broken by Xavier. "That's the power of art, is it not? It speaks to our souls."

If Xavier seeks further discussion, it'll have to come from others, I resolve.

"It's getting late," he proclaims, "and the day has been long. I suggest we meet first thing in the morning to plan tomorrow. Will seven a.m. work for all?"

Heads nod.

"Very well, a goodnight to each of you; we shall meet in the sitting room at seven in the morning."

In the foyer, our party disbands. While Xavier escorts the twins up a wide staircase to the second floor, our contingent from Saysha descends another to a lower level where a series of guest rooms span the length of the lodge.

Innocent Mbewe is the first to peel off into a room which leaves me walking behind Annette, Amu, and Thandi. Although I'm only feet behind Annette, I feel a wide gap separates us. The tension from our dinnertime discussion has distanced us, but I'm willing to attribute it to fatigue as much as to words.

We stop before the room occupied by Amu and Thandi.

"Girls," Annette says, "get ready for bed; I'll tuck you in shortly."

"Good night, *nudume*," the girls say, poking their heads around Annette.

"Sleep well," I tell them. "See you in the morning."

The girls enter their room and close the door to leave me alone with Annette. She looks at me and whispers, "I'm sorry for singling you out the way I did about my painting." Her eyes glisten.

I cup her elbow to start her on a walk with me down the hallway. We pass her room before stopping in a spacious lounge that faces the same sloping hill we looked upon from the sitting room only now, with night fallen, the outside world is cloaked in black.

"Can we talk for a moment?" I ask her.

She looks relieved to sit but before I can do the same, I hear Xavier's voice from the end of the hall.

"Paul, may I have a moment with you?" he calls.

I glance at Annette who wears a look of disappointment.

"Of course, Xavier," I reply.

In moments, we're joined not only by Xavier but by Martin and Alexander. I find the impromptu gathering awkward.

"Oh, I'm sorry," Xavier says, holding up his hand. He motions to Annette and then to me. "If you like, we can have this discussion later."

"No, no," Annette says, standing. "I was just about to tuck Amu and Thandi into bed."

She departs and, in the momentary silence that elapses, I hear Xavier shuffle his feet.

"If it's alright with you, Paul," he says, "I'd like to gather in the privacy of your room."

"By all means," I reply.

I lead them to my room at the end of the hallway. Without delay, Xavier closes the door after all have entered. "Please forgive me for the abruptness of this encounter," he says to me.

"Not a problem," I assure him.

Xavier points to the two single beds in the room for us to sit on while he turns a chair from a desk to face us.

"Paul," he says, taking a deep breath. "I have a big favor to ask of you."

"What is it?"

"I'd like you to fly to Lusaka tomorrow."

"With Innocent, you mean?"

"Yes, and accompanying you will be Alexander and a bodyguard. My airplane is plenty large to carry all of you."

"Why do you want me to go to Lusaka?" I ask.

"Because I need you to do something that could help us tremendously. Earlier today, I told you that a telephone number for an office operated by International Mines in Lusaka appeared on a jihadist's mobile call list."

"Yes, I recall that."

"Well, we recently learned through a pilot-friend of Martin's that International Mines recently moved a fleet of airplanes to Lusaka to support a stake they've taken in our nation's copper industry."

"Yes…," I say, drawing him on.

"It appears one of their airplanes landed near Saysha a few days ago."

My heart races. "How do you know that?"

"Martin's contact verified it. He's privy to flight logs out of Lusaka."

"Why did they fly to Saysha?" I ask.

"I don't know, but that's where you fit in. In Lusaka tomorrow, I'd like you to help us gather information about International Mines."

"How could I possibly do that?"

"You'll assist Alexander as he breaks into their computers while Innocent delivers my specimens to the laboratory."

I look at Alexander on the other bed. He nods confidently while Martin sits beside him stoically, a man whose training to navigate stormy skies will, I hope, see us safely through the proposed mission.

Xavier again: "It's very important that you keep what I'm about to ask you to do in Lusaka secret. I don't want Innocent to know the details. From his standpoint, he'll think you're conducting business at the American Embassy."

He informs me that the office we'll visit is one International Mines established recently just outside the airport in Lusaka while they wait for permanent quarters in the city to be refurbished. In the meantime, a skeletal crew at the airport office prepares for the move and the imminent arrival of the company's staff. He concludes with an overview of the task I'm to undertake, one that makes me shudder.

"You can do it, Paul," he assures me. "I have faith in you."

5

I'M A CREATURE of habit, particularly upon arising.

"Creature" is apt because, since moving to Zambia, I've grown accustomed to beginning each morning in the company of three animals. Before getting out of bed, I listen to the clattering of the shoebill stork in its nest on my roof; its soliloquy tells me the sun is about to rise. Then, as I sit on the patio outside with tea, I wave at the hippopotamus in the river upstream. That's followed by a visit with a large male baboon I've come to call "Jimmy" who swings his way down the acacia tree in front to watch me make my final preparations for the day. On his first visit after I moved into the shack, I rushed inside for protection because I knew baboons can be vicious, but Jimmy proved to be tender. Like the sculpture by Auguste Rodin, *The Thinker*, Jimmy sits beside my water tank with his chin resting on his hand which, in turn, is supported by an elbow propped on his thigh—and he just stares at me as if he's amused. Over time, I've relied on that look to reassure myself that all's well and that the day may begin in peace. In stressful moments at the hospital, I often think of Jimmy's eyes which convey utmost serenity.

I awaken now at the crack of dawn in Xavier's lodge. From above, I hear neither clattering nor shifting of sticks in the shoebill stork's nest. Unable to sleep any more, I dress and go to the sitting room where I hear the sounds of plates being stacked in the kitchen. I find the same woman there who rang the bell for dinner the previous evening. She greets me with a smile.

"Tea, Dr. Rider?" she asks.

"Would love some."

"I'll bring it now."

The savanna I look upon through the west-facing window has yet to receive the first rays of sun, but through a veil of mist I make out the blurry form of an elephant drinking from the watering hole. After leaving its trunk submerged, it lifts the appendage and sprays its back with a torrent before leaving the scene. I remain at the window to see who might take its place but am greeted by a cautious voice.

"Good morning, Paul, am I allowed in your presence?"

I turn to find Annette. She wears an impish smile.

"*Allowed*?" I repeat.

"Really, the way I treated you last night while discussing my painting; my questions were so intrusive."

"Yes, you deserve a time-out," I chuckle. I sit on a sofa before the window and tap a cushion beside me.

She accepts the offer. "I want you to know that last night I was talking more to myself than to you about the painting. You were my alter ego."

"What was your discussion about?"

She wrinkles her brow. "It was a rehash of my young adult life." She looks out the window. "You see, the island I painted belongs to my family. We've owned it for generations. It lies off the coast of western Ireland where I grew up. I went there often to hike and to fish."

"Is there anywhere to stay on it?"

"No longer; we took daytrips and returned before nightfall. Over time, the island became my soulmate. It questioned my ways and helped me forge a path while growing up. I rode my bicycle only a short distance from our house to see the island. It sat off the coast like a loyal friend, beckoning me to view it as often as possible. Later, after I left home to attend university, I made a point of visiting the island when I returned at vacation time. The stones in the painting once formed a monastery; a storm destroyed it fifty years ago."

"A monastery," I repeat, noticing that she wears the same necklace as last night, one with a cross. "Is there a religious thread in your family?"

She laughs, sending hair across her face. "*Thread*?" She clears her eyes. "More like a rope; my family has produced priests for the Presbyterian Church in Ireland for a century."

"Is your father one?"

"He is."

I glance at the cross. "And you?"

She smiles, a reflective tug of the lips. "Yes, I'm an ordained priest but no longer serve in the traditional way."

"Did you leave the ministry to become a photojournalist?"

"I never *left* it. I acquired additional skills to *help* me minister—skills as a photographer I combined with those of journalism I studied at university. I've used the combination to minister to those with special needs." She looks out the window at a gazelle drinking from the watering hole. "The animals of Africa are my parish now."

I allow her space to commune with the gazelle. In the silence, I envision her symbolically breaking bread and serving wine.

"But the painting," I whisper. "What discussion were you having with yourself about it last night?"

She turns to me, but there's an adjustment she seems to make, one, I surmise, that requires her to move from the world of animals to humans.

"I created the painting in my mid-twenties after being ordained. At the time, I was consumed by serving a parish but wasn't happy with my work because I didn't have enough time to myself. During a rare week off, I returned home and propped an easel on the hill overlooking the island. With each stroke of a brush, I realized the island represented a part of me that longed for freedom. As I painted it, I felt I straddled the sea with one leg on the island and the other on the mainland. One leg tugged at me to pursue solitude while the other beckoned human interaction—the classic introvert-extrovert battle."

She looks at me longingly. "So, when you said you found loneliness and austerity in the painting, you struck a chord. Those were the two factors that spoke to me as an introvert, ones that led me to a career in photojournalism which I hoped would allow me to express my introvert and extrovert sides. And then when I witnessed the poaching incident I described earlier—the one in Tanzania where a mother elephant was massacred beside her calf—I knew I was called to minister to animals. Thanks to a chance encounter with Xavier, I combined my skills in photojournalism and ministry to become a missionary serving African wildlife."

My tea arrives.

"Miss Wilson, may I bring you something?" the woman asks.

"That's alright, Helena," Annette replies. "I'll get it myself shortly."

Annette waits for us to be alone again. "So, that was the dynamics of the discussion last night. I hope it explains my intrusiveness." She moves to the edge of the sofa as if to stand but doesn't. "May I ask you something?" she says, looking back at me.

"Go ahead."

"I don't mean to offend you by raising the topic of the text that Xavier indiscreetly projected on the computer yesterday, but it has intrigued me ever since I received it from you."

I feign ignorance. "Which text was that?"

"The one you sent me two nights ago when we were in Saysha. You said, *For the first time, I want to stay put.* What *did* you mean by that?"

I grimace. The text spoke from my heart, but I regret sending it now.

"Paul?"

"I trust you're familiar with the adage, 'A rolling stone gathers no moss,' " I say.

"Of course, one I interpret to mean that activity keeps a mind sharp."

"That's one view, but a vagabond such as I sees it as meaning a wanderer knows no home."

She tilts her head. "Is the vagabond in you changing in some way?"

I breathe deeply. "Let me put it this way: While I've always strived to be like the wind —coming and going as it will—I may be ready for a respite."

She looks ahead and I see her Adam's apple move from a swallow. "Ah, the wind…," she says. "Do you know the verses, *The wind blows wherever it pleases. You hear its sound, but you cannot tell where it comes from or where it is going.*?"

I shake my head.

"What if I add this: *So it is with everyone born of the Spirit.*"

"It sounds biblical," I say.

She nods. "It's a verse from the Gospel of John." She looks at me. "Do not let the wind weary you."

"Easier said than done," I reply. "One pays a price for living in the wind."

She slips back into the sofa. "Is there more you'd like to tell me?"

I chuckle, but it's little more than a nervous tic. Looking out the window, I say, "My wife left me because I followed the wind. She wanted children, yet I wasn't ready to start a family. She said it was unfair that I changed my mind after marrying, and she was right: Before we exchanged vows, I told her I'd have kids with her."

"So, what happened?"

I hold up my ring finger, bare now. Motioning a ring slipping onto it, I say, "A wedding band can change things."

"Did a wedding band change things, or did you face a truth always present within?"

"Both, perhaps: I changed in a way that allowed me to view a truth. I told her I needed more time to grow before I became a father, but she felt her biological clock was ticking too fast to wait any longer."

"How old was she?"

"Thirty-four when we divorced."

"And you were…"

"Thirty-three. We'd been married for three years when our marriage ended, but before marrying, we'd lived together for three years."

"That *was* a long time to wait for a woman who wanted to start a family."

"Yes," I say. "I hold nothing against her for leaving me."

In the silence, I feel Annette take my hand. "Paul," she says, "I wonder just a bit about your feelings toward having children. Why *did* you change your mind?"

"I'm not sure I *changed* my mind. I told my wife I simply needed more time to think about it."

"That could be viewed as a change of mind, especially by someone who has waited a long time to start a family." She squeezes my hand before releasing it. "But it hasn't changed an underlying truth."

"What truth is that?"

"That you'd make an amazing father. I've watched the way you treat the orphans. You're tender and patient and care for them greatly. They love you for that. Is that why you told me, *For the first time, I want to stay put.*?"

"Partly," I reply. "Those orphans bring me so much joy."

"*Partly*? What else makes you want to stay put?"

"You, Annette. You make me want to stay."

Her eyes, calm and serene, hold mine even as I clench my teeth.

"A job in Indonesia will not draw you away from us?" she asks.

I close my eyes for Xavier's probes of my electronic communications have laid me bare. "Time will tell," I say.

She places a hand on my forearm and then stands. "Take the time you need, Paul. The rest of us will remain here. We have no plans to leave."

HAVING PACKED MY bag, I join others assembled for breakfast. Xavier is quick to pull me aside before I sit.

"I want you to know I checked the storage areas of the lodge and found no rat poisons. I'm told our two cats have done an excellent job keeping mice and rats away." His eyes widen. "More importantly, we found an empty container of pesticide used to treat the beams for the infesting beetles. It corroborated what I showed you in the photo: the product contained arsenic."

"Did the label specify the form of arsenic present?"

"Yes, the technical term was 'chromated copper arsenate.' I looked it up online and learned it's a form of arsenic still used occasionally to protect wood from insects. In the United States, it was registered for use in the 1940s although the industry shuns it now."

"Excellent work," I tell him. "It supports your hypothesis that arsenic sickened you."

"If I'm right, how will you treat me?"

"With a drug called Prussian blue. It binds arsenic in your body to inactivate it."

He nods and leads me to a table holding tea, rolls, and fruit. "Let's feed you before you leave for Lusaka."

After serving myself, I join Martin and Alexander at a small table. They've finished eating and drink the last of their tea.

"Don't mean to hurry you," Martin says, "but timing is critical this morning. We'll leave as soon as you've finished eating." He departs with his dishes.

Alexander beckons me now. "Our plans stand as discussed yesterday, only we'll have less time than I thought to carry out the mission. You'll need your A game today." He leaves as well.

I nibble on papaya when Amu and Thandi appear. "Must we go home today?" Thandi asks. Her expression conveys protest.

"Yes, you missed school yesterday, and you'll do so today; that's too much truancy."

The girls frown.

"You know the word, 'truancy,' don't you?"

Their heads shake.

"It means absence from school. I don't encourage truancy on your part." I smile smugly for adding to their vocabulary.

The girls fetch their breakfasts, and I eat what I've taken, but it's a perfunctory meal I consume because my thoughts are on Annette. Looking about the room, I'm puzzled why I can't find her. Only moments ago I'd seen her when I entered the sitting room, and I'd hoped to eat with her, but then Xavier pulled me aside. I carry my empty plate now to the kitchen.

"Helena," I say, "have you seen Annette?"

"She's feeding the elephants out back. You can find her there."

I make my way to the conference room from where I first saw the elephant calves through a window the day before. Beside the window is a door that leads outside. I open it and walk a short distance along a path that brings me to a mango grove enclosed by a chain-link fence. Ten meters inside the enclosure, I see Annette standing beside an elephant calf with her back to me. Unaware of my presence, she speaks to the calf in a monologue that I can't decipher. Beside her is a cabinet holding bananas, heads of lettuce, and cabbage.

"Annette?" I say

She turns. "Paul! Come join me." She points to a gate.

When I step into the enclosure, I look about for other creatures.

"It's alright," she chuckles. "But approach slowly."

I stop beside her as she holds a palm full of pellets that the calf takes from her hand.

"He's a three-year-old male," Annette says. "We rescued him after poachers killed his mother."

The shoulder of the calf stands close to four feet, making it a comfortable height for Annette to hold out her hand. After each palm of feeding, she rubs the elephant's head.

"He weighs about four hundred kilos and eats five times a day," she tells me. "Would you like to feed him?" She reaches for a head of lettuce and hands it to me, but the elephant lifts his trunk before I offer it.

"George, behave!" Annette says firmly.

The elephant drops its trunk obediently.

"Okay, now present it," Annette says. "He needs to mind his manners."

A trunk wraps around the lettuce and it disappears into the elephant's mouth.

"He obeys you well," I say.

"As he should!" She smiles and strokes the animal. "I've been one of his regular caretakers for the past six months. Calves bond fairly quickly and deeply to those who care for them."

"I saw another calf here yesterday," I note.

"That would be Felix. He's a bit older yet smaller than George. We adopted him because his mother was overly aggressive and began shunning him." She points to a stall at the far end of the grove. "We feed them separately so they don't fight over food."

Mindful of time, I say, "Annette, regarding our discussion earlier this morning, there's something I wanted to tell you."

She gives me her full attention as she massages the top of George's head. "Yes?"

"You're probably wondering about the voice mail I left with my sister that Xavier played yesterday."

She shakes her head. "I'm not happy with Xavier for doing that."

"What's done is done. The point is, I suspect you think I'm cruel for not returning to the U.S. to see my father even though he was diagnosed with terminal cancer."

"I was going to ask you about that, but I didn't think it was my business to do so. But I am familiar with the novel, *The Great Santini*. Is your father stern?"

"He's brutal."

A voice calls from the gate: "Dr. Rider, we need to leave!" It's Alexander who summons me.

"Coming!" I reply. To Annette: "We can talk about this more later."

"No," she says, "walk with me one time around the enclosure. It'll only take a minute and George needs the exercise."

I look to the gate and see Alexander has disappeared. "Alright, one round," I agree. There's much I want to tell her but I choose my words cautiously. "I know it's not right for a son—a physician, much less—to say anyone deserves terminal cancer, but that's the way I honestly feel about my father."

"Here, take the leash," Annette says.

The ground is dry and the leaves that have fallen from the previous season make a crunching sound as George's feet flatten them. I adjust my footsteps to fall in line with his.

"I hear anger in your voice, Paul."

"I *am* angry…angry at the way my father treated me!"

She says nothing as she looks ahead. A breeze blows her hair to the side to reveal the fair skin of her neck. "Your wind's blowing for us this morning. Isn't it nice?" She looks at me over George's back. "Perhaps it can lift your anger and carry it away."

"Can the wind carry such a heavy burden?" I ask.

"It sculpts mountains, forms waves, and pushes sand into towering dunes," she replies.

A lump forms in my throat. "But scars, Annette, can the wind remove scars?"

"Dr. Rider!" Alexander calls again from the gate. "We really must go!"

We've reached the end of our loop, and I feel the need to leave. I return the leash and turn to go, but Annette grasps my arm.

"Paul, there's an African proverb that says, *Show me your friend, and I will show you your character.* I want you to think about that proverb today as you travel."

She releases me, and I depart.

♛

FROM TWELVE THOUSAND feet, Zambia is a carpet of gold. I sit in the middle row of a six-person twin-propeller Beechcraft Baron G58 airplane that Martin flies with Alexander beside him. Innocent Mbewe is next to me in a two-seat row that faces the rear of the aircraft while a bodyguard named Ansel occupies one of two seats in the third row facing us. This is Innocent's maiden voyage in the air, and he's not happy with it. He turns from the window, and having declined a headset Martin offered us prior to take-off, misses the sights Martin points out as we fly across the country.

I don't blame Innocent for being edgy. We left urgently because a surveillance officer at the lodge had spotted an object resembling a drone on radar. It was approaching the lodge and we wanted to take off before cameras on the drone spotted the Beechcraft's hiding place, a canopy near the lodge. We were airborne before Innocent had a chance to buckle, and he was thrown about during a rough patch while climbing. Ansel had to lean forward to secure him. Now a bout of nausea afflicts Innocent.

Through the headset, Martin says: "Uku-tetema, a wildlife paradise."

Looking west, I'm treated to an aerial safari. I see herds of zebra, wildebeest, and antelope graze; giraffes and elephants march; and water buffalo rim a lake. Then the airplane banks and I steal a glimpse out the opposite window. It offers a fleeting view of two ranges of low-lying mountains that form the crescent of Uku-tetema. As they converge, they form a funnel that ends abruptly before a separate set of dark mountains that take the shape of a four-pointed star enclosing a black crater. My imagination soars as I wonder whether a prehistoric meteor crashed into the site to mold the present-day earth, much as a large rock hurtled into a pond creates ripples.

"What's that star-shaped area in the distance?" I ask Martin through the headset.

"The eastern portion of Uku-tetema," he replies.

"What gives the central area its black color?"

He says nothing.

I look across to Ansel for an answer but receive a blank stare. After allowing a few moments to pass for Martin to handle any navigational issues, I repeat the question.

"It is best you ask Xavier," he replies.

The curtness of his response surprises me. I make a mental note to broach the subject with Xavier later.

After flying over the Amalumbo River, the cabin falls quiet until we begin our descent to Lusaka two hours later. I hear a voice in the headset: "Dr. Rider, this is Alexander. I'm speaking to you, Ansel, and Martin privately. Can you hear me?"

Beside me, Innocent Mbewe sleeps without a headset.

"Yes, I can hear you," I reply.

"Good. Let's review our plans. After Innocent departs the airport for the city, Ansel will accompany you while Martin and I go separate ways. If you need to reach either of us while we're apart, have Ansel call us."

"Will do," I respond.

"And remember, create as much of a delay as possible to give us time."

"I'll do my best."

The descent into Lusaka is smooth, although the landing startles Innocent. He sits up with sleep in his eyes while we taxi to an area reserved for private aircraft. Together, we walk to the immigration area where Ansel and I part ways from the others under the guise that I need to consult an official regarding a visa matter. In the meantime, Alexander and Martin escort Innocent through the terminal to help him hail a taxi. Arrangements have been made for us to meet again in the late afternoon for the return flight to Uku-tetema.

At the immigration counter, Ansel receives a call from Alexander informing us that Innocent has departed. We proceed to a men's room where I enter a stall while Ansel goes to a urinal. Setting a bag on the floor, I unpack the casting materials within it.

Normally, casting is a routine task for me, but applying a short-arm cast in a bathroom stall on my own arm is different. I begin by cutting a cloth sleeve that I fit over my thumb. I then cut a segment of stocking which I slip over my forearm from palm to just before the elbow crease. Satisfied with its fit, I wrap a roll of soft cotton gauze around the stocking.

"Ansel," I whisper. "Are we alone still?"

"Yes," he replies.

"Fill this halfway with water." I slide a pail under the door of the stall.

When it returns, I soak a roll of fiberglass cast wrap until it's moist. I then wrap the fiberglass around my forearm and a part of my palm. The trickiest part comes in cutting the fiberglass at points where I angle it around my thumb. After applying the initial roll of fiberglass, I fold back the margin of stocking and cotton gauze to neaten the appearance of the cast and then complete the procedure by applying a final roll of fiberglass.

I hear someone enter the men's room. Sitting still, I wait for Ansel to give me the all-clear before I clean the stall of scraps and wrappings. I slide the pail under the door again for Ansel to empty it while I pack the bag.

With a fresh cast on my forearm, I leave the bathroom with Ansel. We proceed to a counter where we rent a small sedan. Another short walk takes us to our vehicle. Before getting in, however, we check the trunk to ensure it contains a spare tire and tools to change a flat.

We depart the airport, but it's just a short ride to our destination: an abandoned cinderblock guard station on the outskirts of the airport along the main road. I stop beside the decaying structure and let Ansel out. He takes immediate cover within the post as I drive off, a set of binoculars hanging from his neck.

On the main road again, I drive less than a kilometer to a convenience store where I park as far as possible from the entrance. I get out and open the trunk. Checking to make sure I'm not being watched, I remove a fat nail with a serrated stalk and wide head that Alexander gave me before we left Uku-tetema.

With the trunk still open, I approach the rear wheel on the driver's side. Stooping, I set the nail upright with sharp end under the rubber. I close the trunk and get into the car. Taking great care, I back up slowly. I grit my teeth expecting a tire to explode at any moment, but it doesn't. I leave the lot and start back toward the airport with window lowered to listen for hissing air. The only sounds I hear are normal ones of rubber meeting road. I adjust the side view mirror to look at the tire, but I'm foiled by a fender that blocks my view of it.

When I reach the cinderblock guard station, I pass it slowly to allow Ansel time to examine the tire. From his position at a bare window along the front of the station, he frowns and makes a looping motion to signal me to encircle the airport. Three-quarters of the way into the process, I detect signs of a flattening tire: a subtle yet audible flapping sound and a diminished ease of forward flow.

I worry now about making it to my destination even though it's close. Questions dog me as I devise a Plan B in case the tire shreds to leave me stranded with a metal rim on asphalt: Will I maintain control of the car? Might an officer pull me over? Will I damage the vehicle?

I reach the cinderblock station again, but I don't decelerate because I've already slowed my pace. This time, I receive a thumbs-up from Ansel. Turning off the main road, I follow a smaller one to a gravel parking lot immediately outside the airport. I park beside a modular office unit that abuts a chain-link fence demarcating restricted airport space. On the other side of the fence a hundred meters away, a South African Airways jet prepares to take off.

There's only one other vehicle in the lot, a jeep with the lettering *International Mines, LLC* on it. The juxtaposition of gravel lot and aluminum modular unit reminds me of construction sites where engineers and architects scurry about, yet here there's no activity at all.

I get out of the car to make sure I've parked in a position where Ansel can see it clearly. I look across a small field to find him standing in the cinderblock guard station some fifty meters away. He waves to me and then in deliberate fashion struts around the structure two times, a pre-arranged signal to indicate the time has come for me to approach the modular unit.

I glance at the rear tire and see it's completely deflated. Feigning exasperation, I proceed to the modular unit and knock on the front door. The *mzungu* who appears makes me do a double take for he looks like a country music singer rather than an office worker.

"Can you help me?" I ask him.

"What do you want?" he responds. He wears his hair in mullet style with short sides, mound atop, and long bushy hair in back.

"I need to replace a flat tire."

He frowns. "Can't you do it yourself?"

I show him my cast. "I would if it weren't for this. I broke my arm."

The cropped whiskers above his upper lip twitch like an antsy muscle, sending quivers along hairy extensions that encircle his mouth. "This really isn't a good time—"

"*Please*," I say. "All I'm asking for is a few minutes to help me get the spare on. I need to get downtown for a meeting that's about to start."

He clucks his tongue. "Do you have a jack?"

"Yes."

He steps outside and locks the door behind him. Gravel shifts under our feet as we walk to the car.

"What about a support for the jack?" he asks. "It'll slip on the gravel if we don't use one."

"That's the one the thing I lack. Do you have one?"

He scowls and looks about. "Let me check the jeep."

While he rummages through the vehicle, I see Alexander slip past a window inside the front of the modular unit. During our preparations for the day, he told me the success of the mission to break into the unit depended on whether a bathroom window in back was ajar. While scooping the unit out beforehand for break-in points, he'd noticed on two different occasions that the window was left open a crack. Seeing him inside now tells me his advance work paid off. A check of my watch shows 1:26 p.m. Per Alexander's instructions, I need to delay mullet man from reentering the unit for at least twenty minutes.

"This should do it," the man calls from the jeep. He extracts a board from the vehicle.

I move quickly to his side before he leaves the jeep. "That's some artwork," I tell him, pointing to the vehicle's hood. It depicts a magnificent bird and, separately, a flowering bush.

"That's Zambia's national bird, the African fish eagle," he replies. "You may have seen it on the nation's coat of arms."

It's an impressive bird whose white head, chest, and tail contrast with its dark forceful wings, eyes, and beak. On the hood, it's shown flying with a large fish in its talons.

"The flowers I recognize, but I can't put a name to them," I say.

"They're bougainvillea, the country's national flower," he replies.

"Is this a company vehicle?"

"Yes."

"Thoughtful of you to celebrate the country's national bird and flower on it."

He assumes a haughty stance. "We're committed to protecting the environment here. Even though we're a mining company, we believe the extraction of oil and minerals needn't harm the environment."

"That's a refreshing attitude."

"We're a progressive company," he replies. "We don't pillage the land we mine."

He appears eager to move on, so I accompany him to the trunk of the rental car where he asks about the spare tire.

"Let me get it out," I say, taking my time to do so.

"What about a wrench and jack?" he asks.

"I'll get them." I explore the trunk for the items even though they're in plain sight.

"Right there!" he says, reaching in to remove the items. He eyes me with scorn.

To redeem myself, I take the wrench from him and place it on a lug nut of the wheel holding the flat tire. Working half-heartedly, I try to loosen the nut without effect.

"Here, let me do that!" he insists.

"Are you sure? I don't want you to get dirty on my account."

"I don't have all day to help you," he grumbles. He kneels beside me and takes the wrench. After loosening one lug nut, he moves to the next. "Have you set the emergency brake?"

"No, I'll do that now."

I start toward the front and steal a glance at Ansel who holds a cell phone to one ear while pointing his binoculars at me with the other.

"Shit, this is messy!" mullet man snarls. "Do you have a rag?"

"I'll get you something." I set the brake and go to the trunk where I sift through my bag.

"Do you have it or not?" the man quips.

"I'm looking!" I pull out a tee shirt and hand it to him. He uses it to clean his hand before loosening another nut. "Six of these damn things!" he gripes.

He's a slight man whose southern drawl tells me he's from the United States. Despite his ire, he appears to be skilled at changing tires.

"What sort of mining do you do?" I ask.

"Different kinds; we're diversified."

"Copper?"

"Of course! That's bread and butter!"

"How about diamonds?"

He looks at me. "Why do you ask?"

"Because, they're being mined across the border in D R Congo."

"Yeah, but not here," he rebuts. "Besides, there's a frickin' war in D R Congo because of diamonds. We're not going to get involved in that!"

"So, what else do you mine?"

"A wide range of minerals, but the money's betting on oil."

I shiver. "*Oil*?"

He loosens the final nut. "That's right, and I'm talking big oil!"

"I live here and I haven't heard a thing about oil," I say.

He reaches for the jack. "Stay tuned, there'll be news shortly."

I want to know more about this man and how he's privy to information that could have enormous impact on the nation. While Nigeria and several countries in North Africa produce oil, I'm not aware that Central Africa has been shown to possess reserves.

"Your accent," I say. "Where are you from in the States?"

"Texas."

"What part?"

"Sugar Land. Heard of it?"

I wince. "Yes, that's just outside Houston."

He looks at me again. "Not bad. Most folks haven't heard of

it." He eyes me with newfound respect. "What about you? Where are you from?"

"New York, originally, but I've moved about."

"What brought you here?"

"Hotel management."

"Which hotel?" he asks.

"A bunch of them; I run a consulting business."

The back of the car rises with each crank of the jack.

"International Mines," I say. "Is your company based in Sugar Land?"

"Yup."

I nod. "Makes sense: that's just outside of Houston, America's oil mecca."

He wipes his brow. "Car's up. Let's get the wheel off."

The time: 1:35 p.m.; eleven minutes more of delay required.

I worry about Alexander inside where his task entails downloading as much content as he can from three laptops. To expedite his job, he created a program that specifies key file extensions to be downloaded and equipped himself with the latest in technology to achieve maximum bandwidth for the downloads. Nonetheless, he expressed concern that twenty minutes was woefully inadequate to transfer everything he needed. From my end, I promised to do all I could to give him his twenty minutes, and more, if possible.

With the wheel removed, mullet man checks it by rolling it forward. "Holy cow!" he blurts. "There's a frickin' nail here!"

He sets the tire on its side and hurries to the jeep. Returning with a pair of plyers, he extracts the nail. "*Damn*, man, where've you been driving?"

"I can't believe it!" I gasp. "How the hell did that get on the road?"

"Probably fell out of a truck, but what's done is done. Let's get the spare on."

"Wait," I say, "let me ask you something."

His impatience grows. "What is it?"

"Does your firm work with TransNational Oil?"

He stiffens. "Why do you ask?"

"I was just curious. I've seen news reports recently that Trans-National Oil is proposing to have a pipeline run from the Arctic to the U.S. Gulf coast."

"That's true," he says. "They're a major international player known for their aggressive exploration projects." He tilts his head to look at me over the rims of his glasses. "But I'm not at liberty to tell you who we work with."

"That's understandable."

Lifting the spare, he prepares to mount it.

"Hang on, before you put that on, let me check so to see if I have a pressure gauge. I want to make sure the tire's properly inflated."

He thumps the rubber. "It is."

"But I don't want to drive out of here only to get another flat."

"What choice do you have? You've got a flat and this is your spare!"

"It'll just take a second." I return to the front of the car and check my watch—1:39 p.m.; seven minutes to delay. I recall Alexander telling me that his previous scouting trips to the modular unit revealed that workers returned from their lunch hour shortly before two p.m.

I fiddle through the glove compartment box. "Damn! I don't see a gauge!"

"Forget about it, man!" the Texan calls.

I return to the rear to find he's already put the spare on and is tightening the lug nuts.

"I'm guessing you're an engineer," I tell him.

"Yup, mechanical engineer."

"Which means you probably know a thing or two about car engines."

"I'm comfortable with them."

"Great, so after we finish with the spare, can you to take a quick look at the fuses?"

"Why, what's wrong?"

"There's a warning light flashing on the dash. I suspect it's a blown fuse, but I'm not sure which one it is."

"Check your owner's manual."

"I did, but it didn't help me solve the problem."

"Shit, man, I'm not your mechanic!"

"You're right! I've stepped over the line by taking way too much of your time."

He shakes his head and tightens the lugs as much as possible with the car raised. As he lowers the jack, I remove my wallet and extract a few bills from it. In the meantime, squeals come from the final turns of the wrench.

"Okay, that's it," mullet man says. "I'll leave it to you to put your shit away."

He stands to face me. "What's this?"

Before him, I hold the equivalent of fifty U.S. dollars. "Take it," I tell him. "I've been a pain in the ass."

"True, but I don't need your money!"

"Take it," I insist.

He waves a hand and starts for the unit but turns abruptly. "How 'bout this: I take the money in return for checking your fuses."

"Deal!"

I join him at the engine under the hood.

He glides to a side of the motor and removes the lid from a plastic box along the chassis. After extracting a small wafer that occupies a slot with a horde of others, he holds it to the sky to explain what a blown fuse looks like.

"When you have time," he says, "go through them one-by-one to see if any need to be replaced, but like I said before, your manual should tell you where the problem is."

"I'll check it again later," I reply. "No time now; gotta go." I hand him the money.

"Good luck," he says. "Stay away from nails!"

I MEET ANSEL at a prearranged spot half a kilometer up the road from the guard station and out of view from the modular unit.

"Good," he says, a long sentence by his standards.

"Did Alexander accomplish what he needed to?" I ask him.

"Somewhat."

My heart heaves. "*Somewhat?*"

"You ask him."

"Where is he?"

"At the airport with Martin."

He directs me toward the terminal, but we exit before we reach it to return the car. I explain to the agent that a nail penetrated the rear tire just outside the airport and forced us to resort to the spare. The agent apologizes for the inconvenience, but I assure her that we were still able to complete our mission. She's relieved as we take our leave.

A short walk brings us to a locked doorway inside the terminal marked *Authorized Personnel Only.* Ansel places a call in Bemba. After a brief wait, Martin opens the door and waves us through.

We pursue a labyrinthine course before coming to a door that begs for a new coat of paint. Martin unlocks it and we enter a musty room to find Alexander busy at work on a laptop.

"Ah, good, you're here," I tell him.

He keeps his eyes on the computer.

I go to his side. "Sorry I couldn't get you more time," I tell him.

"It wouldn't have been possible because other workers returned from lunch just after we left." He informs me about his session there, beginning with his entry through a window in back with a broken lock.

"What about you?" I ask Martin. "Were you successful?"

He points to a box on the floor.

"You got it?" I ask.

He nods.

While Alexander, Ansel, and I did our thing, Martin remained at the airport. Advance planning he did with a friend of Xavier's from the Department of Civil Aviation identified International Mines as the owner of a twin-engine Cessna that landed on a grass strip outside Saysha on the day I discovered the jaguar blood in my shack. Digging deeper, Martin used airport records to ascertain when the Cessna would be on the ground in Lusaka. It was a matter then of pinning a time to sneak aboard the airplane to exchange the cockpit voice recorder for another one. The timing of our flight from Uku-tetema to Lusaka was based largely on the window of availability of the Cessna for this covert operation.

"Can I see the voice recorder?" I ask.

Martin opens the container, but before he can remove the device Alexander addresses me.

"Paul, I just ran a quick search on files I collected from the modular unit. While I'll examine them exhaustively at the lodge, I wanted to see if I could find any mention of extremist or jihadist groups given a number for International Mines appeared on the mobile owned by the jihadist we killed in Uku-tetema."

"What did you find?"

"No mention of any such groups."

"Are you surprised? It'd be foolhardy for computers at International Mines to carry files that referred to a terrorist group."

He puckers his lips. "Perhaps, but there was something else I found that was intriguing. It was a document that referred to a term I'm not familiar with."

"What term was it?"

" 'VIPOR,' " he replies. He spells it for me. "Do you know what it stands for?"

"No. How would I know it?"

"Because the term was mentioned in the context of your former employer, TransNational Oil."

Suddenly, the matter becomes personal. "Who authored the document?"

"It was anonymous."

Sweat breaks out along my brow and I feel my fingers tingle. "*Shit*! I've gotta get this cast off."

WE REMAIN IN the musty room at the Lusaka airport waiting for Innocent Mbewe to return from downtown. He's forty minutes late now and I call him.

"Where are you?" I ask him.

"On the way," he replies. "I was delayed by traffic downtown."

"Did you deliver Xavier's urine and blood to the toxicology lab?"

"Yes, and they told me they'll begin testing the specimens immediately for the presence of heavy metals, including arsenic."

"What about the medications?" I ask him.

"I have them."

At my request, he stopped by a hospital pharmacy to purchase drugs I may use to treat Xavier depending on the outcome of his tests.

Behind me, I hear a knock on the door. Martin opens it to allow a young man to enter.

"This is Rodney," Martin tells me. "He works at the Department of Civil Aviation. He was the one who discovered that International Mines owns the Cessna that flew to Saysha four days ago."

I shake hands with the man. He's young and fit, a mold that seems to apply to Xavier's recruits.

"Rodney will fly with us to Uku-tetema to analyze the cockpit voice recorder there," Martin says.

"We're fortunate to have him," Alexander adds, "because he's the number one expert in this country to do such analyses."

Alexander removes the voice recorder from the box and hands it to Rodney who, within an instant, identifies the manufacturer and model number.

"This is the one from the Cessna?" he confirms.

"Correct," Martin replies.

A snore comes from the corner. Sitting on a stool with his back slumped against the wall, Ansel awakens. A glance about tells him all's well. His eyes close again.

I address Martin: "Aren't the folks at International Mines going to realize someone exchanged a cockpit voice recorder on their Cessna?"

"Not immediately," Martin replies. "While voice recorders are checked for maintenance purposes, it's not that often and besides, the recorder I installed is identical to this one in make and model."

"But with a different serial number," I say.

He's unfazed. "We'll be long gone when they discover that."

I remain concerned because of the words scrolled along the bottom of the device: *FLIGHT RECORDER DO NOT OPEN.* While the presence of an official from the Department of Civil

Aviation takes the edge off my discomfort for what we've done today, I still feel uneasy. Knowing Xavier's independent streak, I assume Rodney is helping us not in an official capacity as an employee of the federal government but, rather, as a friend or paid consultant. Before flying to Lusaka, I had a spirited discussion with Xavier about the ethics, legality, and practicality of securing privileged data. In the end, I agreed to move forward with his plan although I expressed to him in no uncertain terms my preference to work with law enforcement officials. Xavier would have none of it; doing so, he insisted, would mire us in bureaucracy.

I hear a tapping of fingernails on metal. It comes from Rodney's fingers drumming the stainless steel shell about the voice recorder. "Shall we discuss this device for a moment?" he asks me.

I approach him.

He smiles. "It's funny people call these 'black boxes' when they're actually orange." He runs a hand over the metal. "Since you're a doctor, let's begin with anatomy. First, note that we're dealing with a platform that holds a box at one end, a large cylinder in the middle, and a smaller cylinder at the end." He points to each before tipping the device on its axis. "This is pretty much a standard-sized recorder."

To my eyes, it measures roughly twelve by six by four inches.

He lowers the device. "In the old days, cockpit voice recorders used magnetic tapes but now they're solid-state—which is to say, they have no moving parts—and they use digital memory chips to store the audio from the cockpit. It's not just the crew's voices they record; they also capture engine sounds, alarms, and the auditory environment at-large in the cockpit."

He lifts the recorder again. "In the box here we have circuit boards while this larger cylinder holds digital memory chips. And this"—he points to a small white cylinder lying on its side perpendicular to the larger cylinder—"is an underwater locator beacon, or what some call the 'pinger' because of the sound it emits when submerged in water."

"My understanding is these devices record for only limited periods," I say.

"To be more precise, they record continuously, but after two hours older data is overwritten."

"Which means the recordings for the flight to and from Saysha may be gone," I state. "After all, those flights occurred four days ago."

" 'Gone' is a relative term when it comes to digital data," Rodney asserts. "Consider a personal computer: When one deletes a file, it remains in the recycle bin until one deletes it from there, but even then, file remnants can be resurrected sometimes. It's no different here." He grins. "What's the title of that racy book—*Fifty Shades of Grey*? With digital data on cockpit voice recorders, we're dealing with shades of grey."

"And we'll examine every shade present," Alexander adds. His cell phone chimes. "Yes, Xavier," he replies. A moment passes, then: "No! That can't be!" Another pause, briefer than before. "Of course, we'll leave instantly!"

He jumps from his seat and slams the laptop shut. "Pack up! We're flying to Saysha immediately!"

"What happened?" I ask.

"Jihadists attacked your hospital! It was retribution for our killing of one of their comrades."

"Are Annette and the girls there?" I stammer. I check my phone for texts but find none.

"I don't know," Alexander replies. "We shall see."

MY PHONE RINGS as we rush through the terminal. It's Innocent who calls.

"Where are you?" I exclaim.

"I just arrived at the airport."

I inform Martin who, in turn, dispatches Ansel to collect Innocent and escort him to the airplane. In the meantime, the rest of us dash to the Beechcraft where Martin contacts air traffic control while Rodney, Alexander and I stow bags. Already in the compartment is an aluminum suitcase Rodney loaded earlier that contains equipment for analyzing the cockpit voice recorder.

The propeller opposite the passenger door whirs by the time Ansel and Innocent arrive. As soon as they've taken their seats, we start along the tarmac. Between Innocent's legs is a backpack he didn't have before, a large one of the type hikers take on expeditions.

"Where did you get that?" I ask him.

"I bought it in town," he replies. "I've wanted a backpack for a long time."

It upsets me that he spent time shopping when his assignment was to deliver specimens and collect medications before hurrying back to the airport. I wonder whether he shopped for other items because the backpack appeared to be heavy when he loaded it.

We lift off into the dusk and turn northeast toward Saysha. When Martin has completed his communications with the control tower, I address him through the headset. "What's our flying time?"

"A little over two hours," he estimates. "We have a bit of headwind this evening."

"Have you landed near Saysha before?"

"No, but I've flown over it many times."

"Will it be a problem to land in the dark?"

"It won't be completely dark because we'll have a waxing gibbous moon," he replies. "Look out the cockpit."

Sitting in the middle row again with my back to the crew, I turn to find a moon that's more than half illuminated along the horizon, a sight that eases my concerns about touching down on a grass strip at night. Of more concern to me as we fly toward Saysha is the possibility that jihadists will remain in the area. Although reports indicate they've left the village, I fret they've taken cover in the darkness.

We level off in a cloudless sky that allows for a smooth ride. I close my eyes to rest, but Martin's voice summons me in the headset. "I have Xavier on the line," he announces. "He needs to speak to you urgently."

I hear a click, then: "Paul, are you there?"

"Yes, Xavier, go ahead."

"I wanted to share with you what I know about the status of Saysha!"

"Go ahead!" I plead.

"The two guards I dispatched to accompany Annette, Thandi, and Amu to Uku-tetema reported that a Humvee commanded by jihadists entered the village shortly after our party arrived. Through a loudspeaker, they heard the jihadists warn residents not to cooperate with you because they said you're an infidel. They then drove to the hospital where they torched one of the wards."

"Which one?" I ask, heart pounding.

"I'm waiting to find out. In the meantime, my guards engaged the jihadists in gunfire before the Humvee drove off. So far, I have no reports of injuries."

"I hope you'll keep your guards in Saysha until we land!" I beseech.

"They'll remain there overnight."

I say nothing as foreboding weighs on me.

"I'm sorry this happened," Xavier says. "We had no warning the jihadists would attack Saysha. Our task now is to stop an incursion that's imminent on another front, and that's why I've called you."

"What front are you referring to?"

"One at the easternmost end of Uku-tetema. Martin told me you asked about it today while flying to Lusaka."

"Are you referring to the black crater?" I ask.

"Yes, it's a place we call 'Intanda,' a word meaning 'star' in Bemba. The name comes from the mountains that form a four-point star about a shallow valley. The only entryways into the valley come at the four points of the star."

"Why's the valley black?"

"Because of its oily sands."

I shiver, just as I did at the modular unit when the Texan spoke of impending news regarding the discovery of oil. I tell Xavier about the encounter.

"He knows what he's talking about," Xavier says. "International Mines has secured a contract to conduct a seismic survey of Intanda for its oil resources should our government give them the green light to proceed."

"But that green light would come only if the vote to turn Uku-tetema into a national park is defeated, right?"

"Not necessarily; rumors suggest a seismic survey could take place at Intanda any day."

"But I've never heard a peep about the country having oil!"

"That's because, until recently, the prospect of Intanda having oil was restricted to legends and folklore, but then a prospector trespassed onto Intanda, and he extracted samples of sand and found oil in them. The word spread rapidly through the energy sector before International Mines began lobbying our government to conduct a formal seismic survey of the land."

"Why would legends and folklore speak of oil being present in Intanda?"

"Ah, I wish we were sipping beer together so I could relay the rich history of storytelling among my people, but I'll give you a brief version now." His tone is tender and reflective, a storyteller's voice that lures me. "It all begins with an Egyptian cat goddess named Bastet. Have you heard of her?"

"No."

"She's often featured in Egyptian mythology as a goddess with a human body and the head of a lion. One part of her was revered as a kindly goddess of domestic cats. Keep in mind that cats were esteemed enough in ancient Egypt to be depicted in tombs and even mummified in some instances. It was the feline nature of Bastet that people worshipped for her blessings and life-giving powers. Another side of her was a war-like goddess who delivered wrath to the wicked."

When he pauses, I use the moment to adjust my headset to hear him as well as I can through the hum of the engines.

He continues: "In Uku-tetema, storytellers speak of a delegation that a queen from ancient Egypt dispatched to travel the world in search of the most beautiful cat. The queen commissioned the team as a tribute to goddess Bastet. As the legend goes, the delegation discovered the most beautiful cat in Intanda, a leopard that resides in the mountains forming the four-point star. Members of the delegation trapped one of the leopards and took it back to Egypt where it supposedly conveyed miraculous healing powers upon the queen. After the animal died, she sanctified the leopard's homeland and instructed members of the delegation to keep the whereabouts of Intanda secret so no one would ever capture another beloved leopard. For this reason, my people revere Intanda and believe a curse will befall anyone who reveals its secrets, including the presence of oil in its sands—oil, by the way, we believe gives our leopards their distinctive black spots."

"Do you *believe* any part of this story?" I ask him.

"Every part," he replies, "and lest you dismiss folklore, let me ask whether you've heard about the remains of a temple that were unearthed recently beneath the streets of modern-day Alexandria, Egypt."

"No, I haven't," I reply.

"Then let me tell you about it. It was a temple King Ptolomy III built for his wife. He ruled Egypt from 246 to 221 B.C. His wife was named Queen Berenike, and researchers believe her temple was dedicated to goddess Bastet because they found some six hundred limestone statues among the remains that depicted the cat goddess. Of particular interest to those of us from Uku-tetema was a statue of a leopard that had an engraving of a four-point star beneath the cat."

"Are you suggesting the star referred to Intanda?"

"Yes, all of my people believe that."

"Other than the prospector you told me about, has anyone else found oil at Intanda?"

"Yes, a company my father hired to conduct a seismic survey of Intanda."

"What were their results?"

"My father wouldn't share them because he feared a curse from the goddess Bastet would befall his people if he did."

"Oh, come now, Xavier! This is the twenty-first century! We're long past legends and folklore!"

"Say what you will, Paul. Our traditions run deep."

"Tell me this, then: Do you know the results of the survey your father paid for?"

"Yes, my father shared them with me from his death bed."

"What did you learn?"

He says nothing.

"Xavier?"

"If I tell you, goddess Bastet may curse the two of us."

"I'm willing to risk it!"

For several moments, I hear only the hum of the airplane, then:

"Very well, come with me to Intanda. There you'll see the sands and leopards for yourself. When we're there, I'll reveal what my father told me, but I'll do so only after you've helped me install laser trip lines to detect trespassers who plan to rape my people's land."

WELL INTO THE flight to Saysha, Xavier asks me to put my physics hat on. "Let's discuss optics," he tells me.

" 'Optics' as in light?"

"Yes, lasers, in particular," he says.

He's convinced International Mines plans to trespass upon Intanda before the government authorizes a survey because just last week after flying over the star-shaped land, Martin spotted a jeep driving toward the area from the south. When the jeep had come within several kilometers of an entrance, Martin swooped down to warn it to leave. In doing so, he took photos of the jeep and recorded the vehicle's license plate. The jeep belonged to International Mines.

"For that reason," he tells me now, "I'm asking you to help me set up laser trip lines at all four entrances. If I can get photos of them trespassing, I'll have a strong argument to present to the National Assembly that oil interests have no plans to abide by the nation's laws when it comes to oil exploration."

"But why would International Mines trespass Intanda rather than wait for the government to authorize a survey?"

"Because there's a *lot* of oil at stake! We've picked up chatter online that oil companies around the globe are vying to be the first to get into Intanda."

When I suggest a less expensive alternative to setting up trip lines would be to station patrols at entry points, he dismisses the idea on account of insufficient personnel. "Besides," he adds, "I've identified an optical equipment retailer in Johannesburg, South Africa, and Martin will fly there tomorrow to purchase the equipment we need." We spend the rest of our time compiling a purchase list for Martin.

Our conversation ends minutes before touchdown. Outside, I see remnants of fires in the distance that were used for cooking dinners in the village. A pair of lights suddenly appears below us.

"That's the hospital truck illuminating our landing strip," Martin informs us.

The combination of light from the moon and the truck guides us to a surprisingly smooth landing, although I attribute much of the smoothness to Martin's skills. He stops only feet from the truck. Within minutes, he has the door open for Innocent and me to exit.

Outside, Bristol waits for us. His characteristic cheeriness is absent. "It has been very difficult here," he tells us.

"Yes, we heard," I say. "Which ward was destroyed?"

"The one where the burn patient was kept."

"Oh, God!" I gasp. "Is she alright?" I fear not just for her life, but, if she survived, for her psyche after experiencing a second traumatic burn event.

"She's no longer here," Bristol says.

I'm beside myself. "What do you mean?"

"Miss Annette just left with her to go by land to Lusaka."

"Why?"

He hands me a piece of paper which I unfold. Using light from a bulb above the exit to the airplane, I read the words…

Dear Paul,

I'm sorry I couldn't remain in Saysha to see you. I felt compelled to escort our burn patient to Lusaka where I'll pay to have her admitted to the university hospital. This is the least I can do for her given what she's gone through. I feel for her so.

Annette

A pit forms in my stomach as I had wanted very much to see Annette. I long to look into her eyes, hear her voice, and watch her move. I also wanted to ask why she shared the proverb, *Show me your friend, and I will show you your character.*

As an adolescent, I had fewer friends than many, and this was largely because of my own doing. After my father sent me to boarding school, I kept thinking he'd bring me home if I did well academically. As a result, I shunned friendships because I felt they were distracting and because, in my pathologic frame of mind, I thought friendships diluted loyalty for home. Over time, I imprinted on aloneness and carried the imprint through college and into medical school. Marriage for me was more responsibility than friendship, and even that was short-lived.

Yet things changed in Africa. Here, I feel as if I'm part of a loom where the land is the warp and people are the weft. Each encounter is a new yarn woven with others. Working at a hospital where the poor serve the poor teaches me that relationships, like earthly resources, are finite and precious. And now, with a new thread coursing through my life, I want to get to know Annette as well as I can in the time that remains. Highly qualified physicians have applied for the position of medical director, and because I'll need to move on when the position is filled, I've exchanged a number of emails with the clinic in Indonesia that wants to hire me.

I fold Annette's note and tuck it into my pocket. "Who's driving Annette and the patient to Lusaka?" I ask Bristol.

"The brother of a soldier you met while traveling to Danjou three days ago," he replies. "The soldier's brother brought their mother to the hospital today. We are treating her for congestive heart failure."

I recall the soldier from the Zambian armed forces who manned a gate near the border of D R Congo as I traveled there with Benji and Oscar. "That was kind of the soldier's brother," I say.

Martin appears at my side. "I must leave. It will be a short night before I fly to South Africa tomorrow to buy the optical equipment you and Xavier need for Intanda."

"I understand," I reply. "Before you go, let me give you medication we purchased in Lusaka for Xavier. Tell him not to take any yet, however. I'm still waiting for results from some laboratory tests."

In short order, Innocent retrieves a packet from his backpack. I open it to make sure the proper medication has been dispensed. Satisfied, I hand it to Martin. "Again, Xavier's not to take any until I instruct him to do so."

The Beechcraft is airborne before Bristol, Innocent, and I get into the truck. A twenty-minute drive through the bush brings us to the village where we proceed to the hospital, but rather than park in the spot the truck normally occupies, Bristol continues to an isolated section where a lone hut stands before a fallow field.

"Why did you bring us to the morgue?" I ask.

"I must show you something," he replies.

We walk to the hut where Bristol lights a candle. He opens the door and we step inside to find a body on the ground. It lies on its stomach with its face turned toward us. A red bandanna encircles the head. Clotted blood stains the man's collar in back.

"What happened?" I ask.

"Benji killed this man."

"*Benji* did?" I gasp.

"Yes, he used the rifle from the truck."

"But...how...why...?" I stammer.

"While the jihadists raced through the village with a loudspeaker, Benji retrieved the rifle and returned to the orphans' quarters. From there, he watched a militant set fire to the ward where Madam Annette was inside with the burn patient. In moments, Annette and the patient emerged at the doorway, but the militant ordered them to return to the flames. When Annette tried to push the militant aside, he struck her in the face and then took aim to shoot her as she lay on the ground. It was then that Benji fired the rifle and killed the man."

"Where were the two guards Xavier sent with Annette?"

"They were tending the village where other jihadists harassed our people."

"This is not good," Innocent says. "They will come back for revenge."

I ask Bristol to drive me to the orphans' quarters where I find the four oldest ones huddled inside with the younger children. A solitary candle illuminates the fear in the room.

Amu, Thandi, and Oscar rush to my side, but Benji sulks.

I embrace the three in silence before releasing them. "Benji, come here," I say.

He looks up from the mat. His eyes are swollen and red.

"I said, come here," I repeat.

The boy stands albeit with trembling legs. He approaches me with his head lowered.

I grasp him by the shoulders and frame him before me. Stooping, I look into his eyes. I search for words, but they emerge on their own through quavering lips: "You are so brave and I love you with all my heart."

He weeps, and I bring him to my chest. Our hearts beat side-by-side. I don't want to let him go.

"I have killed a man," he wails.

"You saved a life," I reply.

I release him. In his eyes I see a form of algebra that a boy his age cannot possibly fathom: subtraction of one life for preservation of another.

My cell phone rings and I release Benji to answer it. It's Raymond Chabala from Lusaka.

"Paul, important news!" he exclaims. "Xavier Treadwill's urine contains thallium! We verified the results repeatedly!"

"What about arsenic?" I ask. "Was it present?"

"Not a trace."

"Any other metals?"

"No, only thallium, and a good deal of it—485 micrograms per liter of urine when normal values range from zero to less than 5 micrograms per liter. A value in the hundreds of micrograms is clearly abnormal because thallium is completely foreign to the human body."

"What about his blood?" I ask. "Did you find thallium in it?"

"Those results haven't come back yet," he replies. "Is there any reason to believe Xavier may have been exposed to thallium through occupational exposures? For example, does he work at a copper smelting plant or handle rat poisons or ant killers?"

"No."

"Is he involved in the manufacture of electronics or optical glass equipment or is he in the medical imaging field where he could've been exposed to thallium in contrast agents?"

"No, none of those apply to him," I reply.

"Then the man was poisoned intentionally! I have to report this to the police as a suspected criminal event!"

"Yes, of course," I say.

I know the ramifications of thallium poisoning all too well. While working as an emergency department physician in Boston,

I evaluated a patient who complained of sudden numbness and tingling in his fingers and soles of the feet. A week later, he began to lose hair and came to the emergency department to be evaluated. I submitted a battery of laboratory tests which led to the discovery of thallium in both his urine and blood. After reporting the results to police, I was interviewed by the FBI. I learned the man had feuded with a neighbor over ownership of a large tree that straddled their yards. My patient wanted to cut it down but his neighbor, a chemist, protested. After a series of shouting matches, the patient felled the tree. As retribution, the neighbor snuck into the patient's garage one night and, after creating a pinprick hole in a liter bottle of soda, injected thallium salts into the beverage. Shortly after consuming the soda, my patient fell ill and died a month later.

"I trust you'll tell Mr. Treadwill he was poisoned," Chabala says.

"I'll call him immediately."

"How are you going to treat him?"

"With Prussian blue," I reply.

"Yes," he agrees, "a good choice."

For thallium to be present in Xavier's urine at such a high level, his body has certainly taken in a large dose. As such, thallium is likely to have spread widely throughout his organs and tissues. The medication Prussian blue will help dislodge and dispose of those stores.

"What about hemodialysis?" Chabala asks. "Do you see any role for it in his treatment?"

Chabala is referring to a process that involves running a patient's blood through a filter to remove contaminants, one not unlike dialysis that people with failing kidneys undergo.

"If we don't detect thallium in his blood, I'm not inclined to make him go through hemodialysis," I say.

"That's reasonable. I'll get back to you when I get the blood test results."

Anxious to reach Xavier, I thank Chabala and hang up.

While I was on the phone with Chabala, Innocent Mbewe has been good to comfort the children. He requests permission now to return home, and I grant it, but I ask that on his way he summon an older woman from the village to come to the orphans' quarters to stay with them for the night.

I watch Innocent lift his backpack and note something heavy still remains within it because of the force he exerts to slide it across his back. His wife, I presume, will be grateful for the shopping he did in Lusaka. In the meantime, after he leaves, I wait with the children until the woman from the village arrives. Sighs of relief come when she appears, and I'm hopeful the children will sleep after a traumatic day.

I step outside to call Xavier.

"Yes, Paul, I'm glad you called," he says.

"We have a diagnosis!" I tell him. "Dr. Chabala notified me just now your urine contains a high level of thallium but no arsenic or other heavy metals. You were poisoned with thallium!"

"*Poisoned*...with *thallium*?"

"Yes, but the good news is Martin will give you a medication called Prussian blue that you need to start taking immediately." I explain the daily dosing schedule I want him to follow.

"How long do I take it for?" he asks.

"Until thallium levels fall below 100 micrograms per liter in your urine. That may take several weeks."

"So I'll need to provide you with more urine samples."

"Regularly," I reply. "Innocent will be a busy man shuttling them to Lusaka."

"My God, Paul, they're coming at me from all directions: poachers...drones...and now thallium. They're dead-set on getting my people's land."

"Perhaps, but our job is to figure out when and where you were poisoned. Do you have a calendar handy?"

I hear his breathing accelerate as he walks. Papers shuffle, then: "Okay, I have one."

"Good, let's begin with your first symptom. You said it was weakness that began roughly a month ago."

"Weakness *and* fatigue; they began right after I came home from Lusaka after speaking at a conference."

"What dates were you in Lusaka?"

"September 28th through the 30th."

"How did you feel during those three days?"

"Fine."

"So when did the weakness and fatigue begin?"

"The first full day I was home, which would've been October 1st."

"Did Martin fly you to Lusaka and back?"

"Yes."

"And where did you stay in Lusaka?"

"At the Intercontinental Hotel. That's where I spoke on the importance of preserving Uku-tetema."

I ask him to refer to his calendar and describe everything he did in Lusaka beginning the moment he left his airplane to the time he boarded it again two-and-a-half days later. Once again, he proves to be a careful historian who provides in painstaking detail his hours of waking and retiring, times of meals, and locations of meetings.

"Did you have a bodyguard with you?"

"Yes, Ansel was with me at all times."

"Tell me about the speech you delivered."

"Ah, the speech...it took place in a conference hall on the afternoon of September 30th. Some five hundred people were in attendance, including virtually all members of the National Assembly."

"And you spoke of the need to protect Uku-tetema?"

"I did, after which the podium was opened for others to argue why the land should be opened to commercial development."

"It was a debate, then?"

"A heated one; passions were high."

"Who comprised the opposition?"

"A number of groups, including representatives from mining and petroleum firms; labor organizations; tourism officials; and transportation interests, among others."

"Were you alone in advocating Uku-tetema be turned into a national park?"

"By no means; I had environmentalists and wildlife enthusiasts supporting me."

"And after the debate, what did you do?"

"I attended a reception outside the conference hall."

"Did you eat or drink anything there?"

"Let me think…yes, I had a bottle of water that I opened myself."

"What about food?"

"I was too riled to eat."

"And after the reception?"

"I went to my room to pack, but Martin called me to say he had a minor repair to make on the Beechcraft which gave me a few hours to kill."

"What did you do with them?"

"I went out for tea with Ansel."

"Where?"

"To a café near the hotel."

"Did you sit or get carry-out?"

"We sat."

"Describe the place."

"It was much like a French café: small round tables, intimate, and a display case with bakery goods."

"Did you eat anything there?"

"No, I only drank tea."

"Did they make it for you or did you do it yourself?"

"I did—from a pot of hot water they delivered along with a tea bag."

"And what about sugar or cream? Did you add any?"

"Sugar, only."

"Was it pre-packed or in a bowl?"

"It was in packets, of which I used two because I like sweet tea."

"What did you do while you drank your tea?"

"I chatted with Ansel until he went to the restroom."

"And while he was gone?"

He chuckles. "I drank more tea!"

I prepare to end the conversation because it's going nowhere and I need to discuss plans for tomorrow.

"But come to think of it, something *did* happen while Ansel was away. Because our table was close to the cashier and display counter, a good deal of foot-traffic passed behind me. A lady somehow dropped her purse on my foot and I stooped to pick it up for her. When I sat back again, I noticed some sugar had spilled on the table beside my cup that hadn't been there moments earlier."

"*Damn*!" I shout. "Are you sure it was sugar?"

"It looked exactly like sugar—small white granules, although less than a packet would hold."

"And you're positive it wasn't there before you retrieved the woman's purse?"

"I'm very certain. If I'd spilled the sugar, I'd have cleaned it immediately." He sighs. "Didn't you appreciate the standards of neatness I hold my lodge to?"

I did: The hardwood floors were immaculate, the counters dusted, and everything in each room was in its place.

"Xavier," I say, my voice in warning mode, "I'm almost positive that wasn't sugar on the table but thallium salts."

"Are you *serious?*"

"Describe the woman who dropped her purse on your foot."

"She was very attractive, indeed, and had a gracious smile. I can still smell her perfume."

"You were smitten! The granules meant nothing to you at the time."

"Oh, come, Paul, don't—"

"Do you know how much a packet of sugar weighs?" I ask.

"I've no clue."

"Then, let me tell you: about four grams. If you poured out the contents of one packet and then divided it into four equal parts, the amount in one part would approximate the lethal dose of thallium for someone of your weight. It's a good thing that whoever dumped the granules into your cup while you picked up the purse spilled some on the table. Otherwise, you'd be dead now."

"Can one taste or smell thallium?" he asks.

"No, it's odorless and colorless; a perfect masquerade for sugar. The question is: Who poisoned you?"

A moment of silence, then: "I may have a place to start to find out," he says.

"Where?"

"A list of conference attendees; I want to know the name of every person who was there."

"But the poisoner may not have been at the conference," I tell him.

"Nonetheless, what can we lose by checking?"

"Can you get such a list?" I ask.

"I'll work on it."

While his focus is on events that occurred before the conference, mine turn to those following it.

"I want to return for a moment to the beginning of your illness," I say.

"Please hurry because I just heard the Beechcraft fly over the lodge. They'll land shortly."

"You said weakness and fatigue were your first symptoms, and that they started on the day you returned home from Lusaka."

"That's correct."

"Think back again to the hours after you drank tea at the café. Are you sure you didn't feel any ill effects that evening?"

He remains silent for a moment. "You're right; I *did* have some issues."

"What sort?"

"Gastrointestinal problems. Before boarding the Beechcraft, I had some nausea and abdominal pain and used the bathroom at the airport twice because of diarrhea."

"How long was that after you'd drunk the tea?"

"About three hours, but I attributed the symptoms to a sandwich I ate at the airport. It tasted a bit stale. Although I was uncomfortable during the flight home, the symptoms ended that night only to be replaced by weakness and fatigue the next day."

I'm convinced now that a cup of tea at the café served as the vehicle through which he was poisoned with thallium. My question now is whether treatment in the form of Prussian blue will prevent permanent neurologic damage and, for that matter, keep him alive.

6

I FEEL REVITALIZED for having slept in my cot again, all the more so because the night passed safely without further attacks by jihadists. Although the canvas cot is narrow and sags below a wooden frame, I know its contours well enough to find positions that foster deep sleep.

I find rejuvenation, too, in my morning rituals. Steam from a freshly brewed cup of tea wafts up as I sit on my patio and watch the hippopotamus in the river upstream. With the sun just rising, I squint to keep the shimmering light from stealing my view, but I won't be denied the pleasure of watching the animal's head rise above the water only to submerge again.

In the meantime, above me, the shoebill stork clatters as it does before flying away to search for food in the marshes. I get up quietly and walk to the clearing where I look up to find the bird standing on the thatch with its eyes peering over the wetlands. I smile at the curious choice nature has made in endowing the bird with a bill as large as a size-thirteen human shoe and then, to boot, attaching a narrow curved beak at its front. For good reason, biologists named this creature a "shoebill stork." Nor have I reason to complain about an occasional bad hair day when my friend, the stork, has one *every* day with its blue head feathers pointing every which way. Admittedly, I anthropomorphize when I conclude the bird looks grumpy, but that's the mood it conveys with eyes partially obstructed by its bill. I watch it move to the edge of the roof where it takes off with gargantuan wings powering it toward the marshes. No doubt there will be frogs, baby crocodiles, or lung fish that succumb to it shortly.

I move to the front of the shack in hope of finding my counselor, Jimmy the baboon. There's a matter heavy on my heart that I wish to consult him on. It involves a text Annette sent while I slept.

I call Jimmy, but he's nowhere to be seen, so I resort to a maneuver that unfailingly summons him. Standing beside the water tank, I rap it with the heel of my hand in a very specific cadence: *bah-bah, bah-bah-bah; bah-bah, bah-bah-bah.* It brings Jimmy scurrying from the bush where he climbs the acacia to sit on a limb above me. He wipes sleep from his eyes but otherwise appears open to consultation.

"I need your advice, Jimmy," I tell him.

He crosses his legs and leans against the trunk, but his fingers hold his interest as he examines them.

"Jimmy, what would you do if you received this from a woman you liked?" I read Annette's text…

It's the middle of the night, yet I think of you. Xavier tells me you'll travel again to Uku-tetema with friends, and for that I'm grateful.

Above, Jimmy is still engrossed in his fingers. He inserts the tip of one into his mouth and gently tugs at it as if removing a splinter.

"Any thoughts?" I ask him.

Apparently not, so I continue…

"I like this woman a lot, Jimmy; she's grown on me quickly. I'm attracted to her in a way as never before which you may think is strange given I've been married. If only I'd met Annette earlier in my life…maybe I'd still be married…but, wait, that's speculation and, besides, timing is everything. And speaking of timing, this is a horrible time to begin a new relationship as I've arranged phone interviews with two applicants for the job of medical director at the hospital. Not only that but the folks in Indonesia tell me the job there is mine if I accept it."

I halt my rambling and look up. I see that fingers are passé now as Jimmy shifts to his position of *The Thinker.* With a hand under his chin and an elbow on his thigh, he looks upon me as if I'm a waif.

"I know I'm lost, Jimmy," I admit. "And, yes, I have decisions to make."

I scrap my meeting with the baboon to leave for the hospital. After visiting the orphans last night, I neglected to see the damage inflicted by the jihadists because of the protracted conversation I had with Xavier. It's time now to see the destruction with the paramedics.

I find my colleagues assembled before the ruined ward. They view the remains with solemnity, much as survivors of a tornado might cluster about homes that've been leveled. Their faces are long and expressions grim.

I greet them quietly. Smiles, gaiety, and optimism are conspicuously absent. This morning, an unspoken question looms on their minds: What did we do to deserve this?

The ward that used to stand before us had served as our intensive care unit because it was the most rainproof hut on the grounds. Although it could house only a few patients at a time, its intact walls and thatched roof shielded our sickest patients from the elements. Now only ashes remain.

I ask the paramedics about the fate of a gravely ill man who'd shared the space with our burn patient before the attack.

"He was burned to death," Bristol replies.

I sigh and lower my head. I want to curse the attackers, condemn their barbarism, and spit on their effigies, but I know to do so would bring little in the way of comfort to those about me.

I splay my arms. "We will rebuild, my friends," I announce, "and not only that, we will build a ward *larger* than the one that stood here before. Our work will not be sabotaged." I lower my arms. "So, let us begin our rounds together, all as members of the same team, and as we do so, let us be grateful for everything we still have. No one can ever destroy the healing powers that reside in our hearts."

As always, we begin our rounds by visiting the newly admitted patients, the first being the mother of the soldier whose brother drove Annette and the burn patient to Lusaka. One glance at her tells me she's very ill. She lies on a mat with her back propped against two large bags of rice. A nasal cannula delivers oxygen. With her failing heart unable to handle the blood that returns from her body, the veins of her neck are engorged. Edema in her feet and ankles is so severe that a paramedic's recent probe of them with a fingertip has left indentations.

I introduce myself to the woman and thank her for what her son has done for Annette and the burn patient. She's a gracious woman who, despite struggling for air, replies, "All of us are here on earth to help one another."

Her words contrast with the ashes we've just seen. I feel a collective easing of tension among the paramedics. I address the one assigned to care for the woman. "What medicines was she taking for her condition before she came to us?" I ask.

"Only one for high blood pressure," he replies.

I examine the woman. The sounds of her heart are distant, and I hear an abnormal one that confirms a failing heart. Additional auscultation reveals the telltale signs of fluid in the lungs.

"She has pulmonary edema as a result of congestive heart failure," I say. "We need to treat her with digoxin, diuretics, and nitrates to reduce the excess fluid in her body and to dilate her blood vessels."

"What about morphine, *nudume?*" the paramedic asks.

Once again, I'm impressed by the instruction that *tata* Murphy provided the paramedics. For decades, intravenous morphine has been used to treat pulmonary edema because of the opiate's ability to dilate blood vessels and thereby decrease work on the heart, but debate exists as to whether to use it uniformly.

"It's a good question," I say. "While I favor its use in patients with congestive heart failure following a heart attack, I'm not inclined to recommend it for our patient here because of its well-known respiratory depressant effects."

I turn to the woman. "May I ask you a question about your son who serves in the armed forces—the one I met a few days ago up north near D R Congo?"

She nods.

"Would it be possible to get his telephone number? I'd like to contact him regarding an important matter."

The woman points to a bag on the floor. After a paramedic retrieves it, the patient extracts a notebook and leafs through it until she finds her target.

"This is his number," she says. She hands me the notebook.

I record the number and thank her. Outside with the paramedics, I explain the reason for requesting it.

"I'd like to call her son to see whether he might ask his superiors to station a contingent at Saysha to protect us from further attacks."

A paramedic waves a smart phone over his head. "*Nudume*, it's in the news this morning—details of the attack on our hospital!

There's much talk about incursions by jihadists into our nation."

"As there should be," I reply. "We're not alone in being attacked; armed militants have crossed into Uku-tetema to poach wildlife."

Another paramedic: "Some are calling for a joint D R Congo–Zambia military offensive to expel the militants from our nations."

"I trust we'll get help," I say, "so let's focus our attention on our patients."

We visit the maternity ward to check on a young woman who delivered a stillbirth overnight. Twenty-four hours before the stillbirth, she developed a low-grade fever and uterine tenderness along with a foul-smelling discharge. This was accompanied by a rapid heartbeat in both mother and fetus. Suspecting an infection, paramedics treated the woman with antibiotics. Their hopes were raised by what appeared to be a normal labor but were soon dashed by an abrupt cessation of a fetal pulse and the delivery of a dead baby. The paramedic who delivered the baby describes the amniotic fluid as pus-like and copious.

"An infection," I agree. We discuss bacterial agents that may have caused the infection. I ask the paramedic what her plans are for the mother.

"We will continue antibiotics and watch her clinically," she replies, "and I will sit with her to talk about what has happened."

I'm especially grateful for the empathy the paramedics show for our patients. I've seen them bring food from their homes for their patients, take children under their wings until the parents have recovered, and visit former patients in far-off villages to ensure they've recovered. The hospital is the heartbeat for the region's poor and the paramedics the life-sustaining blood flow.

Because it's Sunday and school's off, the orphans are out and about playing. I see Amu weaving a ball around opponents in a football game and Thandi standing before an easel painting a bouquet of flowers arranged in a vase. Thanks to Annette, she's become impassioned with painting and treasures the supplies Annette brought from the lodge. Thandi isn't the sole benefactor of Annette's giving: The ball that Amu and the boys play with was another gift, and in the school there's a newly carpentered shelf holding books she donated.

Across a clearing, I see Oscar lying on the ground beside a mechanic beneath the truck. I know little about vehicle repairs, but this morning I was told that a problem with part of the suspension called a "strut assembly" developed while Bristol, Innocent, and I drove to the village last night from the grass strip where the Beechcraft left us off.

Conspicuously absent is Benji, and having completed rounds on the patients with the paramedics, I set off to find him. I look no further than the floor of the orphans' quarters where he lies. A plank wedged in a crack in the wall partially blocks sunlight from entering.

"Benji," I say. "It's late. Aren't you going to get up?"

"No, *nudume,*" he replies. "I do not feel well."

I remove the plank to allow more light to enter. "Tell me what's wrong."

He sits up. "My head hurts."

"Do you mean you have a headache?" I ask. By instinct, I watch his neck for stiffness as a possible sign of meningitis.

"No, I feel heaviness in my head and heart."

It's clear to me now. "You're troubled by what happened yesterday, aren't you?"

"Yes."

I sit beside him and wrap an arm around his shoulders. "You've every reason to be sad and even angry," I tell him. "Bad people came yesterday and did unspeakable acts. Our bodies and feelings respond to such events in ways that can make us feel heavy."

"I don't know how to make it go away," he says.

"You can talk to me and to others about how you feel. That often helps."

"But my thoughts are not happy now."

"Can you share any with me?"

He looks at a bar of light that streams through a crack and falls upon his feet. "If I had a family, this would not have happened."

"What do you mean by that?"

"I have no mother or father to live with. If I did, I would not have been here at the hospital yesterday to see the man raise a rifle to shoot Miss Annette."

"You have no mother or father, Benji, but you belong to the same family I belong to in our village. We're a family together. That's why I ask you to call me *nudume*."

My words surprise me. After my father sent me to boarding school, "family" became a foreign word to me, an alien concept. I've been estranged from it since.

"And after you leave here, will we still be brothers?" Benji asks.

I feel a pit in my stomach. "What makes you think I'll leave?"

"I have heard the paramedics talk. They say you will go when another *mzungu* arrives to take your place." He looks at me with sad eyes. "Do you know about the sable antelope?"

"No."

"One time, when a ranger visited the hospital, he told me about this antelope. The animal used to come to our land from Kenya in past days but no longer. They are large and strong as some weigh over two hundred kilograms. They have ringed horns that arch backward with pointed ends and have been known to kill lions with them."

I'm wondering where he'll go with this story.

He continues: "When they are three years old and their fur starts to turn from brown to black, the young males are sent away from the herd. The juvenile males band together to form a group. This is what happened to me when my parents died."

"You weren't sent away, Benji." I motion about the quarters. "You're in a safe and friendly place where you live with friends and grownups around you."

"But I feel like a juvenile sable antelope, left to fend for myself." He peers into my eyes. "When you leave, can I come with you?"

I shake my head gently. "I don't want to talk about leaving, Benji. Instead, I want to talk about traveling together—you, Oscar, and I."

He sits bolt upright. "Traveling…*where?*"

"In an hour, we're leaving for Uku-tetema together."

A look of doubt creeps upon his face. "What about Amu and Thandi?"

"No, they'll remain here. I need you and Oscar to come with me on this journey because there are things I need your help with."

Last night, after learning Benji had killed a jihadist, I suspected he'd be emotionally distraught and for that reason I asked Xavier if I could bring him to Uku-tetema with me.

"What sort of help do you need from Oscar and me, *nudume?*"

"You shall see. For now, I want you to tell Oscar to prepare for our departure. Both of you are to pack a few days' worth of clothes. Come to my shack in an hour. We will leave from there."

Benji rushes away and leaves me seated beside his mat. In the crepuscular light, I watch dust particles float in random fashion through a miniature cosmos of their own. I feel a bond with Benji as if we're particles floating through a larger universe of celestial bodies. At the present, we happen to share time and space, but I ponder for how long that'll be the case.

BENJI AND OSCAR are the first to arrive at my shack. I put them to work filling water bottles and packing food for our journey to Uku-tetema. Before long, the two guards Xavier sent to Saysha with Annette the day before show up at my door. They're large, strong men I met earlier at the hospital as they patrolled the area. Each wears khakis of the type donned by others on Xavier's staff. Automatic rifles hang by their sides.

"Dr. Rider," one says, "Xavier is asking that we leave immediately."

"We'll do so just as soon as Innocent Mbewe shows up," I tell him.

While talking to Xavier the previous evening, he asked if I could bring a paramedic with me from the hospital to help a nurse at a clinic located thirty kilometers from the lodge deal with an outbreak of diarrheal disease afflicting residents of one of Uku-tetema's villages. When I asked for a volunteer this morning at the hospital, Innocent Mbewe was quick to step forward. I accepted his offer because of his familiarity with Uku-tetema and because he seemed to get along particularly well with Xavier.

I'm relieved now to see him arrive. He travels lightly with a small carry on suitcase and explains his tardiness results from swinging by the hospital to retrieve supplies he'll need at the clinic in Uku-tetema.

We descend the path to the river and retrieve the Zodiac from a hiding place in a marsh where Annette and the guards had left it. Before long, we set off upstream to the same ledge we stopped at two days earlier. This time the transfer from Zodiac to ridgetop is easier because of its familiarity. Three Land Rovers await us in the grass below. I see Oscar's eyes widen at the sight.

"*Nudume*, I have never ridden in a Land Rover," he confides.

I pat his back. "I think you'll like it very much but, unfortunately, you won't be able to shift gears because I won't be driving."

His excitement is undiminished.

As we descend the slope toward the vehicles, I recognize one of the drivers. He waves to me and I feel at home in Uku-tetema.

"Henry, good to see you again," I call.

He comes forth to greet us and shows particular interest in the boys, assessing them, it seems, for their strength and agility. I conclude he's satisfied for he smiles and introduces himself to them.

I watch Benji and Oscar shake Henry's hand and am pleased with their performance. Each stands straight, looks Henry in the eyes, and says, "Very nice to meet you, sir." Shortly after arriving in Saysha, I summoned the orphans in order to give them practice introducing themselves in public. Because some were particularly shy in my presence, I thought a good way to instill confidence and familiarity in them would be to have them practice handshaking.

After meeting the boys, Henry nods at me and raises his eyebrows approvingly. "Let's split up now to go to the lodge," he says.

While riding in the Zodiac, I prepared the boys to travel in separate vehicles along different paths for security purposes. Although Oscar didn't bat an eye, Benji appeared apprehensive initially but warmed to the idea when I told him each driver was an expert in wildlife.

I pull Henry aside and ask if he'd be willing to escort Benji and stop to see animals as he'd done for me. "He'd like to be a wildlife ranger one day," I inform Henry. In hushed tones, I tell him also about how Benji saved Annette's life in Saysha.

"Oh, my word!" he exclaims. "By all means, I will take him. We'll see rhinos that I passed on the way here."

We split the savanna with vehicles speeding in different angles. My driver, a reserved man, explains that he's been instructed to drive to the lodge without delay. For that reason, we'll not stop to view animals. The lament in his voice tells me that he, like his colleagues, has a deep-seated love and respect for the wildlife of his homeland.

Our drive is two hours shorter than the previous one, and unlike before, there's no greeting party at the front door of the lodge.

"Please go in," my driver says. "You will find Xavier in the conference room."

I climb the stairs and leave my bag in the foyer before stepping into the conference room which now looks like a command and control bunker. A pair of waist-tall speakers frames the entryway while, beyond them, the once orderly conference table holds laptops and papers in disorderly array. An acknowledgement of my entry comes only after I've taken several steps into the room, a hearty greeting from Xavier.

"Paul, I trust your journey was uneventful!" He stands to shake my hand.

At the table, Alexander and Rodney remain riveted to their work. While one peers at a screen, the other listens with eyes closed to a set of headphones.

"My trip was beautiful," I tell Xavier.

"A man of my liking," he chuckles. "One who appreciates what the day brings."

He points to his office and beckons me to follow. After we enter it, he closes the door.

"I want to update you without disturbing the progress of the two gentlemen in there," Xavier says, pointing to the door. "They've worked pretty much non-stop since arriving last night and have made some startling discoveries."

"Like what?" I ask.

"I'll get to that, but first I want to tell you that last night I started taking the Prussian blue capsules you sent. So far, I've taken three doses, and I think I'm beginning to feel better. Is it possible the medication could produce results so quickly?"

"That's pretty fast improvement," I say, "but the proof of success will be falling levels of thallium in your urine over time. Let's collect another specimen tomorrow. In the meantime, are you having any problems linked to the medication?"

He blushes. "My feces are blue, which you warned me they'd be, so I was prepared for that; otherwise, no issues."

"Good, so let's do this: Double the number of capsules you take for each dose for the next few days. Let's see how you fare on a higher dose."

"Will do," he says, taking a seat. "Now, as to our progress..."

He lifts a black marker and swivels to face an erase board on the wall. Along the top of it, he pens the words, *Data Sources*. He then draws three vertical lines to create columns of equal width which he labels, *Hard Drive Files*, *Cockpit Voice Recorder*, and *Conference Attendance List*.

He swivels to face me but points over his shoulder. "The information we can extract from those three data sources could determine whether we live or die." He shows no signs of tempering his words but, rather, sharpens them by adding, "We're in same boat from here on, Paul. That radioactive sample of jaguar blood you received was only a shot across the bow; worse will come."

I peer at the board and wonder how three column headings could hold such power over two lives. "Why do you believe worse is to come?"

He nods as if he's prepared to speak but demurs. "I'll tell you why, but first you'll have to bear with me while I go through a process."

I lean back to listen.

He swivels to the board. "Let's begin here at the left-most column, *Hard Drive Files*. Thanks to your efforts at International Mines' office at the Lusaka airport, Alexander copied a number of files from laptops in the modular unit. You'll recall Alexander asked before if you knew what the acronym *VIPOR* stands for." He writes it in the first column.

"Yes, and I told him I'd never heard of it."

"That's too bad because a number of files on those hard drives refer to *VIPOR* as if it's a source issuing assignments to the staff in the Lusaka office of International Mines."

"Probably an entity in the company's corporate headquarters," I suggest.

"Doubtful because other communications from headquarters were clearly labeled as such."

I grow uneasy with the recollection of Alexander telling me that the acronym had appeared in the context of TransNational Oil in some regard. "What sort of assignments are you referring to?"

"I can't tell you precisely because they were vague but still came across as tasks to be undertaken."

"Give me an example."

"Alright, one involved keeping an eye out for a package sent by international courier labeled as *Fragile* and *Urgent*." He adds the words to the erase board under *VIPOR*.

"Sounds pretty routine to me," I say. "What's the big deal?"

"Would it be 'routine' to describe the contents of the package as something that was 'cooked to sizzling hot by a laboratory'?" The phrase goes to the board.

"What laboratory?" I ask.

"We don't know."

I worry that if the findings he populates the columns with are as murky as those presented thus far, he'll be in no position to substantiate his claim that the data sources hold sway over our lives.

"You're unimpressed," he notes. "So, let's get to the crux of what we discovered on the hard drives." He inks the words *delivery instructions* and then turns to me. "We found a document that instructed the staff at International Mines in Lusaka to fly the contents of the package to a remote village in northeastern Zambia."

I straighten in my seat. "What village?"

"Saysha."

"Oh, God…" I mutter. "Was there a date on the document?"

"Yes, three days before you discovered the blood in your shack."

I feel palpitations. "So, that airplane which our paramedic saw land outside Saysha was responsible for delivering the blood." I dart my eyes to the board. "And the words *cooked to sizzling hot by a laboratory* almost certainly refer to a lab irradiating the specimen with P-32."

"That's how I view it," Xavier says.

As soon as I learned the blood had come from a jaguar, I suspected the tube represented retribution for the measures I took to protect jaguars in the Amazon. With evidence referring to this blood specimen coming now from laptops belonging to a subsidiary of my former employer, I feel shackled to a ball and chain that reach across the Atlantic from Ecuador.

"Among those you pissed off in the Amazon, was there someone in particular you angered the most?" Xavier asks.

I huff. "The security guards in the oil fields, I suppose. They were furious at what I did."

"Do you think they were the ones who sent you the radioactive blood?"

"Hell, no, they were semi-literate at best. It had to be someone else."

"So, move up the chain. Who supervised them?"

"A local guy in the rainforest who didn't want to deal with the feud I had with the guards."

"Who was *his* boss?"

"A mid-level manager at TransNational Oil's regional office in Quito."

"Could he be the culprit?"

"Doubt it; I barely dealt with him."

"Another notch up," Xavier insists. "Who's next?"

"I don't know the personnel structure of the regional office that well, but ultimately, the boss in Quito reported to a honcho in Houston, Texas."

"Do you think someone in Houston shipped the blood?"

"Possibly, but I suspect I was just a minnow in a pond to them as they have far bigger fish to fry. After all, the folks in TransNational Oil's office in Houston oversee operations throughout Latin America, and in doing so, they contend with hot-button issues like guerilla forces attacking oil rigs and politicians resenting a multinational corporation for exploiting their resources."

"Yet they were the ones who fired you, right?"

"No, to be precise, my letter of termination came from a physician at TransNational Oil's global headquarters in Geneva, Switzerland."

"What's the name of that person?"

"Hermann Albershadt, M.D."

"Why would TransNational Oil have a physician in their Geneva headquarters?"

"Because the corporation has over thirty health care providers working at drilling sites throughout the world. Most of the sites are so remote they require a doctor or nurse to be present to care for the oil workers and their families as I did in the Amazon."

"Did you ever meet Albershadt?"

"There was no need to."

"Did you speak to him by phone?"

"Sure, he warned me repeatedly to refrain from dealing with the jaguar matter."

"And you blew him off."

"Damn right. You'd have blown him off, too, if you'd seen a security guard skin a jaguar ten meters away."

Xavier says nothing as he looks out a window at the garden. In the silence, he holds his hands interlocked on the desk before him. I notice the muscles at the base of his thumbs show subtle signs of wasting, a finding that concerns me because it suggests thallium poisoning has led to sufficient nerve damage to cause muscle loss.

Xavier returns his eyes to mine. "I don't think Hermann Albershadt is our man," he says.

"Why not? As a physician, he'd have ready access to a lab that could've irradiated the blood."

"He's a two-bit player. I think someone far more consequential threatened you with the radioactive blood, someone responsible also for poisoning me with thallium."

"Got any ideas who that might be?"

He sucks air through his teeth. "I'm almost positive I know who it was."

"*Who?*"

He gestures over his shoulder. "We've got two more columns to complete to identify our suspect."

A KNOCK COMES on the door of Xavier's office.

"Who is it?" Xavier asks.

Alexander opens the door. "Helena brought us tea and biscuits. Would you like to join us?"

We move to the conference room and serve ourselves before sitting at the table where the dismantled cockpit voice recorder lies.

"Very well," Xavier says, pointing at Rodney. "What did you find?"

Stationed before a laptop, Rodney plugs in a cable that connects to the large speakers I'd noticed earlier. "Before I delve into details, let me give you some background on this particular voice recorder," he says.

He slides the laptop aside to gain an unobstructed view of me.

"As we discussed briefly in Lusaka, this recorder from the Cessna operated by International Mines uses digital techniques as opposed to magnetic tapes employed by earlier models. As with magnetic tapes, however, digital techniques record data for limited periods before overwriting old material. Current devices, including the one from the Cessna, record two hours of data before older data is overwritten. This cycle is called an 'endless-loop principle.' "

He sips tea.

"Because it took the Cessna two hours to fly from Lusaka to Saysha and then another two hours to return to Lusaka, two entire two-hour recording cycles elapsed. To complicate matters, the day after flying to Saysha, the Cessna made another hour-long flight before Martin removed the recorder."

"So that means three-quarters of the data we're interested in was overwritten," I note.

"Correct; only the final hour of the flight from Saysha to Lusaka remained intact."

"What did it reveal?"

"Very little." He takes more tea.

"Couldn't you at least hear the crew's voices as they approached Lusaka to land?" I ask.

"Yes, the co-pilot's voice is audible, but it is only routine landing instructions he receives from the control tower."

"So what kept you up all night?" I ask.

He smiles wanly. "I used sophisticated techniques to recover overwritten data."

"Is that *possible?*"

"It comes down to two factors. The first involves the precise overwriting techniques a cockpit voice recorder uses, and the second is whether one has the necessary software programs to recover overwritten data that's salvageable."

He finishes his tea.

"As it turns out, the Cessna's recorder uses software that generates smaller files to replace larger files that contain older data, and in doing so, portions of the larger files remain intact. I was able to identify those intact sections and restore them to audibility."

"Mind you," Xavier says, "what Rodney recovered were snippets of voices for the flight from Lusaka to Saysha. As such, sentences are incomplete and voices are cut-off." He nods at Rodney to resume.

"Let's begin by listening to the pilot," Rodney says. He taps the laptop which brings the speakers alive. Although a mechanical hum from the engines forms a constant backdrop, the voice is loud and clear. It asks for a weather update and is steeped in a southern drawl that I recognize immediately.

"Hey," I blurt, "that's the guy who helped me replace the tire at the modular unit!"

"Yes," Alexander confirms, "he's a pilot for International Mines."

"But he told me was a mechanical engineer!"

"He lied," Xavier interjects. "He's a pilot."

I confront Xavier: "Why'd you expose me like that?"

"We needed to see whether he'd recognize you, and because he didn't appear to, we conclude he's merely a delivery man. The question is: Who helped him find your shack?"

A chill goes up my spine. "Do you have an answer?"

Xavier's face turns stern. "Yes, a local accomplice."

"In Saysha?"

"Very likely."

"Oh, *God*..." I mutter. I search for reasons why this couldn't be possible. "He wouldn't necessarily have needed an accomplice to find my shack because the village is small. From the air, he'd readily have seen my shack stands alone."

"I know you want to trust your people," Xavier says. "It's natural to do so, but the facts suggest otherwise. Take, for example, the Cessna's flight times. Four hours elapsed from the time it left Lusaka to fly to Saysha and back again. Since it takes about two hours each way, the airplane was on the ground at Saysha for minutes only, enough time to hand the blood to a local who knew exactly where you lived and when you'd be away from your shack."

Xavier bores his eyes into mine. "You need to make some inquiries."

THE MATTER OF a Cessna's cockpit voice recorder seems inconsequential now as I contemplate the possibility that someone in Saysha delivered the jaguar blood to my home.

Rodney interrupts my private thoughts. "Please forgive me for raising a subject you've been asked about repeatedly," he says. "It regards the acronym, *VIPOR*."

The acronym has become an incessant intruder, much like a mosquito that's found its way into bed netting. "Yes, and I've said repeatedly I know nothing about it!"

"I understand, but we hear the term several times on the cockpit voice recorder. Listen, let me play a section..."

"*I'm pissed with the viper*," a voice barks through the speakers. It's a different voice from the one I heard before, one belonging to an American male from an area without defining accents.

"Who's that speaking?" I ask.

"The Cessna's co-pilot," Rodney replies.

"Does he explain why he's pissed?"

"Let me play another snippet."

"*The viper doesn't even work for us yet he—*"

The voice abruptly ends, leading me to say: "Keep it rolling."

"I can't. It cuts off there, but listen to this…"

"Yeah, if it was up to me, I'd make the viper walk to this pissing hole called Saysha." The words drip in the pilot's southern drawl.

"Now, this," Rodney says, "a sequence from different parts of the recorder…"

"…piss on his hot blood…"

"…pour the blood down the viper's throat."

"…radiate the viper's asshole."

"Yeah, so it shines in the night."

The recording ends with laughter.

Speakers silent, Rodney asks: "What do you make of all this?"

"The viper's not a popular guy," I reply.

"More importantly," Xavier interjects, "they speak of 'hot blood' and 'radiate.' It's clear these men were tasked to fly the jaguar blood to Saysha."

Rodney's fingers move to the keyboard again. "Let me play the final pieces…"

"Better be there to meet us…"

"Wanna get back into the air as fast as—"

"…carry it with gloves…"

"…Rider's place."

"There you go," Rodney says. "That's it, a night's worth of work for what you just heard."

My heart pounds from hearing my name in the final snippet. "But none of this tells us whose idea it was to send the blood," I say.

"We're circling in on that person," Xavier insists. "Shall we move to the final data source to make the kill?"

RODNEY CLOSES THE laptop and pushes it aside. This opens space on the table which Alexander fills with sheets of paper he aligns side-by-side. After laying each sheet down, he lifts a finger to tongue to snare the next one.

"Make sure there are fifty-one in all," Xavier tells him.

In the meantime, Rodney clears the cups and saucers. Before long, the table is a sea of white.

"I apologize for the paper format of our next dataset," Xavier says, "but I thought it'd help to see the names and affiliations of attendees at the conference I spoke at last month in Lusaka." He remains seated as he points to the sheets. "Each page contains names, titles, and contact information for attendees. A friend of mine who organized the conference gave me the list. You'll note that members of the National Assembly are grouped together followed by individuals from industry, the press, non-governmental organizations, universities, churches, and other groups. In all, there were five hundred eighteen people present."

"How long did the conference last?" I ask.

"Five hours were dedicated to presentations and discussion which were followed by the reception."

I stand to get a better view of the sheets, starting at one end and moving across the table. "I see numbers beside some names. What do they signify?"

"Speakers," Xavier replies. "A '1' refers to invited speakers such as myself, a '2' to members of the panel discussion, and a '3' to anyone who approached a microphone to ask a question or state a position on whether Uku-tetema should be designated as a national park."

"Was there anyone particularly outspoken in opposing your bill?"

"A number of people, yes, but their positions had been staked out publicly well in advance."

"I see a disproportionate number of representatives from the oil and petrochemical industries," I note.

"Which one would expect," Xavier replies. "The belief is Intanda holds great promise in terms of oil and gas."

"It's a global belief," I note. "Attendees came from every continent save Antarctica."

"Yes, but turn your attention to surnames beginning with 'S,' " Xavier says. "Do you recognize any of them?"

In alphabetical order, I track the names and again note the differing nationalities: *Salazar, Sampson, Schröder, Segreti, Sevčik, Shen, Simsbury…*

My eyes halt. Backtracking, I read the first name and middle initial for *Simsbury—Gary Y.* I finger the name and pivot. "I know him—*Gary Y. Simsbury*!"

"I expected you would," Xavier replies. "You worked for his company, TransNational Oil, when you were in the Amazon."

"Yes, and I met him in Ecuador, too. He flew from Houston to meet with staff in the company's regional office in Quito. I was asked to be present to meet him."

"Why?"

"By that time, I was embroiled in the matter of protecting jaguars. The story you're familiar with about my work had appeared online. Simsbury expressed his displeasure with the story and, in particular, with my refusal to work through company channels to address the issue."

"How displeased was he?"

"Enough so to summon me to Quito, but overall he was reasonable about the matter."

"That was it? You didn't discuss anything else?"

"Not really, except that he thanked me for the medical expertise I provided his employees in the rainforest. He left rather abruptly to catch a flight back to Houston."

"Okay, so look at his official title at TransNational Oil. Do you see anything notable about it?"

I return my attention to the sheet. "No, it's well known he's a senior vice-president for oil resources."

"Look more closely. Read the title aloud."

"*Vice-President, Oil Resources.*"

"If it had an acronym, what would it be?"

My jaw drops. " 'VPOR,' " I say, listing the letters.

"Or 'VIPOR' if you add an 'I' as in the word 'Vice,' " Xavier interjects. "And how would you pronounce this term?"

Heart pounding, I say: " 'Viper,' " That mosquito in the bed netting has turned into a rabid bat.

"Yes," Xavier agrees. "So, it was Simsbury who ordered the blood to go to your shack in Saysha."

"*Shit,*" I mutter.

"It makes total sense now," Xavier continues, "because International Mines is a subsidiary of TransNational Oil. As such, it's not surprising Simsbury was in touch with the International Mines office in Lusaka."

"And tell Dr. Paul about the transcript!" Alexander gloats.

"Yes, the transcript," Xavier says. "We found a speech Simsbury gave at a convention hosted by a non-governmental organization called America's Volunteers about a year ago. In it, he joked about how his title at TransNational Oil made him uniquely equipped to—and I quote here—'slither through bureaucratic channels and reams of red tape to get funding to outstanding organizations such as yours.' In the very next sentence, he asked the audience rhetorically why they thought he used the word 'slither' to refer to his ability to procure funding. 'Because, people call me a snake,' he went on to say, 'and that's because, as Vice-president of Oil Resources at TransNational Oil—a title shortened to *VIPOR*—folks call me a 'viper.' "

I shudder at the revelation.

"Last but not least," Xavier adds, "Alexander discovered a blog Simsbury maintained until recently. It carried a long list of posts pertaining to technical issues dealing with oil exploration and his company's role in expanding frontiers for oil production." He addresses Alexander: "Tell Paul what you found."

Alexander shifts uneasily. "I read its lengthy entries and found something Simsbury posted not long after the story about your work with jaguars appeared online." He files through a stack of papers from which he extracts a single sheet. "I'll read it to you, but first let me tell you this comes from a lengthy post about the challenges oil producing companies face in an era of climate change. The entire post until this point was filled with rebuttals to views that burning fossil fuels is responsible for recent temperature increases. Simsbury then says…

Of course, the myth of climate change linked to fossil fuel combustion is not the only challenge companies such as TransNational Oil face these days. Other obstacles can suddenly arise to command our attention, an example being recent publicity about poaching jaguars in the Amazon Jungle of Ecuador by employees at one of my company's oil fields. Like a spark on a tinder bed, stories like these can ignite conflagrations on social media among wildlife fanatics who, it should be said, depend on cars, airplanes, and other modes of transportation fueled by petroleum products. Nonetheless, these obstacles can be radioactive for those of us who have dedicated our lives and careers to advancing the field of oil production."

I feel as if Alexander has grasped my hand and pushed a finger into an electrical socket, forcing me to recoil from the shock.

"Read the last sentence again," I demand.

He does so, confirming what I'd heard.

"*Radioactive?*" I repeat.

"What more do we need?" Xavier asks. "Simsbury's our man until proven otherwise. I hold him responsible not only for sending you radioactive jaguar blood but also for poisoning me with thallium."

"Are you suggesting *he* poisoned your tea in the café in Lusaka?"

"Either he or a proxy."

"Which means he shadowed you throughout your stay in the city leading up to that café visit."

"That wouldn't have been difficult," Xavier asserts. "I made an inquiry of the same friend who sent me the conference attendee list to ask where Simsbury stayed in Lusaka. Guess where that was?"

"Intercontinental Hotel?"

"Yes, on the same floor as I, no less." He eyes Alexander. "Tell Paul what else we learned from your Internet search."

"TransNational Oil recently requested permission from the U.S. government to launch oil exploration activities in eastern Ethiopia, not far from the border of Somalia."

"That's gotta be risky!"

"They're an aggressive firm. Where they smell oil, they drill."

My cell phone vibrates and I see a text from the soldier I called yesterday while traveling from Saysha to the lodge. "Xavier, you'll want to hear this." I tell him about how I met the soldier while driving to Danjou to look for Annette and how the soldier pursued my offer to have his mother travel to Saysha for evaluation.

"The soldier just informed me that discussions are under way to send a military unit to Saysha. There's concern a larger attack by jihadists may be coming."

CANDLELIGHT FLICKERS THROUGH the lodge. In the cavernous hallways, my body throws shadows upon stucco walls, each shadow expanding and collapsing with every candle passed. I ponder the rich history that would be revealed if shadows from the past had imprinted themselves in a fashion that could be peeled away to learn who their creators were. Which of Xavier's relatives would I meet? What secrets might unravel—affairs consummated, lusts fulfilled, passions pursued?

I enter the sitting room to find Benji and Oscar standing at a bay window overlooking the watering hole, an attraction to all who enter the room. From Benji's body language, I'm certain he sees something interesting because he leans so far forward his nose touches a pane. In contrast, Oscar, less enthralled, stands back a foot or two.

"Boys!" I call. "How was your journey today?"

Both respond with smiles.

"*Nudume*, look!" Benji implores. "There are elephants wrestling!"

I stand between the boys and wrap an arm around each. "That's you and Oscar there," I chuckle. While adults drink and bathe, two smaller elephants tussle in the background.

"They are young males," Benji observes. "Females don't fight like that."

Oscar has other thoughts: "*Nudume*, I learned how to change a spark plug today. My driver taught me how to do it."

"And I saw rhinos!" Benji exclaims.

They're eleven-year-olds, a future mechanic and wildlife ranger, yet they revert to six-year-olds when vying for attention.

Behind us, I hear Innocent Mbewe and Xavier enter the room. They speak in animated tones about scores from recent soccer matches. When the discussion turns to an upcoming game pitting Argentina against Brazil, both profess hopes for an Argentine victory. In a booming voice, Innocent promises to mix Xavier a blue lagoon at cocktail hour should the Argentinians prevail in their striped, sky blue jerseys.

Xavier seals the deal with a pat on Innocent's back before making a beeline to the boys. "Which of you is Benji?" he asks.

I rest a hand on Benji's shoulder. "This gentleman."

Xavier extends a hand which Benji shakes.

Always the diplomat, Xavier is prompt to acknowledge Oscar as well, saying, "I will address you shortly, but let me first pay my respects to Benji." Straightening, he holds Benji's eyes as he commends the boy for the courage he exhibited in saving Annette's life. "When you are grown, you have a job here in Uku-tetema as a wildlife ranger if you want it."

"Really?" Benji exclaims. "*Nudume*," he says to me, "I am ready to work here now!"

"I believe Mr. Treadwill said 'when you are grown,' " I reply.

"As for you," Xavier says to Oscar, "I understand you have a passion for mechanics. I can use good mechanics all the time."

I admire Xavier for the ease with which he engages the boys. Both stand before him with rapt attention.

Rodney and Alexander arrive next. They wear a veneer of fatigue from the long night and day but look eager to eat dinner with the group.

"Please," Xavier calls, "let's move to the dining room as supper is served."

Standing at the table end, Xavier assigns Alexander and me to sit beside him while Rodney, Innocent, and the boys form the flanks. I feel a void with Annette's absence and think of her now, wondering whether she remains at the hospital in Lusaka with the burn patient. As for the twins, Xavier informed me earlier that he'd sent them to the capital to stay with friends of his there.

It's a working dinner we have, one during which Xavier discusses plans for the following day. While Innocent will assist at a village clinic, a caravan will depart to Intanda to install laser trip lines. Traveling in the caravan will be drivers, guards, electricians, a mechanic, a cook, Benji, Oscar, Xavier, and me.

The boys cannot contain themselves at hearing the news.

Xavier is quick to address them. "Boys, I have invited you to go to Intanda with me, but you must view the journey not as a vacation or field trip but, rather, as a sacred mission to a site considered holy by my people. Very few in Uku-tetema have visited Intanda, partly because it's so remote but also because the land is reputed to house ancient spirits."

I see Oscar shrink as he did when we were at the cemetery in Danjou with Felice. Beside him, the table cloth lifts momentarily as he slides a hand under it to take Benji's. The boys lean closer as if numbers provide protection.

"Are the spirits kind?" Oscar asks.

" 'Kind' is not how I would describe them," Xavier replies. "The spirits were sent to Intanda to protect it from pillagers so they must be watchful at all times."

"Do you know what 'pillagers' means?" I ask Oscar.

"People who steal?" he replies.

"Yes," Xavier says, "people who steal and destroy. It was a cat goddess worshipped by ancient Egyptians who sent the spirits to Intanda centuries ago. They remain there to protect the leopards that live in Intanda. So, as we embark for that holy land tomorrow, we do so with utmost respect and, yes, fear."

The boys look at one another with wide eyes. Oscar pushes his plate aside as if his stomach will hold no more.

"Why did you invite us?" Benji asks.

"Because I know *nudume* Paul will value your presence."

Yesterday, after consoling Benji in his room at the orphans' quarters, I asked Xavier for permission to bring Benji and Oscar with me to Uku-tetema. My motivation for doing so was to divert their thoughts away from the attack on the hospital. But Xavier is insightful: I do value their presence as friends.

Benji leans forward to address Xavier. "A wildlife ranger once told me a story about the great leopards of Intanda," he says, "but even the ranger had not seen them himself. He had only heard about them. Will we actually see the leopards when we go there?"

"Oh, yes," Xavier replies, "for it would be a very bad omen if we did not."

THE BOYS APPROACH me immediately after Xavier dismisses us from dinner.

"*Nudume!*" Benji whispers, looking about sheepishly. "We are afraid to go to Intanda because of the spirits."

"Spirits can be our allies," I suggest to him.

"But we may find mean spirits!"

"Come," I say, "I want to show you something."

I lead them to the bay window in the sitting room where they stood earlier watching the elephants at the watering hole. I extinguish a candle nearby.

"Look into the sky," I say. "What do you see?"

"The moon," Oscar replies, pointing to the horizon.

"What else?"

"Stars," Benji answers. He cranes his neck, adding, "And over there, the Southern Cross."

"And what is the English word for 'Intanda'?" I ask him.

" 'Star,' " he replies.

"Yes, and look at all of them up there! Do you see a single one that looks mean to you?"

"No, but they are far away."

"It doesn't matter. In my life, I've found few things that shine to be mean, and if it was a falling star that formed Intanda, we have nothing to fear tomorrow."

The boys are silent, yet in Benji's face I still see doubt.

"There's another reason why I believe we'll find only friendly spirits in Intanda," I tell him.

"What is it?" he asks.

"We're going there to protect leopards."

"Who is disturbing them?"

"No one at the moment, but there are people who want to go there and strip its wealth, and if that happens, the leopards will die."

Already close to the window, Benji inches forward until his chin grazes the glass. Looking up, he gazes at the sky. "Then, I will go," he says, his breath fogging the glass.

I place a hand on his shoulder. "In that case, I suggest we get a good night's sleep. I'll tuck you boys into bed tonight."

Benji steps back from the window and joins Oscar in smiling as if to say my overture is unnecessary although neither declines the offer.

We make our way to the guestrooms where I tell the boys I'll return shortly to say goodnight. In the meantime, I go to my room and place a call to Bristol. He picks up promptly.

"Any news?" I ask him. Before dinner, I'd called him to tell him that an accomplice in Saysha must've delivered the jaguar blood to my shack. Because I trust no one more than Bristol, I asked him to check the schedule of workers at the hospital to see if anyone had missed a shift around the time the Cessna landed. He was dismayed by the news and promised to check his records immediately.

"*Nudume*," he says now, "I have thought about another possibility."

"What is it?" I ask.

"Someone could have flown in the Cessna from Lusaka and then remained to deliver the blood to your home."

"But, surely, that person would've been spotted in the village, don't you think?"

"Not necessarily; your home is remote."

In his tone, I detect irritation for, shortly after I arrived in Saysha, it was Bristol who was most adamant that I live in the village in order to be close to the hospital.

"If your theory is correct," I say, "this stranger would've had to make his way to Mposto to return to Lusaka, and that's a long way."

"I understand, *nudume*, but I raised the idea only because my search of the hospital records showed no one missed a shift on the afternoon the Cessna was spotted."

"Let me ask about two people, in particular," I say. "In no way am I suggesting they played a role in the delivery of the jaguar blood; I just want to be sure you accounted for them."

"Go ahead."

"The first is Innocent Mbewe. I trust him so much I've allowed him to come with me to Uku-tetema twice, but can you verify he was at work on the afternoon the Cessna was spotted?"

Bristol's response is immediate: "Yes, Innocent was at the hospital overseeing the pediatric ward while I attended to adults the entire day."

I think back to that day. "Yes, and he was with me as darkness fell when I examined the burn patient. She'd just arrived by car at the hospital."

"And the other person, *nudume*?"

"Cynthia," I say. "Since she was the one who saw the airplane, she must've been in a part of the village away from the hospital."

"Cynthia was at the hospital the entire day working with maternity patients."

"But how could she have seen the small airplane land in the distance if that's the case?"

"You are forgetting about Cynthia's other job! She is the one who ensures we have sufficient water at the hospital."

"I know that! What's that got to do with the matter before us?"

"Cynthia saw the airplane from the water tower," he replies. "She climbed the ladder to the tower to deal with a small leak she noticed there, and while she was on the highest rung, she could see above the trees into the distance where she saw the airplane about to land."

I sigh. "Okay, Bristol, thanks for the update."

Eager to see the boys to bed, I ask him to think about how we might investigate the possibility that a villager not employed by the hospital might have assisted in delivering the jaguar blood.

"I will think about that," he promises.

I leave my room to join the boys. They're nestled in a single bed with the remaining one empty. A candle on a table beside them still burns.

"We feel safer sleeping near each other," Benji explains.

"Of course," I say, blowing out the candle. At the orphans' quarters in Saysha, the boys and girls share separate rooms with mats on the floor where bodies comingle; sleeping side-by-side is the norm in quarters as cramped as theirs.

I lie down in the spare bed.

"*Nudume*," Benji says.

"Yes?" I reply in the darkness.

"I am sorry I angered you yesterday."

"Angered me about what?"

"About your plans to leave us soon. You have every right to go. Oscar and I only want you to know that you will always be our *nudume*, even from afar."

I place a hand to my forehead and squeeze it. I'm in no mood to discuss my imminent departure. "Benji, I'll make a promise to you and Oscar at this moment."

"What is it?" they respond together.

"As I asked you to look at the stars tonight, I'll do the same. I'll turn to them for guidance."

I hear a boy get out of bed and walk across the floor. A curtain opens along the side of the room to reveal a sky full of stars.

"Good night, *nudume*," Benji says, returning to bed.

"Good night," I reply.

I PASS THE lounge to reach my bedroom at the far end of the hallway. An uneasy feeling accompanies me as I slip into bed. Earlier, while talking with Bristol by telephone, he informed me that a committee of paramedics that had formed to review applications for the position of hospital medical director had voted unanimously to recruit a young husband-wife physician team from Canada to replace me. The pair would come to Saysha with four-year-old triplets and a commitment to dedicate their careers to the hospital, one as a pediatrician and the other a general surgeon. Opportunities like these, Bristol reminded me, come rarely.

I fall asleep into a zone of aloneness, one I know well. In it, I dream of lying on a raft adrift at sea as, beneath me, waterlogged twine that interlaces the planks cuts into my sunburnt skin. After days of drifting, the twine leaves lines that crisscross my raw chest, back, and thighs; even the skin of my calves, arms, and feet is grooved. I look like a piece of meat removed from a sizzling grill, only the lines are red and the skin surrounding them swollen. I lie as still as I can hoping the winds will die and the seas calm, but that doesn't happen. Instead, heaving swells force me to grasp the twine to keep from sliding off the raft, and I turn myself about regularly to spread the sun's wrath.

A knock is a foreign sound in my dream, but I'm sure I hear one tonight. I attribute the sound to a shark probing a plank on my raft or a wayward buoy striking it. When the knock comes again, I awaken to hear a voice that whispers, "Paul, may I come in?"

"Who is it?" I call, sitting up.

I fumble for the matches on the bedside table but knock them to the floor. In the darkness, I hear the door open. A flashlight casts a beam upon the floor which moves into the room.

"Annette?" I ask.

"Yes, Paul, I'm so sorry to wake you at this hour."

I glance at my watch—3 a.m.—and adjust the sheet to cover my briefs.

Annette approaches, but before she reaches my bed, she stoops to collect the box of matches which she uses to light the candle.

"Xavier told me you wouldn't arrive until later this morning," I tell her.

She sits beside me. "I asked Martin to fly me back early from Lusaka."

"Why? You had to fly through the night."

She places a hand on my forearm, a maneuver I've grown accustomed to. "There's something I need to tell you."

"What is it?"

"While I was in Lusaka, I received a call from my friend, Felice, in Danjou. You remember her, don't you—the older woman who shielded me from the jihadists?"

"Of course! What did she say?"

"It seemed quite trivial at first, but then afterwards when thinking about her tone of voice, I became concerned. She told me she was having a spat about money with her cousin, Innocent Mbewe. Apparently she borrowed a sum from him a year ago with the promise that she'd repay him by now, but she hasn't been able to muster the funds."

"Was she hoping you'd help her?"

"No, she made it clear she'd refuse money from me. She believes Innocent has blown things out of proportion and wanted me to convey this observation to you in case you see changes in Innocent's behavior."

"I've seen no changes at all," I say. "To the contrary, I'm happy that he and Xavier have struck a friendship over professional football. They've discussed the matter passionately both times we've been here."

"That's good," Annette says. "Perhaps this will blow over." She shifts her weight as if to stand but only tepidly.

"Wait," I tell her. "There's something else I'd like to talk about."

She slides further onto the bed and crosses her legs. The hem of her white linen dress rides halfway up her tan thigh. Buttons run down the front of the dress from an open collar to her waist where a beige belt encircles her. A pair of Espadrille platform sandals with linen straps completes her wardrobe.

"What is it you want to discuss?" she asks.

Shirtless, I lean against the wall. "Two days ago, before I left for Lusaka with Martin and Alexander, you shared the proverb, *Show me your friend, and I will show you your character.* Why did you do that?"

She looks at the candle on the table beside me. Its light creates embers of orange, red, and yellow in her wavy hair that falls to her shoulders. The same light finds a slit between her lips and glimmers upon the moist surfaces. Before long, the lips move but only barely as she whispers, "You tether me, Paul, don't you?" she says.

"What do you mean?"

"You hold me accountable for things I say, and I like that; it grounds me."

In the silence, she peers at me with her head tilted as if to test my resolve to hold a gaze. We come to a draw.

"The painting I did of the island in Ireland," she continues. "You wanted to know all about it and how it fit into my life, and now, you ask about the African proverb."

"Yes, because you provided no context with it."

She chuckles but it's more an act of reflection than humor. "I find myself saying things to you, Paul, that are really directed to me. You have that effect on me."

"Are you saying you shared the proverb for your own benefit?"

"In a sense."

"What were you seeking by reciting it?"

Gazing upon the candle, she repeats it now: "*Show me your friend, and I will show you your character.*"

I wait for her to continue, but because she doesn't I reach for her hand. I succeed in drawing her eyes but she appears distant now, drawn, it seems, to a far-off land.

"Annette, the proverb," I remind her.

"Yes, the proverb," she repeats. "I shared it with you because I've fallen short."

"Short of what?"

"Who I'd like to be."

I squeeze her hand. "Go on..."

"Choices...*my* choices...they've left me where I am," she says.

"And where's that?"

"Bereft."

"*Bereft?* That implies deprivation or lack of something. Is that what you mean?"

"Yes."

I sense the need to be cautious as her responses, curt as they are, warn me she may flee at any time to that far-off land.

"What are you deprived of?" I ask.

"Respect," she replies. "I've lived without it forever, it seems."

"No, that can't be," I tell her gently. "The work you do commands respect from many, myself included."

The candle lures her again but only after a tear streaks her cheek. I wipe it with the back of my fingers before gathering her hair on one side which I tuck behind an ear so I can see her face unobstructed.

"Respect must come from within, Paul, and I lost it long ago."

"Why?"

"Do you know the term, *laicization?*"

"I've heard of it. It has to do with priests, doesn't it?"

"Yes, it refers to clergy losing privileges of ministry, but it's important to distinguish it from *defrocking* which implies a forced removal by a governing body. In my case, I requested revocation of my rights to exercise the functions of an ordained minister."

"Why did you do that?"

"Because I did something terrible," she replies. "It was totally unacceptable behavior for a pastor."

I wait for her to continue, but she remains silent with her eyes upon the candle. "Annette, what did you do?" I ask her.

She runs a hand through her loose hair on the side opposite me. "I ruined a marriage."

I slip out from the sheet and swing my legs over the bed to sit beside her. Holding her, I feel her shoulders undulate as she weeps. "How long ago was that?" I ask.

"Twelve years ago," she cries. "I was twenty-five at the time and recently ordained."

I feel completely ill-equipped to counsel someone who in the course of her professional training has garnered skills far greater than mine. "Forgiveness, Annette," I say. "Isn't that what it boils down to?"

"Can one *be* forgiven for shattering a marriage which cast three children away from their father?" She looks at me, her eyes red now. "Before that happened, I sneered at the power of lust but no longer."

I squeeze her tightly and rest my head against hers.

She clenches my hand. "But for the first time in a long, long while, Paul, I see the possibility of liking myself again, and do you know why?"

I shake my head gently, feeling the warm skin of her temple against my cheek.

"Because...I feel...*you* have allowed me to become your friend, and if that's true, I see character within me with which I can live again." She removes a tissue from her purse and wipes her eyes. "Isn't that what the proverb means when it says, *Show me your friend, and I will show you your character?* You're helping me find a part of me to like again."

I place a hand under her chin, lift it gently, and kiss her lips. My heart throbs in the act of kissing again not just because months—years, really—have passed since I pressed my lips to a woman's this way, but also because the last I knew of love, it was to fall out of it. I cup her cheeks in my hands and feel warmth no less than that created by the circles she makes with her palm along my bare chest. With each revolution, she alters the contour of her hand, at once using the heel before switching to fingertips. As if to keep me guessing what her next move might be, she traces an arc alongside my navel in the shape of the moon outside. She becomes playful, then, dabbing my belly button before grazing its inner lining with a sole fingertip. For a moment, she retracts to peer at me with smiling eyes, but the attraction of our mouths reunites us as I pull her atop me.

After two, I lose count of the buttons I undo along the front of her dress, perhaps because my hands stray to explore the curves beneath the fabric. In one ear, I feel Annette introduce the tip of her tongue which she slides along the aural perimeter. I refuse to allow my ear to indulge solely in her mouth which I reclaim with mine. If there are sounds to be heard, they come from straps unsnapping, buttons relinquishing, and clothes falling upon the floor. They are soft sounds that befit the softness of Annette's skin which I now lay upon.

Through an open window comes the music of Africa's night—frogs that peep rather than croak; cicadas that screech, scream, and warble at the same time; and, most pleasing to me, a doleful beat of a drum from a village far away. Together, the sounds are a chorus to my ears, and I allow my body to writhe in their rhythm, a rhythm that rises and falls, gives and takes, and comes yet refuses to leave.

7

A KNOCK ON my door awakens me, and I panic at the prospect of greeting a visitor with Annette beside me in bed. I rub the sleep from my eyes to gather my wits. In growing lucidity, I realize Annette is no longer with me because she slipped away before sunrise to return to her room.

I don a pair of briefs and go to the door. "Who is it?" I ask.

"*Nudume*, we are awake!" Benji announces.

I open the door to find the boys' faces beaming. "It's six o'clock," I inform them.

"Yes, but we cannot sleep anymore! We are excited to leave for Intanda!"

"Very well, make your beds and get packed. I'll meet you in the sitting room after I shower."

After dressing, I carry my bag upstairs where I find Innocent Mbewe with the boys drinking tea in the sitting room.

"Good morning, *nudume*," Innocent says. "Help yourself to tea."

"I see our group from Saysha is on an early schedule," I reply.

"I wanted to make sure I saw you before you leave today," Innocent says. "Should we collect another urine specimen from Mr. Treadwill now that he has been on Prussian blue capsules for two days?"

"That's an excellent idea, particularly since we may be gone for three days."

"I will ensure the specimen is collected," Innocent adds, "and I will ask Martin when he will fly to Lusaka next so I can deliver the urine for testing as soon as possible."

I'm impressed with Innocent's attitude and work ethic. I see no evidence whatsoever of resentment spilling over from his financial quarrel with his aunt, Felice, in Danjou.

"You'll be a busy man, Innocent," I tell him. "Helping in the village clinic and traveling to Lusaka as you can."

"It is good, *nudume*," he replies. "I am enjoying being in Uku-tetema."

I pour a cup of tea but have barely added milk when Benji summons me to the window. He points excitedly toward the watering hole where a thin veil of mist hovers above it.

"Can you see what is happening?" he asks.

With the sun having yet to rise sufficiently to cast rays directly upon the area, I see only mist and a grove of trees on each side of the water. "What are you referring to?" I ask him.

He shuffles excitedly. "At the far side of the water, do you see the lions?" He hands me a pair of binoculars.

I lift them to my eyes and after orienting myself I find the target of his excitement. "I do," I say. Five lions congregate at the water, some drinking while others rest, among them a cub.

"Now, look to the right side of the water among the trees," Benji instructs. "What do you see?"

I scan the area and detect motion. Looking more closely, I see a herd of elephants approaching the watering hole. "Oh, oh, conflict!" I warn.

"No, there will be order," he states. "Just watch."

Even from a distance, the elephants bring distress to the pride. The lions at rest stand while those that had been drinking lift their heads and turn toward the open grassland beyond the watering hole. A lioness creeps closer to her cub and hovers beside it protectively. Undeterred, the elephants continue toward the watering hole, their leader an enormous male. In the middle of the herd, sandwiched between adults, a calf scurries to keep pace. When the elephants emerge from the trees and begin crossing a grassy section toward the water, the lions slink away without the slightest sign of protest. For now, the elephants reign at the site.

"Ah, the watering hole," Xavier Treadwill says, patting my back.

I lower the binoculars. "Quite a scene," I reply. "I've never seen lions bow to any other animal before."

"There's a pecking order, for sure," Xavier says, "and that becomes very clear at watering holes." He steps forward to address me more directly. "In fact, we shall use an online watering hole to become predators ourselves."

"What do you mean by 'online watering hole'?"

"You're not aware of the term?" he asks.

"No."

He displays a look of resoluteness. "I'll explain what it is as we travel to Intanda. For now, let me just say this: We're going to ambush your buddy, Gary Y. Simsbury, using a digital watering hole because I hold the bastard responsible for poisoning me." He reaches for my arm as he addresses Benji and Oscar. "Come, boys, let's get you a hearty breakfast before we depart."

INNOCENT MBEWE SITS proudly beside his good friend, Xavier Treadwill, at the breakfast table. No hour is too early or late to discuss football, and they do that now with vigor. In less than thirty-six hours, the national squads of Argentina and Brazil will play a World Cup qualification match. The men root for an Argentine victory because a starting striker wearing the blue and white of Argentina was born in Zambia before emigrating to Argentina as a youth.

I want to interrupt their conversation to ask whether Annette will come with us to Intanda but refrain from doing so. After our liaison hours earlier, I can't take the chance of exposing our romance by showing interest in her.

Xavier concludes our breakfast with a review of Innocent's duties while we're in Intanda: He's to assist at a clinic this morning in a village thirty kilometers away and then return to the lodge to fly with Martin to Lusaka to deliver a urine sample. Following that trip, he'll return to Uku-tetema to continue helping at the clinic. We'll reunite in the lodge three days from now.

"And there'll be much football to discuss then," Innocent declares.

"Happy discussion, I hope," Xavier adds, pushing back from the table.

We part ways with instructions to meet in the driveway in fifteen minutes to leave for Intanda. I rush to my room where I place a call to the soldier from the Zambian armed forces.

"Dr. Rider," he says upon answering, "thank you for helping my mother. She is breathing easier now."

"I think she'll be fine with the new medicines," I reply. "My larger concern is the safety of Saysha. Will a unit be deployed there to protect it?"

"No," he replies, "our troops are needed along the border with D R Congo."

"But Saysha was attacked already. I'm worried it's still vulnerable." I inform him of my partnership with Xavier and how our alliance has fueled the jihadists' commitment to kill us.

"I'm aware of your work in Uku-tetema," he replies. "I will approach my superiors again regarding Saysha."

I thank the soldier and leave the room to start for the driveway but stop at Annette's door. I knock on it softly.

"Who is it?" Annette calls.

I open the door and quickly slip in.

"Paul," she says, sitting up in bed. She collects her hair and directs it behind her shoulders. "What time is it?"

"It's early still," I reply, sitting beside her. "We're about to leave for Intanda, and I wanted to see if you'd be coming, but obviously you're not."

"No, Xavier asked that I accompany a team of guards elsewhere to ward off poachers." She takes my hand. "But I really wanted to come to Intanda. I'm sorry I can't."

With time running, I feel the need to go. "When you and I drove from Danjou to Saysha the night we met, you told me you had a daughter but have said nothing about her since."

She frees her hand and looks away.

"Tell me about her," I plead. "I want to know who she is."

"Paul, this really isn't the time—"

"It *is* the time! I have decisions to make, and I really want to know more about you!"

"Some things are best left untold," she replies. Tenacity grips her voice.

"Very well," I say, standing. "I thought our intimacy might have meant more to you." I start for the door.

"Don't leave!"

I stop with my back to her.

"You met my daughter three days ago—*both* of them, actually."

I grimace. When I turn, I find Annette sitting on the side of the bed in a nightgown.

"The *twins?*" I ask. "They're yours?"

She nods.

"But I asked Xavier about them when I first arrived and who their mother was."

"I know what his answer was: He told you the mother of the twins had died. That's how he describes our relationship."

"You're *dead* to him?"

"Yes…"

I reach for the door knob. "I'm sorry, I had no business asking—"

"You had every right to ask! I should've told you about the girls earlier! The reason I didn't was because Xavier doesn't want people to know I'm their mother. Still, I do what I can to remain in my daughters' lives, but he's the one who makes the decisions as to their welfare."

"That's not the Annette I know, the photographer who risks her life to document the abuses of wildlife. You're a veteran of conflict, yet I hear abdication."

"*Abdication?* You have no children, so you wouldn't know what I'm going through! My daughters' marrow is my marrow and their hearts my heart. *You* chose to forgo such biologic connections, but I will cherish them the rest of my life even though I've been relegated a diminished role by their father." She pauses. "Did you notice the night the twins were present they didn't call me 'mother' or nestle with me?"

"Of course. It made me dismiss the notion you were their mother even though my initial impressions suggested otherwise."

"What do you mean?"

"The similarities are obvious! They have your beautiful eyes, your zest, and they carry themselves with the same hope and promise you hold!"

She lowers her eyes. "Xavier's trained them well. They know when company is present to keep their distance from me."

"Xavier told me last night that he'd sent the girls away."

"That's right, because he didn't want them to be an issue here. He's uncomfortable with our present estrangement."

She stands and goes to an antique roll top desk that holds a sealed envelope. Delivering it to me, she says, "Take this. I wrote it after we made love, and every word stands."

I slip the envelope into my pocket. "I need to go."

She points to my pocket. "I inked those words rather than text or email them to keep them from Xavier. He monitors everything I transmit electronically."

I open the door.

"Paul."

I stop but refrain from turning. In the silence, I hear her approach. From behind me, she lifts a hand and rubs a palm across my cheek. "Be safe."

SHOCKED BY WHAT I've learned, I climb the stairs to the foyer. I feel like a courier carrying a secret document containing highly sensitive information. I remove the envelope from my shirt pocket and transfer it to a more secure one in my trousers. I do so none too soon as Xavier meets me halfway down the steps.

"I was just coming to look for you," he says.

"I was on the phone with the soldier from the Zambian armed forces," I tell him. I summarize the outcome of our discussion.

We exit the lodge where I see a caravan of seven Land Rovers parked in the driveway. The final one is a combat vehicle with a gun turret. Standing beside each vehicle is a driver and one or more guards armed with assault rifles. Before the lead Land Rover, Oscar and Benji wait with other staff members I've not seen before. With a wave of his arm, Xavier assembles the group at the base of the steps.

"Good morning, all," he says. "I will make introductions and provide a brief overview of our mission to Intanda so we may depart without delay."

He introduces Oscar, Benji, and me before turning to his staff. Each raises a hand when called, eighteen in all. In addition to drivers and guards, a cook, a mechanic, and three electricians will travel with us.

"As for the vehicles," Xavier continues, "we will travel together because of the difficult terrain. We're amply stocked with fuel, food, and water for three days, and because our mobile phones will not work, each vehicle is equipped with a satellite phone." He points to the vehicles. "The antennas will help the satphones connect to satellites in low orbit about Earth."

"How secure are the communications?" I ask.

He smiles. "A while back, I would have said 'not very,' but that was one of the accomplishments of my software firm: We developed an encryption algorithm to secure satphone communications. So far, hackers haven't been able to reverse-engineer the algorithm." His smile broadens. "Of course, it costs a pretty penny to subscribe to the service."

He completes the briefing with seating assignments which, to the delight of Oscar and Benji, put them with their accustomed drivers as I join Xavier in a vehicle in the center of the caravan.

A short distance from the lodge, the unpaved road disappears altogether and we weave through tufts of grass and around rocks and trees flush with new leaves awaiting the rains due to begin any day. Our route is a steady uphill one that presses our backs to the seats, all the more so when we encounter especially steep sections. A half hour after departing the lodge, we reach a summit and stop for a brief view. In the distance, I see ever so faintly the outline of the ridge above the Amalumbo River where we began our journey into Uku-tetema. Stretching before it is a golden plain we crossed to reach a series of low-lying hills that led to a meandering river valley where Henry and I stopped to watch a black lechwe fall prey to lions.

We drop through woodlands to reach a savanna where herds of zebra and antelope graze only to stop at a river bed. With the dry season at its peak, the water level has receded to a fraction of its maximal flow, leaving sand banks on both sides.

"Come," Xavier tells me, "let's stretch."

Members from the other vehicles are already walking toward a mound of plant material along a sand bank. Among them are Benji and Oscar who, along with their drivers, crouch as they move slowly toward the mound. Before long, we stop by their side some fifteen meters from the site that captures their attention.

"A crocodile," Xavier whispers. "Do you see it?"

Stretched across a flat rock beside the mound is a tan and black croc roughly two meters long with a distinctly slender snout.

"*Crocodilus cataphractus*," Xavier mutters, "one of four species of crocs found in Africa, the others being the Nile, desert, and dwarf crocodiles. Note the distinctly slender snout which gives rise to its better-known name, the 'slender-snouted crocodile.' "

Benji, hearing Xavier speak, shuffles to his side. "Is the mound a nest?" he asks.

"It is," Xavier replies, "which tells us this croc is a female. In the nest are eggs which will hatch before the rains begin and the river floods. In the meantime, the mother will guard the nest against predators such as the monitor lizard, badgers, and even hyenas."

Henry, Benji's driver today, joins us. "When the juveniles hatch, you can sometimes hear them chirp. It is then the mother helps them clear the nest."

We return to our vehicles and cross the river which, at its deepest points, reaches the undersurface of our chassis. When the rains come, Xavier tells me, it will be impossible to make this crossing. "There will be much more to see as we drive," he tells me, "but for now I need your attention for a pressing matter regarding your former employer, Gary Y. Simsbury."

He removes a pad of paper, opens it to a blank page, and readies a pen. "This morning I told you that we planned to ambush Simsbury using a technique called a 'watering hole.' Let me explain what I mean by that."

He draws a box at the top of the page and prints *TransNational Oil* within it. "Simsbury's employer," he says. Below the box, he adds a circle and labels it, *HelpOurOilWorkers.com*. "This," he says, running his pen around the circle, "is a website established recently to solicit donations for oil workers laid off in the United States as a result of falling prices. Simsbury has been a vocal proponent of the effort. For example, within TransNational Oil, he matches employee donations dollar-for-dollar with his own funds."

"He can afford to," I observe. "He's paid millions."

"The bottom line is this: *HelpOurOilWorkers.com* is a trusted website visited not only by the public but, most important to me, by employees of TransNational Oil." He draws a bold line to connect the box and circle. "I'm taking advantage of this trusted relationship."

"How?"

"By launching what's called a 'watering hole attack' on the website. While we travel to Intanda, Alexander and others are coordinating the attack. They've begun by inserting an 'exploit'—clandestine computer code—into *HelpOurOilWorkers.com* so that when employees of TransNational Oil visit the site, their computers become infected with a malware that allows us to access TransNational's network." He smiles wryly. "That's why it's called a 'watering hole attack': like lions waiting in hiding at a watering hole, we attack unsuspecting prey that comes for a drink."

"Surely the company has defenses to ward off such attacks."

"Defenses, yes, but the question is: How robust are they? Having worked with computer security for over a decade, I've learned that vulnerabilities exist in every system. From an attacker's standpoint, the goal is to identify the vulnerabilities before they're patched."

"I don't know," I reply. "I'm skeptical."

His eyes round into fiery balls. "Put a target before me, Paul, and I'll hit it eventually. It may take several attempts, but I always get what I want."

I detect the same hostility I encountered in Xavier when he displayed the text I'd sent Annette reading, *For the first time, I want to stay put.* Then, as now, his angry eyes made me feel I was his opponent. I appreciate anew Annette's concern for his ability to monitor electronic communications.

He stirs as if discomfited by being too harsh with me. "Remember, I earned over a billion dollars for selling my software security firm in Silicon Valley."

"Was it your hacking tools or defenses against such attacks the buyer sought?" I ask.

"Are they not two sides of the same coin?"

"I don't know; cybersecurity isn't my forte."

"It *should* be. We're all prone to attack, yet few understand the importance of behavior in preventing such attacks. Let me give you an example, one involving a former director of the Central Intelligence Agency in your country who had his personal email hacked."

He relays the details of an episode that culminated in hackers discovering classified documents the CIA director had sent to his personal account. Shaking his head, he concludes, "The guy was terribly careless, but things like this happen all the time. As a security specialist, I seize upon lapses like these to pry into others' lives. I'm doing that now with your ex-employer's wife."

"Simsbury's wife?" I ask.

"Yup."

"What are you doing to her?"

"I'm digging into her personal data." He pauses. "Do you recall the speech I told you about earlier that Gary Simsbury delivered to a group called America's Volunteers?"

"The one in which he joked about his title at TransNational earning him the moniker 'viper'?"

"Yes, that one. Turns out, the venue for the speech was a fundraiser, and he spoke right after a cocktail hour. I'm guessing he had one too many drinks because he divulged his wife's mobile phone number."

"Why?"

"It was in jest. Citing his admiration for the work America's Volunteers did, he invited employees of the non-governmental organization to call him at any time if they thought he could help them. He added that if he didn't return their call within twenty-four hours, they could call his wife. He shared her mobile number with them at that point. In the transcript of the speech, one sees the word *laughter* in brackets following the sharing of the number. I doubt he'd laugh if he knew what we're doing with his wife's number now."

"What *are* you doing with it?"

"For starters, we used a reverse call directory to identify the service provider in Houston. With that piece in-hand, I called an actress yesterday I know who lives in Los Angeles. She's an incredible impersonator. I asked her to deliver a script Alexander and I wrote to weasel key information from the mobile phone service provider regarding Mrs. Simsbury's account."

"Oh, come on! Companies train their employees to resist such requests."

"Tell my actress friend that. Posing as a subcontractor to the service provider, she said she was working on a high-priority client account and needed access to the provider's customer database. The timing couldn't have been better because a nasty storm had just deluged the Houston area and had downed trees, power lines, and a cell phone tower. All hands were on deck to repair the damage."

"Still," I protest, "the technician at the service provider would've demanded certification of some sort before releasing access to a customer database."

"The actress was prepared for that. She provided a four-digit code of the type the service provider issues to its employees and subcontractors."

"Was it a valid code?"

"No, but it did the job. Immediately after providing the code, my friend began sobbing about the stress she was under dealing with irate customers who demanded immediate restoration of service. In an attempt to console her, the technician gave her access to the customer database."

"So she cracked the system."

"Yup, which allowed us to go into the database and get what we needed: Mrs. Simsbury's account number, a four-digit PIN, her email address, and the last four digits of a credit card. Our actress friend then called the internet service provider and told them she was Mrs. Simsbury and had locked herself out of her account after forgetting her password. When a technician asked for the last four digits on Simsbury's credit card, the actress provided it. That got us a temporary password which allowed us to infiltrate the account. We're scouring it as we speak."

"She'll realize soon she's been locked out of her own account."

"So be it. We'll have gotten everything we need by that time." He raises a hand to his chin in thought. "What did I tell you earlier about human behavior? It opens doors for people like me to conduct social engineering attacks of this sort." He looks out the window before returning his eyes to mine. "And now, a question about Annette's behavior," he says.

My pulse quickens.

"What did she mean when she sent you a text saying, *It's the middle of the night, yet I think of you?*"

"I didn't realize you were copied on that text."

"Come, Paul, let's be honest with each other."

"Okay, I'll be honest: Texts are a private matter."

"Am I not privy to the emotions of the woman who mothered my children?"

He might as well have punched me in the stomach. Breathless, I reply: "Only if she chooses to share those emotions with you."

He smiles. "Thank you, you answered my next question. I needn't ask it."

"What was it to be?" I riposte.

He studies me before responding. "I was going to ask whether Annette told you the twins are her girls. It's obvious from your response to my question that she did because, otherwise, you'd have shown surprise when I told you."

As skilled as he is with cybersecurity, he failed to decipher my breathlessness. "I showed no surprise because I was thinking about the remaining words of the text you referred to, ones that went something like, *Xavier tells me you'll travel again to Uku-tetema with friends, and for that I'm grateful.* My guess is Annette was thinking of me in the middle of the night because she was glad I'd be traveling with Oscar and Benji."

He ponders the response. "Alright, I'll give you the benefit of the doubt on that, and for that reason, I owe you an apology for being impertinent."

"Why didn't you tell me earlier that Annette mothered your girls? When I examined you in your office the day we met, I asked where the mother of the twins was."

"Yes, I recall that, and I didn't answer your question because I found it to be intrusive."

"*Intrusive?*" I ask derisively. "You pry into others' communications like a voyeur!"

He grimaces as if he detects a foul odor. "Well, now you know the truth: Annette is the mother of my twins. And lest you think

I'm withholding other key facts, I will tell you now that we never married. I proposed to her repeatedly, but she demurred."

"Why?"

"Cultural differences kept us apart." He peers through the windshield and appears to be relieved by what he sees. "Ah, we're nearing our lunch stop. I hope your appetite is good."

Indeed, my stomach grumbles, but not from hunger. It twists with concern about how much Xavier knows about my involvement with Annette. I think of the walls of the guest rooms at the lodge and wonder whether they harbor microphones or hidden cameras. A burning sensation sears my thigh at the spot where Annette's envelope presses into my skin.

THE SATPHONE IN the Land Rover rings. The call comes from Alexander at the lodge who reports that the National Assembly in Lusaka has scheduled the vote on Uku-tetema for three days from now. More troubling, a friend of Xavier's in the capital with ears to the ground reports a team of oil surveyors is about to leave Lusaka for Intanda to conduct a clandestine assessment of the land for oil. The team is confident bountiful supplies will be proven to underlie the surface which, in turn, will sway legislators sitting on the fence to vote against the bill to designate Uku-tetema as a national park.

"No time to stop!" Xavier announces. "We will eat lunch as we travel!"

Between bites of sandwiches, we finalize plans for setting up laser trip lines at all four entryways to Intanda. I express concern that, unlike the Amazon rainforest with its ample supply of trees, the barren slopes of Intanda will offer few places to secure sensors, cameras, and other instruments. In addition, I remind Xavier that a camera-based surveillance system will have to perform twenty-four-seven, meaning its nighttime shots need to be as lucid as those taken during the day. Because we couldn't get the resolution we desired with equipment on-hand in South Africa for nighttime infrared photographs, we decided to wire the trip lines to spotlights powered by rechargeable batteries to generate the needed flashes;

that meant solar panels would have to be wired to the batteries. Overall, not an easy setup with limited time in hostile terrain.

"We'll do what we can do," Xavier replies. "My land is about to be invaded!"

In the hours that pass, the sun morphs from a ball that blinds us through the windshield to a scalding iron overhead. Every mile is hard-fought, a journey of starts and stops, climbs and descents, accelerations and decelerations. Although we have air conditioning, it's insufficient to keep the backs of our shirts from sticking to the seats. Dirt cakes the vehicles. At one point, we stop long enough for Benji and Oscar to climb atop a Land Rover where they lie on their stomachs with their bodies tethered by canvas belts to the rack. It's a transfer Xavier and I approved so the boys could search for cheetahs known to inhabit the area. To protect themselves from dirt and blowing debris, they wear aprons tied around their heads with slits for the eyes. The fabric flows over their necks in a fashion that reminds me of the traditional Middle Eastern headdress, the keffiyeh, but rather than having the distinctive standard checkered pattern, theirs are solid white. As I watch them several vehicles ahead, heads turning one way and another in search of elusive cheetahs, I recall scenes from *Lawrence of Arabia*, only here the horse the boys ride is metal.

From the ground, I get a much closer view of the mountain ranges that comprise the funnel-like formation I first noticed while flying in the Beechcraft. With each kilometer traversed, the mountains close in as we approach the funnel's spout. They are rugged, inhospitable mountains that support only grass and a few low-lying trees. Periodically, narrow grooves sliced through the mountains provide corridors through which herds of antelope and zebra migrate to Lake Tanganyika during dry seasons. The dirt kicked up during these migrations explains why the corridor walls are darker than the tan of higher elevations.

As we drive further, the mountains taper into hills, but the lower elevations do little to stymie claustrophobia I feel from being squeezed into an ever narrowing valley. Contributing to my unease is a darkening sky ahead which threatens to unleash the season's first rainstorm, one that, if strong enough, could trigger flash flooding. I point to the sky, but before I speak, I notice the black comes not from clouds but from a mountain range running perpendicular to the direction we travel. Using binoculars, I see the mountains are lifelessly gray, jagged to the point of hostility, and devoid of plants. On closer inspection, the jags along their peaks consist of knife-like projections that remind me of glass shards cemented to the tops of brick walls that enclose expensive properties in some nations. I wonder whether nature has mounted the rocky blades to prevent travelers from crossing the mountains.

In short order, we drop in elevation, and this causes my ears to pop at several points. Through the windows comes a heavier, warmer, more humid air that leaves my hair sticky and matted. Without regret, we leave what has been a relentlessly bumpy, rocky ride for a smoother course along an increasingly sandy surface. Against the windshield, I see a small blob strike the glass to leave a black smudge. I watch the guard in the front seat extract a rag from the glove compartment box. After moistening it with isopropyl alcohol, he leans out his window and reaches across the windshield to remove the smudge.

"What was that?" I ask him.

"Oil," he replies.

"From the engine?"

"No, from the sand."

I turn to Xavier for an explanation, but he dismisses me by saying, "You'll understand shortly."

After driving another hour, we reach a sandy cul-de-sac several kilometers wide which is framed on two sides by the hills we've just traveled between while the dark mountains I saw earlier through the binoculars enclose it. Stopped at the base of those dark mountains now, I can see that whatever it was that struck the Earth millions of years ago to create them left towering deposits of greyish-black rock that stretch as far as the eye can see in both directions. Curiously, a ground-to-sky opening slices through the mountains in the middle of the cul-de-sac in a manner that makes me think of the Red Sea's parting in biblical times. The aperture resembles a gateway that, at its base, is wide enough to allow several vehicles to pass through side-by-side. Forming the floor of the gateway is a bed of sand blacker than any I've seen before. Its surface is rippled from an incessant wind that blows at us from the interior of the gateway. Although I crane my neck, I cannot see what lies beyond the gateway because of its higher elevation from where we're parked.

We remain in our vehicles in silence, foreigners in a strange land. About us, strewn across the cul-de-sac, are black rocks of varying sizes and shapes. I unleash my imagination and envision the rocks dropping from a giant celestial pepper shaker that hovered over the cul-de-sac. In doing so, a pepper corn must have spilled from the shaker which explains why a massive boulder now rests about forty meters before the gateway.

"Intanda," Xavier whispers, pointing to the gateway. His tone is reverent, his demeanor spiritual, and he clasps his hands before his chest as if praying. Before long, he opens his door and walks slowly to the boulder where he stops to face the gateway. In like style, his compatriots leave their vehicles to join him while I remain behind with Oscar and Benji.

From the gathering beside the boulder, Xavier summons us with a wave. I take the boys by the hand across the sand to the boulder where we stop along the outside of the group. Before us, sunlight strikes the mountains to ignite the slopes in orange and red, yet there is more to the palette: somehow, whether from mineral content or simple light diffraction, the reds and oranges shed hints of blue, green, and yellow. Meanwhile, through the gateway come miniature bursts of windswept black sand that sparkle like glitter before settling. In all, the dazzling lights and colors combine the beauty of sunsets, fireflies, aurora borealis, and more.

Xavier leaves the center of the group to stake a position in front where he falls to his knees. Behind him, others follow suit, each holding arms outstretched and palms skyward. Out of respect, the boys and I do the same, our knees sinking into a bed of salt-and-pepper sand. Together, we form a pew of three in a church whose faith is yet to be defined.

From the front, Xavier begins to chant in Bemba, only snippets of which I understand.

Oscar, kneeling beside me, edges closer and, lifting his head to mine, whispers in interpretation. Because of the whistling wind, he moves so close I feel his lips graze my ear. Using a finger, I plug the opposite one to hear him as well as I can.

Through my interpreter, I hear a story I know well by now, one about an Egyptian queen who revered a cat goddess named Bastet. Xavier praises the goddess for creating the leopards of Intanda and the queen for dispatching a delegation to search the world for the most beautiful cat only to find it here.

Suddenly, there's singing from the group as the congregation sways with clapping hands.

Oscar looks at me apologetically. "I do not understand because they are singing in the dialect of Uku-tetema."

On my other side, Benji leans into me before withdrawing as both he and Oscar join in the swaying and clapping, each, it seems, lured by a primeval rhythm that speaks to their souls. I feel I've become the orphan now as the boys find spiritual parents in their African brethren. As hard as I try to immerse in the moment, I remain apart, perhaps because I'm foreign to spiritual events, but also because I'm awkward at dancing and ill at ease expressing emotions with body movements. At the same time, I'm drawn to the afternoon light on the mountains, light that now features a collage of yellows and golds. I think of Annette and wonder whether she, too, has knelt here among the parish of Uku-tetema, and if she has, whether the worship rekindled the flames that led her to become a minister in the first place.

The singing ends, and Xavier turns to his parishioners. As I look about, I see faces transfixed by the service he's led so far. He instructs us to sit, and I wiggle side-to-side to create a comfortable contour in the sand.

"Before we begin our work," Xavier tells us, "it is only right to remember why we are here. This land is our mother and our father, our aunt and uncle, our grandmother and grandfather. We may divorce the land, but the land never divorces us; it keeps our feet to the ground as long as we exist. 'Ah,' you may say, 'but what about Earth's waters? Are they not our mother and father, aunt and uncle, grandmother and grandfather?' To that I answer: no, they are not. The waters are merely the tears of heaven cradled by the land, for beneath the rivers, lakes, and oceans is more land, forever holding the waters as an urn holds ashes."

He turns briefly to the mountains before facing us again. Raising his arms, he makes a scooping motion as if to lift us onto his palms. "In each of us resides a mountain, one that becomes taller with every challenge we face. We spend our lives along the mountainsides, sometimes climbing, other times resting. At times we slip, fall, and injure ourselves; debris strikes us from above; storms drench us; and gales knock us down. Yet all of this grooms us for our true calling in life—to be stewards of the earth."

Before me, I view a different Xavier Treadwill from the one I've come to know. Gone is the cold and calculating efficiency of a wealthy entrepreneur and businessman, replaced by a caring teacher and leader. Absent, too, is the subtle yet unmistakable drive to command his surroundings, replaced by an earnest submission to a higher good. At the gateway to Intanda, a software mogul has become a shepherd. Figuratively, I find myself standing between Annette on one side and Xavier on another, each tugging me in different directions—Annette pulling at my heart, Xavier at my soul. I want to abide in each, yet I cannot because of the gaping divide which separates them.

My thoughts yield to Xavier's benediction. I center myself on his raised arm and extended palm as he instructs us with the words, "Now go forth into Intanda, my brothers. Love the land; respect the land; protect the land; and may the blessings of our goddess, a queen, and the leopards keep you forever."

Suddenly, I'm moved to tears. Although I was unable to connect to the moment earlier, I connect now. Xavier's benediction has lassoed me and brought me into the fold, and I feel one with the flock. I stand, wipe my eyes, and allow my fellow congregants to pass me to return to the vehicles. Although the terrain I occupy differs starkly from the Amazon, déjà vu overcomes me: Once again, my principal mission is to protect a cat, and I'm one with nature. I view the mission before me as being more important than any aligned with my day-to-day work. It transcends earthly duties, elevates me to inter-planetary domains, and lures me deep into the cosmos. If there's to be order in the universe, I seek to do my part to uphold it.

"Paul, when you're ready, I need your help," Xavier says.

I lower my eyes from the mountain to see him accompanying the boys across the sand. He's been patient with me as if he knows I need time to return to the here-and-now.

I cross the sand to the convoy abuzz now in activity. As some pitch tents, others unload supplies. Beside the vehicles, Xavier sits on a stool while the boys carry equipment for the trip lines to a central collection point.

"Are you alright, Xavier?" I ask, concerned about his paleness.

"It has been a long journey," he replies. "Allow me to catch my breath."

I take his pulse. With fingertips pressed into his skin, I draw comfort in feeling his heartbeats. Our connection deepens. "Yes, catch your breath," I tell him. "You'll be fine."

A ring comes from the satphone.

"Henry, attend to that, please," Xavier tells the driver.

As Henry departs, Xavier addresses me: "As you can see, we're establishing base camp here. Shortly, you and I will work with a team to install the first trip line in the opening before us." He glances at his watch. "With luck, we'll finish before dark. That will leave us all day tomorrow to install trip lines in the three remaining access points to Intanda."

From a satchel, he removes a map of northern Zambia which depicts the crescent and star of Uku-tetema. Pointing to the star, he slides a finger across Intanda to its westernmost point. "This is where we are," he says. His finger moves successively to the star's other three points. "Since these entryways are seventy-five to ninety kilometers apart from each other, and because it's virtually impossible to travel across the interior of Intanda on account of its sticky terrain, we'll divide into smaller teams tomorrow to install the trip lines at each entryway."

Henry reappears. "Alexander called to confirm the convoy has departed Lusaka for Intanda to survey the land for oil."

"Did he say what route they're taking?"

"They will go through Malawi and possibly Tanzania to approach Intanda from the northeast."

"Clever of them," Xavier states, "leaving Zambia to decoy their destination." He reflects a moment. "By going that way, they'll reach Intanda after dark tomorrow which will allow them to begin their survey under the cover of night."

On the map, I point to Intanda. "Which entryway do you think they'll choose?"

"Logically, it'd be the eastern one since it's closest to Malawi and Tanzania, but there's no telling." He points to the mountains. "They could even choose to drive around Intanda to enter through this gateway."

"That leaves us little time," I note.

"About thirty-two hours according to my calculation," Xavier replies, "which means we have to get trip lines installed at all four entryways by sunset tomorrow so we can leave before they arrive. I don't want to lose this chance to prove they've trespassed upon our land."

"I'm astounded they're moving forward without government permission," I note.

"It's a calculated gamble. If they can prove vast oil reserves exist here, they will sway votes in the National Assembly, and trespassing becomes meaningless."

"What about Zambian border authorities? Won't they inquire where the convoy is going as they leave the country?"

"They may inquire, but the drivers will provide fictitious destinations, and once they're in Malawi, they'll almost certainly re-enter Zambia at an uncontrolled site where no one will see them. The entire operation will be done in a stealthy fashion."

I seize the moment to call on a promise Xavier made to me. "Two days ago, while I was flying from Lusaka to Saysha, you told me that years ago your father had hired a surveyor to assess Intanda for oil. You promised you'd tell me the results of that survey when we reached Intanda." I glance about. "We're here."

Xavier winces in a fashion that tells me I've been indiscreet to call on his promise in a public arena. "Yes, I did, but you will recall I said I would do so only after you helped install the trip lines."

With effort, he stands.

"Henry," I say. "Do me a favor: Call Alexander at the lodge to confirm the urine specimen Xavier provided this morning was flown to Lusaka. I want to make sure it's there."

I STAND WITH others around a cart stacked with boxes containing supplies for the first laser trip line. Xavier and I have decided to involve everyone except those assigned to set up base camp in order to devise a strategy we'll replicate at the remaining three entryways tomorrow.

We march together across the sand with the cart in tow. Wide, inflatable wheels allow it to glide over the sand with a puller in front and a pusher in back. For good measure, Benji and Oscar attend to the sides to ensure the supplies stay put.

We pass six canvas tents in various stages of sprouting. In the center of the tent circle, the cook monitors a portable gas stove which heats two pots. Thirty meters beyond the circle perimeter, we halt at the base of a sand berm leading to the entryway.

Forming a line akin to ones used to pass sandbags in flood situations, we transfer the contents of the cart to the top of the berm. Xavier and I help each other with the climb, a tricky one because of sands that shift under our feet. With each step, a thickening layer of sticky black sand adheres to our boots to make successive steps harder. By the time we reach the top, I focus on my lead feet rather than the view ahead.

"What do you think?" Xavier asks.

I lift my eyes but find no words to respond. Before us, a channel cuts between mountain walls that rise to receive sky—no, not to *receive* sky but to *beckon* it. Here, nothing is passive; all is dynamic and purposeful. Here, ground pulls atmosphere to bring heaven to Earth; lungs inflate with inspiration and awe along with oxygen.

"Worshipful, is it not?" Xavier says.

Shifting light makes it difficult to ascertain the channel's length, all the more so because at the far end heat waves rise from a sea of black to blur the passage. For a moment, I feel I'm in a sizzling desert where mirages abscond with not only my eyesight, but my sense of reality.

A tug from an invisible force pulls me toward the heat waves until an arm restrains me.

"No, we'll go there later," Xavier says. "First we install the trip line."

Behind me, the equipment lies on a tarp: laser emitter, sensor, cables, cameras, and more. I ask for the electricians to join me. Three men step forward.

"We're fortunate," I tell them, "because we have grooves and ledges in the walls where we can install our equipment in hidden fashion."

"How high above the ground should we place the laser line?" an electrician asks.

"A meter and a half," I suggest. "That way, cameras will be triggered by the passing of humans or vehicles."

I address Xavier: "What do we know about the vehicles in the convoy?"

"There are about a dozen of them that range in size from jeeps to trucks."

"Tell me more about the trucks."

"All I know is some are very large and have enormous tires."

I recall my days in the Amazon when I watched a seismic survey take place in a remote region of the rainforest. I share my observations with the electricians now: "Seismic surveys have changed in the past few years. While the general strategy remains the same—sending vibrations into the earth and then recording seismic signals reflected from underground structures—the way the vibrations are created has changed. In former days, dynamite explosions were used, but now large trucks with vibrator pads send vibrations deep into the earth. The reflected waves are then captured by sensors laid over wide swaths of land. The sensors run to a recording truck where they're analyzed. The end product is a three-dimensional map of the area surveyed."

From behind the group, Henry appears. He breathes heavily from climbing the berm. "Xavier, you are needed on the satphone! Alexander has important news from the lodge!"

"Get things started!" Xavier implores as he leaves.

We examine the walls for sites to place the laser emitter and sensor. To my relief, we find them, but there's additional equipment to plan for—cameras, spotlights, laptop, solar panel, batteries, and even a satellite dish. Taking photos is only one task; transmitting them via satellite Internet to the lodge yet another.

Hidden cables will have to connect all the parts.

I prepare to assign tasks when I hear a falling object. The sound comes from a wall several meters into the channel, a clattering of the sort a walnut might make while dropping through a jagged crevice. Before long, a rock hurtles onto the sand.

I pick up the rock and search for its exit point. Looking up, I find a narrow passageway that rises at an angle through the wall. Although I can't see sky, light streams through the crack.

"The wind dislodged a rock from above," an electrician notes. "It fell through the crack."

"This could be good," I say. "Perhaps we can place our solar panel and other equipment at the top of the crack and drop the electric cables through it to the laser emitter, sensor, cameras, and spotlights."

Energized, the electricians begin working in the channel while I scale the slope in search of the crevice opening. The climb is challenging because of the slippery surface and sharp rocks. In one groove, I nearly place my hand on a scorpion that hides under a stick.

I come to a patch of rounded rock that reveals a crevice wide enough to swallow the leg of an unwary hiker. Stooping to look into it, I note the passage curves in a fashion that prevents me from seeing its entire trajectory, so I reach for a small rock and drop it into the opening. A series of pings follows as the rock descends. Placing my mouth over the crack, I shout, "Can you hear me down there?" Shortly, a voice below answers: "Yes, we hear you!"

I begin my way down but halt abruptly when I hear whistling from above. Searching the slopes, I discover two sets of arms waving at me from a ledge far up the mountain.

"Benji, Oscar!" I shout. "Come down right now!"

Even from afar, I see Benji place a finger across his lips for silence while he summons me with his other arm.

I rush up the incline but pay for my haste by tripping on a jutting stone. With knee skinned and heart racing, I pass boulders that seem primed to roll down the mountain but remain in place from stunted ridges beneath them. Against my better sense, I push off them to propel myself up and, in time, I reach a new geologic feature, one comprised of ledges that form a terrace along the mountainside. Looking up, I see a series of them separates me from the one Benji and Oscar occupy. Above the ledges, the mountain crests in knife-like projections.

One by one, I scale the ledges by placing my palms and stomach along their edges before swinging my legs up. A short crawl brings me to the next ledge which I mount in similar fashion. Along the way, I cut my hands and rip my shirt. For their part, the boys admonish me to climb as quietly as I can and, thankfully, they offer me their hands to conquer the final ledge.

Breathless, I ask, "What are you doing up here alone?"

Benji hands me a pair of binoculars and points to a spot lower on the mountain in a direction opposite from the one we've come. "Look carefully," he says. "Do you see the cave down there?"

I lift the binoculars and search the area he pointed to. "Yes, I see it."

"Look inside it now and tell me what you see."

I find it challenging to visualize the interior because part of the cave is illuminated by bars of sunlight streaming through cracks whereas other parts are relatively dark. As I adjust to the lighting, I make out a leopard and two cubs along the floor. Beside them is a carcass, an ungulate of some type.

"*Incredible!*" I whisper.

"The Intanda leopard," Benji announces, "the most beautiful cat in the world."

Until now, I'd dismissed the folklore of an Egyptian queen from ancient days who dispatched a delegation to search the world for the most beautiful feline. All malarkey, I concluded. Yet now, with legs trembling, I undergo a conversion as goddess Bastet speaks to me through the leopards.

"Miss Annette told me you are an expert in jaguars," Benji says. "How do they differ—jaguars and the Intanda leopard?"

"A jaguar is stockier and more muscular than a leopard, and its tail is shorter." I lower the binoculars to engage him. "If we use football as an analogy, a jaguar would be a defender because it's solid and fearless. In contrast, a leopard would play forward because it's sleek and graceful."

"And their fur?" he asks.

I raise the binoculars. "Both have golden fur although some are black in which case they're called 'melanistic.' "

Benji perseveres: "And their markings?"

The question sets me at unease because of what I see.

"*Nudume*, the markings?" Benji repeats.

I stammer: "Both have rosettes but they differ in a key way: Whereas jaguars have spots inside their rosettes, leopards don't." Keeping the binoculars to my sockets, I wince.

"What is it?" Benji asks. "Why do you moan?"

I feel a deep revulsion from what I see. Across the floor of the cave, the mother leopard carries a cub in her mouth and deposits it in a nook before returning for the second cub. When both are in place, she lies on one side with her flank, chest, and shoulder facing me as the cubs nestle onto her teats.

"*Nudume*, are you alright?" Oscar asks. He comes to my side and looks up at me.

"I'm moved by what I see," I reply, my voice cracking. I squeeze the binoculars to cup welling tears.

" 'Moved' hardly expresses the rage I feel for nature's cruelty. I curse the goddess Bastet for creating a leopard with rosettes arranged not as they are in other leopards but in lines which stretch across the feline's flank and chest before coalescing into the shape of a cylinder along her shoulder. I find it bitterly ironic that the pattern should resemble a medieval whip known as the "cat o' nine tails," or "cat" for short. Mentally, I hear the plaited ropes of the whip swish through the air before a whistling blow cracks my back. One after another, the cat's tails rip into my flesh.

A hand reaches for the binoculars. "*Nudume*," Benji says, holding them, "you are in pain, so we must go."

I wipe my tears and look to the western sky. Remnants of jet trails scratch the horizon and blur a lowering sun. "Yes, let's go," I say.

The boys are tender to offer me support as we descend. At points, they exchange possession of a rifle they've brought as we drop ledges or negotiate passages. I accept their hands and arms because there is a place for the assistance of Sherpas in the life of every wounded climber.

When we reach the base of the mountain, Xavier confronts me. "Why did you go up there?" He taps his watch. "We have only two hours of light and there's much to do!"

"I didn't want the boys to be up there alone!"

Xavier scowls at them. "Return the rifle to Ansel! I do not want you to climb the mountains again because leopards abound there."

Alone now, I take a moment to compose myself. I feel depleted from the hike and even more so from emotions unleashed on the ledge. My inner being lies raw and exposed, my deepest pain laid bare. Whatever healing occurred following the lashes I took during elementary and middle school has been reversed by the sight of rosettes taking the shape of a cat o' nine tails whip. My wounds gape and burn from sweat that saturates my shirt.

I climb the berm to the channel where I find the electricians have installed the laser emitter, sensor, cameras, and spotlights. This allows us to divide into two teams, one of which climbs the slope to the crevice opening above the channel where they wire a satellite dish and solar panel to a rainproof container that holds a laptop, batteries, and other electrical gadgetry, none of which can be seen from the ground below. In the meantime, I remain inside the channel with others to connect cables that descend through the crevice to the laser emitter, sensor, spotlights, and cameras.

Having completed the electrical circuit, we assemble in the channel to test the system. We stand silently in darkness as Benji and Oscar push a cart toward the trip line. As they approach the invisible beam, my pulse quickens. I count the meters that remain—three, two, one...

Instantly, flashes illuminate the night and cheers erupt, but I remind the group that we haven't finished our job until the photos transmit. I ask Henry to phone Alexander at the lodge.

Silence befalls the channel as we wait for news to return from the Land Rovers below. It finally comes from a worker who announces the photos have transmitted. "But, wait!" I shout before anyone can cheer. "What exactly did Alexander see in the photo?"

Another delay, then the worker's voice again: "He said the photo showed a cart being pushed by two boys, one wearing a green shirt and the other a blue shirt."

"We're good!" I exclaim, raising my arms. I join the celebration this time.

When the group disperses to return to camp, I remain in the channel with Xavier who appears ill at ease. "What's the matter?" I ask him.

"It's something Alexander told me in a call while you were on the mountain."

"What did he say?"

"Do you remember I told you about a social engineering attack we undertook to break into Mrs. Simsbury's email account?"

"Yes, the one in which your actress friend played the role of subcontractor to Mrs. Simsbury's mobile service provider."

He nods. "We discovered a troubling email Gary Simsbury sent from his wife's account. He probably hoped to hide it by using that account."

"What did it say?"

His brows furrow. "That he was extremely concerned about the outcome of the imminent vote on Uku-tetema."

"That's it? Why would he feel the need to hide such an email in his wife's account?"

"Because he also said he'd heard from a reliable source that I was still alive despite being poisoned."

"*Shit!*" I mutter.

He grasps my arm and looks about. "Can the boys be trusted?"

"Oscar and Benji? Of course they can! Why would you think otherwise?"

"Because, I'm absolutely convinced there *is* an informant among your people."

"And not among yours?" I quip.

"Impossible! They know I'd shoot them on the spot if I caught them betraying me."

THE AROMA FROM a roasting boar stirs my appetite. While traveling earlier in the day, a guard spotted the animal in a thicket beyond a drying creek. A single shot felled the animal, and with impressive speed the cook slit the animal's belly, removed its entrails, and dragged the carcass to a Land Rover where he tied it to the rear of the luggage rack to bleed while we drove.

A skewer runs through cut-up sections of the boar to a pair of posts with U-shaped grooves that allow the cook to rotate the sections as they roast over coals. With each turn, drops of fat spit up flames that cast a yellow hue on tents which encircle the pit. A day-is-done lull pervades the camp as my fellow travelers relax in the pre-dinner hour, one man whittling a stick, another laying out blankets, others wiping metal plates in preparation for dinner. Calm as it is, a trio of armed guards manning the perimeter of the camp reminds me this is no jamboree but, rather, a mission laden with danger.

I warm my hands over the coals when Xavier approaches me. "Let's take a walk before dinner," he says.

I rise to find him holding a rifle similar to the one Benji and Oscar carried on their mountain sojourn. We collect a kerosene lamp and depart camp, passing a sentinel just beyond the tents. The course we take is a familiar one that leads to the sandy berm and the channel above it.

"You haven't seen the crater of Intanda up close," Xavier reminds me. "I want to take you there to share the secrets I've promised to tell you."

Although I anticipate them, the flashes from the trip line blind me and I slow to allow my eyes to adjust. I acclimate to walking with soles caked with sticky black sand and pause periodically to kick one boot against the other. Above, the channel walls frame a crystal clear corridor of stars.

As we trudge on, Xavier asks, "Did you notice how the wind has ceased? That's because the crater cools at night. During the day, the sun beats on its tar sands to create updrafts that blend into winds, and with only four outlets through which to escape, the winds barrel through each gateway. That's why sand blew at us from the channel when we arrived. And I'm sure you noticed heat waves rising from the end of the channel. Over time, my people have reported seeing mirages in them—serpents, dragons, and even multi-headed giants, mirages so eerie they never set foot here again."

I look about warily.

Xavier continues: "The boys told me you saw Intanda leopards on the mountain."

"Yes, a mother and two cubs."

"What did you think of the mother?"

"Sh…sh…she moved me enormously," I falter.

"You are one of very few *mzungus* to have seen our leopard. The sight of it may change your life."

I put my arm out to stop him from walking. "Why do you say that?"

"Because, the two *mzungus* I know about who *did* see the leopards experienced life-changing transformations."

"Who were they?"

"The first was the British businessman who built the lodge I live in now. Not long after he constructed it, he visited Intanda where he was attacked by a leopard while hiking in the mountains. Elders have told me they believe the only reason the man survived was because the leopard possessed extrasensory perception that allowed it to decipher the man's intent to flee Uku-tetema if he escaped."

During my first journey into Uku-tetema, I recall asking my driver, Henry, how the lodge had come to be owned by Xavier's family. At the time, I found his response to be evasive—namely, that Uku-tetema could be unfriendly to outsiders—but now, having heard Xavier's story and having seen the leopard myself, I understand his answer.

"Extrasensory perception," I repeat. "That's quite an attribute to bestow on an animal."

"Say what you will. My people are not alone in believing our leopards possess great powers. As I told you before, Queen Berenike concluded the Intanda leopard endowed her with miraculous healing abilities."

"Who was the second *mzungu* to be transformed by the leopard?" I ask.

"Annette Wilson."

My curiosity soars. "How did she become transformed?"

With one foot, he makes a circle in the sand, a laborious process because of its stickiness. After a prolonged silence, he addresses me.

"I must confess, Paul, I have not been a perfect companion for Annette. I have strayed from her repeatedly, yet she has chosen to stay with me for the benefit of our daughters. There was a time, however, when she came close to leaving not only me, but Africa in addition, but then, after we moved from Lusaka to the lodge, she visited Intanda and encountered the leopards. In her words, they changed her life. She decided to settle in Uku-tetema to help battle poachers. Although she resides in Danjou part of the time, she will tell you that her heart remains in my homeland, and not just because our girls live here, but because of the communion she feels with the leopards of Intanda."

"What does she see in them?"

"A number of things, among them the loving care the mothers provide their cubs."

"That's maternal instinct," I reply, "no different from what mothers express throughout the animal kingdom."

"Oh, there's much more. She sees in the leopards a natural balance between motherhood and independence, community and self-reliance, and agility in toeing the line yet walking alone when needed. I will let Annette explain in more detail how the leopard speaks to her."

I turn to walk again, but Xavier takes my arm.

"The transformational power of our leopards is far-reaching," he says. "It transcends those immediately impacted."

"How do you mean?"

"After Annette decided to remain with me in Uku-tetema, I began to change. I knew it was time to stop taking her for granted, to respect her more, and to turn our relationship into a partnership. Those were no small changes for me. I found it difficult to transition from CEO of a billion-dollar firm to an equal partner in a relationship."

He releases my arm and places a hand on my shoulder as he peers into my eyes. "Paul, there's a request I have of you, but please don't feel obligated to fulfil it; I know it's a lot to ask."

"What is it?"

His expression turns from confessional to petitionary. "Can you talk to Annette…ask her how she feels about me…where she stands in our relationship?"

"You need to ask her directly," I reply.

"In an ideal world, yes, but that's not where we live. Ever since I became ill from the poisoning, I've been reevaluating my life, and it's become clear to me how much I love Annette. I really don't want to lose her. To the contrary, I want to make amends with her, to heal our wounds, to move forward in unity."

Throughout his petition, he has left a hand on my shoulder which he now squeezes. "I need an opening through which to approach her," he continues, "an indication that she is still receptive to me, and I believe you are in a unique position to create that opening. I beg of you, will you do it for me?"

My heart sinks. In the dim light of a lantern whose rays barely reach the channel walls, I feel trapped between the closing jaws of a vice, one whose handle has two hands upon it, one—Xavier's—depressing the handle to close the jaws while the other—Annette's—lifts it to free me.

I reach into my pocket and grasp Annette's envelope, soggy now with sweat. All day, I've wanted to read it, but the right moment hasn't come.

I squeeze it now with such force it rips.

WITH EACH STEP I take, the expanse of silver-on-black grows closer. Under moonlight, it seems to stretch forever and resembles a gigantic puzzle comprised of infinite black pieces with silvery saw-toothed edges. It lies below the level of the channel as if an enormous extraterrestrial flattener visited Earth to stamp the region several meters into the ground.

With Xavier at my side, we come to the end of the channel. He extinguishes the lantern.

"The moon is our light now," he says.

Our final steps to the channel's end were awkward ones not only because the sand had become stickier as we walked but, more so, because I became estranged from Xavier after rejecting his plea to engage Annette regarding her feelings for him. It wasn't a simple "no" I rendered but, rather, an assertion that it was his duty, not mine, to address Annette about their relationship. The excommunication I received was one I imagine Annette confronts regularly from Xavier yet my hope is that she, like I now, receives periodic reprieves.

"The crater of Intanda," Xavier professes. He falls to his knees in prayer.

I wait for him to stand again. "So, this is what I glimpsed from the air while flying to Lusaka."

"Yes, and had it been nighttime you'd have seen a million shifting lights from moonlight falling upon sands in perpetual motion."

"But if there's no wind at night, what keeps the sand in motion?"

"A geologic upwelling of oil from beneath," he replies. He hands me a pair of pocket binoculars. "Look at the crater surface and tell me what you see."

I raise the binoculars and adjust them. "A lot of black, gooey topsoil," I reply.

"Yes, the black comes from bitumen which is a semi-solid form of petroleum. The crater surface consists of oil sands which are a mixture of bitumen, clay, sand, and water."

I move the binoculars across the surface until I come to a silvery jagged groove. Focusing on the junction of black and silver, I notice a faint jiggle in the sand. I still the binoculars to make sure it wasn't my hand that created the jiggle. Holding my breath as an added measure, I see an unmistakable trickling motion. It reminds me of a time in Ecuador when I visited a beach along the Pacific. While walking along it at low tide, I came upon an array of tiny sand balls encircling a hole a crab had dug. Stepping back, I watched the hole for signs of life and before long, a crab emerged and began pushing a sand ball away from its burrow. In doing so, the drying ball crumpled and sent sand trickling into the hole.

I think of that trickling motion now. "Something's moving," I tell Xavier.

He sighs. "Yes, that's the heartbeat of Intanda."

I remove the binoculars to look at him.

"What you're seeing," he explains, "are the effects of oil under pressure below pushing up against the crater's surface. Through this process, liquid oil changes to bitumen which gradually sheds its sand in the trickling motion you see. Moonlight reflects from the sand to create the black-on-silver pattern before us."

"So, there *is* oil here," I confirm. "How much?"

Sadness fills his eyes. From a shoulder bag, he extracts a plastic tarp that he lays across the sand. "Sit with me," he says.

We take our places overlooking the crater.

"I'm weary," Xavier says, his eyes directed ahead, "and I don't know how much longer I can carry on."

"A long time," I reassure him. "You're as strong as a horse. You've been set back by thallium poisoning, but you're recovering, I believe."

He looks at me. "Paul, I appreciate what you've done for me, but when I say 'carry on' I'm referring not just to my health but—quite literally—to a load that's weighed me down for a long time. I need to share that burden with someone else, and I've chosen you to be that person."

"What load are you referring to?" I ask.

His lips tremble. "You and I, Paul, are sitting on *tremendous* oil reserves. My father told me this before he died."

"How tremendous?"

He looks pained, as if a knife pressing against his abdomen is about to pierce it. "I'll leave it at that for now; 'tremendous' is the right word."

"If that's true," I exclaim, "how could these reserves have remained secret for so long?"

"Uku-tetema is clothed in secrecy. We're apart from the world."

"So is the Amazon, but that doesn't keep people from extracting its oil. Why should Uku-tetema be any different?"

He inhales deeply and looks away.

I place a hand on his shoulder. "I meant no offense by challenging you. It's just that what I saw in the Amazon convinced me no land is safe from commercial interests."

"Not even national parks?"

"Ask yourself," I say to him, "who creates national parks? In my country, the answer is Congress, and while no national parks have been disbanded, I worry future circumstances will compel

Congress to sell one or more parks to investors. One can't rule that possibility out."

"I have more faith in humanity than you, Paul, because I believe that when a land such as Yosemite speaks to so many souls, a spirit protects it forever."

"Souls may change, Xavier! Those in communion with Yosemite today may be replaced by others in the future that lust for its wealth, and then the park will fall."

"That won't happen! There's no lust in soul. Soul is neither fad nor trend nor temptation. It infuses us at birth and releases us at death. It pumps the heart, stirs the blood, and waters the tears." He turns quarter-circle. "The trip line we installed today... it speaks to the soul."

"How?"

"Its line is one with the leopard's lines."

I flinch. "What do you mean?"

"Although the trip line runs *above* the sand, figuratively, it is a line drawn *in* the sand, one that, if crossed wrongfully, will lead to destruction. If we allow humanity to cross the line for commercial purposes, the leopards will be the first, but by no means the only, casualty. Wildlife across Uku-tetema will vanish as will our language and culture. And it won't stop there. If Intanda is exploited, we'll drive another stake into Earth's climate by burning more fossil fuel. We can't let that happen. The leopard's lines must stop it."

THE COALS THAT roasted the boar now serve as our campfire. We gather around it to eat a dinner of *nshima* and meat. Soft voices blend into a hum that plays second fiddle to the fire's crackling.

Seated between Benji and Oscar, I listen to them converse in Bemba. I let my thoughts wander as their laughter tells me they're content. The same can't be said for Xavier across the circle who sits with a look of discontent. I can't tell whether the fire in his eyes comes from reflections or from the discussion he carries on with his assistants. Before long, he summons me. I carry my plate to fill a space vacated beside him.

"More news from the lodge," he tells me. "The lion has struck at the watering hole."

I know by now that the lion he speaks of is a digital one. "And its prey?" I ask.

"TransNational Oil," he replies. "Alexander succeeded in ambushing the corporation's network using the fundraising website I told you about earlier. He hacked into Gary Simsbury's emails. He's downloading them now."

"Any preliminary findings?"

"Not yet, but he'll work through the night and call us as needed." His expression softens. "On another note, Martin and Innocent flew to Lusaka to deliver the urine specimen."

"That's good."

He hands his plate to the cook. Standing, he says, "See you at sunrise."

I return to the boys who yawn now. "To bed," I tell them. We go to our tent where we find our bags, a flashlight, and three water bottles along with blankets and pillows. I ask the boys to take the two interior spots so I may occupy one closest to the door.

From outside we hear a clattering of dishes being washed, dried, and stacked, but this is replaced soon by singing accompanied by drum beats and strums from a guitar. Earlier, while eating, I'd noticed the instruments resting against a box and took delight in their originality. The drum was made from a wood barrel and had rawhide stretched across one end secured in place by a metal band. The guitar, on the other hand, was created from a large metal can and had three wires that appeared to have come from a discarded radial tire. It was the artwork on the drum that caught my eye, however, for it depicted animals of various kinds, the most prominent being a leopard in full sprint with rosette lines streaking across its side. For a moment, I felt the sting of acid reflux.

The singing I hear now has a familiar call-and-response style where a leader prompts and others respond, but there's a novel component in that I hear multiple forms woven into the music—blues, gospel, and even hip-hop. The soporific effect of the voices and beat put the boys fast asleep as their chests rise and fall beneath their blankets.

I cherish the alone time. Finally, I'm able to extract the envelope which Annette gave me before I left the lodge. While I'd almost opened it when I was on the bluff above the channel earlier in the day, the sight of the boys on the ledge up the mountain forced me to leave it in my pocket.

The envelope and its contents are in two pieces now as a result of my ripping them after Xavier petitioned me to intercede with Annette on his behalf. My anger with him renews.

Settling my mind, I piece together six halves of a three-page hand-written letter. The sheets are still moist from sweat, forcing me to handle them with care.

I lift a flashlight and shine it on the words…

Dearest Paul,

It's four-thirty in the morning as I write this letter, and I've just returned from your room. Making love with you was so beautiful I felt I had to write to tell you things you need to know about me.

First, because I never told you the details of how I came to know Xavier, it's time I do so…

As we rode together from the border of D R Congo to Saysha the night you rescued me in Danjou, I told you that I'd traveled to Tanzania as a photojournalist to complete an assignment for a travel magazine. I also described a poaching incident involving elephants that I saw while returning to the capital. Witnessing that event led me to quit my job with the travel magazine to become a freelance photographer. I focused on poaching and licensed killing of African wildlife. When you asked me whether that supported me financially, I admitted that it didn't and that there was a man in Uku-tetema named Xavier Treadwill I worked for. All of that is true.

What I didn't reveal was that I met Xavier in California nine years ago when I gave a speech at Stanford University about how a distinct species of gorillas known as Grauer's gorillas has become endangered in recent decades in D R Congo. They are beautiful primates, larger than their cousins, the mountain gorilla. As a photojournalist, I spent much time in

D R Congo documenting their declining numbers. My speech at Stanford addressed the social and political forces fueling their endangerment.

At the time I gave the speech, Xavier was working nearby in Silicon Valley. He attended the speech because he'd seen a flier for it and had a passion for African wildlife and because his birthplace in Zambia was located just across the border from D R Congo. I will spare you the details of the long-distance relationship that ensued and my decision to leave Africa to live with him in Silicon Valley. Shortly after moving in with him, I became pregnant with the twins. Three years later, we moved our family to Lusaka where, as I told you before, Xavier started a school for disadvantaged children. After a year and a half of running the school, he felt compelled to move to his family's lodge in Uku-tetema to address the problem of poaching on his homeland.

I'm sure you've assumed that I married Xaiver, but the truth is I didn't. And the reason I didn't was because shortly after we had the twins, we began to disagree on fundamental issues about rearing children. Those disagreements gave me second thoughts about marriage. One of our first points of contention was whether to vaccinate the babies, I being an ardent proponent and he a disbeliever. (I found that incredulous given his level of education.) The schism deepened when I expressed a desire to have the infants baptized. He objected, arguing that it would be better for them to steer clear of institutionalized religious doctrine. (Even though he moved away from Uku-tetema at an early age to attend a Christian school in Lusaka, he never abandoned his ancestor's tribal views on spirituality, ones that espoused the existence of a supreme creator but also lesser deities and ancestral spirits.) With time, other disagreements arose with regard to things like nutrition and rules and consequences. Growing discord led me to plead for counseling, but he refused to participate. For the sake of unity, I acquiesced on this account and on many others and even celebrated his proposal to move to Lusaka to launch a school for disadvantaged children. With the twins having just turned three years old, I saw the move as a chance to start anew.

Shortly after we arrived in Zambia, however, a disagreement arose that set us apart for good. It stemmed from Xavier's professed right to see other women, a right, he contended, that was steeped in Uku-tetema traditions. My vehement opposition brought me only exclusion as I became an afterthought to him. Concerned he might banish me from the household, I walked a fine line between advocating what I thought was best for my daughters and abiding by decisions he made unilaterally. What I found most painful was his reference to me as a 'helper' rather than a mother, a distinction that led the twins to view me as a member of the domestic staff.

After we moved to Uku-tetema, however, a glimmer of hope arose when I realized I could help fend off poachers. Because many incursions came from D R Congo, I offered to collect intelligence in Danjou. I spent a good deal of time in D R Congo, some of it rekindling work I'd done earlier with Grauer's gorillas located in forests north of Danjou. I kept an apartment in Danjou and rented office space there from a wildlife conservation group. That's where I befriended Felice, the office cleaning lady and Innocent Mbewe's aunt.

Around the time tata Murphy died and left the hospital in Saysha without a medical director, a colleague in Danjou showed me an online report of your work to save jaguars in the Amazon. I took an immediate liking to you when I read one of your quotes, one that went something like, "... every jaguar killed in the rainforest removes a tuft from the world's carpet of grace." I forwarded the report to Xavier because I knew he would be intrigued by your use of laser trip lines. To my delight, Xavier ensured you received a notice of a job opening for medical director at the hospital in Saysha. He even donated a large sum to the foundation that runs the hospital to encourage them to recruit you; that's how keen he was to have you nearby as a technical consultant for trip lines he envisioned setting up to protect Intanda.

Oh, my eyes are getting heavy, but I need to ask you about something that troubles me greatly...

As we made love, I passed my hands along your back and felt lines, long, deep ones that spanned nearly the entire width of your body. And so many of them. Then, when you lit a candle to help me find my way to the door, I saw the lines with my own eyes. They brought me to tears when I reached my room.

And so I ask you this: Might there be another time when I can lie with you to rub, massage, and caress your back with the most tender love I possess?

In the meantime, I implore you to do one thing for me: While you're at Intanda, commune with the leopards. Be with them in a state of heightened sensitivity, awareness, and receptivity, and as you view them through binoculars, take special care to look at their sides, for they have called you to Africa.

With my deepest love,
Annette

I close the letter, restore the halves to the envelope, and tuck the papers into the pocket again. Outside, a single voice sings without response now. It's a doleful solo sung in the dialect of Uku-tetema and accompanied by the tin guitar whose wires twang loneliness. After each verse, a short refrain follows with a word I recognize, one the soloist pronounces *eeng-weh, eeng-wey*. It calls me to put on my shoes and step outside.

The space about the fire pit has been abandoned save for the soloist who sits on a three-legged stool with his back to me. As he strums the guitar, he waves his head back and forth in gentle motion while his chest heaves from breathy singing. It is an incantation I hear, one laboriously delivered in which every word seems to drain, to deplete, to leave both soloist and listener breathless. Yet the singing continues.

Eeng-weh, eeng-wey…

I don't know if the man's eyes are open or closed, but the direction he faces tells me he sings to the mountains. With the moon well along its arc, it drapes the slopes in velvety white. I lift my eyes to the ledges I scaled earlier to retrieve Benji and Oscar. Draped in moonlight, they no longer look like slabs of rock but, instead, like successive steps in a waterfall which flows with light.

Eeng-weh, eeng-wey…

In Bemba, the word *ingwe* means "leopard."

Under the stars of Uku-tetema, two men sing to the leopards of the mountains, one in audible solo and another in silent wails that tear his heart.

8

A RASP FROM the canvas startles me. It's followed by a command: "Paul, wake up! We need to go!"

I open the tent flap to find Xavier strutting away with a flashlight guiding his steps.

It's four o'clock in the morning, well earlier than I intended to arise for a dawn departure. I dress and leave the boys asleep. In the center of the tent circle, I meet Xavier standing where the fire pit had been, its depression covered by sand. All about, activity bustles—tents collapsing; supplies packing; crates loading.

"Why the rush?" I ask Xavier.

"The intruders from Lusaka are traveling faster than expected. That leaves us less time to complete our mission."

He barks at his assistants.

I've seen Xavier accommodating, gracious, and diplomatic; I've seen him pensive, reflective, and inquisitive. Add a new persona: combative—a general in civilian attire.

I leave him to his tasks to return to the tent where I awaken the boys. They grumble at the intrusion.

"We need to go," I tell them. "Xavier's orders."

The tent falls as soon as they emerge, but they find an unexpected treat awaits them: hot tea. Still half asleep, they hold the cups with a tilt but manage to drink without spilling.

Today, there's no pre-departure briefing because duties have been assigned. Engines start, doors close, and wheels turn.

Headlights pierce the darkness in differing vectors, some pointed north and others south, all tracing the base of the mountains that encircle Intanda. Behind me, the two seats that were lowered the day before to make room for supplies have been raised to accommodate Benji and Oscar while, beside me, Xavier rides deep in thought.

"We're splitting up, I see," I observe.

Reluctantly, Xavier leaves his world of thought. "Yes, divide and conquer."

We're in three teams today, each assigned to install a trip line at the remaining entries to Intanda. My team will drive to the most distant entryway, the eastern portal. It harbors the most risk because, in addition to being the furthest away, it's the gateway most likely to see the convoy of oil surveyors due to arrive later in the day. For this reason, Xavier has delegated the combat vehicle to continue driving with us after we leave a second team at the northern portal. Behind us, the third team travels in the opposite direction to the southern gateway.

Because the oily sands of the crater are too difficult to traverse, we travel outside the mountains that form Intanda. By the way the crow flies, this perimeter measures roughly three hundred sixty kilometers with the four entryways located roughly seventy-five to ninety kilometers apart. By ground, however, the distances increase because of the zigzag nature of the course required to circumnavigate the star-shaped land. Ideally, one would seek to shorten the distance between entryways by hugging the base of the mountains, but doing so entails negotiating rocky, slippery inclines pocked by drop-offs. For this reason, we leave the mountains to pursue a more circumferential route through shrub lands that separate the mountains from savannas further away. But even in shrub land, the speedometer rarely exceeds forty kilometers per hour because sudden decelerations are required to traverse ravines that appear with little warning. From the back, the boys cheer with every drop that sends them flying into their shoulder belts.

Beside me, Xavier's knuckles turn white from clenching the satellite phone. In the hour since leaving base camp, he's spoken to Alexander repeatedly, each time in his native tongue. On the present call, he switches abruptly to English. "What did it say?" he asks Alexander. A moment passes before he curses. "Keep reading the emails and call me with news!"

He addresses me: "Trouble's mounting, Paul."

"What sort?"

"Talk of attacks."

"On us?"

"Yes."

"By whom?"

"Unclear at this point." His mind seems to be locked in gear from the conversation he just completed with Alexander.

I search for a verbal lubricant to shift the gear. "What brings this up?" I ask.

"A kill from the watering hole that Alexander just told me about."

I glance out the window for a reality check. We're in Africa, alright, but our watering holes remain digital.

"You said last night that Alexander had succeeded in ambushing TransNational's network and was downloading Gary Simsbury's emails. Was there a particular email that spoke of an attack?"

"Yes, it came in the form of an attachment to an email Simsbury sent to over two hundred people. It was one of his regular updates on the petroleum sector." He scrolls the touch phone. "Listen, I'll read it to you…

"Africa may be the next frontier in oil exploration as new technologies allow us to attack old challenges. With seismic techniques improving at breakneck speed, plans are underway to apply these techniques in hinterlands that promise great progress."

He stops and looks at me.

"Keep reading," I tell him.

"No, that's it. Didn't you catch the threat?"

"What threat?"

He hands me the phone. "Look at the words closely."

I peruse the lines he read. "I don't see what you're concerned about."

He grows agitated. Taking the phone from me, he fingers four words he reads aloud: *Africa…attack…plans…progress.* You didn't see those words?"

"Sure, but you picked them out from the text; they didn't appear side-by-side the way you read them!"

He becomes defiant. "In my business, Paul, we examine words in all directions—up-down, transverse, and even reverse; forward alone is insufficient."

"If you're suggesting Simsbury's intent was to convey a secret message through those four words, how could he be sure his targeted audience would recognize them as such?"

He scoffs at the question. "The select members of the audience he targeted to receive the message had been given a list of specific terms to look for; all they had to do was pick the words out from the larger narrative to derive the message."

I scrunch my face. "You're suggesting Simsbury targeted a subset of people in a general industry audience to convey an update about an attack?"

"Yes."

"Why wouldn't he have just called them or emailed them directly?"

"Calls and emails leave trails," he replies. "Even though this was an email, the message was buried in an attachment that looks innocent to untrained eyes and went to two hundred people."

"Okay, let's say you're right. How do we identify the members of Simsbury's targeted group?"

His expression softens. "We check the identity of every recipient of the email."

"Two hundred of them?"

He nods. "Alexander's a busy man."

DAWN ARRIVES WITH a subtle awakening of sky over the Intanda mountains. Because the peaks block the rising sun, daybreak is slow to find us. Nonetheless, with every added photon, Henry presses the accelerator a hair more to speed our pace, and before long he and the other drivers in our convoy are able to extinguish headlights while behind me, the boys fall asleep from the smoothening course.

The enormity of Africa strikes me anew through my window. Looking down upon a savanna, I make out an animal herd in the distance. Thousands of bodies dot the land to create a painting in pointillism, yet on this canvas there's a hint of motion that makes me strain to get a better look. Intrigued, I borrow the guard's binoculars.

Focusing on the herd, I see fairly large animals, wildebeests being my guess. At one end of the herd, the animals graze in serene fashion, but as I scan over their backs the opposite way, I see signs of agitation. Animals cease grazing and begin running, some even leaving the herd. Looking further, I discover what spooks them: a vehicle racing directly toward the herd's center. Although I can't make out the model, the vehicle appears to be a light weight utility truck with a metal grate across its front and a cargo bed in back from which the tarp has been removed. Its green conveys the look of a militarized vehicle although I see no weapons or insignias other than a large red circle along its chassis.

"Uh, Xavier," I say. "You might want to see this."

He takes the binoculars and looks upon the savanna. Freezing on the spot that holds the herd, he barks an order to stop. Saying nothing, he gets out of the Land Rover and, with an unobstructed view of the horizon, studies the scene. I hop out and stand beside him.

"What do you make of the vehicle?" I ask.

By now, even without binoculars, a trail of dirt can be seen rising into the air behind the speeding truck.

"A man in the rear wears something on his head that I can't make out," Xavier observes.

"Let me see." Peering into the eyepieces, I notice two men standing at the back of the truck with arms clenched to a crossbar that spans the vehicle. From each head, a red bandanna waves in the wind. "Benji!" I call. "Come here!"

In no time, Benji appears at my side. I hand him the binoculars. "Take a look at the truck in the distance that leaves the trail of dirt."

A moment passes before Benji finds the target. "No, no!" he cries. "They are the bad men who came to Saysha! I see the large red circle on their truck. It is the same marking I saw on the Humvee in Saysha!" He lowers the binoculars. "We must hide! They will kill us!"

"No, we're safe here," I assure him. To Xavier, I say: "Jihadists!"

He seems more concerned about Benji. Putting an arm around him, he escorts Benji to his seat. After closing the rear door, and with both of us still outside, he asks: "Why did you traumatize the boy?"

On the move again, I nurse my guilt by staring out the window at the new course we take, one carved through shrub that's tall enough to obscure our presence but not so dense to obstruct our way. By phone, Xavier informs the other drivers of what we saw and, in a separate call to Alexander at the lodge, instructs him to report the sighting to national military authorities. With the jihadists traveling south toward Uku-tetema, I'm haunted by the earlier report of a village near Danjou having been razed by jihadists.

I turn my attention to a compass along the dashboard. With each turn we make, it swivels one way or another but the predominant direction we travel is north, one consistent with the orientation of Intanda as a star tilted slightly to one side. Based on the time elapsed since departing, I expect we'll reach the northern portal to the crater before long.

We leave the shrubs for a more arduous course along the base of the mountains, and our pace slows considerably on account of gullies carved into rock through eons of water rushing off the mountains. The concavity of the gullies makes me imagine a giant from the past has taken a cylindrical file to the rock to etch each depression. I worry for the Land Rover's axels which moan with every descent. On one particularly long and difficult ascent, we scale the gully diagonally which causes the vehicle to tilt. I fret the tires will slip and send us careening down the slope but the rugged treads and balanced weight keep us moving forward. The motor, grinding vociferously, sighs upon reaching the top.

We drive a short distance across a flat rocky stretch before rounding the mountain beside us. Through my window I gawk at what looks like an enormous gun barrel pointing at us.

"The northern gateway to Intanda," Xavier announces.

It's little more than a hole at the inflection point of a mountain range that, after running north-northwest for ninety kilometers, abruptly turns south-southeast. I think of the giant who etched the groove-like gullies, only now I envision it blowing a hole through the mountain. Unlike the western portal, this is a round opening that leads immediately to the dark oil sands of the crater, an aperture that reminds me of a doughnut-hole MRI scanner of the type used for patients with claustrophobia who can't tolerate the tunnel-like counterparts. Here, as before, dark sand lines the entryway to the crater, only it takes the form of a doormat rather than a berm.

I'm allotted only a brief visit to the entryway for the purpose of advising the team how best to install the trip line. Together, we map out sites for the laser emitter, sensor, cameras, and spotlights before turning to the supporting equipment. All the while, Xavier watches us from a vehicle as he attends to a satellite phone.

Satisfied with the plan in place, we leave our colleagues to press on. Only two other vehicles accompany ours now, one with supplies and the other with a gun turret. Eight men and two boys comprise our team as we journey on.

Xavier taps my arm. "Alexander just spoke with Dr. Raymond Chabala from the hospital lab in Lusaka. We have results for my most recent urine specimen."

"Chabala works fast!" I note. "What do the results show?"

Xavier hands me a notepad with a value on it.

"Excellent!" I proclaim. "The Prussian blue capsules are eliminating thallium from your body."

My patient smiles in a rare display of levity since departing the lodge. "I must say, I'm feeling better," he admits.

I instruct him to continue the same dose of medication. "We'll submit another urine in a week."

In the meantime, I'm struck by the stark changes along Intanda's eastern perimeter. Whereas earlier the mountains dropped to shrub lands that fell to savannas, here low hills comprise the border of Intanda and give way to drylands that extend forever. Gone are the hovering knife-like protrusions along the peaks, replaced by rounded summits formed from the same dark rock that created the earlier jags. The changes make me wonder whether, when creating Intanda, goddess Bastet chose two styles, one hostile and imposing and the other meek and mild. From what I know of the goddess, I find it befitting that the land should have two contrasting faces given that Bastet herself underwent a transformation from lioness warrior deity to protector deity represented as a cat.

We travel at a rapid clip now along drylands. Beneath us, the surface is flat and hot, not unlike the Bonneville Salt Flats of Utah, only here there's an occasional prickly bush withered from lack of rain. To my chagrin, the air conditioning has broken which forces us to leave our windows open. The sound of the blowing wind leads

Xavier to use a headset to work the phone. He engages me presently over a matter which seems to upset him.

"More news," he utters. "Read this."

I take the satphone…

> *In our quest to expand the world's oil supply, we have identified Africa as the next frontier. This is not a task for the weak, but, rather, a job for attackers—assaulters of skeptics; ambushers of naysayers; assailers of those who say the mission is impossible.*

I know why he's asked me to read the words: there's a secret embedded within them that he expects me to decipher. I analyze the narrative with care, parsing it into phrases, examining sequences, assessing punctuations. A number of words trouble me—among them, "Africa" and an additional quartet beginning with the letter "a" near the end of the text. I share my observations with Xavier.

He nods approvingly. "Better," he says. "You chose two of the five words that comprise the message Alexander decoded."

"What two are they?"

" 'Africa' and 'attackers,' " he replies.

"What were the three I missed?"

" 'Identified,' 'job,' and 'for,' " he states. "The message is: *Attackers for Africa job identified.*"

"Is this from another Simsbury pontification?"

"Yes."

I sulk. "I don't understand how Alexander decodes messages from entire documents so readily when I can't find them in a few lines!"

"He wrote a software program to help with the task."

I contemplate the message—*Attackers for Africa job identified.* "Africa's an enormous place," I remind Xavier. "The message doesn't specify *where* in Africa the attack will take place."

"I know, but it's a warning nonetheless!"

"Yet there's no mention that we're the targets."

He looks at me with disdain. "Don't be naïve, Paul! Are the hit list, radioactive jaguar blood, and my poisoning not enough to persuade you we're targets?"

I prefer to think that what Xavier calls naivety is a desire on my part to live simply. Believing I'm a target of attack undermines that goal. Once again, I stare out the window for solace. I watch the beige drylands gradually turn green. Trees appear, and in a telltale sign of change, we cross a small stream that splashes across the arm I hold along my window.

"The landscape's changing," I say, a peace offering I extend to Xavier after licking my wounds for being called naïve.

He's kind to accept the offer. "Yes, a garden lies ahead."

We pass tall reeds where birds chirp and cattails swish. Beyond them are groves of fruit trees native to this region of Zambia where sour plums, monkey-oranges, and water-berries grow. A tree I've never seen before piques my interest. It stands roughly forty feet tall and has a short trunk with flaking bark. Its lower branches are spiny, droop, and bear an oval fruit some four inches in diameter with a woody shell. I ask about the tree.

"A bael fruit tree," Xavier replies. "The way I identify it is by the shape of the fruit and by the clear, gummy sap that exudes from wounded branches. You can see strands of gum hanging from some branches."

"What's the fruit like?"

"It's fleshy and somewhat orange when ripe. I scoop it out and mix it in water with a bit of sugar. It's good for the digestive tract."

For a moment, I view myself as a traveler hurtling through time back to a Garden of Eden, one that, in this case, abuts a crater which allegedly holds one of Earth's largest oil reserves.

Detecting my wonder, Xavier says, "The goddess Bastet was artistic; she provided the leopards with a paradise."

Artistic, indeed; she used both oils and water colors to paint this garden.

Xavier launches a description of how the beauty came about. It began with the goddess Bastet directing a meteor to strike Earth on a desolate land that was to become Africa. The impact left a star-shaped hole into which rain collected to form an inland sea. With the passage of millions of years, the sea took in the remains of plants and animals with their energy-laden carbon molecules. Gradually, layer by layer, sediments were laid and subjected to heat and pressure that converted the biomass to oil. The cataclysmic strike that started the process also created subterranean veins through which oil extends beyond Intanda.

"Where does the water come from for these gardens?" I ask.

"From an aquifer," Xavier replies. "The meteor's impact created channels with ceaseless springs."

We cross another stream, this one wider than the first, before climbing a gradual incline that returns us to the hills surrounding the crater. After traversing a grove of tamarind trees, we stop before a highway of black sand that spills from an abrupt opening to the crater.

"The eastern portal to Intanda," Xavier announces.

Each entryway is unique, this one coming from the blueprints for a skateboarder's park. On each side of the entryway is a hill whose rocky core has been scooped away to leave a concavity. In reality, the surfaces are too rugged for skateboarders, but if this were a snowy clime, I could envision adventure skiers dropping from the top of the concavities into gravity-defying free-falls before rocketing into the air from the lower lips.

Separating the two concavity-carved hills is a river of black sand studded with rocks, more peppercorns from the spill of the Great Grinder eons ago. I grow concerned when I look at the walls of the entryway because they're little more than cliffs.

"I call this the 'boulevard,' " Xavier says, pointing to the sandy highway.

We stop near the base of the nearest scooped-out hill. Without delay, Xavier goes to the back where he opens the door to summon the boys. "I have an assignment for you," he tells them. "I want you to climb to the ridge overlooking the entryway to keep a lookout to the east." He points in the assigned direction. "You have my permission to take a rifle with you."

"What do you want us to look for?" Benji asks.

"Traveling vehicles." He hands Oscar a pair of binoculars. "From the ridge, you will see the garden extends to the horizon. There are no roads, so if you see any vehicles, you are to blow this whistle." He places a lanyard around Oscar's neck. "But it's critical that only one of you keeps a lookout at a time; the other is to watch for leopards. They frequent the ridge and attack from behind."

"Xavier," I say, "I'm not comfortable with the boys going up there alone."

"What 'boys' are you referring to?" Xavier quips. "Oscar and Benji have become men on this journey. You must release them."

While we've talked, unpacking has begun. Benji and Oscar are brisk to assist, and when the task has been completed, they take a rifle and some food and water and hop onto the roof of a Land Rover. A driver backs the vehicle to the base of the concavity where the boys clamber onto its base to begin their ascent. The final lip of the concavity proves to be challenging. Handing the rifle to Oscar, Benji grasps a ledge and pulls himself up. He then takes the rifle from Oscar who duplicates the maneuver, and it's only when the two stand atop the concavity that I understand why Xavier assigned the mission to them rather than to adults.

With urgency, Xavier leads an electrician named Matthew and me into the entryway. It differs from the other two I've seen in being far wider, a good hundred meters separating its walls that reach to the sky like those of the western portal.

When we reach the closest wall, I rub my hand along its smooth surface. Looking up, I see the smoothness persists without accessible grooves the entire way to the ridge above. "It's going to be difficult to find places for our equipment," I say.

We walk another thirty meters to the crater where, peering around the end of the wall, I find a rocky shelf situated at a perfect height to hold the laser emitter. "This'll work!" I declare. "Let's check the other side."

While traversing the crater rim, we hear a shout from above. I turn to find Benji's face poking out from the ridge above the entryway, a height equivalent to a ten-story building. A hand waves at us.

"Get back!" I holler.

"No, it's fine, *nudume*," he volleys. "Oscar is holding my legs."

Xavier minces no words: "That is not your lookout point!" he shouts. "Move back now!"

The face promptly disappears, and we hear no more from the boys.

We continue along the crater rim with frequent stops to knock sandy clumps from our soles. At each stop I stoop to the level of the rocky shelf I discovered earlier to ensure no obstacles will block a laser's path. When we reach the distant wall, however, it becomes clear our options are restricted because if we choose a site too far in from the crater rim, the laser will be disrupted by the end of the first side. As a result, we focus on spots along the final section of the second wall, ultimately settling on a rocky horn at its terminus.

Given space limitations at the first side, we opt to place only the laser emitter and a small battery to power it on the rocky shelf and transport the remaining equipment across the boulevard. Matthew is concerned that, unlike at the previous portals, the equipment here can be seen readily by intruders if they approach the crater along either wall, but I remind him such notice will likely come only after the trip line triggers.

I lead a team of four to undertake the installation. After the job has been completed, I ask Henry to bring a Land Rover to the crater's rim to test the trip line. As the vehicle moves forward along the boulevard, I take a final peek through a camera mounted along the rocky horn to ensure its view covers the entire span of the entryway. Reassured, I watch the final approach of the Land Rover.

A sharp crack diverts my attention. A second one follows that explodes glass from the Land Rover's rear. I watch the vehicle come to a stop before it reaches the trip line. Through the front window, I see Henry slumped against the steering wheel.

The staccato sound of rapid fire from the boulevard entrance draws my attention to the armored Land Rover that accompanied us. Sparks fly from the twin barrels of the machine gun mounted to its turret as cartridges enter one side and spent shells eject from the other.

"My God!" I shout. "What's happening?" Scanning the area, my eyes dart to the ridgetop where I see a body creep forward, a hand held to its brow as if to scout the scene below.

"Oscar!" I scream. "Get away from there!"

Gunfire across the boulevard drowns my voice. My throat burns in the dry air. Keeping my eyes locked on Oscar, I see he drops to his knees but keeps one hand to his brow while the other goes to his mouth. Between gunshots, a whistle blows.

"Oscar!" I shout again. "Get—"

In a volley of fire, the boy slumps forward before somersaulting over the cliff to make a free fall to the sand.

"No!" I shriek. I leap from the rocky horn onto the boulevard, but before I can take a step I'm tackled to the ground.

"Don't be crazy!" Matthew shouts. He pins me to the ground with his muscular frame. "They'll kill you if you go out there!"

Face to sand, I smell petroleum and feel sick to my stomach. "Get off me!" I cry.

"Not until it's safe!" Matthew heaves his chest along my back to secure me.

More automatic rounds come. When they end, I feel the weight on my back lift. I stand to find Xavier speaking on the satphone. His face is pale and his lips quiver.

"Come!" he beckons. "We must go to Henry immediately!"

I feel torn between attending to Oscar or Henry, but when I see others running toward the boy, I set off for the Land Rover. "Who attacked us?" I shout to Matthew who runs beside me.

"Jihadists," he replies. "They waited in the garden on the far side of the boulevard."

As fast as our feet allow, we plod through sticky sand. I think of the utility truck we saw earlier speeding across the grassy savanna, and while I know that vehicle couldn't have beaten us to this entryway, another contingent of jihadists had to know we were coming. I fear for the safety of our colleagues at the other entryways.

Even before we reach the Land Rover, my stomach twists when I see Henry's body slumped against the steering wheel. Separating ways, we open both front doors to approach him. Clotting blood runs from the back of Henry's head to his collar. I feel for a jugular pulse. "Henry!" I shout as I dig my finger into his neck. No pulse is present.

Squatting on the passenger seat, I grasp Henry's shoulder and shake him. His head wobbles across the wheel. Gritting my teeth, I probe the back of his head and discover a hole in his skull. Across from me, I see Xavier and the electrician peering stoically at their fallen comrade. In their faces I see heaviness and pain yet, oddly, their eyes hold what I can only call "acceptance." It's not a word I choose lightly, for I know it's not human nature to accept the death of a loved one, and had I not seen the very same look in the eyes of a young mother during my training as an emergency medicine resident, I'd attribute the look to denial or shock.

In the case of the mother, her look came when I was asked to inform her that her six-year-old daughter had died in a car crash. Both mother and daughter had come to the hospital by ambulance after a drunk driver struck their sedan side-on, crushing the girl in the back seat. While the team I worked on attended to the girl, another treated the less-injured mother in the next room. It became apparent immediately there was no way to save the girl because her injuries were catastrophic; opening her chest for manual compressions of her heart only produced feeble squirts through severed organs and arteries. When my attending asked me to tell the mother her child had died, I entered her room with trepidation yet encountered serenity. For this mother-daughter pair, no hospital wall could separate their hearts and souls; they were joined inextricably. Before I said a word, the mother told me she knew why I'd come. I took her hand, but it was really she who took mine. She asked if I'd wheel her to her daughter's side so she could see the girl before the morgue claimed her. I rolled her gurney to her daughter's room. Side-by-side, the two laid in silence, and in the mother's eyes I saw the look of a shepherd who mourns yet accepts the loss of one of her flock.

I watch Xavier press a hand gently between the steering wheel and Henry's chest. Tenderly, he pushes the body back against the seat. "Paul, help us move Henry to the back," he says.

I circle the vehicle and, working with Matthew, carry Henry's corpse to the rear compartment. With my attention turned to Oscar, I rush to see him, but my heart sinks well before I complete the twenty-meter sprint because I notice the three guards who surround Oscar's body stand idly as if nothing's to be done.

I squeeze between the guards and kneel beside Oscar. He lies on his back with his face turned to one side and his legs and arms splayed apart. Blood mixed with spinal fluid trickles from his ear. The blue fabric of his shirt has turned dark red over the area of the heart. In my shock, I want him to end the nightmare by standing or, better yet, by moving his arms and legs to create an angel in the sand, but he does neither. Instead, he remains lifeless.

I pull up his shirt to expose the gunshot wound. It stares at me like an angry eye, scolding me for allowing an eleven-year-old to travel to such a hostile place. I take his hand and cup it. Gently, I squeeze the cooling skin, so different now from the warmth it exuded each time we shifted gears together in the truck. I lift his palm to my cheek, and while I feel unworthy of wiping my tears with his fingers, I do so in a plea for forgiveness.

I lift my eyes to the wall. "*Why?*" I cry. I shriek at my father in the hopes the prevailing winds will carry my voice across the equator to his cancer-ridden body some six thousand miles away. "I never lived up to your expectations, did I, dad? So you robbed me of my childhood and made me never want to have kids of my own!"

I stand, strip off my shirt, and tear it to pieces. "And your curse continues to this day! Just when I began to discover the joy of children, you ripped Oscar away from me! I hate you, dad! I hate you so much because I loved Oscar as if he were my child!" I lift my arms to the sky before wrapping them around my back where I rub the scars my father left by whipping me with his favorite tool, a cat o' nine tails. "I *hate* you for what you did to me!" I scream.

I fall to my knees. My sobs blend with a howling wind to create a chorus of desperation. From beneath Oscar's shirt, I extract the whistle he still wears. Removing it, I place the lanyard over my head and cup the whistle in my palm. With eyes closed, I hear a faint whistling, one I attribute to Oscar's final breath accompanying the wind to another place.

WE DEPART THE eastern portal two men down. The electrician, Matthew, has replaced Henry at the wheel as Xavier sits up front with him. From my place behind them, I tighten my embrace on the youngest yet bravest man to remain in our presence.

It was Benji who insisted on lifting Oscar from the sand to place him in a compartment of the armored vehicle. After laying him there, he removed his green shirt and placed it over Oscar's chest as a tribute. He told me later he did so because he wanted more than ever to be my brother, my *nudume*. Unbeknownst to me, he'd stationed himself behind me as I wailed at my father and mourned Oscar's death. Since I was shirtless, he wanted to follow suit.

I hold him now as if we're blood brothers. He tells me that had it not been for Oscar's keen eyes on the ridge, we wouldn't have known about the convoy of vehicles approaching Intanda to conduct the seismic survey. While scanning the horizon, Oscar had noticed a faint line of vehicles, but the line was so indistinct Benji wasn't sure it existed. Partially obscuring their view were a hill in the distance and a canopy of trees in the garden through which the convoy traveled.

As the boys debated the sighting, they heard gunfire on the boulevard. Creeping toward the end of the ridgetop, they couldn't make out what was happening so Oscar kneeled to get a better view. Cupping his brow to peer across the boulevard, he saw men with red bandannas firing at the Land Rovers. Concerned the attack was timed to precede the arrival of the convoy, Oscar scanned the horizon a final time before blowing the whistle. It was then a bullet tore through his chest.

Starting down the hill, Benji took cover when shots came his way. Lodged behind a boulder, he returned fire but in little more than a minute the shooting ceased after the guards in the armored Land Rover unleashed a barrage of automatic rounds. While descending the remaining way, Benji counted a dozen fallen opponents along the sand. Sprinting to join us by Oscar's corpse, he warned us of the approaching convoy. Although we wasted no time in departing, Xavier regretted leaving the jihadists' vehicle unharmed and not collecting their cell phones.

With the eastern portal well behind us now, we learn from our colleagues that they've departed the southern entryway for the lodge after installing the trip line without event. The same is true for the northern team. Xavier warns each group to take exceeding caution as they travel through the night.

He turns now to Benji who stares ahead wide-eyed. "I want to assure you again that my offer of a staff position holds forever."

I feel Benji nestle closer to me. A faint smile crosses his lips.

"As for us," Xavier says to me, "we'll travel through the night, but first we'll bury our beloved comrades. I've picked just the spot to do so. We'll get there before sunset."

He lifts the phone, but I preempt his call. "The message Alexander deciphered from Simsbury's documents," I say. "They proved to be true threats."

"Indeed," Xavier replies. He recites them: " 'Africa attack plans progress' and 'Attackers for Africa job identified.' " His expression sours. "And more will come before the National Assembly votes."

"But why would Simsbury take the risk of recruiting a jihadist group to attack us?"

"Who says Simsbury recruited them?"

"*He* issued the threats," I remind Xavier.

"That doesn't mean he recruited the attackers. Someone at International Mines could have done that. Why else would the number for the company's office in Lusaka be on a jihadist's cell phone?" He shakes his head. "Unfortunately, we may never know for sure who arranged the attacks because the IT folks at TransNational patched their system. We can't access Simsbury's emails anymore."

"So, what's our next step?" I ask.

"We turn out the lights."

"Give up?" I rebut.

Xavier smiles feebly. "I'm referring to an email Simsbury issued just before we lost access to his account. All it said was 'Going dark...' "

"What did he mean by that?"

He turns to Matthew who has requested his attention. The men peer at a slope on our right.

"Yes, this is the place," Xavier tells him. "We will bury our fallen ones here."

THROUGH MY WINDOW I see a hill that rises into a series of crags before cresting in a rugged peak. I wonder what it is about this spot that earns it the right as a burial site. I leave my seat to join others standing outside who pass binoculars from one to another.

"Take it," Xavier says, handing me his pair.

I look in the direction the others examine but see only a hillside with crevices.

"Up a bit," Xavier directs me.

I feel intense angst as through the eyecups I see a leopard carrying its prey up a slope.

Xavier nudges my elbow. "Come, let's find a quiet spot."

He leads me to a rock on which we sit apart from the others. Taking the binoculars, he observes the leopard. "He killed a baboon in the lowlands." Inserting two fingers into his mouth, he whistles loudly before passing the binoculars. "Look now," he says.

I see the leopard has stopped in its tracks and looks down the hillside at us. For reassurance, I glance at the Land Rover.

"Focus on the leopard," Xavier says. "I want to tell you something."

The leopard resumes its ascent only now moves in reverse up a steep section with the baboon in tow. Its rippling muscles accentuate the lines of rosettes along its flank and chest.

"You are a savior to the big cats of the world, Paul. I trust you know that."

"I did what I thought was right in the Amazon," I reply.

"And you've done right by us as well."

I remove my eyes from the oculars. "Perhaps, but animals seem to lose out to humans over the long-run."

"Nonetheless, I live in the moment, and at this moment I'm in the presence of a magnificent leopard." He nods at the slope. "Look at it again."

As I do, he places a hand on my shoulder. "I was moved by your emotion for Oscar today, and I couldn't help but notice your back after you removed your shirt. You've experienced great pain in life."

I remain silent.

He speaks again: "I often remind myself that despite the suffering we inflict on animals, they remain a source of healing for us."

The leopard has reached its dining spot, a ledge in full view. It lies on its stomach with front legs propped over the lifeless baboon and rips into the primate's abdomen. The upward tug causes the baboon's head to swivel, bringing its dog-like muzzle into view.

The sight reminds me of my friend at home, Jimmy, The Thinker, who, I suspect, would cringe at what I see.

"Yes, animals can heal us, Paul, even the great anger you have for your father. It mustn't remain inside you. The leopard can resolve it."

"Bullshit, Xavier! The leopard is a wild animal with no connection whatsoever to issues I have with my father!"

He takes the binoculars and puts them aside. "You underestimate the link between animal and man. Because of what you've done for the leopards of my land, you shall remain connected to them forever, and from that connection comes healing. Look no further than the ancient queen of Egypt who received miraculous healing abilities from one of our leopards."

"That's folklore, Xavier! In my profession, scientific proof is required before concluding something has healing powers."

"Step aside from science for a moment." He points to the hill. "You and my leopards are connected forever because of lines—rosette lines along their sides, trip lines above the oily sands of Intanda, and…" He inhales deeply. "…lines across your back."

He places the binoculars in my hand. "Take one more look."

Through the lenses, I see a medley of intestines, muscle, and bloody fur beneath the leopard's chin. But it's not the kill that attracts my eyes; instead, it's the rosettes.

"Healing for you will come from the leopard's lines, Paul. Allow the lines on your back to become one with those of the leopard, and in doing so, the leopard will draw out your pain, your suffering, and your anger."

When I was a child and knew my father was about to whip me, I'd cower and cry. It wasn't a sobbing cry but a whimper mustered from a sense of pain to come. The sides of my mouth would quiver as I groaned and sniffled. My father interpreted the motions and sounds as whines which only angered him more. Not infrequently, he'd tell me that my mouth resembled a cat's mouth as it watches a bird through a shut window. Then the whipping would start, and the only feline to be present would be a cat o' nine tails.

"Xavier," I say, "may I be alone for a moment?"

He stands. "Take the time you need. Join us when you're ready."

I watch him walk to the vehicles from which others remove shovels. Before long, digging commences and piles of dirt and rock collect beside a pair of graves.

I return my gaze to the leopard which continues to devour its prey. As I watch it eat, I think about Xavier's words. Although I'm not a psychiatrist, I know that when he speaks of allowing the lines on my back "to become one with those of the leopard," he invokes the principle of transference. In this model I'm the patient and the leopard is the therapist. Healing, if it's to come, results from my transferring to the leopard feelings I harbor toward my father.

While I respect the specialty of psychiatry, I see no place at the moment for its therapeutic tools. I rise from the rock and begin walking toward the vehicles yet, inexplicably, I feel compelled to stop.

Jaguars in the Amazon...leopards in Africa...and a cat o' nine tails deep within my psyche. I remove the shirt I put on after ripping apart my previous one and weep with my back to the leopard.

9

FROM THE REAR view mirror, the sun's reflections strike my lids like branding irons. I shift sleepily in futile attempts to avoid the rays but the bumpy terrain makes it impossible to find an escape. Reluctantly, I surrender to the dawning day.

It has taken all night to reach the final stretch of savanna before the hills that hold Xavier's lodge on their western slopes. Cramped in a Land Rover for ten hours, I stretch my legs as I can without waking Benji who sleeps across the back seat with his head on my lap. From the front, Xavier notes my awakening and promptly engages me.

"The other three teams have reached the lodge safely," he announces.

Our last place position comes not only from the longest distance driven but from time taken to bury our dead. At the base of the hills where we watched a leopard devour a baboon, we laid Henry and Oscar to rest. Taking turns with shovels, we dug side-by-side graves, one smaller than the other. It was a solemn sunset-to-starlight burial. After lowering the bodies into the ground, we assembled to listen as Xavier, holding a lantern above his head, extolled the virtues of each of the fallen. My heart sank when it came my turn to pitch dirt onto the bodies. The thud of earth striking a corpse is not one I want to hear again, especially when one is a child.

Touchingly, Benji laid the shovel down when it came his turn to pitch.

"You don't have to do this if you don't want to," I told him.

"I want to, *nudume*, but first I'd like to leave something with Oscar." From his pocket, he pulled a small wrench. "Mr. Treadwill, may I place this wrench on Oscar's chest? I removed it from the Land Rover."

My eyes watered as Benji stooped to leave the tool with his friend in a final farewell.

After departing the burial site, I sat in the back with Benji as Matthew drove and Xavier worked the satphone. At one point well after nightfall, Xavier turned and, seeing Benji fast asleep, pointed into the darkness. "Over there in the distance is the southern entryway to Intanda."

I peered into the night but saw nothing. For prudence, we'd swung far to the south of the portal to stay clear of the oil survey convoy in case it chose to enter the crater from that point.

But now, as we leave the grasslands to ascend the hills, I notice Xavier has relieved Matthew at the wheel. It brings me comfort to see him there for it makes me think his recuperation continues. With one hand on the wheel, he drinks coffee that Matthew has passed around. I confront him now on a point of unfinished business.

"Yesterday you told me about an email Alexander discovered from Simsbury's account that said something like 'Going dark.' You didn't explain what you thought it meant."

Xavier's eyes appear in the rear view mirror. "I can tell you exactly what it means," he says. "Are you familiar with the 'deep web'?"

"No."

"When people think of the Internet, it's the clearnet or surface web they're referring to, a space combed over and indexed by browsers such as Google, Internet Explorer, and the like. In contrast, the deep web is everywhere online outside the clearnet, a vast expanse of hidden sites untracked by search engines and unvisited by most web surfers. For this reason, some call it the 'hidden web' or 'invisible web.' "

"How does one access it?" I ask.

"Different areas have different requirements, but one popular program is called TOR that can be loaded onto individual computers."

"TOR?"

"Yes, an acronym for 'The Onion Router.' His eyes turn large. "The name refers to the many layers one would have to peel away to figure out the identity of users of the deep web. After installing TOR, one uses it just as any other web browser only TOR exposes sites ending in *.onion* which are hidden from search engines that ply the clearnet. For those who demand even greater privacy and security, there's a TOR operating system called TAILS. Alternatively, some people use a Virtual Private Network, or VPN, along with TOR for added privacy. VPNs hide IP addresses which are unique codes assigned to individual computers."

Talk of software and computers does little to clear the mental cobwebs from a poor night's sleep.

"By no means is everything on the deep web sinister," Xavier continues. "While the name conjures thoughts of child pornography and markets for stolen credit cards, the deep web also hosts academic databases, corporate portals, and a host of other legitimate sites that users seek to keep private."

"Come to the point," I tell him. "What's Simsbury doing on the deep web?"

"He's communicating through an area of the deep web called a 'dark net,' a computer network that links trusted peers that's exceptionally difficult to penetrate by outsiders."

"How'd you figure that out?"

A smile appears in the mirror. "You've forgotten my past. Among other things, I spent time dealing with decentralized digital currencies such as Bitcoin, a cryptocurrency, so to speak. These virtual currencies have no direct link to specific nations or central banks. They're created to enhance peer-to-peer commerce without the need for credit cards, currency exchanges, or other market barriers."

"And, from what I've read, they're used for nefarious purposes."

"So are regular currencies! The point is, my firm did an enormous amount of work to enhance the security of virtual currencies and markets based on them, many of which conduct transactions on the deep web, and in doing that work, we became one of the world's leading experts in deep web cybersecurity. Alexander's using the fruits of that work to infiltrate sites once thought to be impenetrable. He's zeroing in on Simsbury's dark net forum."

"Who are Simsbury's peers?" I ask.

Angry eyes shoot into the mirror. "Alexander will tell us when we get to the lodge."

Xavier's phone chimes. "Yes, Alexander," he says, "I was just telling Paul about the work you're doing with Simsbury and the dark net." He pauses to listen, then declares, "*Really?* How clear are they?" Another pause, then: "I'm sorry to hear this."

He hangs up but remains silent.

"Is there something you'd like to share?" I ask him.

Large sad eyes appear. "The oil surveyors have trespassed upon Intanda. Photos just arrived showing their convoy entering the western portal." He turns to look at me directly. "The trip lines don't lie, and neither do the leopard's lines."

MY MOOD IMPROVES the closer we get to the lodge. From a ridge high above it, I catch a glimpse of the curved, three-story structure with the gardens surrounding it. The brief sighting conjures the feeling of returning to a beloved home after a long journey. The simple, irreplaceable elements of home still win the heart—a bathing place, potable water on demand, a roof overhead, and a comfortable pillow.

"Feel free to check your phones," Xavier announces. "We should have coverage now."

I've looked forward to this moment all night, hoping to find a text from Annette. My heart leaps to find one...

Paul, I'm in Lusaka now. I came here to visit my twins and to see our burn patient because she faces difficult surgery ahead. I think of you ever so fondly.

I turn to an email next from the hospital in Indonesia which has offered me a job. A contract is attached which I'm asked to review and sign at my earliest convenience. It proposes a starting date in just two weeks from now.

I feel Benji tap my thigh. He wears doleful eyes and a look of exhaustion. "When will we go back to Saysha?" he asks. "I miss my friends."

"Soon, I promise. I want you to be with your friends, too."

I recoil at the prospect of telling him about my plans to leave Africa. I know that doing so on the heels of Oscar's death will only deepen his wounds. I cringe, too, at the idea of holding a memorial service for Oscar only to follow it with a departure announcement. The orphans deserve better than that, I tell myself.

Before putting the phone away, I open a text from Bristol...

Nudume, please call me at your earliest convenience!

I delay calling him because I'm sure he wants to discuss logistics pertaining to the imminent arrival of the husband-wife physician team from Canada. A nap, a shower, and a bite to eat will put me in a better frame of mind to engage in such a discussion. Better yet, I'm hoping Martin will fly Benji and me to Saysha later in the day so I can talk to Bristol in person.

We arrive at the lodge just after seven. The other Land Rovers sit in the driveway with dirt caked along their sides, but there's no sign of their occupants who, I trust, have gone home to rest.

Dressed in fresh whites, Helena commands the top step with an especially wide smile for Xavier who returns her greeting with a wink. After climbing the steps to join her, he announces that Helena will have a meal prepared for us in two hours.

I accompany Benji to his room where he plops onto his bed and falls asleep instantly. I follow Benji's lead by dropping onto my own mattress moments later. Within seconds, I enter a sleep so deep I remain on my back without shifting until my alarm sounds ninety minutes later.

I shower and slip on a pair of trousers when a knock comes on my door. It's Xavier: "Paul, we need to speak!"

I open the door to find him looking distraught. "Come in."

He walks to the window where he remains with his back to me. "He's back," he says.

"Who is?"

"Gary Y. Simsbury. He returned to Zambia last night."

"How do you know?"

He pivots. "A contact in immigration just called Alexander to let him know."

"This is bad!" I mutter.

"*Very* bad."

"What purpose did Simsbury declare for his visit?"

"Business, of course."

"Where's he staying?"

"At the Intercontinental Hotel in Lusaka."

"Where he stayed a month ago when you spoke at the conference on Uku-tetema."

"Correct."

"What do we know about his schedule?"

"Nothing yet, but that'll change. I'm sending Ansel and another guard to Lusaka today to shadow Simsbury twenty-four-seven."

"Why endanger them? You should leave that task to federal security officials. Have you presented them with the email Simsbury sent from his wife's account indicating his concern you were still alive after being poisoned?"

He becomes defiant. "I'm not going to rely on anyone but myself and my men to protect me!"

It troubles me that Simsbury has arrived in the capital when Annette is there. While I'd like to inquire how Xavier intends to protect her, I say nothing. Instead, I ask: "When Martin flies Ansel and the other guard to Lusaka, can he drop Benji and me off in Saysha?"

"Yes, but first we need to meet with Alexander."

I finish dressing and knock on Benji's door. A shower and clean clothes have lifted his spirits.

"Breakfast," I tell him. On our way to the sitting room, I inform him that Martin will fly us to Saysha after I meet with Alexander and Xavier.

He's pleased, adding: "I will be outside with the young animals. Come get me when we're ready to go."

We enter the sitting room where Innocent Mbewe approaches me. "*Nudume*, welcome back!" He hugs me but only loosely, and when he steps back, I see he looks haggard and has one hand wrapped with gauze and tape.

"What happened to your hand?" I ask.

"I cut it yesterday while slicing a mango."

"Do you need sutures?"

"No, *nudume*, the cut is superficial. The dressing will suffice."

"Still, may I see it?"

"Later today; I need to go to the clinic this morning."

I notice that his face is pale and apprehensive. Crusted blood lines a tip of one nostril. "Did you have a nose bleed?" I ask.

"Yes, I struck my head against the door during the night when I went to the bathroom. I meant to use my flashlight, but I was half-asleep."

"Are you sure you're alright?"

"I may have caught the diarrhea bug at the clinic. It kept me up last night."

"You shouldn't work today!"

"I'll be fine," he insists. His shoulders droop. "But I'm very sad about Oscar and Henry." He pats Benji on the back.

"You need to come back to Saysha with us today," I tell Innocent. "Martin will fly us."

"I will ask Xavier if I may go." He looks past me, and his eyes widen. "There he is now!" He crosses the room to greet Xavier.

Once again, football is a catalyst which transforms the two from men to boys. Backs are slapped, laughs shared, and words spewed giddily. The power of friendship impresses me as Innocent heals before my eyes.

"We must celebrate Argentina's victory over Brazil!" Innocent announces. "And to do so, I prepared special drinks; allow me to serve you one from the kitchen."

"An alcoholic beverage?" Xavier asks.

"Of course!" Innocent giggles. "A special occasion to celebrate our favorite team!"

Xavier addresses me from across the room. "Will it be alright with the doctor if I have a drink even though I am taking Prussian blue?"

I nod. "It shouldn't be a problem."

Innocent returns shortly with a tray holding two highball glasses that contain attractive blue drinks. Handing a glass to Xavier, he keeps the second for himself before setting the tray down. "To the blue and white of Argentina!" he gushes. Glasses clink, and the men drink heartily.

"My word," Xavier effuses. "I don't think I've had a drink this early in the morning!"

I approach the men. "It looks like a blue lagoon," I say.

"How rude of us to exclude you!" Xavier exclaims. He looks about as if to summon Helena from the kitchen.

"No worries," I reply. "I'm not as passionate about football as you."

Pleased with himself, Innocent raises his drink to the light. "A heavenly combination, isn't it—vodka, lemonade, and Blue Curacao liqueur?"

The men hook elbows and drink.

"Gentlemen," Helena calls from the dining room, "breakfast is served."

Innocent gulps the rest of his drink and, noticing that Xavier has set his down half-full, asks, "Come now, will you not finish it?"

"Moderation, my man," Xavier replies.

We eat a simple meal of *nshima* thinned with milk and sweetened slightly with sugar. Hot tea rounds out the affair.

"The day moves on!" Xavier says, standing. "Innocent will drive a vehicle to the clinic to work for a couple hours and then return to fly with you to Saysha."

We part ways, Innocent to the clinic, Benji to the garden, and Xavier and I to the conference room where we find a weary-eyed Alexander toiling before a laptop.

Alexander rises to greet me with his usual formality.

"Great to see you again," I tell him. "You've been hard at work, I hear."

He's modest, taking a seat only after Xavier and I've done so.

Xavier puts him to work instantly. "Bring us up-to-date on your activities with the dark net. Where are we currently?"

"It is not good," Alexander replies. "I've identified Simsbury's peers on a dark net forum they're using to communicate with one another."

"How many peers are there?" Xavier asks.

"Four, including Simsbury."

"Who are the other three?"

Alexander winces. "Like Simsbury, they're executives at oil companies." He hands Xavier a sheet of paper. "Here are their names."

Xavier's complexion lightens. "My God, the four firms these men work for collectively produce two-thirds of the world's oil!"

"What have they been discussing in the forum?" I ask.

"I have found only two postings so far, one a blank to ensure the system was running, and a second in which Simsbury confirmed his arrival in Lusaka."

Xavier's attention remains on the names. "We're at war," he declares. "These people will stop at nothing short of conquering my homeland."

"Not true," I say. "It's up to the National Assembly to determine the fate of Uku-tetema."

"You're dreaming, Paul!" He snaps the paper. "These are some of the most powerful people on Earth!"

My phone rings. I glance at it but set it down.

"Who was it?" Xavier asks.

I wave a hand. "It's my lead paramedic, Bristol; I'll call him as soon as we're done."

"No, call him now," Xavier insists.

"Why?" I'm perturbed by his meddling into my affairs. "It's just logistics he wants to discuss."

"Logistics pertaining to what?"

"My leaving for—" I say no more, dropping my eyes to a text Bristol has just sent.

"Indonesia?" Xavier asks. "Are you still planning to leave us?"

"Oh, *shit!*" I exclaim.

"What is it?" Xavier asks, leaning forward.

"Bristol thinks he knows who delivered the jaguar blood to my shack!"

"Call him!"

I do so immediately. "Bristol! I've got you on speaker phone. You think you know who delivered the jaguar blood to my shack?"

"I can't be sure," he replies, his voice loud and mechanical, "but I just learned that Innocent Mbewe was gone from the hospital the afternoon the airplane landed outside Saysha."

"Innocent?" I repeat. "No way! He and I examined the burn patient together that afternoon!"

"It was early evening when you examined her. He was away from the hospital part of that afternoon."

"Why didn't you notice this earlier?"

"Because only last night Cynthia told me she worked in Innocent's place for three hours on the afternoon the airplane landed. He told her his goats had gotten loose and that he had to round them up."

"Who's Cynthia?" Xavier asks.

"She's one of our paramedics," Bristol explains. "She was the one who reported seeing the airplane land in the countryside outside Saysha on the day Dr. Paul found the blood at his home. She was standing on a ladder of the water tower when she saw it."

"Why didn't your records of staff work hours register that substitution?" I ask.

"Because the paramedics were paid last night, and it was only then that Cynthia caught the error. She came to me immediately after noticing her pay didn't reflect the hours she'd worked for Innocent."

"Did you verify this with Innocent?"

"I called him last night and early this morning, but he didn't answer either time. That led me to go to his home an hour ago to ask his wife whether Innocent had truly spent an afternoon recently rounding up lost goats. She told me she knew nothing about goats being lost; moreover, she said she'd be the one to find them if they were lost."

I shake my head. "I don't know, Bristol, this is a serious charge you're leveling."

"There's more, *nudume*. I discovered something strange at Innocent's home when I went there this morning."

"What was it?"

"Do you know the shed where he keeps his goats at night?"

"Yes, I do." It's a tumbledown structure sitting across a dirt patio from Innocent's hut.

"Well, this morning I found a metal canister in the new backpack Innocent had purchased recently in Lusaka that had fallen over in the shed. Sunlight reflected from the canister so I went to see what it was. It proved to be a cylinder made from dense metal, and it was heavy—some twenty kilos. After removing it from the backpack, I stood it on end and noticed it consisted of a cylinder within another cylinder. The outer one had a hole in its side, and when I realized I could rotate the outer cylinder about the inner one, I discovered a hole was present in the inner cylinder, too. When both holes were aligned, I saw a deep blue color in the core of the canister—an eerie blue that looked almost supernatural."

My pulse quickens. "What did you do with the canister?" I ask.

"I rotated the outer cylinder until no blue was visible and then carried it to the hospital to show it to Katrine."

"Katrine?" Xavier asks.

"She runs our hospital lab," I explain. To Bristol: "What did Katrine think about it?"

"She was very wary of it from the beginning but became alarmed when I showed her the blue color in its core. When she placed a battery-powered Geiger counter that she kept from her training days beside the hole, it went crazy!"

My body jerks as if I've been electrocuted. "Where's Innocent?" I shout.

"He left for the clinic," Xavier replies, grasping my arm. "What's the matter, Paul?"

I disconnect the call and, extracting myself from Xavier's hold, sprint from the room.

"Stop!" Xavier calls. "Where are you going?"

I race to Innocent's guest room and rifle through the contents of his open suitcase. I discover wrappings from a packet of gauze and a roll of adhesive medical tape among his clothes. A tube of topical antibiotic ointment rests on a table nearby with its cap missing.

Hurrying to the kitchen, I find Helena preparing the next meal. "Dr. Paul," she says, "may I help you?"

"I'm looking for something Innocent Mbewe may have left here this morning!"

"What is it?" she asks.

"A container of some kind that held a glowing blue substance!"

She puckers her face. "I haven't seen such a thing. What was the blue substance?"

I don't want to alarm her. "A dye Innocent added to the drinks he mixed this morning."

She grins. "The blue lagoons?"

"Yes, were you in the kitchen when he prepared them?"

"No, I was outside picking fruit, but Innocent told me he was going to prepare the drinks to celebrate a football victory."

I check the trash but find only discarded papaya peels and other rubbish. "Is there a refuse area outside?" I ask.

"Yes, let me show you." She takes me to a screen door and opens it.

I raise an arm to keep her from proceeding. "Just point to it; I'll go there myself."

She indicates a shed that's partially hidden behind a tree in a patio. "Over there," she says. "A gardener removes the refuse each evening."

I go to the tree and take cover behind its trunk. Peeking around it, I examine the shed. It's built from wooden slats with six-inch gaps between them.

Looking about, I see a stick across the patio which I retrieve. From behind the trunk, I poke the stick through a gap between the slats. Being early in the day, there's little refuse present—empty cans, crumpled papers, and what appear to be dust, dirt, and hair from sweepings. Discouraged, I prepare to leave but then see a small soiled cardboard box standing in a corner of the shed, a box of the sort that might hold a bottle of liquor. Extending the stick to its full length, I pierce the box easily because its cardboard is moist.

Bit by bit, the box comes apart. Before long, a metal thermos falls to the floor. Its cap is missing and as it rolls toward me, a clinking sound comes from inside it. I pause from the challenge before me. Somehow, I need to tip the thermos upside down to free whatever it contains. If I err and send the thermos out of reach, I'll lose my chance to retrieve its contents.

I look about the patio again. Along a wall I see a hoe leaning against the lodge. Setting the stick aside, I retrieve it.

I return to my perch behind the tree and, lifting the hoe, direct its blade between two slats. Reaching further, I position the blade behind the thermos and roll it to the refuse I examined earlier. When it comes to a rest against the heap, I reposition the hoe's blade ever so carefully to lift the thermos onto its open end. As it rises, my arms begin to shake and I struggle to keep from toppling the thermos. When it finally stands, I remove the hoe and exhale.

I struggle to relax as I used to do before entering the operating room during my two years of residency training in surgery. Even though the surgical theater here is a wooden shed and my scalpel a hoe, I feel immense pressure from the final operation that remains.

Lifting the hoe again, I push it against the top of the thermos, causing it to fall. A small, transparent, plastic vial of the sort we use at the hospital in Saysha to centrifuge urine specimens comes into view. The vial has a screw-on cap but it's the contents that terrorize me—a glowing blue powder, one that, to borrow Bristol's word, has a *supernatural* beauty.

Suddenly, blue becomes sickening to me, a stark transition given the color used to be my favorite—the color of the sky, the ocean, and the eyes of the first girl I had a crush on. Now, I detest the color. Nausea wells within, and I feel like vomiting.

Dropping the hoe, I flee the tree and run toward the lodge as I shriek.

WHILE I'VE NEVER treated a patient with radioactive cesium poisoning, I've read about the condition. An account that caught my interest, in particular, described a disaster that took place in 1987 in a city called Goiânia in Brazil. Two thieves entered an inadequately guarded and partially demolished hospital where they dismantled a metal device called a teletherapy unit that held highly radioactive cesium-137. They stripped the device to isolate a heavy metal canister consisting of an outer cylinder that rotated about an inner one called a "capsule" that held the radioactive cesium.

Using a wheelbarrow, the thieves transported the heavy canister home thinking it had scrap metal value. Dismantling the unit further, they freed the capsule from the outer cylinder but were exposed to significant radiation released through a small hole in the capsule placed there by the manufacturer to release metered doses of radiation for medical purposes. That night, the men began to vomit, have diarrhea, and become dizzy. One of them successfully enlarged the hole in the capsule by jamming a screw driver into it. After extracting some of the glowing blue powder from the capsule's core, he tried to ignite it thinking it was gunpowder, but it didn't explode.

Five days after stealing the capsule, the men sold it to a scrapyard but not without consequence. Both men sustained serious burns, one involving a hand that was burned in a shape and size that matched the hole in the capsule. His partner developed severe ulcers on an arm that required amputation. From there, things worsened. Fascinated by the blue glow in the capsule, the scrapyard owner took the capsule home where he invited friends to visit him to see the blue substance. With further work, several glowing grains removed from the capsule were distributed among the community, leading to further illnesses. Naturally, interest in the material and the illnesses that resulted from exposure to it sparked significant publicity, and in the end, an estimated 130,000 people overwhelmed hospitals in the area with the fear they'd been exposed. Two hundred fifty people were shown to be contaminated, twenty of whom experienced radiation sickness, and four died, including a six-year-old girl who ate a sandwich that contained blue dust from cesium powder spread over a concrete floor where she ate the sandwich.

This Brazilian account convinces me Innocent Mbewe somehow acquired a canister of cesium-137 similar to the device from the Brazilian event. Because the canister was heavy and risked detection if he brought it to Uku-tetema, he transferred its radioactive payload to the plastic vial I discovered in the refuse shed and then slipped the vial into a metal thermos. Carrying the thermos to the kitchen, he unloaded the vial and extracted some of its contents to prepare Xavier's blue lagoon. From whom and where he obtained the canister I don't know, but with rampant global strife, I can easily envision industrial or medical sources of cesium-137 falling into hostile hands. Nonetheless, I'm aghast that someone of Innocent's stature in an area as remote as Saysha should come into possession of such a lethal substance.

My shrieking from the patio has drawn Xavier and Alexander to the kitchen where they stand with Helena in disbelief as I rush into the lodge.

"What in God's name is wrong with you, Paul?" Xavier asks.

I stop before him to catch my breath. "You've been poisoned!" I shout.

He grasps my arm and twists it to the point of pain. "What are you talking about?"

"Just get Innocent Mbewe! He poisoned you!"

"Poisoned with *what?*"

"Get him!" I repeat.

Xavier turns to Alexander. "Dispatch the guards! Have them bring Innocent here straight away!"

As Alexander departs, I tug on Xavier's arm. "Come with me to my room!" I tell him. "There's a medicine you need to take!"

"But you haven't told me how I was poisoned!" he protests.

"You drank radioactive cesium in the blue lagoon Innocent prepared for you! I discovered a vial in the refuse just now that contains a glowing blue powder, and I'm sure it's cesium-137. You must tell your gardener and the rest of your staff not to get near the shed!"

"*Cesium*, did you say?" His face is grim.

"Yes, cesium-137. It emits a blue glow and deadly gamma radiation, and you drank some of it just forty minutes ago!"

"Oh, God!" he gasps. He turns limp as I escort him arm-in-arm out of the kitchen.

When we reach my room, I tell him, "Sit down; I'll get you the medication."

From my medical bag, I retrieve a pair of gloves and, after donning them, pull out a vial of black liquid. I pour out a cupful and hand it to Xavier. "Drink this. It's activated charcoal; it'll help absorb the radioactive cesium you ingested."

He swallows the liquid and rumples his face.

While walking to my room, I weighed the pros and cons of giving Xavier syrup of ipecac first to induce vomiting, but I decided the cons outweighed the pros. Since more than forty minutes have passed since he drank the blue lagoon, I assume most of the cesium has passed through his stomach already to enter his intestines. Moreover, I don't want to take the risk of having induced vomiting lead to aspiration or tear his esophagus.

I hand him a water bottle. "Drink it. It's critical you consume a lot of water today with this medicine." I lift the container of activated charcoal. "And continue taking a dose of this every four hours throughout the day."

"What about the other medicine, Prussian blue?" he asks.

"Take it without interruption. As it turns out, Prussian blue is the antidote for cesium poisoning as well."

I instruct Xavier to remove his clothes, wash his body with soap and water, and leave the clothing and towel in my bathroom. Before he begins, however, I ask for directions to his room so I can get him clean clothes.

As I walk to Xavier's room, it dawns on me that the entire lodge may be radioactive if Innocent spilled cesium-137 throughout the premises. High-energy gamma rays from the isotope would readily penetrate passing bodies in contaminated areas. The driver who accompanied Innocent in the Land Rover from the Amalumbo River near Saysha to the lodge must be checked immediately to see how he's doing because the plastic vial and metal thermos which Innocent used to transport the cesium-137 would have done nothing to contain the deadly gamma rays. In the meantime, the guest room where Innocent slept is surely contaminated in a major way, as is the kitchen where he prepared the blue lagoons. I'm concerned for the butler who carried Xavier's half-consumed blue lagoon cocktail back to the kitchen and poured it out into the sink. As for Innocent, I'm sure he's taken an enormous dose of radiation through his skin; he may have ingested some cesium as well from hand-to-mouth movements. The process of transferring cesium-137 from the capsule to the small plastic vial was surely an arduous and exceptionally hazardous task, one that, without doubt, placed Innocent at great harm.

But it's Xavier who most certainly ingested the largest dose of radioactive isotope, creating a potentially lethal situation. Within his body, his intestines are absorbing radioactive cesium from where it migrates to soft tissues, and particularly muscle. Everywhere it disseminates, the radioactive substance is destroying DNA and other vital structures. As a result, he's at risk for developing acute radiation syndrome, an illness characterized by symptoms that range from nausea and vomiting to more life-threatening bleeding and infection.

I try to recall the half-life of cesium-137. The exact number eludes me, but I know it's roughly thirty years.

After returning to my room with clean clothes for Xavier, I pack my bag while he dries and dresses in the bathroom. When he steps out, I ask to meet with him in the privacy of his office. We pass through the conference room where I see a young woman seated before a laptop across the table from Alexander. Both raise their eyes nervously, but we continue to Xavier's office where I close the door.

"I owe you an apology," I say. "I'm to blame for not smelling a rat in my presence, especially after you warned me there was an informant in Saysha. I can't *believe* Innocent did this!"

Xavier sighs. "Water under the bridge; we move on."

I peer at him. "No, we move *out!*" I say. "We have to assume the lodge is contaminated, and we can't take the risk of having others getting even more exposed." I pause. "And you…" I point at him. "…*you* need to go to Lusaka immediately. You've been poisoned internally with an exceptionally dangerous isotope and require specialists to treat you! I want you to go there before you fall ill."

He swivels to look at the garden. "What are the first symptoms I should expect?"

"Diarrhea, most likely," I reply. "Although you've taken activated charcoal, the cells further down in your intestines are getting bombarded with radiation."

"And after diarrhea?"

"Your bone marrow will take a beating, which will cause your platelet and blood cell counts to fall. You'll bleed and be at risk for serious infection."

"Over what time will these things happen?"

"It all depends on how much cesium-137 you ingested; could be hours, could be days, but once the process starts, you'll be in no shape to travel."

He turns from the window. "Uku-tetema is my home, Paul, my castle. I shall not leave it."

I shake my head and exhale a long, deep breath. "I can't be here with you the entire time. I need to return to Saysha to attend to matters there."

"I'm not asking you to stay. I know you have other business to attend to. You've already given me more time than I deserve. I shall be grateful to you forever for accompanying me to Intanda and for what you did there. I sent the trip line photos to all members of the National Assembly and to the press at-large. All hell's breaking out as a result."

We look at each other in silence. I feel a brotherhood with the man. He has a few years on me, but we're at similar stages in life: our young adulthoods have given way to middle years when careers and children often dominate one's time, and while he has twins and I'm childless, for both of us the present is a pivotal time, one in which we know our lives could change decisively. We face an uncertain future together.

I speak now: "For the record, I disapprove of your decision to remain in Uku-tetema, but I won't fight it any longer. If you'll allow Martin to fly me back and forth from Saysha, I'll attend to you as I can, but we'll have to meet at a place other than the lodge. It's too dangerous here now. In the meantime, your staff needs to evacuate the premises immediately."

He grimaces. "*Evacuate* the lodge?"

"There's no question about it: Remaining here is hazardous to the health of your staff and to you." The thought crosses my mind as to precautions I'll need to take to protect myself as I care for Xavier in the future. I will contact Raymond Chabala at the hospital in Lusaka to see if I can acquire appropriate gowns, gloves, and masks to shield me from radiation Xavier's body may emit.

Xavier shuts his eyes. In wrinkles, I see years add to his age. "But the lodge can be remediated!" he cries.

"Over time, perhaps, but only with expert help." I say this not out of conviction but from a desire to instill hope; the man has already taken a beating.

"Paul, I will do as you say because I cannot allow my staff to be in harm's way."

"Xavier!" Alexander calls from the conference room. "May I come in?"

I open the door. Before me, Alexander holds a phone to his ear. After addressing the party on the line, he lowers the phone. "It's one of our guards," he says. "Innocent Mbewe abandoned a Land Rover and took off in a small truck with a group of men."

"What truck are you speaking of, and who were the men?" Xavier asks.

"The guards didn't see what happened. They only found the abandoned Land Rover. While searching the area, however, they came upon a shepherd who told them he saw a man who fit the description of Innocent get into a military-like vehicle and speed away."

"Did the shepherd describe the truck?"

"Yes, it was green and had a large red circle on its side."

I lock eyes with Xavier's but speak before he does: "Did the men in the truck wear red bandannas?"

Alexander relays the question and delivers an answer shortly: "Yes, they wore red bandannas."

"Jihadists!" Xavier thunders. "They are the men we saw in the truck racing across the savanna as we drove toward the northern portal to Intanda."

"If it's any comfort to you," I tell him, "I suspect Innocent Mbewe is gravely ill."

"Why do you say that?"

"Because, he looked terrible this morning and admitted to having diarrhea last night. Although he attributed the distress to a bug he caught at the clinic, I'm sure he's suffering from the early stages of radiation sickness. He had far too much contact with cesium-137 without proper precautions *not* to become ill. As a matter of fact, I don't think he cut his hand as he claimed; I'm sure he sustained radiation burns from handling the isotope!"

"Do you really think so?"

"Absolutely, the timing fits perfectly with radiation sickness. If he acquired a canister of cesium-137 in Lusaka while we were there four days ago, he probably transferred the contents to the plastic vial just before we left Saysha to come here. In doing so, he exposed himself to significant radiation and has now fallen ill. He's already showed signs of bleeding from his nose, and he'll only worsen with time."

"But what about the rest of you who were in the Beechcraft with him on the flight from Lusaka to Saysha?" Xavier asks. "Were you exposed?"

"My guess is not if Innocent picked up a canister designed to transport cesium-137 without leakage." What concerns me more is the half hour Innocent spent in our company as we rode the Zodiac to the ledge across the Amalumbo River to meet our drivers to travel to the lodge the following day. During that half hour, gamma rays certainly penetrated the plastic vial and thermos which transported the radioactive cesium he carried in his bag.

While Xavier and I've conversed, Alexander has attended to another call. He ends it now and solicits Xavier's attention. "A development on the military front," he announces. "It appears an attack on our nation is imminent."

"An attack by whom?" I ask.

"Jihadists," Xavier replies. "We're privy to communications taking place between the armed forces of D R Congo, Tanzania, and Zambia. They're planning a joint military deployment to preempt the attack."

"Why would jihadists attack Zambia?"

"They want to seize a wide swath of our land along our northern border that they can hold until their demands are met."

"What are they demanding?"

"Access to the Amalumbo River in Zambia for diamond mining."

"No way!" I shout. "That's a non-starter!"

"Let me remind you, Paul, we're not a wealthy nation," Xavier replies. "Our defense forces are limited, and the jihadists know our vulnerabilities."

"Still, certain things stand supreme, among them sovereign land!"

"I know that!" Xavier bellows. The muscles of his jaw contract to form knots along the sides of his face. His eyes morph into round balls that remind me of lead spheres used once by musketeers. He pulls the trigger: "I sense an easy readiness on your part for war, Paul, one that comes from a foreigner with resources to flee our nation should hostilities erupt. Don't get me wrong; we'll fight the jihadists to the end, but these aren't *your* brothers and sisters, mothers and fathers, and uncles and aunts whose lives are at risk. You're a short-termer—here today, gone tomorrow! It's the rest of us who'll remain to dig the graves for the loved ones we'll lose."

"Dig graves?" I volley. "I just helped dig *two* of them last night! Don't talk to me as if I don't care about the people of your nation! I give everything I have each day to take care of some of the sickest and poorest here. All I'm saying is that when it comes to fighting oppression and tyranny, we're *all* brothers and sisters, mothers and fathers, uncles and aunts. I don't care if the color of my skin is white and yours is black; I don't give a damn whether your native tongue or religion differs from mine; I came here because I thought I had something to give, and while I'm here, I'm not going to succumb to extremists who seek to mine diamonds along a river I live next to!"

By now, Alexander has retreated to the conference room where he braces himself for more battle should Xavier seize the offensive. None comes, however. Instead, Xavier goes to the doorway and calls, "Madeline, do you have a minute?"

The woman I'd seen earlier sitting across the table from Alexander appears.

"Madeline, please meet Dr. Paul Rider," Xavier says. "Madeline has a doctorate in computer science with a concentration in cyber security. She's keenly skilled at navigating the deep web."

Xavier has not looked at me once since we argued. For all I know, I'm invisible to him.

I shake what little there is of the hand Madeline offers me. I can see her spending hours working in the most secret places of the Internet for she's just a wisp of a woman with dark complexion who appears to be far more at ease with bits and bytes than with handshakes and niceties. Her hand remains in mine for a record short time among hands I've shaken. It's clear she longs to return to her laptop rather than stand in a demilitarized zone that separates Xavier from me.

"Madeline, it's very nice to meet you," I say.

"Madeline's taking the lead in cracking the dark net which Simsbury and his peers are using to communicate," Xavier says. He speaks to her rather than to me, and this clearly augments her discomfort. "That frees Alexander to keep abreast of developments on the military front."

And then it comes: a glance from Xavier; I exist after all. "Let's move to the conference room," he says.

After we've taken our seats, he addresses Madeline: "What have you learned from Simsbury's forum on the dark net?"

"He checked into the Intercontinental Hotel in Lusaka and

will be spending time at the temporary office quarters of International Mines near the airport."

"Doing what?" Xavier asks.

"Using it as his office for now."

"That's it? No specifics?"

"Yes," Madeline replies, "there was another thing, actually. He told his peers they mustn't give up in their joint effort to drive oil prices into the ground."

"What's that supposed to mean?" I ask.

She shakes her head and turns her palms up.

"Continue to follow him online," Xavier says. To Alexander: "Assemble the entire staff from the lodge here. We'll meet right after Paul leaves to discuss our need to evacuate the building."

THIRTY-FIVE MINUTES IS the flight time from the lodge to the bend in the Amalumbo River where my shack sits above the riverbank, and I savor every minute in the air to gaze at the beauty below—grazing wildebeest, buffalo, and zebra; loping giraffe; and marching elephants. It seems inconceivable the flight should be so short when it took nearly seven hours to travel the same distance by land. Remorse sets in as we begin our descent, for the peace of the skies has been a welcome relief from the tumult of land.

Through the headset, Martin calls my attention. "I have Annette on the phone for you," he says. "I'll connect you to her via a private line."

A moment later, I hear Annette's voice: "Paul, I'm so glad I reached you. I understand you're about to land shortly, so I won't keep you."

Her voice is like a balm. "Are you still in Lusaka?"

"Yes, but I just heard from Xavier. He told me the terrible news about being poisoned by Innocent Mbewe with radioactive cesium."

"You mustn't return to the lodge; it's not safe," I warn her.

"I won't, but Xavier refuses to leave. He insists on remaining at the lodge even though he sent the entire staff home."

"But he told me he'd leave as well!"

"Only to appease you; he intends to remain there to test the facility for radioactivity. I've purchased a Geiger counter at his request here in Lusaka that Martin will deliver to him later tonight."

"Madness! I'll call him straight away!" I say.

"Let him be, Paul. There's something else I want you to do." Urgency fills her voice.

"What is it?"

"Jihadists are driving in hordes toward Zambia with the threat of invading the northern rim of the country. You need an escape route should they reach as far south as Saysha. I've asked Martin to drop you off on the east side of the Amalumbo River so you can collect the Zodiac from the spot where you left it when you, Benji, Oscar, Innocent, and the guards last traveled to Uku-tetema three days ago."

We hit an air pocket on our descent that throws me back against the seat. I feel a burning sensation on the left side of my back midway between my pelvis and rib cage. Leaning forward, I slip a hand behind me, pull up my shirt, and detect a swelling the size of a golf ball along my back in the area where I felt the discomfort. When I press the area gently, it brings exquisite pain. I think immediately about an abscess as a possible cause. I'll have Bristol examine it as soon as I return to Saysha.

"Yes, I'll collect the Zodiac from beneath the ledge," I tell Annette.

"And one more thing, Paul…"

From the cockpit, Martin waves to me to end the call.

"Annette, I need to sign off because we're about to land. What is it you wanted to say?"

"Only this," she replies. "Are you really leaving soon for Indonesia?"

FROM THE PILOT'S seat, Martin warns us to ensure our seatbelts are tightly fastened. "The landing is short, rough, and sloped," he tells us.

He circles a familiar bluff along the Amalumbo River. Banking one way and then another, he peers out the window at a narrow grass strip nestled between rocky outcrops. Through the headset, I listen to his stream of consciousness: "No new holes…no debris… wind light…no bones from recent kills…all systems go…"

In a stomach-dropping swoop, he brings the Beechcraft to the ground where we come to a bumpy halt. It's a landing that, while not as abrupt as those that take place on aircraft carriers, is more truncated than any other I've had, one which throws me back in my rear-facing seat.

Martin is at the rear of the airplane unloading our luggage by the time I exit with Benji. We take our bags and step away from the fuselage.

"I must leave," Martin informs me. "You'll find the Zodiac in its usual spot."

Benji and I have just reached the top of the bluff when the Beechcraft takes off. I feel a sense of loss with its departure for Martin and the rest of Xavier's staff has grown on me. Having come to know them, I feel welcomed in a land that once seemed inhospitable.

We descend the bluff through the transverse fissure that drops to the river. With Benji leading the way, I recall Xavier's proclamation in Intanda that Benji had become a man. Only days earlier, when we were in this same fissure, Benji climbed it wide-eyed and tentatively, but now he jogs his way down. When we reach the river, he lowers himself through the ledge into the Zodiac. I hand him our bags before joining him onboard.

Manning the motor, I ease the Zodiac into the current. Without Annette's capable hands, I feel a heavy responsibility on my shoulders. Up front, Benji lies on the bow to watch for logs; when he sees one, he lifts an arm to point the way to go.

I feel less claustrophobic passing between the cliffs this time because the current whisks us through each vice-like narrowing. Mentally, I prepare for the upcoming challenge of mooring at our destination, a challenge that arrives quickly although not before I meet a good omen: a glimpse of the hippopotamus at the river's bend. Steering well clear of the animal, I approach the shoreline where I raise the motor while Benji paddles us to a stopping point. Together, we pull the Zodiac from the water and drag it over a sandbank to a small pond where we hide it among reeds, all the while keeping an eye out for crocodiles.

In the shade of the patio in front of my shack, I make a jug of lemonade from fruit picked a week ago that has ripened in the interim. I sit with Benji and Jimmy the baboon who appears from the trees to watch us. After seeing the fate of the baboon along the slopes of the eastern perimeter of Intanda, I'm grateful to see Jimmy alive and well.

I accompany Benji to the orphans' quarters where we meet a bevy of children who surround Benji in an offering of unity. Thandi and Amu soon emerge to envelope him. All three cry as Oscar's death weighs heavily upon them.

"After dinner tonight, we'll have a service for Oscar," I tell the children. "I want everyone to come prepared to share what's in your hearts."

I leave the children for the wards where I find Bristol among the patients. "It's your day off," I remind him. "What are you doing here?"

He's somber. "My soul is heavy because of Innocent."

Before leaving the lodge, I texted Bristol to let him know about how Innocent had poisoned Xavier Treadwill before running off with jihadists.

"His wife was taken away last night," Bristol adds. "A jeep appeared in the middle of the night to take her and the children away."

"What did the jeep look like?"

"I can't tell you because only one person saw the rear of it as it raced away from Innocent's home."

"We'll overcome this by moving on together," I tell him.

"But you won't be among us," he reminds me. "The Canadian doctors will arrive soon."

For the first time, I hear regret in his voice. "Let's make the most of the time we have together," I say. "And there's something I'd like to do with you immediately."

"What is it, *nudume?*"

I lead him to a small office beside the pharmacy where we're alone. Lifting my shirt, I ask him to examine my back.

"What happened?" he asks, circling a fingertip about the lump.

"It just appeared," I reply. "I noticed a burning sensation in the airplane today."

"The skin is swollen," he observes. "Did something strike you here?"

I think back to the activities of the past few days, recalling an episode where I scraped my back while descending the mountain with Benji and Oscar after watching the mother leopard with her cubs. The scrape brought little more than transient discomfort. "I can't think of anything unusual," I tell him. "Does it have the feel of an abscess?"

He pushes a finger into the swelling, eliciting exquisite pain. "No, it's not an abscess. Could it be a burn?"

I twist my head and torso as far as I can to try to see the affected area, but it remains out of sight. "Hand me that," I tell Bristol, pointing to a pocket-sized mirror sitting on a desk.

Holding the mirror along my side, I take another look and see the lesion—a mound of tense red tissue with irregular borders. The sight reminds me of a postcard I once saw of Ayers Rock, the large sandstone rock formation in central Australia that often appears as a glowing dome with the first or last rays of the day. My stomach churns at the sight.

I set the mirror down. "Bristol, where is the canister you found at Innocent's property?"

His face tightens. "I hid it in the bush, why?"

"Take me there; I want to see it."

"But, *nudume*, it's dangerous!"

"We'll take Katrine's Geiger counter. If it registers radioactivity as we approach it, we'll go no further."

We swing by the laboratory to collect the counter. Before long, we reach the outskirts of the hospital but continue along a neglected path that takes us past thorn bushes and small trees. Carrying a stick and swiveling his head to look about at all times, Bristol warns me to watch for snakes.

While I've never been here before, I've heard others speak about it, a place seldom visited because of a highly venomous snake that resides in the trees. Locals call the snake *nalukunilumo*, but in English it's known as the twig snake. It's slender and has a long profile, pointed snout, and greyish-brown skin with faint light and dark markings that help it camouflage in branches. When a breeze blows as it does now, the snake can sway like a twig, and thus its name. From the trees, it keeps a lookout for terrestrial prey in the form of frogs, lizards, and birds. When threatened, the snake inflates its throat to look especially ominous. The hospital staff has great concern for the snake because no anti-venom exists to treat people bitten by it.

The path soon climbs a knoll with blowing grass and clusters of rocks, one of which forms a semi-circle around a hole in the ground. At first sight, I wonder whether the hole descends to a cave, but upon closer inspection I see it's simply a depression about a meter deep.

"There it is," Bristol says, pointing to a backpack in the hole.

Because a flap has been pulled over the top of the backpack, I'm not able to see its contents. Removing two pairs of hospital gloves, I hand one pair to Bristol. After donning the other, I push the probe of the Geiger counter toward the backpack as I listen to its console. Because I hear only occasional and random clicks which I attribute to background radiation, I move closer.

"You *did* close the hole in the canister that you described earlier, right?" I ask.

"For sure!" Bristol replies. "I didn't want radiation to escape."

With no evidence of increased radioactivity, I set the Geiger counter down beside the depression and lift the flap on the backpack. The maneuver brings the canister into view. It stands on its end and appears just as Bristol had described, a two-unit device in which one cylinder lies within another.

"Give me a hand," I say. "Let's lift it out."

Bristol demurs.

"You can hear the meter," I tell him. "There's no evidence of leakage."

Together, we extract the canister and stand it on the ground. It's roughly half a meter in height and half that wide, a chunky, cumbersome unit with a gleaming smooth surface.

Kneeling, I tilt the unit to inspect its undersurface. Seeing no markings, I set it on its side to study its features. It has a small aperture along its outside that has been widened with a drill or some other device, leaving scratches on the surface around it. When I look into the hole, I see it runs the width of the exterior cylinder before ending along the interior one. At the top of the outer cylinder is a finger-size hole that allows me to insert the tip of my index finger to slowly rotate the outer cylinder.

"No!" Bristol exclaims. "You'll let out radiation!"

"I won't turn it enough to align the holes," I assure him.

As I rotate the outer cylinder, I peer through the hole to see what appears to be very fine lettering along the surface of the inner cylinder. Because the hole is small, I can see only one letter at a time. I tilt the cylinder until the sun shines directly into the hole to enhance my vision. With continued turning, I read the letters aloud…

S…h…e…f…f…i…e…l…d…R…a…d…i…o…l…

Suddenly, the Geiger counter comes alive with an outburst of clicks.

"Stop, *nudume!*" Bristol cries. He points to a digital meter on the instrument which registers increased radioactivity.

Immediately, I rotate the cylinder to its full-close position.

"Have you heard of this name, *Sheffield Radiol?*" I ask Bristol.

He shakes his head.

"Neither have I." Then again, as an emergency medicine physician, I've had little exposure to radiotherapy for any purpose, so I'm not surprised the name eludes me.

"*Nudume!*" Bristol wails. "Were Katrine and I harmed by opening the hole all the way?"

"Did either of you look directly into it?"

"I did briefly, yes, when I first aligned the holes at Innocent's shed. That's when I saw the glow come from inside."

"What about when you and Katrine examined it together?"

"We didn't open it all the way because, like now, the Geiger counter registered radioactivity."

"What about your hands? Did you place them over the hole?"

"No!"

"And you didn't sustain any burns on your arms or body?"

"None."

While I'm concerned about Bristol's view of the glowing blue when he was at the shed, I'm relieved his exposure was very brief. "I think you'll be fine," I tell him.

As for me, I grow alarmed that the lesion on my back may be a burn from cesium-137. How and where I was exposed I don't know, but if my thinking is right, I'm in serious trouble.

I'm not alone in having these thoughts, for Bristol asks: "*Nudume*, the burn on your back. Could it be…?"

I lift the probe from the Geiger counter and hand it to Bristol. "Run it across my back," I tell him.

While I take comfort from the counter registering only background levels of radiation, I know I'm not in the clear by any means. It's possible I was exposed to cesium-137 at the lodge before showering this morning, and if that happened, I may have sustained the burn I now feel before washing away the blue powder that caused the burn. Alternatively, it's possible I was burned by the cesium-137's gamma rays through my shirt without the powder ever coming into direct contact with my skin as might have happened, for example, if the back of the chair I sat on during breakfast this morning had been contaminated. I discount the burn having occurred four days earlier while I rode in the Zodiac with Innocent across the Amalumbo River to go to the lodge because I'm sure the burn would've appeared before now had that been the case.

I say nothing as I try to recall all possible exposure points. They could be myriad if Innocent Mbewe had spilled or deliberately placed cesium-137 in my path. I think about the chair I also sat on in my guest room this morning while taking off my boots; the rug on which I'd stretched briefly after doing so; and even the back of the toilet I'd used before napping.

As there's no cell phone coverage here, I tell Bristol: "Let's go back to the hospital. I need to call Xavier Treadwill."

Together, we set the canister back into the backpack and close the flap. "Keep this a secret!" I say. "I don't want anyone to come here and get exposed!" At some point, we'll need to dispose of the canister properly, but that will be another time.

We retrace our steps to the hospital where I call Xavier.

"Paul!" he answers. "I was just about to call you."

"Serious problem," I respond.

"What is it?"

"I have a radiation burn on my back. The area is swollen and very painful. I'm concerned about damage to underlying structures."

"Such as?"

"A kidney, the urine collecting system, and major blood vessels, among other structures."

"Oh, God, Paul!"

"I spoke to Annette," I add. "She said Martin is bringing you a Geiger counter from Lusaka later today."

"Yes, he just arrived in Lusaka with Ansel and the other guard. He has a Geiger counter and is about to leave for Uku-tetema shortly."

"Two favors I ask of you," I tell him. "First, when you get the Geiger counter, test the back of the chair I sat in at breakfast this morning and then go to my guestroom and run it all over the place—bed, rug, chair, bathroom, closet. And test the back seat of the Land Rover I rode in to go to the air strip around noon."

"This is why I'm staying at the lodge!" he declares. "I want to determine the extent of contamination."

I'd argue with him about the judiciousness of his decision to remain but, selfishly, I want to know what he finds with a Geiger counter.

"And the second favor?" he asks.

"Look up a company called *Sheffield Radiol.*" I spell it for him. "I found the name etched into the canister of cesium-137 that Innocent Mbewe brought to Saysha."

"Do you mean Sheffield Radiology?" he asks.

"I gave you the lettering I saw before we had to close the canister; I'm not sure of the rest."

"Good enough," he says. "I'll look it up."

Changing topics, I ask him: "Did you take another dose of activated charcoal?"

"Yes, but what about you? You need help!"

"I have some Prussian blue here that I kept from Lusaka. I took a first dose an hour ago."

I'm not convinced Prussian blue will do me any good, however, because if my lesion resulted purely from gamma rays burning my skin from the outside, I'm not likely to have cesium-137 inside my body as Xavier has. "Gotta go," I tell him. "I want to wash myself as soon as I can."

"By all means!" he replies. "But call me back when you can. I have news from the military and dark net fronts."

BENEATH THE WATER tower at the hospital is a stall where staff may shower. I stand under a stream of cold water after lathering my entire body. The cool water soothes the skin over my burn but does nothing to quell the internal pain. Neither acetaminophen nor non-steroidal anti-inflammatories have dulled it, either.

I dry off, dress, and return to the office beside the pharmacy where I call Xavier.

"You said you had news," I remind him. "What is it?"

He speaks with urgency: "On the military front, I've been informed that jihadist vehicles are converging on remote spots along our border with D R Congo and Tanzania for select strikes within Zambia. Their intel appears to be excellent as they're avoiding areas where we and our allies have positioned our defenses."

"And from the dark net—what have you learned there?"

"Yes, the dark net," he purrs. "Madeline struck the mother lode! Are you familiar with a group called Al-Shabaab?"

"Al-Shabaab!" I exclaim. "They're an Al-Qaeda offshoot with roots in Somalia!"

"Yes, a group whose goal is to create a fundamentalist Islamist state. In recent years, their cells have migrated from Somalia deeper into Africa. You may recall an attack they conducted at an upscale mall in Nairobi, Kenya where they killed more than sixty people. Their cells are in Danjou now mining diamonds along the Amalumbo River. Al-Shabaab's current leader is a man named Shimbir Awaale Sa'id who's pushing to expand mining into Zambia because of its lucrative potential. He's communicating with Simsbury to advance this goal."

"Wait a minute! Are you saying the two are in contact?"

"In direct contact, yes, and we have proof of it! Madeline discovered a string of communications between Simsbury and Sa'id on the dark net. Simsbury's the point man for a cabal consisting of four oil magnates I referred to before who're using the dark net as a forum to discuss mutual interests with Al-Shabaab. Among other things, they've discussed the oil deal I told you about earlier where TransNational is seeking to drill in eastern Ethiopia, not far from the Somali border. As the U.S. government deliberates the petition, TransNational is acting as if approval is imminent. Simsbury reached a deal with Sa'id to share profits from the venture in exchange for a promise from Al Shabaab not to attack TransNational workers in Ethiopia."

"That's outrageous!"

"There's more: In addition to receiving a share of profits from the Ethiopia project, Sa'id extracted a promise from Simsbury to lobby our National Assembly to open the Amalumbo River in Zambia to diamond mining. Simsbury sweetened the deal by promising to lobby not just for opening the Amalumbo River but *all* of Uku-tetema to mining and licensed killing of wildlife. To push for this, he and his three partners in the oil cabal have infused millions into our ailing copper industry. That's why the vote on Uku-tetema could go either way."

I'm beside myself: "But it makes no sense! Why would Simsbury and the other oil magnates risk going to jail for colluding with a terrorist group?"

"The rewards are huge!"

"What rewards? A two-bit deal in Ethiopia and access to Uku-tetema for minerals and animals?"

"You're forgetting about Intanda!" he retorts. "For Simsbury, it's *all* about oil!"

"Dammit!" I shout. "You still haven't told me how much oil Intanda has! Your father *must've* told you!"

He says nothing.

"Come on! Fess up!"

When he speaks, his voice is subdued, little more than a whisper: "The reserves of Intanda are equal to those of the Arabian Peninsula."

"*Shit!*" I whisper. "Are you serious?"

"Absolutely serious."

"But how could Simsbury know about those reserves? Certainly the prospector you told me about earlier—the one who trespassed upon Intanda to collect specimens of sand—couldn't have defined the true size of reserves at Intanda!"

"That's true. Simsbury had another source of far more reliable information."

"What was it?" I ask.

"As it turns out, the company my father hired to conduct the seismic survey of Intanda decades ago was a one-man firm based in Lusaka. When that man passed away a few years ago, his widow sold the company to International Mines. Not surprisingly, Simsbury learned of the results and made it his number one goal to secure rights to drill at Intanda."

I shake my head in disbelief.

"And another thing," Xavier adds. "It was Simsbury who generated the kill list with our names on it, and he's the one who's encouraged Sa'id to launch poachers into Uku-tetema to punish me for my drive to protect Uku-tetema."

"What about the poisonings? Was there mention of them on the dark net?"

"Not specifically, but Simsbury made it clear those who vote in favor of designating Uku-tetema as a national park will be dealt with forcefully."

"I trust you've shared these dark net communications with authorities here and in the U.S.!"

"Not yet, but I will shortly."

"*When?*"

"Tomorrow when I speak before the National Assembly in Lusaka. They just invited me to present a final argument for why Uku-tetema should be preserved as a park in perpetuity, and I've decided to accept their invitation. The members of parliament will vote immediately on my bill after I speak."

The news reassures me because, finally, I know Xavier can receive the care he needs in the nation's capital.

IT'S THREE O'CLOCK in the afternoon, yet my body drags. With the sun still high, the hot, dry air leaches my breath and sweat to leave me parched even though I drink one bottle of water after another.

With a radiation burn on my back, I know I must leave Saysha for the capital to seek specialized care. Thankfully, I look forward to tomorrow morning when Xavier has graciously promised to stop by Saysha to pick me up on his flight to Lusaka.

I leave the pharmacy and walk to the orphans' quarters where I find the children sitting in the shade of a mango tree. While the older girls braid the hair of younger ones, the boys stoop in games of marbles in the dirt. I ask Benji, Amu, and Thandi to step aside for a moment.

"I need your help," I tell them. "Tonight after dinner, we'll have a memorial service for Oscar and I want you to plan it with me."

We discuss options to celebrate a life gone by. I say very little, encouraging Oscar's friends to empty their hearts. After shedding many tears, we draft a service which I believe Oscar would have approved.

With plans to meet Bristol at my shack in forty-five minutes to discuss the arrival of the Canadian doctors, I begin my way home to start packing my belongings. They're sparse and will fit into a single suitcase, but I want to begin the process now because I suspect the memorial service may keep me up late tonight. I grow sad with the thought that the marks I'll leave along the ground tomorrow morning as I pull the suitcase behind me will be the last tracks I make in Saysha.

As I pass Innocent Mbewe's hut on my way home, I notice the door to the shed is open and the goats have disappeared. In front of the hut, the patio is littered with fallen leaves. Emptiness pervades the space.

My phone rings with a call from Xavier.

"The surveyors trespassed Intanda from all four entryways!" he announces. "We have photos to prove it."

"All *four?*"

"Yes, and I just sent you a photo of one of the trespassers. Tell me if you recognize him. He's a *mzungu*."

I pause along the path in a shady spot to check the photo. It shows a man standing on black sand beside a truck. From the camera placement, I know the photo was taken in the channel of the western portal. The man glares at the camera as if it belongs to a paparazzo who's taken his photo without permission. By instinct, I draw back to keep him from spitting into my face.

"I know this man!" I exclaim. "He helped me change the flat tire at the office of International Mines near the Lusaka airport."

The hairstyle gives him away. Although the mound atop his head is disheveled, as is the long, bushy hair in back, the sides of his scalp have been freshly cut to accentuate the mullet hairdo.

"I recognize him, too!" Xavier announces. "He was at the café in Lusaka the day I was poisoned with lithium! I recall him walking past my table several times behind the woman who bumped me."

"Oh, Lord!" I mutter. "So, *he's* the one who slipped the lithium into your tea!"

"Yes, and his employer, International Mines, just trespassed upon my land! They're sending Simsbury provisional results from the seismic survey they've begun. Simsbury's at the modular unit near the Lusaka airport studying the results as we speak." Xavier's breathing deepens to the point I can hear each breath. "Not only that, but he's forwarding the results to a very select group of National Assembly members in the hopes of bolstering opposition to my bill."

I'M PACKING MY suitcase when Bristol arrives. He's clearly agitated. "What's wrong?" I ask him.

"A large military contingent is passing through the village now. They're traveling north toward the border. They're heavily armed to defend against a possible invasion by extremists who want to extend diamond mining into our nation."

"Is Saysha in danger?"

"Not at the moment; the talk is the jihadists will attack west of us. That's where the military contingent is going." He looks at my suitcase. "Why are you packing so soon? The Canadian doctors will not arrive until next week."

"I'm feeling worse by the minute," I explain. "I just peed out blood. I need to get help in Lusaka."

"*Nudume*, that's serious!"

"Yes, I'm worried my kidney's damaged."

"How will you get to Lusaka? The journey by land is too long in your condition!"

"Xavier's flying to Lusaka tomorrow to speak before the National Assembly. He offered to stop here tomorrow morning first thing to give me a ride."

Bristol's face saddens. "But you must return to Saysha! You cannot leave without saying goodbye!"

"I'll do my best to get back because I want to meet the Canadian doctors and help them settle in, but at the same time, the folks in Indonesia are pressing for me to get started there."

He shakes his head. "We'll miss you, *nudume*."

My emotions well. To keep them at bay, I switch subjects. "The canister in the backpack," I remind him. "We need to have it disposed of safely. When I'm in Lusaka, I'll speak to experts to see what they advise."

From outside, we hear a faint hum.

"Is that an airplane?" Bristol asks. He leaves the shack to step outside. "Yes, it *is* an airplane!" he confirms. "It looks like the one Mr. Treadwill owns." He looks at me. "I thought you said he was coming here tomorrow morning."

"Yes, that's right. I don't know why the airplane is here now."

Bristol places a hand on my shoulder. "Rest, *nudume*. I will go to see why it has come."

THE DINNER HOUR approaches at the orphans' quarters and I want to eat with them. I close my suitcase and wheel it to a corner where it will remain for the night. Before leaving, I collect the sole photo I've nailed to my wall, one I plan to share this evening. As I step out of the shack and close the door behind me, I think about how I'll miss hearing its creaking hinges and feeling its wobble and rebellious bounce-back whenever I shut it too hard. I'll also miss the peek-a-boos of the Amalumbo River through the blowing leaves of banana trees along the perimeter of my patio. And with particular tenderness, I'll miss Jimmy, The Thinker.

The baboon sits now on the lowest bow of the acacia tree with his gaze upon me.

"Gotta run," I tell him.

He looks at me with utmost patience. Perched with his back against the trunk, he alternates his attention between the pedicure he affords himself and my departure. With his eyes, he asks, "Why do you *run?*"

I pause to look at him. Running appears to be the last thing on his mind. He's comfortable being where he is and who he is. From his seat in the sky, he lets the earth turn, the sun droop, and the river flow. In the stillness of his gaze, he asks me, Are these not the basic tenets of life? Isn't perpetual motion really a distraction from something else? Live where you are, he tells me; live with what you have; and live with *who* you are. In a cosmos of spinning planets, racing comets, and streaking meteors, isn't it enough just to *be?*

I leave Jimmy's questions unanswered and start down the path. Around me the light fades but not from the coming night. There's a sway in the bushes unlike any I've seen before, one that comes from a determined wind that brings dark clouds. Tonight will be unlike any I've spent in Africa, for rain will come; a sweetness in the air tells me this is so.

Outside the orphans' quarters the children sit on the ground for dinner. They form a circle by age, the youngest starting the circle and the oldest—Benji, Thandi, and Amu—closing it, only the circle isn't entirely closed because a gap remains between the youngest and oldest. A village elder, a woman who has prepared dinner tonight, directs me to fill the gap.

I take the hand of the little girl beside me and, on my other side, Amu's. Around the circle, hands find their neighbors'. Together, we sing a song of praise for the land and water that have graced us with another day of life. And then we eat, fingers dabbing balls of *nshima* into a vegetable stew. I've eaten this meal on countless occasions with the orphans, but tonight is different for the chatter and laughter that normally enliven the meal is absent; in their place come silent stares that tell me the children know that the *mzungu* who sits with them has taken the first step of a journey that will lead him away from their village.

When the meal is over, I ask Thandi, Amu, and Benji to lead us to the place they've chosen for Oscar's memorial service. The last light of day guides us to the flatbed truck Oscar tended like a shepherd tends his sheep.

I'm overwhelmed by the sight of flowers arranged along the hood in the shape of the letter, "O." How fitting, I tell myself, that Oscar's name begins with a letter that embodies the circle of life. But I also feel emptiness commensurate with the center of the letter until I remind myself that the letter "O" is by its very shape expansive, inclusive, and encircling and that, tonight, we gather together along its infinite arcs in a ceaseless flow of love for Oscar.

As I'd requested, Amu, Thandi, and Benji lead the service. They ask us to form a semi-circle around the hood of the truck. From the back of the vehicle, Benji carries three paper bags, one of which he keeps as he hands the other two to Amu and Thandi. Together, they distribute glow sticks and bracelets to the children but instruct them not to set either aglow yet. Taking the lead, Benji slips a bracelet over his wrist while holding the stick in his hand. The rest of us follow suit.

Amu takes a spot directly before the truck to face us.

"*Nudume* Paul has asked us to come together to celebrate Oscar's life," she begins, her voice wavering. "I will speak before Benji and Thandi, and then *nudume* Paul will do the same."

She looks up at the sky. Cracks of moonlight appear between coalescing clouds. Lifting her glow stick, she bends it to bring it alive in the color red. "Red was Oscar's favorite color," she says. "And red is the color of blood which gives us life. May we remember Oscar's life forever."

Thandi goes to her side. Behind the semi-circle, I notice several adults and children from the village have joined us. Others behind them make their way toward us as well.

Thandi lights her stick and lifts it. "Green is the color of grass when it rains," she says. "Oscar loved to play in tall grass. May we remember Oscar when we play."

Benji joins the two girls. Cracking his stick, he raises it, saying, "Yellow is the color of the sun. Oscar brought us warmth with his friendship. May Oscar's light shine upon us forever."

Addressing the entire group, Amu says, "Please join us in turning on just your glow sticks and lifting them to the sky. We will light our bracelets shortly."

After a moment of silence, with raised glow sticks lighting the night from uplifted arms before her, Thandi speaks: "Even though the clouds are setting in, we hold up our shining sticks to the stars so that Oscar may look down and see us smiling at him."

The three older orphans shuttle to the side of the truck in a signal that my time to speak has come. I take a place before the hood and look at a sea of endearing faces beneath glowing sticks. "I cannot match the beauty of the words and deeds we've heard and seen from Thandi, Amu, and Benji," I tell the assembled, "so I will keep what I say short and simple."

I pause as more adults and children arrive. Among them are paramedics and teachers accompanied by their families. Others I barely recognize, all compressing into an arc behind the orphans.

"I'd like to begin by reminding all of us, myself included, that there are times in life such as now when it's okay to be sad and to cry. Losing a friend—a brother, really—like Oscar is so hard and so painful. Do not feel alone in your pain; you are accompanied by the rest of us as we walk together along the road of loneliness and sorrow."

I lift the framed photo I brought from my shack but do not show it yet to the group.

"I've heard it said a person's life shouldn't be measured by the number of years lived but by the fullness of the days passed. By that measure, Oscar lived a very full life! Each day, he filled the minutes and hours with activities that brought him joy, be it helping the mechanics with the truck, playing with friends, or assisting with chores at the hospital. But what I especially liked about Oscar was his inquisitiveness. He had an endless desire to know how things worked. If he had his way, he would've dismantled everything about us only to put it all back together again, such was his passion for mechanics."

My throat dries. Each word becomes a struggle to deliver.

"I feel particularly fortunate that Oscar and I crisscrossed in one particular activity—driving the truck. As you know, he loved to sit on my lap and take the wheel or, sitting beside me, shift gears. He was skilled at both, so much so he knew exactly when to shift by the sound of the engine; I wouldn't have to say a thing."

I turn the photo around and, illuminating it with a flashlight, hold it up for all to see.

"Teacher Daniel, who is among us tonight, was kind enough to take this photo of Oscar and me. As you can see, it shows only our hands and a portion of our arms. Together, we hold the knob of the gearshift, Oscar's hand beneath mine. Teacher Daniel took the photo shortly after Oscar began learning how to shift gears. I shall keep this photo in my presence forever because I feel Oscar's hand will remain in mine for as long as I live."

I know when it's time to stop speaking, and the time has come. While there's more I could say, I fear breaking down, and I don't want that to happen. Instead, I turn to Thandi who recognizes my subtle plea for help and intervenes seamlessly.

"It is time now to light our bracelets," she says. "Let us sing together as we raise our arms in light."

The children sing a song in Bemba as they sway their arms with bracelets aglow. Before long, others from the village join the chorus with arms asway. Looking through an ocean of arms, I see a solitary glow stick rise from the rear of the crowd. The bare arm which holds it is unmistakably fair. Beneath the glow, a woman's hair blows in the wind. Although thirty meters and dozens of bodies separate me from Annette, I feel one with her in heart and soul.

THE MEMORIAL SERVICE ends with each orphan collecting a flower from the hood. I make my way through the dispersing crowd to Annette who greets several paramedics she's befriended during her brief visits to Saysha. When I reach her, she's providing an update on the burn patient in Lusaka. I wait by her side until we're alone.

"I wanted so much to see you I asked Martin to leave me here on our way back to Uku-tetema," she tells me. "I'm very worried about your radiation burn."

I tell her I've packed and inform her that Xavier has agreed to swing by in the Beechcraft tomorrow to pick me up on his way to the capital.

"Yes, I heard about that," she replies. "But I fear for his safety in Lusaka. There's so much tension there as war looms."

Having dispensed the last of the flowers, Thandi joins us. She places a flower in Annette's hair. "Thank you for bringing the glow sticks and bracelets from Lusaka," she tells her. "I only wish you'd had a chance to know Oscar better."

"I feel fortunate to have spent time with him walking through the bush of D R Congo," she replies.

The two hug.

"Come," Annette says, "let's walk home together to see the young ones to bed."

As we set off, Thandi walks between us. "*Nudume*," she says, "Bristol told us you'll be leaving soon and that new doctors from Canada will be arriving in your place. Must it be so?"

"My coming here was always to be temporary," I remind her. "That was the nature of the job."

"But you could have applied to stay permanently," she notes.

I say nothing, for I can't talk my way past Thandi; she's too smart.

"Let's live one day at a time," Annette says, wrapping an arm around the girl. "Tonight first, then tomorrow..."

We walk the remaining way in silence. When we reach the orphans' quarters, I see the boys to bed while Annette accompanies the girls. We meet outside after the last candle falls dark.

"We need to talk," Annette tells me. "Can I come to your place?"

"Yes, but let's swing by the pharmacy first," I reply. "I need some stronger pain meds."

In the pharmacy, I unlock a cabinet that holds a stack of individually-wrapped suppositories and take a handful of them.

"Oxycodone," Annette observes from the label. "You *are* hurting, aren't you?"

I close the cabinet and lock it. Lifting the back of my shirt, I show her the wound.

"Oh, my God!" she gasps. "It's horrible! Bristol didn't mention there was a blister!"

"It just formed." I tell her about the bloody urine and increasing fatigue. "I need help soon."

She takes my arm, and we leave the pharmacy but not before I collect a tourniquet, a liter bag of saline, an intravenous catheter, and plastic tubing to run the saline. Along the path to my shack, Annette blows the whistle for me as I save my breath for walking. When we reach the shack, I light a candle in the kitchen and drink some water but vomit it shortly.

"Oh, Paul, leave it!" Annette enjoins. She takes the cloth I use to clean my mess. Before long, she joins me on my cot where we sit side-by-side. I ask her to help me as I insert an intravenous line into my arm. "I need the fluids," I explain. "I'm getting dizzy from dehydration."

She shows no discomfort with needles. I suspect this stems from her having seen blood shed by countless animals in poaching events. With saline flowing through the line, she places a palm across my forehead. "No fever," she observes.

I worry about whether one will come. If it does, it will signal infection, a potentially fatal turn of events.

"How can we make you comfortable?" she asks. She fluffs my pillow. Kneeling before me, she says, "Here, let's take off your shirt so you can lie on your stomach." After undoing the upper buttons, she lifts her head to look at me, and her eyes betray concern. "Just hold on until tomorrow; help's on the way."

I place a hand beneath her chin. "I never thought I'd say these words again, but I must: I love you, Annette."

She comes to my side and kisses me, caressing my cheeks with her palms. In her kiss, I feel emotion and tenderness, and she's careful to keep me from moving. We hold hands and look into each other's eyes. In hers I see patience. Flashbacks of our brief relationship race through my mind. My lips part in a faint smile as I recall thinking early on that she was irritatingly prim if not capricious and domineering. And then everything changed.

"What is it, Paul?" she asks. "You're smiling, aren't you?"

I look up at the door which remains open to the patio in front. A light rain falls now, the first of the season. With each drop that strikes the earth, I hear a plump patting sound that comes from water bouncing off a ground so dry it's almost impenetrable. From above comes the shoebill stork's high-pitched whine, one announcing the arrival of the latest visitor, the rain.

"My animal friends," I tell Annette. "I'll miss the stork that lives up there."

"Who else lives with you?" she asks.

I point to the patio. "Jimmy's out there somewhere in the trees. He's my baboon buddy. I just had a talk with him earlier this evening."

"What did you discuss?"

My heart heaves. "He asked why I always feel the need to run."

"*Do you* feel that way?"

I look away.

"Paul?"

"Yes," I whisper. "I'm always running…have been since I was young…and always will as long as I live."

"What are you running from?"

"My past."

Annette takes my hand and cups it in hers. "Did you read my letter? The one I gave you before you left for Intanda?"

I point to the torn envelope on my bedside table. "I've read it so many times I've almost memorized it. Let me show you." I glance at the saline bag; a third of it has flowed into my veins. "In your letter you told me, and I quote now: *And so I ask you this: Might there be another time when I can lie with you to rub, massage, and caress your back with the most tender love I possess?* Those were your words, weren't they?"

Because she says nothing, I turn to look at her. Tears stream along her cheeks. She scrunches the skin about her eyes in a futile attempt to stem the flow.

I kiss her, tasting the salt of her tears. "I'll take those fingers, palms, and hands now," I tell her. "I need them more than ever."

She rubs her fingers through her tears before spreading them across my cheeks. "Lie down," she says. "Let me deliver on my promise."

Shirtless, I stretch along the cot on my stomach. From the kitchen, Annette brings a stool that she places beside me. I feel her palms rest upon my shoulders.

"I'll be careful," she says, "but tell me if I hurt you in any way."

I surrender my body to her. She places her palms below my neck where they remain long enough to make me lift my head to look at her. I see she looks to the ceiling with her eyes shut. Her lips move ever so slightly, yet I hear no words.

And then her hands begin to move across the top of my back, at first only fingertips but then palms as well. She is gentle yet probing, and her skin is soft and smooth. With each crossing of the back, her hands drop lower until they come to the first scar. By instinct, I tighten.

"Let go, Paul," she whispers. "Release yourself to me."

Ever so softly, she traces the upper margin of the top scar only to reverse course along its lower margin. She repeats the maneuver only this time using the tips of her middle three fingers which she presses into my skin in circular motions. After moving across the scar in both directions, she kisses it.

The sequence begins anew with the next scar down, but this time she sings quietly as she traces and rubs...*Dapples and greys, pintos and bays, all the pretty little horses*

"My father used to sing me those words every night when I was little," she whispers. "I loved the lullaby because my mother owned horses before she died when I was four years old."

"That's a young age to lose a mother," I say.

"Far too young; I was old enough to remember her but too young to have known her well."

"So your father raised you?"

"Yes, and I love him dearly for the way he did so. Even after my self-destruction as a minister, he stood by me. He's encouraged me more than anyone in my work as a wildlife photographer."

She works another scar but stops short of its end on account of its proximity to the burn.

"Paul, from the voice mail you left with your sister that Xavier played for us, I know your father must've been cruel to you. In that voice mail, you referred to him as 'the Great Santini,' and you said he deserved to have terminal cancer."

"That's right. I hate my father. Hate oozes from every scar he left on my back."

She sings anew…

When you wake, you shall have, all the pretty little horses

"There's no curse on you, Paul," she says. "*No one*, especially not your father, can deny you the joy of having or being around children. In fact, from what I've seen, you're incredibly gifted with them and they draw great love from you."

TO MY BLEARY mind, the buzz from Annette's phone sounds like an enormous insect has entered the shack and hovers over my ear. I open my eyes and see that Annette has made a bed from a spare blanket that stretches across the floor beside me.

The light from her phone illuminates her face. Glancing at me, she says, "It's Xavier calling."

I'm woozy, but the awkwardness of the moment doesn't escape me. Beside me in my home at the midnight hour is a woman who takes a call from the man who fathered her children, a man who, just days earlier, had pleaded with me to help him reunite spiritually and emotionally with her. I vow to remain silent to prevent him from knowing that Annette and I are together at this moment.

Although the oxycodone suppository I inserted two hours earlier takes the edge off my pain, I occupy a hazy world between sleep and alertness as Annette converses with Xavier.

"Yes, I'm in Saysha," she tells him. "I wanted to deliver some art supplies I purchased in Lusaka to the orphans."

I hear a faint tinny voice from the other end.

"Oh, no, that's terrible!" Annette mutters. "Yes, keep me posted as you can!"

She hangs up.

"What did Xavier say?" I ask. Stiff from lying on my stomach, I turn gingerly onto my side.

"He did a first pass through the lodge with the Geiger counter. He found several hot spots, including the bed in the guest room you occupied."

Even in my foggy state, I understand the implications of what she said. "Thus my burn: Innocent seeded my bed with radioactive cesium!"

"Xavier said the kitchen was hot, too."

"What about the airplane?" I ask, thinking about our upcoming flight to Lusaka.

"It's clean."

I shift the pillow in a futile search for comfort. From the floor, Annette rubs my side.

"On the military front," she says, "Xavier's getting mixed messages."

"In what way?"

"Some reports indicate the jihadists are well west of us, but others suggest a splinter offensive is heading our way."

"What about our soldiers? Bristol saw a convoy pass through the village today."

"I can't tell you where they are, but there's ferocious fighting going on along the border. Xavier will leave the lodge at daybreak to come get us."

"That's it? Any other news?"

"Yes, something about how Alexander installed keystroke recorders on laptops at International Mines last week when he broke into their office near the airport. Those recorders are allowing Xavier to monitor everything Simsbury's doing on their laptops."

THIS NIGHT IS endless.

The pain medication has worn off, and my back throbs. If I could whittle away the remaining hours of darkness by tossing and turning, I'd do it, but the pain keeps me from moving.

I insert another suppository. My cell phone rings before the medication takes effect.

"Xavier, how are you?" I ask. I fear the ingestion of cesium-137 must be scorching his insides by now.

"Get out of Saysha!" he blurts. "They're almost there!"

"*Who's* almost here?"

Beside me on the floor, Annette awakens. I place the call on speaker.

"Jihadists!" Xavier exclaims. "They're going to raze the village!"

"How do you know that?" I ask.

"I have before me a series of communications from the dark net between Simsbury and Shimbir Awaale Sa'id that span the past eight hours. Last night, Simsbury ordered Sa'id to divert some of his forces to Saysha to destroy it in retribution for the trip lines we installed."

"Did you say Simsbury *ordered* the attack on Saysha?"

"Yes! He's furious we have photos of International Mines trespassing Intanda."

"Has he sent jihadists after you, too?" I ask.

"I've seen no mention of it," he replies.

"But you can't *assume* you're safe!" I tell him. "I doubt he'd attack Saysha without going after you, too!"

"Listen!" he shouts. "Do as I say! You will take the Zodiac down the Amalumbo River about ten kilometers to a field along the western shore where Martin and I will be waiting for you in the Beechcraft. We're leaving Uku-tetema shortly to get you."

"Why don't the two of you use the field outside Saysha? It's closer!"

"Innocent Mbewe informed the jihadists about that field. They'll have it staked out! Now go!"

ANNETTE IS DISTRAUGHT. "Where's the Zodiac?" she demands.

"Among the reeds by the river," I reply.

"Let's get in it and go!" she exclaims.

"I can't!" I say.

"Why not?"

I try to stand, but my knees buckle, forcing me to grasp Annette's arm.

"Paul! Are you alright?" she cries.

"I've never felt so weak," I reply.

"I'll help you get to the river!"

"No, I first need to check on the orphans!"

"But jihadists are coming!" she wails. "We won't survive unless we flee now!"

"You go!" I tell her. "I'm already responsible for losing Oscar; I can't let any of the others die."

"*You're* not responsible for Oscar's death! The jihadists killed him!"

I check my watch—four forty-five a.m., just about the time human adrenal glands squirt adrenaline into the body to boost energy for the dawning day. "I know why I'm weak," I say. "The radiation fried the adrenal gland over my kidney. It'll take a couple of days for the gland on the opposite side to compensate."

"So let me help you!"

"Just go to the river," I repeat. "Get the Zodiac ready while I retrieve Amu, Thandi, and Benji. I'll bring them there with me."

"You're asking to die!"

I go to the kitchen to get the rifle Bristol left there the day before while visiting me. Departing the shack, I take no more than three steps before Annette interlocks her arm with mine to walk alongside me.

"Go to the river!" I tell her.

She remains at my side. "I'm not leaving you, Paul."

The rain has stopped and while the clouds are lifting, the path is enshrouded in darkness. Using a flashlight, we reach the outskirts of the village where we hear screams come from the direction of the hospital. They're followed by the roar of approaching vehicles whose horns blare as whoops and jeers come from their occupants.

"Jihadists!" I whisper, stooping with Annette behind a bush.

Suddenly, the thatched roof of a hut erupts in flames. A pickup truck with a large red circle on it races to another hut which soon ignites as well. Triggering each fire is a torch brandished by a man wearing a red bandanna who leans over the truck at each passing hut to set it afire. One by one, the dwellings of Saysha burn as more vehicles arrive.

"Come! I know another way to the hospital!" I whisper.

We backtrack along the path a short distance before cutting through dense bush that offers the narrowest of passages. It brings us to the rear of the hospital grounds where we slink alongside a roofless one-story cinderblock building that serves as the facility's laundromat. The sight that meets me when we reach the front of the building sickens me.

"Oh, God!" I cry.

I feel Annette's arm pull me close. "There's nothing to be done, Paul!" she insists. "They've destroyed the place!"

Freeing myself from her, I limp to a line of bushes that transects the hospital grounds. As I creep through them, I hold the rifle diagonally to keep it from snagging a branch. Along both sides, I see huts which once housed patients now lay completely demolished. A crushing thought comes to me: The jihadists overran the huts without regard for their inhabitants. From the rubble, I hear moans and cries for help.

At the end of the bushes, I look across a courtyard to where the orphans' quarters once stood. The arrival of dawn leaves no doubt the building has been destroyed. The only structure remaining is a cross beam that juts to the ground from the remnants of a wall.

"Let's go!" Annette implores. "We need to see if anyone's alive there!"

While stealing through the bushes, I assumed Annette had remained behind. Now I scramble to keep up with her as she darts toward the fallen quarters. As I hobble, I expect gunfire to take me down, but none comes. Instead, an eerie quiet pervades the grounds as sounds of bedlam come from the village.

Ahead of me, I watch Annette comb through debris before she kneels. By the time I catch up to her, she holds a four-year-old girl named Darla whose whimpers tell me the child has sustained serious trauma. Moments pass before the whimpers cease. Annette lays the body down.

"*Nudume*," a voice cries.

I know the voice well and look about desperately for its source. Lifting a section of corrugated tin, I find Amu lying face down. I turn her over. She has cuts across her face and winces when I move her leg.

She rises slowly and looks at the lifeless form beside Annette. "I tried to save Darla, but I couldn't!" she cries.

I take Amu into my arms and hold her tightly. "Can you walk?" I ask her.

"I think so," she replies.

"Where are the others?"

"Everyone got out except Darla," she explains. "I saw her in the headlights of a truck that ran over us as we slept. Darla was trying to escape before the truck struck again. I ran in to help her, but everything fell upon on us."

Beside Darla, I see one of the crutches that helped her walk as a result of a congenital hip defect.

"What about Benji and Thandi?" I ask. "Where are they?"

"Thandi went with the paramedic who stayed at the hospital all night."

"Which paramedic was that?"

"Cynthia. She took the children to her house outside the village."

"Did Benji go with them?"

"No, he told me he was going to blow up a fuel truck."

"*What?*" I gasp.

She points to a grove beside the remnants of the pharmacy. "Over there, just behind the trees, there's a truck. Benji recognized its lights as a fuel truck. He told me he knew how to blow it up."

"When did he go there?"

"Minutes ago. He said he needed to get something first in the ruins of the pharmacy."

"What did he need?"

"Wire and a battery."

"Oh, no!" I mutter. "I've gotta stop him!" To Annette, I say: "Go with Amu. She'll show you a way through the bush to Cynthia's. It's set apart from the other huts not far from the field where

Martin landed the airplane. But be careful! Jihadists will be all over the place!"

"And you, Paul?" Annette asks. "Where shall we find you?"

"At the river. Have the Zodiac ready to launch! I'll get there as soon as I can."

We part ways, but before I reach the ruins of the pharmacy, I glance behind me to see Annette and Amu have disappeared into the bush.

I find utter destruction at the pharmacy. Littering the ground are medication vials, patient instruction brochures, a blackboard used for recording the arrival of new supplies, and, to my dismay, broken solar panels. I follow a cable from one of the panels. It dives into the wreckage, but I'm able to track its course by lifting debris, all the while looking about for signs of the invaders. In short order, I come to the charge controller, an instrument that monitors battery voltage, and I know then the batteries are nearby.

Lifting an overturned desk, I find the battery bank although one is missing. Looking further, my eyes catch a movement in the grove nearby. I crouch to see Benji approaching the fuel truck Amu spoke of. It idles audibly just beyond the trees. As he moves forward, Benji carries a large spool of wire that he unwinds as he advances. He springs from one tree to another, peeking around each before moving on.

I lumber into the grove where I almost trip on a lone battery. It sits on the ground with a wire running from one of its terminals toward the truck. I know now exactly what Benji has in mind to do, and I prepare for disaster should he make the slightest error in carrying out his task.

At the distant end of the grove, Benji peers around a tree. Just meters ahead of him, a pair of legs moves along the far side of the fuel truck. A militant soon appears at the rear with an assault rifle. He moves along the near side of the truck before disappearing around the engine.

Benji rushes forward from the tree as he unwinds more wire. Stopping beside the truck, he removes the cap to the fuel tank serving the truck's engine and cuts the wire with a splicer. After stripping both ends of the cut wire, he twists the two ends together and then pushes them into the fuel tank. He can't see it, but along the opposite side of the truck, the militant's legs move toward the rear in what I'm sure will be another roundabout. I want to call out to Benji to run, but my better senses tell me not to.

The task of pushing wires into the tank while unwinding a spool proves to be slow and onerous, and while Benji toils, the guard reaches the end of the truck. I lift the rifle and take aim at the fender nearest to Benji in preparation to shoot the guard if he reaches that point. Sweat pours from my forehead, and it takes all I have not to tremble. Peering through the scope, I see the guard's legs halt at the end of the truck. Two more legs appear and stop beside the guard's. A conversation begins.

Having completed his task, Benji returns to the grove. His job is far from complete, however, because he needs to unwind wire from the spool all the way back to where I stand beside the battery. In the interim, I fear the militant will notice the wires emerging from the tank and follow them to discover Benji. I keep my rifle aimed at the guard's legs, waiting for them to move again.

The conversation between the jihadists continues long enough for Benji to approach me. So as not to frighten him, I whistle softly. The sound causes Benji to halt and look about.

"Over here!" I whisper. I wave my arm until he sees it.

"*Nudume!*" he whispers back. "You're alive!" He unwinds more wire as he backs up to the tree behind which I stand.

"Yes, as are you!" I grasp his shoulder and squeeze it affectionately. Pointing to the truck, I add: "You've taken on a dangerous project! Let's finish it and get out of here!" I hand him the rifle and take the spool. "Cover for me!"

I unwind several more lengths and cut it with the splicer Benji hands me. "You connected the two wires loosely at the fuel tank, right?" I ask.

"Yes," he replies. "I remember when we installed solar panels on the pharmacy roof you showed us how loosely connected wires can throw off sparks when current flows through them."

I'm amazed by Benji's diligence. While working together on the solar project, he and Oscar paid particular attention to my warnings, one of them relating to the spark potential of loose electrical connections.

I strip the end of the wire coming from the truck. To be safe, I hold it far from the battery while I address Benji. "We're ready to make the final connection, but before I do so, I want you to get farther away."

With rifle at the ready, he backs away to the point where I entered the grove. After I see him stake a position behind a tree, I prepare to short-circuit the battery by touching the wire to the free terminal.

Putting my fate in the trees that separate me from the truck, I lower the wire toward the battery. The last few inches between wire and terminal become miles as I dig for the courage to bring copper to lead. I flinch as a spark jumps from the terminal when the two meet. It's a good sign because it tells me we've successfully short-circuited the battery by connecting its negative and positive terminals. The lack of an explosion at the truck, however, suggests the short circuit hasn't created sparks at the loose electrical connection in the fuel tank. Only one solution remains: to hold the wire to the terminal for a longer period to send continuous current through the circuit to generate sparking at the loose wires.

Seeing a stick nearby, I wrap the wire around it several times but leave the exposed end free. I step behind a tree and extend the branch to a point above the battery, only then lowering it slowly until the wire touches the terminal. Sparks ensue, but this time I press the wire onto the terminal to keep the connection intact. Smoke with the aroma of lead wafts from the terminal as sparks continue to fly. And then it comes, a duo of explosions, the first from the smaller fuel tank that feeds the engine and a second, massive detonation from the reservoir. The latter hurtles me backward.

Dazed, I look up to find a yellow curtain of flames where the truck once stood. Above it, a plume of black smoke rises into the sky. My ears ring with such force I can't hear Benji who speaks to me at my side. For a moment, I forget where I am. When I try to stand, I fall forward, eliciting a sharp pain at the burn site.

"*Nudume*, come with me!" Benji pleads.

I take his arm and follow him out the grove and past the ruins of the pharmacy. Before long, we crawl through the same bushes I traversed earlier. Passing the laundry area, we enter the bush and take the narrow path back to the main one that leads to my shack. When we come to a straightaway, however, we see three armed jihadists running ahead of us toward my shack.

"We can't go this way!" Benji whispers.

Ducking into the bush, I say, "We need to get to the river somehow! Annette is waiting for us there at the Zodiac with Thandi and Amu."

"They should set off on the water before the jihadists find them!" Benji warns. "Call her and tell her to leave in the Zodiac, but they must float and not start the motor or they'll be heard! Have them stop around the first bend downstream. I know a way to get there from here."

Trudging deeper into the bush and out of hearing range, I call Annette.

"Where are you?" she asks frantically. "We've been waiting for you here at the river!"

"Get into the Zodiac and go!" I tell her. "Jihadists are on the path headed toward my shack. They'll see you from the bluff if you stay by the river. Float downstream and stop after the first bend. Benji is with me and knows how to get there by land."

"Okay, we'll leave, but I have terrible news from Xavier to share when I see you!"

My heart sinks as the call ends. I feel a loyalty to two places yet have little to offer either: Saysha is under siege, and Xavier Treadwill is in trouble. All I can do is to flee both.

I follow Benji through bushes that give way to a steep descent lined by acacia trees where baboons roam. I look about for Jimmy but don't see him. At the base of the descent, we come to wetlands, and I think about the shoebill stork on my roof that frequents the area for fish.

"Be careful!" Benji whispers. "There may be crocodiles here!"

After sloshing through reeds and water that reaches my knees in places, we come to drier land which we follow around a hill. Pointing to the summit, Benji says, "The river wraps around this hill. We should find Miss Annette at the other side of it."

While the first rain of the season came last night, it was a short one that leaves no reprieve from a rising sun and warming air. As I begin to sweat more, I lament leaving the shack without water. In my present condition, symptoms will worsen with dehydration. One thing I didn't forget, however, was my pain medication. When an appropriate opportunity comes, I'll take another dose for what seems to be shortening periods of relief.

Nearing the river, we push through grass so tall Benji disappears at points. I follow in the trail of bent stalks he leaves behind but do so with considerable difficulty as grasshoppers whiz by. Because the blades are sharp, I hold my arms up to keep my face from getting cut.

Finally, the grass thins, and we come to the river. Looking both ways, we see no sign of the Zodiac.

"Where are they?" I ask, worried they've been detained by the jihadists. I lift my phone to call Annette when Benji grabs my arm.

"Over there, *nudume!*" he exclaims. "I see them!"

I follow Benji's outstretched arm to make out a head poking over a boulder beside the river. A pair of arms rises to wave at us.

"Thandi!" I call, waving back at her.

We reach Annette, Amu, and Thandi in short order and push off in the Zodiac. Instantly, Annette has the engine started and steers us into the current.

"Did the jihadists see you leave?" I ask her.

"No, because we hid beside the raft in the reeds until they left your shack." Her expression saddens. "But they burned your home entirely."

"No!" I cry. "The stork—"

"The stork is fine, *nudume*," Amu interjects. "I heard it whine as the militants approached and then saw it fly away."

From the bow, Benji helps Annette steer clear of debris.

I address her now: "You told me you had troubling news from Xavier. What is it?"

She grimaces. "He's very ill, Paul! He told me he's passing blood from his rectum and has intense abdominal pain. He can barely walk at this point."

I lift my phone to call him but discover I have no service.

"A call wouldn't change anything," Annette asserts. "It's over."

"What are you talking about? If he can keep himself hydrated, we can get him to a hospital!"

She shakes her head.

"Annette! You're not telling me something! What is it?"

She begins to cry even as she steers the Zodiac. "Just before Xavier was due to leave the lodge to fly here with Martin, he noticed a string of vehicles with jihadists making its way across the savanna toward the lodge. He decided to remain there to defend the place. He's alone now without any help, and that's the way he wants it. He refused to endanger his staff by keeping them there."

"But he told me he had no indication the lodge would be attacked!"

"It's true; he didn't, but the jihadists came nonetheless."

"But Martin can get us there in half an hour once we take off!" I insist. "All Xavier has to do is get to the air field so we can pick him up! Although the Beechcraft will be full with our present numbers, I'm sure Martin will squeeze Xavier in given the circumstances."

Annette sobs now. "I begged Xavier to go to the air field, but he refused! He insisted on remaining at the lodge."

"How can he possibly defend it *alone?*"

She says nothing, keeping her eyes on the river as wind streaks tears across her temples.

I turn to face the bow for I've had enough of this discussion. I'll address Martin directly when I see him.

With five people in the Zodiac, we motor more slowly than I'd like, but the rain from last night has quickened the current. Unlike the section of river north of my shack which posed hostile narrows and jutting protrusions, here we glide along open waters which, on close inspection, host whirling eddies indicative of dangerous undercurrents capable of sucking one under. I check to ensure that life vests are worn securely by all.

The currents are not the only hazard we'd face if we capsized. Along the surface of the water near the shorelines are crocodiles which float effortlessly as they watch us cautiously. With sufficient air in their lungs to keep their heads up, they angle their bodies into the water largely out of view save for limbs which they splay as stabilizers to keep from rolling. Every so often, we startle one which causes it to it lash its tail before it disappears altogether.

We pass not a single dwelling or sign of humanity the entire way. Here the river is a tan thread upon a barren brown tapestry. I search the terrestrial fabric for the field where the Beechcraft waits, but Annette is the first to spot it.

She steers the Zodiac to the western shore where we stop along a muddy bank. Benji is quick to hop out onto a slippery surface. After securing the vessel to a small tree, he helps the rest of us exit. We meet a relieved Martin at the top of the bank.

"I was getting ready to fly along the river to look for you!" he exclaims.

I tell the children to board the airplane which they do with Annette. Remaining outside, I plead with Martin: "We *must* go back for Xavier! This is our last chance to rescue him!"

Martin is anguished. "I tried to persuade him this morning to leave the lodge with me but he refused! He insisted on remaining there, saying nothing could force him from his ancestors' land!"

"I'm not asking him to leave it permanently—just long enough to evade the jihadists!"

He shakes his head. "There's no time to rescue him. Only an hour ago, I stood with him in the garden overlooking the savanna to the west. We saw jihadist vehicles coming straight for the lodge."

"But that's tricky terrain to traverse! I've traveled it twice on my way to the lodge. It took us great effort to keep our axels from cracking on its rocks and gullies."

Martin's anguish deepens. "Okay, we'll fly back to the lodge, but only because I know how much Xavier reveres you. Get in!"

I limp to the airplane and take the seat beside Martin. Even before closing his door, he hands me a manila envelope. "Xavier asked me to give this to you."

"What is it?"

He shakes his head. "I was only asked to deliver it."

We put on headsets. Within moments the engines rev, and we pull into the sky. On one side of the airplane, the Amalumbo River fades as we bank to the east.

"Martin!" Annette calls through the headset. "Where are you going? Lusaka is the other way!"

"I'm sorry, Madam," he replies. "We're returning to the lodge."

"Paul!" she shouts. "You're violating Xavier's wishes! He explicitly told me not to allow you to return to the lodge!"

I say nothing as my eyes rake across the contents of the manila envelope. It holds a speech Xavier had prepared to deliver to the National Assembly before the vote takes place on Uku-tetema's future.

"Water!" I beg. "Do you have any, Martin?"

He points over his shoulder toward Annette. "Madam, on the floor beside you is a case of water. Please distribute a bottle to everyone."

Annette frees herself from her belt, opens the case, and disseminates bottles to all but me. Leaning forward over her seat behind me, she removes her headset and mine. Her lips come to my ear. "Paul, I'll give you water, but first I want to convey how upset I am with you."

Through the sound of the engines, I barely hear her words. I crane my neck to look at her.

She turns my head to regain access to my ear. "The thirst you have for water is the thirst I have to see justice done for Xavier. I *promised* him I'd get you to Lusaka in time for you to deliver the speech he prepared for the National Assembly. Yet now you've put that in jeopardy! Uku-tetema may fall as a result."

I turn to address her: "Why didn't he ask someone in the National Assembly who supports his bill to deliver the speech?"

"Because, he believes you hold the most credibility to speak for him."

"What about *you?*" I ask in disbelief. "Talk about credibility..."

"I'm just relaying what he told me this morning. He considers you a brother because of the way you've cared for him during his illness and for what you did for his people by installing the trip lines."

She hands me a water bottle which I empty readily. Returning Xavier's papers to the envelope, I gaze out the window at a now familiar sight of animal herds in savannas below. They beat like a heart, creating a pulse on the land.

Through the headset, I hear a buzzing sound and then Martin's voice. "I've placed a call to Xavier," he says, looking at me. Our eyes lock as the call goes unanswered. He shakes his head in despair.

In the distance, I see the outline of hills upon which the lodge sits. I search the savannas below for a trail of dirt coming from vehicles traveling toward the lodge but see none.

After beginning our descent, Martin lifts a pair of binoculars and points them toward the hills ahead. "Not good!" he says, passing the binoculars to me. "Not good at all!"

I peer through the windshield at grasslands that slowly climb to a watering hole I've come to know well. Unlike earlier views of it, however, there are no animals stooping to drink from it. Instead, just beyond the water, three jeeps weave a path around rocks in a steady ascent toward the lodge.

"Hurry!" I tell Martin. "They're almost there!"

I search frantically for a place to land beside the lodge, but no such spot exists. The slope beneath the lodge is too steep and rocky, the gardens too congested, and the driveway too narrow. If we land at the air field, there'll be no way to get to Xavier before the jihadists arrive.

"I can't go too low," Martin declares. He leans forward to track the vehicles. "They may have rocket-propelled grenades!"

He lifts us in a steep ascent toward puffy clouds above the lodge. When we enter them, the airplane begins to shake, but the turbulence is short-lasting because we suddenly turn and descend in a stomach-wrenching arc toward the lodge.

"Martin!" Annette cries. "We can't land here!"

"I know, Madam!" he replies. "But we *can* salute Xavier's courage!"

He levels the airplane just above a hillside I was sure we'd strike. Scenes flash by: woodlands; a garden; a pen where two juvenile elephants play among mango trees; the lodge with its massive wood beams and cream-colored mortar; and then another garden where a man dressed in a white robe limps with a cane toward a drop-off overlooking the watering hole in the distance.

"There's Xavier!" I cry.

"Yes, he is dressed in our ancestral white garb," Martin states.

I look ahead at the approaching vehicles. "We can't let this happen!"

Seconds pass before we fly over the three jeeps from which men jump out with rifles.

"Jihadists!" Benji cries. "Bandannas and red circles!"

The window beside me cracks.

"We've been hit!" Martin shouts. He makes a steep ascent to avoid further fire.

"Get us out of here!" Annette cries.

The pilot beside me is shaken yet systematically checks the instruments before him. "Nothing vital hit," he declares. He glances at my window. Its cracks hold for now.

I turn to look at the children. Terror fills their eyes.

"To Lusaka!" Martin declares. He banks the airplane in a new course that allows us to see the lodge one more time. Sickeningly, I watch jihadists scale a wall to the garden where Xavier stands defiantly. A jihadist confronts him shortly. From Xavier's body language, I see he addresses the militant with contempt before he swings his cane at the man. The militant strikes Xavier with his rifle. Stumbling, Xavier manages to keep his feet, but another militant takes aim and fires. Xavier's robe becomes bloody over his stomach, and he falls to his knees. As he bends over, his body jerks with bullets before he lays limp.

Behind me, I hear Annette weep.

10

SMOKE BILLOWS FROM the direction of the Amalumbo River. As we approach the western border of Uku-tetema, I know where it comes from—Saysha's conflagration. At my request, Martin has agreed to fly over the village but at a high altitude to avoid gunfire. Having lost Xavier, I want to pay my respects to the place I called home for the past five months.

The prevailing winds blow the smoke to the west in a two-tone column. A black band rises from a burning fuel truck while silver comes from smoldering huts and fields. Although I've never seen such sheer destruction, I'm reminded of controlled burns I saw from the air in the Amazon when petroleum workers set fire to lands to clear them for drilling. Here, however, there's no concept of *controlled* burning; everything is decimated, including the hospital. I writhe at the thought of patients crushed or burnt to death.

I search for the marauders but see none. Instead, I discover a wave of humanity migrating along grasslands away from the village. A fortunate few walk with cows or goats by their sides. A boy pushes a bicycle. Belongings are few as the pre-dawn attack left no time to collect personal effects.

I turn to Annette who consoles the orphans. They weep in separate tones that express unspeakable anguish. Unable to commune with them from where I sit, I look to the sky.

"Don't be alarmed when you see a military jet approach," Martin announces. "It will escort us to Lusaka."

I feel selfish for not thinking of Martin's pain. Without exception, he has tended to our safety in the face of assault on his land and on his employer. More, he risked his life by returning to the lodge and yet again by altering course to fly over Saysha at my request. Not once did he capitulate to emotions, not even while informing air control authorities that Xavier Treadwill had been killed. There'll come a time when he confronts emotions, I know, but for now they remain at bay.

Presently, he nods at my window. Through the cracks, I discover a sleek silver jet alongside us, so close I see a thumbs-up from its pilot.

"An F/A-18 Hornet," Martin says. "Just like the kind your country's Blue Angels fly."

"Why the escort?" I ask.

His face tightens. "Our nation has lost one of its most beloved men. The escort is in his honor."

It strikes me then how greatly Xavier Treadwill was esteemed. Never in my presence did he allude to his popularity or access to pillars of power in this nation or any other. His wealth alone placed him in rarified circles, but one wouldn't know it from his demeanor. He was simply the man he wanted to be, one impassioned to make the world a better place.

I grimace. In the higher altitude, I wonder whether shifts in oxygenation play havoc with the damaged tissues of my burn. Having consumed four bottles of water since taking off, I feel the need to urinate but fear the moment I do so I'll see more blood come out.

A hand rubs the base of my neck. "Paul, you're sweating profusely," Annette says.

While motoring along the river, I began to feel feverish. I attributed this to dehydration, but neither water nor cool air blowing at me through an air vent relieves the feeling. Infection at the burn site comes to mind; more worrisome is extension of that infection to the bloodstream.

"I'll start antibiotics as soon as we land in case there's an infection brewing," I tell Annette. It's not the way I like to practice medicine, however, because normally I'd submit specimens of urine and blood for microbiologic culture before beginning antibiotic treatment. In this instance, though, I'll resort to stopgap measures in order to fulfill Xavier's request that I speak before his country at the arranged hour.

"No, you need to go straight to the hospital!" Annette insists. "You've ignored yourself for too long!"

I lift the manila envelope and wave it. "Have you read what's in here?"

"No, but—"

"The world needs to hear this!"

"Others will have access to the material," she counters. "Xavier told me he'd made arrangements to share his speech with everyone in the National Assembly."

"True, but they won't receive the speech until the moment I begin speaking. He told me in a note that he instructed Alexander to email the speech the moment I take the podium. He didn't want any of its contents leaked before then."

"So be it," she says. "It's your health!"

"I'll go straight to the hospital after I speak," I assure her.

I remove Xavier's speech to review it in full this time. Along the margins I find hand-written notes encouraging me to substitute my own words as I see fit. One note underscores this freedom…

Paul, speak for me as the spirit calls.

I finish my review just as we begin our descent. A glance out the window shows our escort has been a faithful one. The Hornet remains with us until the very moment before touchdown when it suddenly roars into a steep ascent. In its place come military vehicles lining the sides of the runway. One approaches the Beechcraft as soon as we exit the main strip.

Martin brings the airplane to a halt. He removes his headset and looks at me with fatigued eyes. "Thank you for all you've done for my people," he says.

"This sounds like a goodbye," I reply. "I hope that's not the case."

He extends his hand. "I promised Xavier I'd get you here safely. My job is done."

I take his hand and hold it. "Martin, you're an incredible man. Xavier was fortunate to have you as a friend and pilot."

"I owe him everything I have," he replies. "He took me from a small village in Uku-tetema, gave me an education, and saw me through flight school. I am who I am because of him."

The door to the aircraft opens, and a soldier asks us to exit. Behind him stands an officer in full regalia who announces, "Dr. Rider, I'm to take you and your contingent by motorcade to the National Assembly, but we'll stop briefly at the terminal to use the facilities."

A short drive in a stretch limousine brings us to a lounge. In the men's room, I seek the privacy of a stall to urinate. As expected, my urine is red and I feel pain as it exits. More than ever, I'm concerned that my damaged kidney has become infected. Grateful to Annette for having collected my suitcase before she departed for the river, I rummage through my belongings for antibiotics which I pop into my mouth. I wince as I bend over the sink to drink from the faucet. Standing before a mirror, I lift my shirt, but the fabric sticks to the wound. Pulling slowly, I moan as I separate the two. With the blister gone, raw tissue is left to rub against cloth, an interaction that irritates nerves and leaves the wound soiled, red, and swollen.

We waste no time leaving the airport. Although it's early afternoon on a weekday, the streets are eerily calm. Along major avenues, we pass troop carriers, Humvees, and trucks pulling artillery trailers. Through café windows, television monitors project images of soldiers fighting the enemy. At a principal intersection, a crowd has assembled to rally the faithful in support of the nation. Held high above the heads I see a photo of Xavier Treadwill. A lump forms in my throat.

Thirty minutes after leaving the airport, the limo stops before a building with the words *National Assembly of Zambia* scrolled across its façade. The structure sits atop a low hill and exhibits a curious blend of traditions. Lacking an architect's vocabulary, I'd describe the building as looking like a matchbox with a chalet in the middle. It's a graceful structure with palm trees in front and columns adorned in colorful wraps. By the time we reach the front doors, I see how it holds space for the roughly hundred fifty members of parliament who meet here.

The officer who accompanied us by motorcade hands us off to a delegation waiting in the reception area. A harried man steps forward to introduce himself as Benjamin Nachula, an "MP" as he refers to himself. He glows as he affirms his friendship with Xavier Treadwill. "I'm the sponsor of Xavier's bill to protect Uku-tetema," he informs us.

He allows the briefest of time to make introductions before whisking us deeper into the building. As we walk, I become acutely aware of my attire. An old pair of running shoes bears mud from the morning's trek while my khakis hold rubber smudges from the Zodiac. Earlier, while checking my burn in the airport, I noticed a circular area on my shirt discolored by wound secretions. I can only imagine I emit body odor after sweating profusely throughout the day. Meanwhile, the delegation who leads us to the building's central Chamber is dressed nattily.

We stop outside a pair of grand wood doors where the delegation peels away with Annette and the orphans. "They'll sit in the gallery," Nachula explains. He links my arm. "Come, it's time for you to take the podium."

The doors open before us. Walking beside Nachula, my legs wobble. As we make our way along a central aisle in the Chamber, we pass MPs who stand and applaud. Above, the gallery teems with observers. Altogether, I estimate more than five hundred people occupy the hall.

Silence befalls the Chamber as Nachula and I reach the stage. Beside us, a screen hangs for the purpose of projecting slides. With butterflies in my stomach, I step aside for Nachula to occupy the podium where he lowers a microphone to the level of his lips. A digital display on the stand shows the hour to be two o'clock.

Nachula speaks: "Mr. President, fellow MPs, distinguished guests, members of the press corps, and citizens of the great country of Zambia, we gather today to vote on a bill that has captured the nation's attention for many months, a bill which will determine whether and how we protect the natural resources of our beloved nation. Some have asked how we can justify voting when our nation is at war. My response is that by voting on this bill now, we may deter future attacks of the sort we've just experienced, attacks which, after all, are nothing more than acts of extortion to force us to relinquish our resources.

"As such, it's critical to distinguish legitimate domestic interests that seek to open Uku-tetema to mining and gaming from foreign invaders who want nothing more than to rape our land."

Nachula shuffles his feet before continuing. "The issue before us is whether to open Uku-tetema to legitimate commercial development or, as Xavier Treadwill implored us to do, to protect the land as a national park for posterity. With the unfathomably sad news that Xavier was killed only hours ago, I believe we owe him the honor of voting on the bill he fathered. I'm convinced this nation has lost a leader of a magnitude we won't fully appreciate until some day in the future."

Nachula extends his arm. "It brings me great comfort, however, to know we have before us a true friend of Xavier Treadwill's. I say this because Xavier called me just hours ago to tell me he'd chosen Dr. Paul Rider to speak before us in his place because of Xavier's decision to remain in Uku-tetema to defend his lodge and people against jihadist attacks. Before hanging up, he told me he looked upon Dr. Rider as a native of Uku-tetema, such has been the dedication and love Paul Rider has shown for the land and people of that province."

Nachula addresses me: "Dr. Rider, an assertion such as this coming from Xavier Treadwill speaks volumes of you. I want to extend my deepest gratitude to you for your willingness to speak to us today. The floor is yours."

I move to the podium. When the applause ends, I inhale deeply.

"Ladies and gentlemen, I want to begin by saying that I'm an angry man—angry because of what I've seen and learned in the seven days I knew Xavier Treadwill. And I'm especially angry because such a great man was murdered in cold blood for greed alone. When you hear the circumstances that led to his death, I trust you'll feel *compelled* to vote 'yes' for Xavier's bill."

I push aside the manila envelope with Xavier's speech.

"Any moment now, you'll receive an email from Xavier's staff with the speech he prepared for today, but since you'll have that speech to read for yourself, I'm going to speak from my heart."

I take a drink of water.

"Late this morning, jihadists belonging to Al-Shabaab drove to Xavier's lodge in Uku-tetema and shot him to death in his garden. I witnessed the killing from the air while flying over the lodge in a last-minute attempt to save him. The shooting was the final episode in a series of attempts to take his life to thwart him from protecting Uku-tetema."

I scan the gallery in search of Annette, for I long to see her. To my disappointment, she's nowhere to be found among the crowd.

Motioning to the screen, I ask, "May I have the slide?" Earlier, while walking to the Chamber, I told a staff member that I'd ask for a photo to be displayed that Xavier provided on a flash drive he included in the envelope.

I point to the photo that appears which shows a *mzungu* with a mullet haircut looking into the camera. "The man you see here was the first person to try to kill Xavier. His name is Felix Atwell and he works for International Mines here in Lusaka, a company that recently committed millions to your nation's copper industry. About a month ago, Atwell poisoned Xavier by pouring thallium salt into a cup of tea that Xavier had ordered at a café in Lusaka. Fortunately, Atwell spilled a portion of the thallium onto the table while Xavier stooped to pick up a purse a woman had dropped onto his foot to divert his attention. Had Xavier consumed the entire amount of thallium intended for his cup, he almost certainly would've died earlier than he did."

Rumblings come from the audience.

I explain how the illness from the poisoning led me to become Xavier's physician and how I'd told him in an early discussion that I was worried his poisoning was retaliation for his campaign to protect Uku-tetema. "Because the poisoning occurred on the same day Xavier delivered a speech to promote his bill," I add, "we reviewed a list of names of conference attendees on the suspicion that one or more of them may have colluded with Felix Atwell to poison Xavier. One name on the list stood out—Gary Y. Simsbury, a senior vice-president at a major oil company called TransNational Oil, which, by the way, owns International Mines as a subsidiary. Before coming to Africa, I worked for TransNational Oil in the Amazon rainforest of Ecuador. Because some work I did on the side there to protect jaguars was ill-received by my supervisors, Xavier and I suspected TransNational might hold similar resentment for Xavier's campaign to protect wildlife in Uku-tetema."

The rumblings escalate.

"For this reason, Xavier used his exquisite cybersecurity skills to dig into Gary Simsbury's past. He discovered several alarming findings. One was a public fundraising speech Simsbury gave about a year ago in which he joked about how his title of 'Vice-President of Oil Resources' at TransNational—or 'VIPOR' for short—earned him the nickname 'viper' because of his ability to slither through bureaucratic channels to strike at money. Another red flag was a blog Simsbury wrote for oil executives in which he referred to wildlife 'fanatics' as 'radioactive obstacles' to the search for oil. Let me repeat that: A senior VP from a multinational oil company called wildlife advocates *radioactive obstacles* to the search for oil."

A chill falls over the Chamber.

I continue: "At Xavier's request, I traveled to Intanda with him three days ago to install a security system to photograph trespassers. The system we installed was similar to one I used in the Amazon to protect jaguars." I point to the screen again. "This photo was taken by our system early yesterday at the western entrance to Intanda. Behind Felix Atwell are trucks owned by International Mines. They entered Intanda to conduct a seismic survey of the land even though your government didn't authorize them to do so."

Heads turn among the MPs.

"While Xavier and I were in Intanda installing the system, Xavier's staff at the lodge uncovered more troubling evidence regarding Gary Y. Simsbury. One item was an email International Mines received here in Lusaka roughly two weeks ago that contained instructions issued by a sender referred to as 'VIPOR' to dispatch a tube of blood to an undisclosed location. A few days after the email arrived, someone left a tube of blood in my home in Saysha. With help from specialists here in Lusaka, I learned the blood came from a jaguar and contained radioactive phosphorus in it."

A collective gasp breaks the silence.

"Then, yesterday morning after we returned to the lodge from Intanda, Xavier was poisoned again, this time by a paramedic at the hospital in Saysha I oversee who turned out to be an Al-Shabaab informant. The method of poisoning involved radioactive cesium obtained from a mobile storage device of a type found in hospitals. The paramedic added the radioactive cesium powder to a cocktail he served to Xavier to celebrate a recent victory by Argentina's national football team. By this morning, Xavier had begun to bleed from his bowels."

I scan the gallery again for Annette only to find her sitting in a front row above to my right. She leans forward with clasped hands on a guard rail and looks at me in earnest.

"By now, I'm sure you appreciate the centrality of radiation as a theme in Gary Simsbury's communications. Yesterday, while I was in Intanda, an employee at the hospital in Saysha called to tell me he'd discovered a metal cylinder in a shed in the village that contained a glowing blue powder. The shed belonged to the paramedic I told you about earlier who poisoned Xavier with radioactive cesium. Even before I had a chance to return to Saysha to inspect the cylinder, I suspected it contained radioactive cesium which the paramedic extracted and transported to Intanda where he poisoned Xavier Treadwill. The question was: How did the paramedic get such a lethal substance? We'd never stock such an item in our hospital pharmacy!"

For comfort, I lift my eyes to Annette but find her peering at her mobile phone with a look of profound concern.

"Upon returning to Saysha yesterday from Xavier's lodge, I inspected the metal cylinder and found lettering engraved along its surface that identified the manufacturer as a company called Sheffield Radiologics. Further inquiry revealed this company manufactures radiation-delivery devices for cancer treatments and is owned by a multinational oil company located in the United Kingdom."

Another check on Annette shows her whispering to the orphans sitting beside her.

"After scrutinizing Sheffield Radiologics online, Xavier's staff turned to a little known part of the Internet called the dark net which traditional search engines don't index. Using software products Xavier developed in Silicon Valley, his staff searched the dark net for communications that referred to 'Sheffield Radiologics.' It led them to a secret discussion group composed of four executives from the world's leading petroleum companies, one of which owns Sheffield Radiologics as a subsidiary. Just recently, the CEO of that oil company had staff at Sheffield Radiologics ship a cylinder of radioactive cesium to operatives at International Mines in Lusaka who passed it on to the paramedic at my hospital."

I hear gasps and see hands go to mouths in the audience, but of concern to me is that Annette has risen from her seat and now makes her way along a row toward an exit.

"Ladies and gentlemen, I'm going to use the term 'cabal' to refer to these four oil executives who Xavier's staff discovered communicating with one another through a forum on the dark net. It's an apt term because their communications were intended to be highly secret, and their organizer was none other than Gary Y. Simsbury."

In the gallery where Annette once sat, I find a void as deep as the dark net I now discuss.

"So, let me pull things together," I say. "From the cabal's exchanges, Xavier learned these oil honchos had a grand plan to flood world markets with crude derived from Intanda's vast oil reservoirs. Why did they want to do this? For one reason: to set back renewable energy technologies worldwide to extend the reign of oil. But one person stood in their way, Xavier Treadwill, and his opposition cost him his life! Despite his courage, Xavier Treadwill died at the hands of a cabal of oil executives directed by Gary Y. Simsbury!"

Pandemonium erupts in the Chamber, forcing me to pound on the podium and shout over the din. The efforts test my strength, and I fear I'll need help soon.

"I know what you're thinking!" I shout. "You didn't know Intanda held such vast reserves of oil, but it does! It's been one of the most closely held secrets of the past century. The jewel of Intanda bears such wealth it drove the members of the cabal to forge an alliance with the terrorist group, Al-Shabaab, to pressure Xavier Treadwill to abandon his efforts to protect his homeland. When it became clear the bill to designate Uku-tetema as a national park would pass despite this pressure and the infusion of millions into your nation's copper industry, the cabal changed course. They paid Al-Shabaab heartily to launch attacks on your nation for one vile purpose: to prime your government to accept millions of dollars from the oil companies for the purpose of strengthening military defenses. In other words, the battles taking place at this very moment against invading jihadists along your northern borders were instigated by a cabal of oil executives that seeks to influence the vote on Uku-tetema. In case you haven't heard the news already, let me inform you of it now: In the past twenty-four hours, Gary Y. Simsbury of TransNational

Oil offered your nation millions of dollars earmarked for your military. This is nothing more than a last-ditch, calculated effort to buy "no" votes on Uku-tetema. But I plead with you: Don't let this cabal of oil executives strip one of the last pristine regions of the world from you! Vote to protect Uku-tetema! Honor your fallen patriot, Xavier Treadwill!"

Groups of MPs now stand in anguished discussions as order in the Chamber collapses. Somewhere in the hall, a gavel strikes a sound block but to no avail.

Leaning forward, I scream into the microphone with all the energy I can muster. "Lest you think your nation is alone in being harmed by this cabal, let me get personal! Two nights ago at Xavier's lodge in Uku-tetema, I slept on a bed that had been deliberately contaminated with radioactive cesium, and I'd like to show you the price I paid for doing so."

I strip off my shirt and walk to the center of the stage. What my screaming failed to do, my half-nakedness now accomplishes: I have full attention of the Chamber. In the silence, I turn around to expose my back. "That's a radiation burn!" I shout as I point to the lesion. "The burn went through my kidney and destroyed—"

My energy flails. Doubling over, I fall to the stage and the world becomes a blur.

AS AN EMERGENCY medicine physician, I'm accustomed to treating patients on gurneys rather than occupying one. On either side of me, I see worried faces of MPs as medics rush me through the Chamber toward the exit. In the lobby, three additional faces appear before a security officer attempts to clear them.

"No, let them stay!" I plead.

The officer backs off.

"*Nudume!*" Benji exclaims, "Miss Annette was right. We should've taken you to the hospital before!"

Amu and Thandi nod with vigor.

"Where is Annette?" I ask them.

The orphans look at one another, none willing to speak.

A door opens. Pain stabs my back when the gurney's wheels strike a metal frame. After descending a ramp, we come to a brief stop before the gurney rises and slides into an ambulance.

I call for the orphans.

"We'll meet you at the hospital!" Thandi shouts.

I'M IN FAMILIAR territory yet it feels utterly foreign. Emergency department doctors and nurses swirl about. One I recognize as a friend.

"Hello, Raymond," I say weakly. "How'd you know I was here?"

Raymond Chabala bends his tall frame over me. "Alexander called me from Uku-tetema. He heard you'd collapsed at the National Assembly and were being rushed here. I hurried down from the lab to find you." His face lengthens. "I'm sorry about Xavier and what happened to your hospital in Saysha."

"Everything's gone," I reply. "So much destruction."

"I know, but right now it's you I'm concerned about. Alexander told me about your burn. May I see it?"

Lying on my side, I lift the gown. I feel Chabala's fingers rest on my hips before they probe the area surrounding the wound.

"You have a raging fever," he tells me. "I see they've taken blood and urine and are about to send you for an MRI. I suspect the next stop after that will be the operating room."

A radiology technician enters the room, unlocks the gurney, and rolls me into the hallway.

"Hang on," I tell my escort. "I need to speak to three children who are in the waiting area."

The technician glowers and parks me beside a wall. In short order, he reappears with the orphans. "I'll give you a minute, and then we go!" he warns. He steps aside.

I address the orphans. "Be strong, do your part while I do mine, and in the end we'll come together." I study the three to see who shows the most resilience. "Thandi," I say, "I asked earlier where Annette had gone, but you didn't answer me."

She glances at Amu and Benji. "Miss Annette went to get her twins from someone who was taking care of them here in Lusaka."

"But she didn't take my call! On the way to the hospital, I gave my phone to a medic and had him call her for me."

I see discomfort in Thandi's eyes. "What is it?" I ask her.

My escort returns. "We need to go! The doctors are waiting for your MRI results."

I see remorse in Thandi but have no time to address it because the gurney moves forward. In the radiology suite, I move to a mobile platform that glides into an MRI tunnel. Although I wear headphones, the loud thudding sets me on edge. After the procedure has been completed, I ask the technician for the results.

"Your doctors will discuss them with you," he replies.

On the gurney again, I meet a doctor shortly, a woman in scrubs who introduces herself as an anesthesiologist. Chabala's prediction bears out: the operating room is my next stop. Along the way, the anesthesiologist elicits my history with urgency.

"Faster!" she barks at the technician who wheels me. "We need to get this man into surgery!"

I EQUATE HOSPITAL recovery rooms with holding pens on livestock farms. In both, captives wait at the mercy of others to be released. For me, it's not just guard rails that confine; when I try to shift to a more comfortable position, a thick dressing encircling my torso restrains me. My throat burns at the site where a breathing tube once connected me to a respirator, and my mind wavers in pharmacologic limbo between wooziness and euphoria.

I scrunch my eyes and blink to confirm that the two men I see beside my bed are real. While one is familiar, the other isn't.

"Paul," Raymond Chabala says, "this is Dr. Samuel Bithwanu, your surgeon."

"Did you leave anything in me?" I ask the surgeon.

Bithwanu is short, muscular, and broad at the shoulders. His eyes are intense and penetrating. "Leave anything?" he echoes. "As in sponges or instruments?"

"No, I was referring to organs," I reply. "I feel like a mummy in this dressing."

Bithwanu's smile is lopsided. Raising a hand, he says, "You came this close to bleeding out. The radiation burned through your skin, muscle, and kidney and almost destroyed your renal artery." He frowns. "I couldn't save the kidney, though; it was too damaged."

"What about infection?" I ask.

"Clearly present; we drained a lot of pus."

"You'll be with us for a while," Chabala warns. "In the interim, my wife and I'll take care of the orphans. She came to the hospital already to pick them up. They'll stay with us until we figure out a more permanent solution." He eyes me longingly. "And is it true you're planning to leave us for Indonesia?"

"I have to work somewhere," I reply, "and I don't have a job here anymore."

"But even before Saysha was destroyed, you were planning to leave, I hear. Why? They loved you there!"

I wince because, before moving to Saysha, I felt I knew only one other loving home. It was the one I moved into in fourth grade where I experienced for the first time what it meant to have parents and siblings, but that loving home soon wilted when my father began whipping me in fifth grade. Through boarding school, college, medical school and even marriage, I shunned love from my living quarters because I'd seen it crushed once and didn't want that to happen again. But then an African village and a hospital with orphans living on its grounds took me in and, once again, I had a loving home.

From my bed, I look up at Raymond Chabala who waits for me to answer his question. I repeat it: "Why didn't I seek to remain in Saysha?"

He nods.

I swallow into a dry throat. "Because, loving homes don't last forever."

AFTER SETTLING INTO my hospital room, I check my phone eagerly to see if Annette has left a message. Secretly, I wished she'd have ridden with me in the ambulance and when I didn't see her in the emergency department before surgery, I began to worry about where she was. That angst grew when I awoke from surgery to find her absent still.

Hope wells within when I find a text from her awaits me...

Paul, I'm so sorry I'm not at your side. I'm praying with all my might that you'll recover from your ordeal. I can only tell you that I'm with my twins and trying to make a life for myself. I shall always hold you close in my heart.
Annette

I feel like a fist has just punched me where I had surgery. I don't know how much of the pain comes from the wound versus the psyche. I feel abandoned, alone, and isolated. Walls close in on me.

Distraught, I compose a text pleading with her to call me, but it goes unanswered. When I call her directly, I receive her voice mail repeatedly. Over the ensuing days, I leave heart-wrenching messages to contact me, but I hear nothing.

Days pass slowly in the hospital. Each begins with fatigue and ends in depletion. In the interim come interruptions—dressing changes, meals, and medical consults. Being on the other side of the doctor-patient fence now, I see value in requiring medical students to be hospitalized for a day to experience what patients go through; such stints could foster empathy.

Fortunately, my spirits are propped by visits from Raymond Chabala and the three orphans. From his end, Chabala has helped run errands for me—securing visas, paying bills, and purchasing clothes for the orphans. Having left Saysha with the clothes on their backs, they need new wardrobes, limited as they'll be. In the meantime, they hang out with me every day. Thandi works on art projects, Amu reads, and Benji...well, I'm concerned about him. He doesn't like living in a city. He misses the wildlife of the country, the marshes along the Amalumbo River, and skylines punctuated by mango trees. To his dismay, he confronts automotive exhaust here along with honking cars and harried schedules. To worsen matters, a pain remains from the loss of his best friend in Intanda.

Ten days from the time I entered the hospital, my doctors release me. I summon the orphans to my room for a final visit. I ask Benji to hang a sign on the door that reads, *Meeting in Progress. Do not Disturb.*

We congregate at a small table in my room.

"I called you here because we have decisions to make," I say. "We've reached a juncture where each of us needs to choose a path to follow moving forward."

"Are you saying goodbye to us?" Amu asks. "Because if you are, I will leave now!"

"No, I'm not saying goodbye. I'm holding a discussion in which I'll present options you'll need to choose among." I lift a sheet of paper on which I've taken notes. "While I've been hospitalized, I arranged a number of possible places where you can live and go to school."

"I want to return to Saysha!" Benji insists.

"That isn't possible because, as you know, it's been destroyed."

"But I've heard the government will rebuild it."

"That'll take time; in the interim, you need a home." I tap the sheet of paper. "So let's run down the list."

"We want to stay together," Thandi proclaims.

"I understand that. Some of the options will allow you to do so."

I review the choices, taking time to explain each. Most elicit tears which leads me to repeat they have a choice in the matter. "Remember, I've promised to help each of you financially within reason until you reach the age of eighteen. You'll never have to worry about food, shelter, or education; I'll make sure you have those things. In turn, I want you to make the most of your lives with the options I've presented." I fold the sheet and tuck it into my pocket.

Standing, I bring the three into my arms. Fighting back tears, I reiterate what I've already told them: "So, in a few days, I leave for Indonesia to begin my new job, but my supervisor there has given me permission to return in three weeks to meet with you to hear what choices you've made. I'll remain here for a short while during that return trip to help you make your transitions."

For the longest time, we stand in a circle with hands clasped, no one willing to let go.

II

I'VE COME TO know the airport in Lusaka well in the past week, only this time I board a commercial jetliner rather than Xavier's Beechcraft. In my economy seat, I look momentarily for a headset of the sort Martin provided each time I flew with him but find none. Takeoff of the Boeing 777 consumes far more runway than the Beechcraft which leaves me anxious about whether we'll ever get airborne. And then we lift.

With a travel time of twenty-two hours between Lusaka and Jakarta, Indonesia, I settle in for the first leg of the trip. While I'm relieved the seat accommodates my back without pain, I find myself fidgeting. A printed version of an examination I need to complete to earn continuing medical education credits for my physician's license in the U.S. sits idle. My mind wanders.

From the time Annette left her seat at the National Assembly two weeks ago to the present, I've sent her over a dozen texts and emails and have called her repeatedly without response. I'm heartbroken she hasn't contacted me because I've heard from Bristol that she's been in touch with him regularly. What they've discussed remains a secret as Bristol won't divulge the details other than to say Annette has left Africa with the twins. I feel excommunicated from people I was once close to. Even the whereabouts of the other paramedics and orphans is a mystery, leaving me to presume they've died or are scattered throughout the country. My only hope is that casualties were few although reports suggest otherwise as government workers survey the widespread destruction left by the jihadists. In the meantime, the husband-wife physician team that was recruited to replace me has returned to Canada.

Once more, I'm a vagabond.

Touchdown in Dubai comes on time, and I depart the aircraft to make my connecting flight to Jakarta. With a two-hour layover, however, I sit for a cup of coffee. Across a busy corridor bustling with travelers, I see a poster depicting a global flight map for the airline I'm traveling with. Bountiful arches spring from a dot representing the hub of Dubai to reach across the world like spider legs sprouting from a cephalothorax. Among the cities at the ends of the arches is London, England.

I take a sip of coffee but almost spit it out. Jumping from my seat, I rush to a service counter where I approach an agent. "I need to change my flight plans," I tell her. "Can you help me do that?" I push a boarding pass for my flight to Jakarta toward her.

She examines it before locating my record on her monitor. "Where is it you want to go?"

I tell her.

"One way or round trip?" she asks.

"One way, no luggage; I've just a handbag with me."

Fifteen minutes later, ticket paid for, I hurry to another terminal where I board the first of a two-legged trip to Ireland.

I'VE NEVER FLOWN into Shannon Airport in County Clare, let alone anywhere in Ireland. The airport serves the western portion of the country, and being as early in the morning as it is, I have the place to myself.

Getting here wasn't easy. My flight from Dubai arrived at London's Gatwick Airport at midnight last night, and since my flight to Ireland departed from Heathrow first thing this morning, I had to shuttle between airports overnight. I slept on the brief trip from London to Shannon and walk now to the car rental desk with a large latte in hand.

My first stop outside the airport is at a petrol station where I purchase a map of Ireland. Although the car has GPS, I prefer paper when navigating terra incognita. I spread it across the steering wheel to map my route to the Connemara coast four hours to the northeast. With an incomplete night of sleep, I rely on caffeine to remind me to drive on the left side of the road.

Driving north, I pass the towns of Latoon, Crusheen, and Shanaglish. To keep alert, I lower the window to allow a brisk wind blow into my face. With the sun still low, its rays dapple farmlands and meadows in a lifting mist.

In Galway, I stop for a traditional Irish breakfast of sausages, eggs, butter-fried veggies, and brown bread which soaks the juices. A strong cup of black tea completes the meal before I hit the road again.

From Galway, I continue on toward Connemara. It's Sunday, and the roads are deserted. I pass lakes, streams, and farms where cattle graze on lush grass. Here and there, I see bogs where bricks of peat have been stacked into neat piles. After following a river, the road takes me over hills covered with purple moorgrass that sways in rippling waves that remind me of their human counterparts in packed stadiums. Where there are barns, homes or livestock, there are stone walls, grey ribbons that parcel the land.

My heart accelerates when I see the first sign for the town of Clifden—forty kilometers ahead now. The name strikes a tender chord because Annette had mentioned it in passing during our first dinner at Xavier's lodge. At the time, she was flustered that Xavier had broached the topic of a painting on a nearby wall that she'd done which depicted an austere Irish island. Keeping her words to a minimum, she seemed more intent on extracting my views of the artwork than divulging her reasons for creating it. Yet I glommed onto every word she uttered, sparse as they were, and 'Clifden' was one of them. She mentioned the name in the context of returning to her home near the town if she ever left Africa.

My introduction to Clifden comes from a summit overlooking the town. I stop along the roadside to look at the picturesque scene below. I see church steeples, colorful buildings, and a quaint traffic circle near the town center. Beyond Clifden to the north are mountains with peaks enshrouded in clouds while, to the west, up and down the coast, narrow peninsulas project into the ocean with islands beyond them.

I scan the islands now for one with features portrayed in Annette's painting, but it eludes me. Disheartened, I tell myself the angle at which I view the islands may be different from the one Annette faced when she created the painting and that this alone could explain why I don't recognize it now. Thinking back to the discussion at Xavier's lodge, I recall Annette saying that while she couldn't see the island from her home, it came into view if she walked up a hill from her house. With that in mind, I survey the scene again and notice that one in a string of peninsulas south of Clifden has a particularly rugged island off its tip.

I drive from the summit to the center of Clifden where I stop before a bakery. Inside, I purchase a piece of coffee cake and a cup of tea. Sitting at a table off to the side, I wait for the woman behind the counter to attend to another customer.

When we're alone, I address her. "Can you tell me whether there's an island nearby with the ruins of a monastery on it?"

She steps out from behind the counter and points through a window. "There's Clifden Castle up that way," she replies, "but it's on the mainland, not on an island."

"No, it's the remnants of a monastery I'm looking for, and they're on an island," I repeat.

"And it's near Clifden, you say?"

"Yes."

"How did you hear about it?"

"I saw it in a painting a friend did. She told me it was near Clifden."

"Who was the painter?"

"Annette Wilson. Do you know her?"

"No, but I just moved here a year ago."

I point in the direction from which I entered Clifden. "On the summit above town, I saw a spit of land jutting into the sea with a rugged island beyond it. It was the fifth projection of land south of here. Do you know what I'm talking about?"

She shakes her head. "I've been to Errislannan Peninsula just south of town but no further. Are you sure the road goes that far?"

"I believe I saw one."

"Then you're only option is to drive there." She provides me with directions to the coastal road running south.

I leave the bakery with doubts about my trip to Ireland. Before boarding the flight in Dubai, I'd emailed my contact in Indonesia to say I needed a few more days before I could get there. I left the reason for the postponement vague. My contact was gracious to allow me the extra time I sought even though my arrival in Indonesia was eagerly anticipated.

The coastal road I take is newly paved. Several kilometers south of Clifden, I see a sign for *Irish Lawn Bowls, Errislannan* that points to the right. The turnoff appears to be one most traffic follows because the new pavement goes that direction while the road I remain on degenerates. I slow to cross an inlet over a one-lane stone bridge. On my left, grasslands ascend to rocky hills that parallel the coast, while on my right, I pass one spit after another extending to the sea.

I count the spits carefully. At the fifth one, I leave the road for a gravel lane, but to my dismay, I can't see the rugged island I'd noticed from the summit because of a low hill that blocks my view. With gravel striking the chassis, I come to a farm where horses graze in a pasture. At the far end of the pasture is a white cottage with a thatched roof. I take a driveway to the cottage and stop before it. A wind chime over the front door strikes its notes.

Because this is the only home I've noticed since turning off the main road, I want to see if anyone's home who might know the whereabouts of Annette Wilson. I approach the front door where I find a hand-written note taped to it…

Daddy, have the girls change when you return with them from church. I'll be home later in the afternoon.

A knock on the door brings no response. Returning to the gravel lane, I follow it toward the end of the spit. When it disappears at the base of the low-lying hill I'd seen before, I park and scale the hill by foot. With each step, I leave earth for sky. Wind blows through my hair while tall grass whips my wrists as if to question my authority for being there.

When I reach the summit, I freeze. An island erupted from the sea in tall cliffs stands before me. Verdant grass encircles its slopes while, just below the peak where grass meets rocks, the remnants of what appeared once to be a castle refuse to die.

I start down the path toward the shore. Hairpin bends take me one way before doubling back. With each turn, I get a better view of the coast, a boulder-strewn stretch that, curiously, throws off a sand bar that links the island some hundred meters away to the mainland. At one turn, I stop to gauge the depth of water covering the sand when I notice a woman standing before an easel on a beach that funnels into the sand bar. Her hair is drawn into a pony tail that lashes about in the wind.

My heart races as I continue along the path to get a better look at the woman's face. Step by step, I assure myself my eyes aren't deceiving me. I stop at the final bend some twenty meters from the artist and wait for the woman to notice me, but she remains engrossed in her painting.

"Annette," I call gently. The wind steals my voice. I call again.

This time she turns to me. Her lips part and her mouth opens, but she says nothing, raising an arm instead to restrain a stray lock of hair.

"Paul!" she states finally. "Is that really you? I can't believe—" The brush falls from her hand, but she makes no attempt to retrieve it.

I complete the final steps and take her into my arms. Her shoulders roll as she begins to weep.

I tilt her back enough to look into her eyes. "*Why*?" I ask.

She wipes her tears. "I've struggled so much in the past two weeks deciding what to do! I've gone back and forth a million times, at once telling myself to respond to your texts and calls only to change my mind!"

I cup her cheeks. "But why'd you leave me in the first place?"

"You need your freedom, Paul! I know that. I never want to be the one to take it from you."

"*Take* it?"

"You're an introvert…a loner…a 'vagabond' as you put it."

My eyes water. "Does that mean I can't love you?"

She pulls me close, running her fingers through my hair before caressing my head.

"Of course it doesn't!" she cries. "That you should even ask that question touches me so." She releases me. "But, let's be practical: My twins just lost their father and you've taken a job in Indonesia."

"Have I?"

She peers into my eyes. "That's what Bristol told me. He texted me while you were speaking before the National Assembly. He told me you'd made your decision to go."

"True, but halfway there yesterday I questioned that decision and flew here to look for you."

"Why did you want to find me?"

"Ever since I met you, Annette, I haven't been able to stop thinking about you! Did you *feel* what I felt the night we made love at the lodge?"

"More than you can imagine! That's why I wrote you that letter at four o'clock in the morning!"

"Yes, your letter," I nod. "It changed my life."

"How?"

"Your last paragraph: Let me recite it…

In the meantime, I implore you to do one thing for me: While you're at Intanda, commune with the leopards. Be with them in a state of heightened sensitivity, awareness, and receptivity, and as you view them through binoculars, take special care to look at their sides, for they have called you to Africa.

I take her hands to form a bridge between us. "I did what you said, Annette. I communed with the leopards, and they've brought me healing; partial healing, for sure, but enough to allow me to live differently than before."

"Healing?" she echoes.

I nod. "You told me in your letter that as we made love you'd felt the lines along my back, 'long, deep ones that spanned nearly the entire width of your body,' as you put it. 'And so many of them.' You said you cried when you returned to your room."

"I did."

I squeeze her hands. "Those scars came from whippings I took at the hands of my father beginning in the fifth grade. He lashed me time and again with a cat o' nine tails whip because he knew how deep its cords dig into human skin. Every time I failed to live up to his expectations, he whipped me. Three years of whippings, Annette; that's what I bore. Thank God he sent me to boarding school in eighth grade."

Annette releases a hand and cups her mouth.

"I'll never forget what my father told me one day as he extracted the whip from a case he kept it in as he prepared to lash me for a 'B' I'd received in seventh grade math. He said: 'Paul, you're a failure because you don't have my genes. I've told your mother countless times that we shouldn't have adopted a stray from the pound.' "

Tears fall from Annette's cheeks. "You were adopted?"

"Yes, and that's why I love those orphans so much! I know what it means to be alone in the world."

I want to be strong, to hold myself from crying, but I can't.

In the blowing wind, we hold each other tightly. Our cheeks seal in wetness from tears that mingle along our skin.

I bring my lips to her ears. "The leopards," I whisper. "They spoke to me just as you said they would. As I watched them on the slopes of Intanda, I found them to be so apart from the world yet so connected to it. In their presence, a voice deep within told me to release the past and to move on in grace. It was as if the leopards lifted the lines from my back, not physically, but emotionally. My lines became the leopard's lines."

I release Annette, turn to the sea, and fall to my knees.

Since starting down the path toward the shore, the tide has lowered to the point of exposing the sand bar. The sun bakes its surface to form a dry crest that extends to the island.

"Your painting," I say, looking at the canvas. "The horse is no longer there."

"That's right," she replies.

"In its place are two figures, a man and a woman, standing beside the monastery ruins."

"Yes," she says, voice cracking.

"Are they part of the ruins or a creation from them?"

She kneels beside me. "You tell me."

I lift my head to the sky, shut my eyes, and inhale the unknown. It's sweet to the mouth and fills my lungs. The sun strikes my lids, creating the image of a fiery ball before which a dark silhouette appears. It takes the form of a man who confronts me before doing an about face. I watch him walk away.

I take Annette's hand, hold it mine, and open my eyes.

I am a vagabond no more.

12

ABOUT FOUR YEARS LATER...

The cool wind blowing up the hillside from the green savannas carries the aromas of lush grass and wildflowers. A month has passed since the rainy season ended and green prevails in the *Uku-tetema Wilderness Conservancy*, a United Nations World Heritage Site and Zambia's newest national park.

Nearly four years have passed from the day Xavier Treadwill was killed and the National Assembly voted to memorialize Uku-tetema as a national park. During those years, the remnants of what was once Xavier's lodge have been reconstructed after being destroyed by jihadists. In several hours, a ceremony will mark the official opening of the refurbished lodge as the park's headquarters, and a part-time junior volunteer ranger named Benji will be among speakers to address government officials and wildlife enthusiasts who've gathered from around the globe to dedicate the site.

After I left Zambia and found Annette in Ireland, I declined the job in Indonesia and flew back to Lusaka to meet with the orphans as I'd promised to do, and upon reuniting with them, I presented them with an additional option to consider: living in Ireland with Annette, her twins, and me. All three orphans accepted the offer. Three months later, after settling in with us in a home along the Connemara coastline, Benji served as a ring-bearer while Thandi and Amu joined the six-year-old twins in sprinkling rose petals at my wedding with Annette.

Although I live and work in Ireland now near a church where Annette is a pastor, I've returned to Uku-tetema every year with Annette since leaving Zambia. The call of Africa remains deep in my blood. Each time we travel, the orphans—and they're no longer that, for they're our children now—come with Annette and me. On each visit to Zambia, we've pitched in to help in the building of a new hospital in Saysha before traveling to Uku-tetema to view wildlife in the new national park. This year, however, we've brought the twins and the newest member of our family, a three-year-old named Cassandra who bears her mother's auburn hair and love for animals.

I stand now on the summit above the lodge holding Cassandra in my arms. With the rest of the family beside me, we watch herds of zebras, wildebeests, and antelopes blanket the grasslands. Although the wind blows into my face, I feel a separate, invisible force pull me from behind. In previous visits to Uku-tetema, I've made it a point to visit Intanda to lay flowers at the site where Oscar died, but this year, with the entire family here, I forgo the journey.

For now, as we savor our views of the savannas, I interpret the push and the pull as Africa moving me—the push coming from Oscar's breath in the wind, and the pull from Xavier's love and respect for a star-shaped land called Intanda.

As happens every time I visit this land, I shall leave a part of me behind when I depart.

Made in United States
North Haven, CT
23 October 2025